For Rosie
because we're rocking and rolling now.

It Was Only Ever You

Prologue

Riverdale, New York, March 1941

SAMUEL KLEIN clicked off the radio and leaned back into his low, soft chair. He sucked deeply on his pipe, releasing a ball of smoke into the still air, then said through clenched teeth, 'You've got to love the British – but they could be right, you know? Churchill reckons that now the Yanks have agreed to come on board we are finally coming to the end of this wretched war.'

His wife Anya shot him a warning look but it was too late. Their niece Sheila was at the door and had already heard him. Samuel did not like to be shushed by his wife, especially not in his own home, but he immediately realized his terrible mistake. He laid his pipe down in the large wooden ashtray on his armrest and leaned forward in his chair.

'The war is ending?' said Sheila.

Samuel and Anya loved their fourteen-year-old niece as if she was their own child. Samuel's brother had been a German opera singer, living in Berlin when Hitler came to power.

Klaus had intended to move his whole family to America, and had sent his young daughter over to New York for an extended 'holiday'. He had kept his son behind so he could finish his studies at the Mendelssohn Conservatory of Music. Then war broke out and it was too late.

Sheila had learned not to think about what was happening to her mother and father and brother. She had been so impatient to see them again that the waiting for them to come had been almost unbearable.

'Soon,' was all they had ever said. 'After the war.' After a while, she could see that her continued enquiries hurt Auntie Anya and Uncle Samuel, so she made herself stop. When her family's faces came into her mind's eye she put thoughts of them to one side, reassuring herself that she would see them again when the war was over. Until then it was best to do what Auntie and Uncle told her to do, and live in the day.

But now, the war was ending! Everything would change. They would be coming home? Five years had been a long time, but now it was over!

Samuel watched Sheila as she stood in the doorway, her arms crossed and her bony shoulders in their long, brown cardigan hunched. She had a strong face, like her father. A long aquiline nose gave way to a broad, generous mouth – alight when smiling, markedly downturned when not. Her eyes were dark brown with luxurious lashes, but their heavy lids gave her the appearance of being slightly bored. Sheila's habitually serious expression made her look older and wiser than her years. An unfortunate fact, in Samuel's opinion, that was in direct contradiction to her sweet, open nature.

Sheila's face was now lit up with such an expression of hopeful delight that it seemed to Samuel as if she held the world in her eyes. If they could only see her, Churchill and

Roosevelt; if they could only see the expression of pure innocence and hope on this child's face they would put an immediate end to this war and find a way of bringing her family back to her.

'Come in, bubula ... sit down.'

Sheila looked at her uncle and there was something in his face that made her not want to do as he said. Why was he not smiling too? He had said it himself – the war was ending and yet ...

She stayed where she was and said, 'When the war ends, then Mama and Papa and Hans ...'

The words trailed off.

Why could she not finish the sentence? Anya and Samuel said nothing. Anya's face was as pale as dough.

The terrible silence hung in the air between them in unspoken words, in assurances. *'Mama and Papa and Hans will be here. Soon. After the war.'*

The war was nearly over. So surely it was safe to say it now.

But they weren't saying it, or telling her that everything would be all right. Why weren't they saying it? Why did she feel unable to say it out loud herself?

'Sit down, bubula,' Samuel said. 'I have something to tell you.'

Sheila looked at her uncle's face with its grey, pointed beard. Her own father wore his beard short and brown. She knew that from the photograph, although she could not picture it from memory now. She could not recall the feel of it pressed against her cheek. Uncle Samuel's eyes were sparkling with tears. Not tears of happiness, like when he listened to Mahler on the gramophone. This was something else. Something she did not recognize and yet she knew what it was. She couldn't look at him, didn't want to look at him. She looked to her auntie for comfort, for a shred of hope, but Anya's face was equally stricken. Sheila felt sick. She steadied herself in the doorway and looked around the room, searching for something to alleviate that awful fear crawling its way into her conscious mind.

This small drawing room was her home. For five years it had been her sanctuary, the safe place where she had come to find salve for the torn skin on her knee from Auntie's medicine box, or to tinker on Samuel's piano. But in that moment it felt as if the room itself was shrinking away from her; the polished mahogany sideboard clung to the flowery wallpaper, the large radio with its constantly flickering light was silenced in shame, the piano lid shut tight as if the keys beneath it were paralysed with dread.

They were dead. Her family was dead. Hitler had killed them. That was why they hadn't written. That was why nobody ever talked about them or the war ending any more. Even as she thought it, Sheila kept telling herself that it could not be true. She was a bad, bad person for even imagining such a thing. You shouldn't tell yourself people were dead unless…

'Bubula,' Samuel said. 'Come, sit down. We must talk…'

He reached out to her, his long fingers outstretched. Tears were streaming down his face and in a sudden moment, as suddenly as if she had been slapped, Sheila recognized the look in his eyes. Pity. They were not the tears of emotion inspired by music or art that she so often saw in her uncle's eyes. They were tears that told her her parents really were dead. Not only that, they told her that she was not loved, only pitied.

Anger flashed through Sheila as she ran from the room. She heard Samuel say to her auntie, 'Leave her, Anya. Give her some time.'

Sheila ran to her room and locked the door. Her heart was

pounding. She felt sick. Where were the tears? She waited patiently for a few minutes but they didn't come. Why wouldn't they come? She wanted to shout out and scream, 'It's not fair! None of this is fair!' but she could not. If she let any of the words out she was afraid they would be too loud, and the whole world would hear her.

Sheila felt a sob building in her chest. Not the kind of sob that comes from having a torn hem or a scraped knee, but something huge and frightening. Black and unknown. If she gave it voice she would pull the house down around their ears. So she took a deep breath and kept it to herself, inside her head. They were dead. All of them. Mama. Papa. Hans. How did they die? By a bomb? How long had they been dead? Why had they not told her? The questions made her feel angry. There were so many of them and yet she did not want to know the answers to them.

Five minutes ago her life had been good. Her parents were not here, but she had everything else that she needed. Five minutes ago there was kugel for dinner and, afterwards, she would be allowed to stay up to listen to a play on the radio with Uncle Samuel. Tomorrow she would go to school and do that rotten maths test, then afterwards go to Margaret's house and flirt with her Irish cousins. In five minutes everything had changed. Her family was dead. They were never coming for her. She was alone. Five minutes ago the people downstairs were her beloved auntie and uncle. Now they were strangers who had lied to her. She hated them. She hated them for not telling her the truth. And she hated them for not lying. They could have told her that her family was still alive. That they would all be coming for her. Soon. After the war.

The pain in her chest just kept getting bigger and bigger but as Sheila lay on her bed and waited for the tears, she realized that she could not cry alone. She had never cried alone. When she was small, she would go to Auntie, wrap her hands around her waist, press her face into her large, soft bosom and weep into the buttery smell of her cooking apron. Or her uncle would sit her up on his lap at the piano and teach her how to play 'Für Elise', complaining and laughing when her frizzy black curls got caught in his greying beard.

But that seemed a long time ago now. Now, in the last five minutes, everything had changed. Love was not the same as pity and she would *not* go downstairs and endure the pity of the two people she had decided, in her sudden, shocked fury, were strangers now.

Big girls don't cry, and she was a big girl now. Her family was gone and she was on her own.

There would be no tears. Not today.

1

County Mayo, Ireland, Summer 1958

I T WAS a hot day and Patrick Murphy was heading down to Gilvarry's lake for a swim with his friends. The small lake was easily accessible from the town, a twenty-minute barefoot stroll across three flat green grazing fields. However, that month Mickey Gilvarry had taken possession of a new stud bull so his fields were out of bounds. The lads had to walk forty minutes at a brisk pace along the stony road in their boots. It had been a good summer, with spells of hot sun between the rain, so the boys' faces and chests were weathered from a hard week's work. Brendan Kelly had been picking and bagging potatoes, his brother, Tony, cutting turf and Patrick bringing in hay on his father's small farm. This was the three young men's day off and as the dusty air stung their burnt skin, they cursed Mickey's bull for making their journey to the cold water of the lake longer than it needed to be.

They stopped at the roadside to strip off their shirts and Brendan pulled a packet of Woodbines out of his breeches and passed them around. 'I've half a mind to take these trousers off,' he said. 'I'm roasted alive.'

'We'd rather you didn't,' said Tony, who, despite his burly physique, had the manner and wit of an old woman. 'I caught sight of your bollocks once and I'd just as soon not repeat the experience.' He pulled a small hand-corked bottle from his shoulder bag.

'Is that tea?' Brendan asked as Tony perched himself on a stile at the side of the road. 'Isn't your mammy great altogether?'

'She's grand, surely,' Tony said coyly, 'and this is the finest and sweetest tea my mammy ever made me.' Then he took a swig from the bottle and grimaced wildly.

'You fecker – it's poitin! Give us a swig!'

The other two made a grab for the flask, as Tony dived under their arms.

'It's tea, I'm telling you!' he said, walking backwards down the road, waving the bottle at them and laughing, urging them to follow.

Brendan chased after him, but Patrick held back and started to pull his shirt off. Of the three, twenty-five-year-old Patrick stood out as the eldest and by far the best-looking. His luxuriant black hair was slicked back from his forehead in a heavy quiff and his white shirt-sleeves were rolled up to his shoulders to reveal muscular tanned arms. He had the tall, broad physique of his father, but unlike other men whose bodies were built more for labour than for love, Patrick carried himself with a nonchalant charm. However, while his peers envied Patrick, they could never hate him. Although he looked like a Hollywood idol and had all the girls round about driven pure daft chasing after him, Patrick was sound as a pound. There wasn't an ounce of arrogance about him, unlike the la-di-da local gobshites that went off to London for a summer working the sites and came back with big ideas and cockney accents. Patrick, with his singing talent and his good looks, could easily go off abroad and make his fortune. But he didn't. He was happy at home, working on the farm, and singing whenever he was asked. He wore his gifts lightly and was always sure to direct attention away from himself. Only last month, at a dance in Pontoon, he had cornered Mary McCarthy and gazed searingly at her, then, just as she was fit to fall into a swoon, gently delivered her to Tony Kelly who had been plucking up the courage to speak to her for six months. Tony didn't mind that she had fallen in love with Patrick first. It was a rite of passage for almost all the girls in the town anyway and, sure, Tony was a little in love with him himself. Mary was engaged to him now and Patrick had made that happen.

Patrick laughed, watching big Brendan make a grab for Tony's poitin flask, but as he went to place his shirt on the stile it fell on to the high soft grass on the other side. Reaching over the wall to get it, something caught the corner of his eye. It was a girl, standing stock-still in the middle of Mickey's field. Facing her, not twenty feet away, was the bull.

'Mother of God,' Patrick whispered to himself. Without thinking, he clambered over the stile. Cautiously but steadily he began to walk towards the girl. Her body was paralysed with fear, he could see that from here. She was doing the right thing, standing still. As Patrick inched closer, the girl turned her head towards him. It was Dr Hopkins's daughter, Rose, his younger sister Sinead's best friend. There was a look of terror on her pretty face.

The bull seemed transfixed by a small, blue bag dangling from her arm. Rose must have been heading down to the lake for a swim and not known to avoid the field. Her flow-ery dress had a solid red ribbon around the hem, which was fluttering slightly as she struggled to hold her shaking legs steady. One gust of wind, and the red hem might set the bull charging.

As their eyes met, Patrick raised his palms up in front of his face and shook his head. He wanted her to stay exactly where she was. He was twenty feet to the other side of her now and knew he had to act fast. So he opened his mouth and he sang.

'The pale moon was ri-sing, above the green moun-tain...' Patrick's broad, impressive baritone reverberated across the empty field.

As soon as she heard his voice Rose felt the frozen edge of her fear melt away. For a few seconds the bull just stood there, confused, then, slowly, he turned his head towards Patrick. As soon as he did so, Rose began to run.

Still distracted by Patrick, the bull scraped the ground with his left hoof. Once Patrick was sure that he had the animal's full attention, he began to wave his arms wildly. Then, still singing 'The Rose of Tralee', he did a little dance before shouting, 'Come over here and get me, ya big hairy bastard!'

As the bull started to charge, Patrick turned and ran as if all hell was after him. He could feel his heart banging in his chest as the galloping hooves of the heavy animal reverber-ated through the soft ground beneath him. His friends were shouting frantically from behind the wall, 'He's up your arse! Run!' Patrick had barely made it over the stile when the bull stopped a few feet short of the stone wall. His nostrils flared as he shook his flat square head.

'Jesus, Patrick, you pure lunatic, you could have been killed,' Tony said.

As the bull began to turn, his adventure over, Patrick picked up a stone from the ground and threw it at his ear.

'Feck. What the hell are you…?'

'I have to go back for her,' Patrick said to his friends, 'make sure she's safe. Keep him busy.'

Before the other two had the chance to object, he climbed over the wall back into the field. As he ran across the flat meadow of daisies and dandelions towards the mirrored glint of the still lake, Patrick could see that Rose was well clear of danger, but he still followed her.

He caught up with her at the old boating jetty where they all swam. She did not seem surprised by his sudden appearance. Perhaps she knew he would follow her. Patrick felt a pinch in his stomach when he thought that.

'How'ya now?' he said.

She looked up at him shyly from beneath long black eyelashes.

'Grand,' she said.

Rose had the type of elegant, refined beauty about which his mother might remark, 'That girl has a touch of Grace Kelly in her.' Sleek blonde hair sat in lush waves across her delicate shoulders. Her skin was pale silk, and her cheeks and lips were tinged with soft pink, as if God had remembered the rouge. She had an almost overt perfection to her appearance, which, when she was younger, had made her appear prim. As she grew into a woman it had made her astonishingly beautiful. He remembered his father and his pub cronies saying about Grace Kelly one night, 'That woman's face is a caution. It doesn't do for a woman to be too beautiful.' 'You wouldn't know what kind of trouble they'd lead you into.' 'A plain woman will never stray too far from the house.' 'Marriage makes a woman plain in any case – that's the proper order of things.' 'All the same, I'd do time for a kiss from them perfect lips!'

Rose was his sister's wee friend. He had never paid any attention to her before now. She was just the blonde quiet girl in the background of his life. Yet now he was noticing that her rosebud lips were set in a closed smile, pouting. He thought of reaching across, touching them gently with his thumb to see if they were as soft as they looked. He had done that a hundred times before with other girls, but with Rose he felt unable to. She was too much for him. Too beautiful.

So, he looked down at his feet and said, 'That was some bull.'

'It was surely,' she replied.

He looked up at her again and she was smiling. Her teeth were straight and white and her blue eyes turning sapphire in the sunlight.

'Yeah, that was some bull,' he continued, gravely adding, 'It might have killed you.'

'Might have,' she said brightly.

'And me too. Did you see the way he was chasing me across the fields? I tell you, he was going at some speed.'

She shrugged, and smiled a little bit. Not a big smile. Just a small one, her eyebrow raised slightly.

She was mocking him!

'That was some stupid thing you did coming through the field like that with everyone in the town told there was a bull in it.'

The happy glint dimmed in Rose's eyes and she lowered them.

He had upset her and immediately felt sorry.

'There was no sign,' she said, still looking at her feet.

Patrick remembered that, being part of the professional

class, Rose's family lived slightly apart from the ordinary town people. As the local doctor, her father was liked and respected, but his wife was aloof. Mrs Hopkins was not interested in local news and Rose was never let out to dances or to the pictures like other girls. It was possible then that she had not picked up news from around the town about Mickey's new bull.

'Well anyway,' he said, making his voice as soft and gentle as if he were talking to a child, 'you're safe now.'

She rewarded him with a smile as dazzling as a film star's and Patrick felt that his legs might go from under him.

'Are you going in for a swim?' he asked.

It sounded like such a stupid thing to say now, but she laughed, as if he were the wittiest man in the world.

'I don't know,' she said. 'What about you?'

Spurred on by her smile and the aftermath of his bull-chasing, Patrick ripped off his shirt, breeches and pants, and then right there, stark naked and in full view of Rose Hopkins – the doctor's daughter – he ran down the jetty and threw himself into the freezing water. When he came back up to the surface he saw her standing there on the edge laughing and clapping. Patrick felt as if he was the funniest, cleverest man in the world.

'Come in,' he shouted. 'It's warm, I promise.'

Rose took off her shoes and laid them carefully on the mossy wood, then sat down on the edge of the jetty and dipped her toes in the water. She let out a shiver. 'It's cold as ice!' she squealed, then said, 'I'm not as adventurous as you.'

He swam towards her, making long broad strokes with his arms, trying to impress her. He trod water in front of her, his breath heavy with the cold. He could feel every inch of his naked body tingling, the chill of the water fighting the heat of his nakedness. Rays of sun bounced off his skin and looking down at his arms he saw how tanned he had become. With his long narrow face, broad nose and coarse curls, Patrick was told he was the most handsome boy in the town. He didn't care much about that, but he also knew when he fixed his vivid blue eyes on something, be it girl or bull, what effect they had.

He fixed them on Rose now and said, 'You're as adventurous as any man, I'm thinking.'

'What makes you say that?'

Patrick's limbs were getting tired and he suddenly regretted his spontaneous urge to strip naked.

'Facing down a big bull, there's not every man would do that.'

He felt stupid having a conversation, with her fully dressed in the warm sunlight and him naked in the freezing lake. What had he been thinking of?

Then Rose did something entirely unexpected. She closed her eyes, pointed her toes and slid herself, fully dressed, into the water with the smoothness of a raw egg sliding down the edge of a cold plate. Before her head went under, Patrick heard her say in a clear voice, yet not much louder than a whisper, 'Save me. I can't swim.'

Rose didn't know why she did such a reckless, stupid thing. It was the same passionate impulse that had led her to take the back route down to the lake, after she had seen Patrick Murphy and his friends taking the road in that direction with their swim bags. Her parents had gone down to Galway for the day and she had stayed behind in the house on her own.

Her mother had wanted her to go with them. She was quite insistent but Rose had said she would prefer to stay at home and sketch. Eleanor Hopkins had no reason not to trust her daughter. Rose was a quiet, studious young woman who, aside from a friendship with young Sinead Murphy stretching back to their first years in school together, spent most of her time drawing and sketching, for which she had some considerable talent. There had been talk of sending her up to Dublin to art school, when the time came. But the idea of that made Eleanor uncomfortable. Rose had grown into a beauty and Eleanor knew all about the great responsibility beauty could bring and the terrible pitfalls that came with male flattery. Including a backstreet abortion in a filthy room above a shop in Dublin's seamy streets, which had robbed a demure young girl of her capacity to have children. It was a dark secret that, as a medical man, her husband suspected, but never referred to. Rose was adopted from a convent shortly before the Cork doctor moved his practice and family to this Mayo town. Rose did not know she was adopted and her parents never discussed it, even between themselves. Although their daughter's astonishing beauty was a constant reminder of her provenance, they kept it a secret from her. It was their shame, not hers.

Eleanor loved Rose even more than if she had given birth to her from her own broken womb. Now she was determined to keep her daughter away from boys for as long as she could.

Perhaps, then, it was a rebellion against her mother's anxiety and persistent cloistering that had caused Rose to chase Patrick Murphy and his friends down to the lake that day. The very moment her mother's back was turned she had faced off a bull and then slid into a lake in the hope that a young man would save her from drowning.

Rose felt the freezing water creep through the roots of her long thick hair as the ends floated up to the surface then, as she sank, tangled about her face in a slimy curtain. She struggled to hold her breath and after a few seconds felt the panic rise up in her, willing her to flail around and struggle against the water to reach for the air again. As she was about to open her mouth, she felt the force of Patrick's body push against her as he carried her in his firm arms up towards the surface of the lake. They burst out of the water and sucked in great breaths together, gasping and clinging to one another.

Rose had not intended to drown. All she had known was that she had wanted to embrace the moment, to keep the adventure alive. When Patrick had saved her from the bull, the feeling of having been rescued was sweeter than she could have imagined. In those moments, as she was running across the fields, heart thumping, blood pumping through her small breasts, her feet running so fast across the soft grass, she felt as if she was flying. So, she thought, this is what love feels like: to surrender and be saved. She wanted to do it again.

Rose had pretended to drown because she had wanted to find a way to make Patrick touch her. She knew she was pretty but she also knew he would never look at her. She was his sister's friend, younger than he was. Rose was the doctor's daughter, and she also knew that put her out of bounds, not just to Patrick, but to all the boys in the town. Rose was considered 'posh' and she hated that. Apart from Sinead, all the other girls thought her standoffish and strange, because she preferred to paint and draw than to talk to people. Sinead said they were just jealous of her because she was beautiful, but Rose didn't think she was especially beautiful. She knew she looked 'different' from the other girls, with her ash-blonde hair and pale, delicate skin. She longed to be earthy and 'ordinary' in the just plain pretty way that the boys liked. She wanted to be teased and tickled and danced with, but it seemed that the local boys were somewhat shy of approaching her and the girls just ignored her. Sinead said not to mind them. She said that Rose's drawing was a special talent. She understood people with special talents because her brother was able to sing like John McCormack. Sinead said that her brother found it hard because people didn't always understand how important singing was to him. Patrick once confided that the only time he was truly happy was when he was singing. Sometimes, he told Sinead, he dreamt of having enough money to go to America and become a big star, but he was afraid of saying it to people in case they laughed at him.

Rose could not imagine Sinead's older brother worrying about anything. But then, no one could imagine Rose Hopkins, the doctor's daughter, being worried about anything either. She was the girl who had everything, and Patrick was the boy who had everything. Yet Sinead had told her that Patrick, too, had that strange space inside him: the space she could only fill when she was drawing.

That was what had started Rose off looking at Patrick Murphy in a different way. Up to then he had just been the good-looking bad-boy in town. Now, it seemed, he was a sensitive artist, like her. An unlikely soulmate. Rose had followed him that day, hoping she might draw him away from his friends and, perhaps, strike up a conversation. She had not banked on the bull. Frightening as it was, the encounter with it had worked to her advantage. She had certainly got Patrick's attention.

Underneath his blather, she knew that Patrick was not the type to put his hands on a girl uninvited, especially not his little sister's friend. Which was why she slid into the water and put herself at risk of drowning.

She had known he would save her. When she felt his strong

arms lift her up towards the air again, towards breath, towards light, she felt the thrill of being saved as acutely as if she had actually fallen to her death.

Patrick put his hand under her torso and swam the few strokes to the edge of the jetty and then told her to hold on to the wooden stilt. He should have asked her why she had done such a stupid thing. She might have got tangled in weeds, he might not have been able to see her in the dense lake water. He should have been angry that she had recklessly put them both in such a dangerous situation. But when he looked at her face and her glistening wet skin, her eyes glittering with the reflection from the lake, with the excitement of simply being alive, he was flooded through with a painful desire. Reaching out, he ran his thumb along her bottom lip and as her eyes half closed, he kissed her, his naked body folded around her, keeping her afloat.

In that moment, the fierce cold and the adrenalin rush dropped away and all Rose could feel was him.

'His clothes are here, he's after going in without us… Murphy! Where the feck are you?'

They had not heard the lads coming down the jetty until they were on top of them.

'Shite,' Patrick whispered.

Rose wasn't worried about getting caught. Nothing in the world mattered to her except being kissed by Patrick Murphy. Nonetheless, she was glad to see that he was worried for her reputation.

He whispered at her, 'Follow my lead.' Then, 'Down here, lads!' he called out. 'She fell in – she can't swim so I came in after her.'

Neither of the boys commented on the fact that he had stripped before diving in for this daredevil rescue, or asked why Rose Hopkins came down to the jetty with a swim bag when she was unable to swim. Either they didn't think of it, or they were too shocked to believe that their friend was forward enough, or stupid enough, to go after the doctor's daughter.

For the rest of that afternoon Rose lay on the jetty with the three lads playing and talking around her; jumping in and out of the water, showing off their smooth, strong bodies. They were kind and respectful towards her, feeding her sweet biscuits and allowing her a taste of their poitin – which burnt her lips. She lay on the jetty, her clothes drying on her skin. When the others were in the water she and Patrick looked across at each other. His blue eyes gazed at her with something she could not name but which made her feel as if her limbs might dissolve with longing. Rose turned on her side and felt the hot sun bake her damp dress. The secret kiss and the passion of her rescue seemed to burn into her very soul over the course of that afternoon. She longed to kiss him again, and again, and to never stop kissing him, but she knew that could not happen while the others were watching. They would have to wait, and Rose knew her life from then on would be spent counting the moments until she saw Patrick Murphy again.

2

Yonkers, New York, 1958

AVA BROGAN was doing the jitterbug, zigzagging with her unnaturally long legs and large feet, and flicking her arms out to her sides in time to the Jack Ruane Band. The dance floor of the Emerald Ballroom in Yonkers was packed tonight, but Ava's limbs were so long that the other dancers left a wide circle around her in case she gave one of them a dig. Another person might have been more self-conscious about flinging herself around like that, but, despite her height and build, Ava was a good dancer, and she knew it. The only place where she had confidence in how she looked was on the dance floor. It didn't matter if she was pretty or not, or that she was wearing pants and a sweater instead of a dress, when she was dancing, it was just her and the music.

Tonight she was mostly dancing with Jamsey Collins, an Irish guy who cleaned windows in her father's office where she and Myrtle worked in the typing pool. Even though Ava was the boss's daughter, she had no airs and graces. Her father was a self-made man, Irish himself, and didn't mind who his only daughter dated as long as she was happy. Her mother was a different story. She didn't think Ava should be working in an office at all, or wasting her time learning to dance when she should be busying herself finding a good husband. Ava shrugged off her mother's concerns but in truth she was hoping that one might lead to the other.

Ava and Jamsey had just done two jives, a cha-cha, the stroll and now the jitterbug – back to back. She could tell he was ready to stop after that crazy jive to 'Rip It Up', but she had challenged him to two more. At one point he had her laughing so hard, messing about during their stroll, that she thought she might have to stop and be sick! Jamsey was a funny-looking guy, gangly, and even taller than she was. He wasn't a looker but he was a charmer all right, what the Irish called 'great craic'. Ava liked him but, more than that, she thought she might be in with a chance – none of the girls in the typing pool was interested in him and so she felt they had that in common. Perhaps he knew what it was like to be left out too.

When they were done, Ava threw herself down into the banquette next to her friend Myrtle, exhausted.

'You are one hell of a dancer young lady,' Jamsey said, panting. 'You have me worn out.' Ava laughed. She felt her face redden with a flush of hope, and was glad to have the excuse of the dancing to cover it. 'Can I get you ladies a drink?' he asked. But as he stood up, the slow set started with a smoochy waltz. Jamsey held out his hand and said, 'May I?'

Ava blushed and was about to accept when she saw that he wasn't holding his hand out to her, but to Myrtle. This had obviously been his intention all along: being friendly with Ava in order to get close to her prettier friend, who would never have looked at him otherwise. It hurt.

Ava flinched then gathered herself before Myrtle sensed her disappointment.

'Do you mind?' Myrtle mouthed as she hopped behind him, her hand in his.

Ava shook her head and made a funny face. Jamsey turned and gave her a friendly wink, as if Ava were one of the boys.

'I'll go and get the drinks,' she said, then called after Myrtle, 'Watch his hands – he's cheeky!'

She felt a stab of rejection, and then shook it off by reminding herself it was always the same.

Ava was the most popular girl in the room for the fast dances, but she never got asked up for the slow set. Even the boys that nobody else liked weren't interested in her. It wasn't their fault. How any boy could take a girl of her height and build seriously, especially, as her mother was constantly at pains to point out, since she insisted on wearing 'those dreadful pants' instead of a dress.

She went up to the bar and ordered two coffees for herself and Myrtle. Jamsey could buy his own drink. Ava was sore, but she was no pushover. He hadn't meant to be cruel but even so, it was a nasty game he had played getting to Myrtle through her. There was no need to reward his cunning with a drink.

She stood looking out at the vast wooden dance floor. The resident band was playing a medley of old-fashioned Irish waltzes. Couples clung to each other. The older men wore suits and ties, only taking their jackets off to dance, draping them on the backs of the chairs. The younger men wore the smart-casual look that was all the rage – slacks and collared sweater-shirts. Many of the younger girls were wearing tight pencil skirts that had just come into fashion. Myrtle was poured into one, which showed off her full bottom and wasp-waist to full effect.

Despite her friends cajoling her to embrace fashion, Ava disliked dressing up. Everything she put on seemed only to draw attention to her height and broad build. As a teenager in those innocent years when she did not realize quite how unattractive she was, she had experienced the humiliation of being left out. So now, during the slow sets, while the other girls sat prettily smoking, waiting for their turn to be asked up to dance, Ava always went straight to the bar. She got asked up occasionally, but only ever by the desperate or the drunk.

Kind-hearted by nature, Ava had endured being fondled and stepped on by the very worst the Irish-American dance-hall scene could throw at her. One night, about two years ago, after a particularly treacherous waltz with a man who had more hair growing out of his ears than on his head, she was slapped on the bottom and told she was 'a fine big heft of a thing that would be a welcome addition to one of the biggest cattle farms in Mayo'. The girls in the typing pool were in stitches when she relayed her ordeal the following morning during coffee break, but as she reached twenty-two, Ava could feel that the self-deprecating humour and her plucky nature had begun to fail her.

She watched the couples on the dance floor. The older married ones gliding in the old-fashioned style, the younger ones with their bodies pressed against each other, shuffling slowly in search of intimacy. A murmured suggestion, a breathless request, might be given permission to slide outside and canoodle in a car before being dropped home. Some girls would be left on their parents' doorstep with the promise of new love. Others would go home alone, carrying with them the hope that next Saturday the handsome prince would find them. But that was never how it was for Ava. Not tonight, or any night.

The Emerald Ballroom was where the Irish came to find love. When immigrants stepped off the boat from Ireland it was the first place they came. The huge dance hall had four bars and was a Mecca not just for the Irish immigrants, but for the children who had been born here. The Irish showbands were just taking off. They took the music that had shaken America – the rock and roll of Bill Haley and Elvis Presley – and were feeding it back to the dance-crazy Irish. While conservative priests preached about the moral dangers of rock and roll, the Irish carried on going to mass and courting each other in dance halls, as they had done since the 1940s.

The New York Irish showbands scene was like a home-from-home for Ava. She and her friend Myrtle were here every Saturday night, without fail. Ava knew most of the staff and many of the band members. The resident band comprised, largely, classically trained musicians. Dating back to the old Glenn Miller days, they kept the regulars busy waltzing and foxtrotting throughout the week. On weekends, the visiting Irish showbands came to town and shook things up; with their sparkly suits and cheeky, cheery grins, they toured a circuit that ran from London, Leeds, across all of Ireland, then to Boston, Chicago and New York. Many of these dance halls were owned by Iggy Morrow – a Kerry man and entertainment mogul who was friendly with Ava's father, Tom Brogan.

Jack Ruane and his lads had cleared the stage and the resident band was playing an old-time waltz. The jiving was over. The rest of the night would be given over to romance.

Ava looked across the crowded floor to see how Myrtle was getting along. With a bit of luck her friend would have shaken off Jamsey and would be ready to go home.

'Worn yourself out, Ava?' the barman quipped as he slid her two coffees.

Ava smiled but found herself at a loss to think of a smart comeback.

It was not that she particularly liked Jamsey, only that she had been foolish enough to think that he had liked her when he hadn't.

'On the house,' the barman said.

Did he feel sorry for her? Ava didn't even mind – she was feeling a little sorry for herself, if truth be told.

As she was walking back to the booth she spotted Myrtle and Jamsey in amongst the mash of couples. Jamsey whispered something into Myrtle's ear and she threw her red curls back and laughed. A wave of sadness washed over Ava as she felt that moment would never belong to her.

Leaving the coffees behind, she picked up her bag and her cardigan and walked back out on to the broad suburban street where she hailed a taxi home.

3

'IT'S AN investment.'

Nessa Brogan had said it straight out, while explaining to her husband, Tom, over breakfast that morning, why almost two hundred dollars of his salary was being spent on a Sybil Connolly gown for their daughter, Ava, to wear to a wedding that wasn't her own. P. J. Dolan was a high court judge and one of the most powerful people in New York Irish society.

Tom Brogan was a successful insurance broker, one of the rising middle class of Irish Americans, but his real passion was his philanthropic work with young Irish immigrants, many of whom came to be employed in the dance halls owned by his friend Iggy Morrow. Tom and the judge knew each other vaguely through their charitable work for the poor immigrant Irish, but it was apparently well enough for the Brogans to be invited to be one of their eight hundred or so guests at PJ's eldest daughter Gloria's wedding. Nessa was determined to make an impression.

The famous Irish fashion designer Sybil Connolly was renowned for her classic designs using the finest Irish tweeds and linens. Jackie Kennedy was a customer. The Brogans were not in the same league as the Kennedys but being invited to Judge Dolan's wedding was a start and Tom could afford to splash out every now and then to keep his wife and daughter happy. Or rather, his wife. His daughter hated shopping.

Nessa opened her eyes wide and nodded conspiratorially. 'It's a big day, Thomas, an opportunity. There will be a lot of important people there.'

Then she mouthed the word 'husband'. Tom shook his head and blushed, embarrassed. He didn't see what the problem was. So Ava was taller, broader and not as delicate and pretty as her cousins, but she was still a great girl. She was sensible, practical and as smart as any man he'd ever come across. She could fire through a crossword in an hour and count as fast in her head as any of the young men he had working under him. Ava was a good, kind person too – worth a thousand of these silly American girls with their bows and big busts and their wasp-waists. As far as Tom Brogan was concerned, any man would be the luckiest man alive to marry his daughter. What she needed to find was a good, solid Irishman, like himself. The fact that she insisted on working in the typing pool of his insurance firm didn't help. She was too independent by far, and men didn't like that either. Ava could afford to buy her own clothes, but most of the time she didn't bother. This was her mother's way of trying to fancy her up a bit. Tom could have told her it wouldn't work. Ava just wasn't that kind of girl.

Tom loved his only daughter more than anything and told her she was beautiful every day. The problem was, she didn't believe him.

'You can stop talking about me finding a husband,' Ava said to them. 'I'll find my own when I'm good and ready.'

Tom laughed. 'There now, Nessa, will you leave the poor girl alone?'

Nessa smiled, taking temporary comfort in her daughter's show of confidence.

'The fitting is in the Plaza at eleven, we'll have time for lunch afterwards in the Palm Court...'

'Steady,' Tom said.

'Perhaps your father might call in with one of his colleagues?'

'She never gives up!' Tom said, smiling, bringing the paper back up to his face.

'And I never will,' said Nessa, picking up her bag, 'until our daughter is as happily married as we are.'

Tom pulled a face behind his paper so just Ava could see and she winked back at him.

It was important to Ava that she let her parents know that she neither noticed nor cared that she wasn't especially pretty. Except that Ava did notice and she did care. Her nose was too long, her eyes were close together and her face was broader than it should have been. She had good hair that set easily – but it was a dull shade of mousy brown and she was nervous to dye it a shade darker for fear of looking ghoulish. Glamorous 'Hollywood' blonde would have been a ridiculous notion on a girl of her size – almost six foot tall, with broad shoulders and long limbs. She was slim, but not curvaceous. Ava had long since decided that she was not going to apologize for her size. She did not want to make herself invisible and shrink into the corners of the dance hall to become a wallflower. She had lots of friends, and people liked her – men liked her too, just not in a romantic way. At least, not the ones she liked.

Ava's favourite film star was Doris Day and since she was a young girl she had tried to emulate the star's feisty, independent manner. Doris had shown her that a girl didn't have to be sultry like Lauren Bacall, seductive like Marilyn Monroe, or romantic like Grace Kelly. She could be tomboyish and plucky and full of fun. But she still had to be pretty if she wanted a man. If she wasn't pretty, a girl didn't stand a hope in hell of finding love. Ava knew, from seeing how happy her parents were, that without love, life was nothing.

The lavishly decorated suite was on the tenth floor of the Plaza Hotel. It had panelled walls and heavy silk drapes at the windows that were closed to preserve the client's modesty. Light was provided by occasional lamps with large yellow shades that threw off a warm, flattering light. Twice a year, Sybil Connolly would take a suite here and New York's wealthiest and most discerning fashion lovers would make appointments to be fitted with her elegant, classical designs. Ava left her clothes in a pile on the thick, navy carpet and came out from behind the ornate Chinese screen in her undergarments. Her long pale limbs were shivering, less from the cold than from the shame of being almost naked in front of a complete stranger.

Sybil's assistant pulled out a magnificent evening gown for her to try on. It was made of Connolly's trademark pleated linen, in a shade of soft, dove grey. Her mother had wanted her to have this dress since reading about it in *Harper's Bazaar*. The handcrafted effect was produced by closely pleating up to nine yards of handkerchief linen to produce one yard of delicate fabric. It could be packed away in a bag then shaken out and emerge as good as new. *Harper's* had declared Sybil's evening dresses both 'modern' and 'practical'.

'Just like you,' Nessa had said, hopeful that the cutting would light a fire under her daughter's lack of interest in how she dressed. Ava had agreed to give it a try and Nessa remained optimistic that this expensive dress would turn her daughter into a princess.

'There now,' Sybil's assistant said, holding open the huge, pleated skirt. 'Step into this, like a good girl.'

Ava loved the way the Irish talked. As if they had known you all their lives. At least half the people at their church were 'full Irish' not just born to Irish parents, like she was. The assistant talked in a kindly, matronly way, although she couldn't have been much older than Ava.

Ava stood in front of the full-length mirror as the assistant pulled the bodice up over her slim hips and narrow chest. The grey dress had a skirt, which spread out in a soft triangle from the waist. The bodice crossed over her bust and the fabric felt as soft and sublime as a cloud. It was, truly, a magnificent gown. However, it looked the same on her as all the magnificent dresses her mother had been making her try on since she was a little girl. Just ordinary. She glanced across at her mother and saw the shadow of disappointment flicker across Nessa's face before she plastered on her usual hopeful smile.

The dress was beautiful, but her daughter Ava was not. Another expensive mistake, she thought. The more elaborate the dress, the plainer her daughter seemed to render it. Ava was plain, and as each year passed, getting plainer. In the year since she had been home from finishing school she went about the house in slacks and her father's weekend sweaters, only putting on a skirt and blouse when her mother forced her into them. Nessa didn't want to destroy her confidence but if her daughter didn't smarten herself up she would never find a husband, and without a husband Ava would never be happy.

'Oh no.' Sybil Connolly swept into the room and stood behind Ava, her dark hair swept back from her face in a high set, her severe eyebrows raised in a look of thoughtful disapproval.

'Oh no – I do not like this dress on you, young lady – at all. This is all wrong.'

Nessa began to bristle. She was paying a lot of money for the dress and did not appreciate the woman's tone. It was one thing for Nessa herself to comment inwardly on her daughter's unremarkable looks, but quite another when somebody else did it.

'We want the finest dress for our daughter,' she asserted. 'Money is no object.'

Sybil smiled at her curtly. 'I don't doubt it – but this dress is all wrong on her.'

'But it's this season,' Nessa objected, adding sharply, 'And the most expensive you have.'

'Seasons mean nothing,' Sybil said. She gave a formidable glare. 'And price is of little interest to me.' Nessa blushed, regretting her faux pas.

Sybil turned her attention back to Ava. 'What this young lady…What is your name, my dear?'

'Ava.' She had never met anyone like Sybil before. So outspoken, so…certain. She reminded Ava of some of the stricter nuns in her boarding school but with lipstick and coiffed hair.

'What Ava needs is something to suit her own style. Isn't that right?'

Ava was not aware that she had a style.

'I suppose.'

'Tell me, my dear, do you like this dress?' Sybil said as

she stood behind her, smoothing down the exquisitely soft pleated skirt.

'Well, it's beautiful.'

'Of course it is. As your mother tells me,' and she arched a perfectly painted eyebrow, 'it's the most expensive dress money can buy. But do you like yourself in it?'

Ava wasn't sure what she meant. She didn't like how she looked in anything and avoided looking at herself as much as possible. Standing in front of a full-length mirror like this was torture. She thought she should answer truthfully if she wanted to get out of it so she shook her head and said with certainty: 'No. No, I don't.'

'Good,' Sybil said. 'So we will find something else.'

The older woman clicked for an assistant to come and undress Ava as she walked across to a clothes rail by the window and instructed another assistant to pull out items for her one by one.

She flicked past dresses, rejecting them with a 'No – not that one, wrong colour. Again...'

Ava felt a curious wave of depression come over her. She had been in this position before. Hours spent in the dressing room of Saks, Fifth Avenue while Nessa and a bevy of shop assistants passed in dress after dress, nothing ever fitting her properly, and nothing ever looking quite right. Hope followed by the humiliation of just not being quite pretty enough, not quite feminine enough to pull anything off. Now this was happening in the rarefied atmosphere of the Plaza and in front of this very important woman.

'STOP!' Sybil said, and then dramatically added, 'Now – what have we got for you here, Ava?'

Her assistant was holding up a tweed suit. It had a straight, slim skirt and a fitted jacket, nipped in tight and flaring into a waved pelmet at the waist, all pulled smartly together by eight mother-of-pearl buttons at the front. But by far the most unusual thing about the suit was its colour: an exquisite shade of pink.

'It's the colour of a rose,' Ava said.

'Well yes,' Sybil said. 'How charming of you to notice. As a matter of fact this tweed was commissioned by me from the wonderful nuns in Foxford Woollen Mills on the west coast of Ireland. It is a match for the wild roses of Mayo, the most delicate flowers you will ever see.'

While her assistant held the skirt open for Ava to step into, Sybil herself pulled the jacket over her bare shoulders and buttoned it up the front with confident speed, pinching the fabric with her strong manicured fingers.

As Sybil stepped back and Ava saw herself in the mirror in the rose suit, she could not quite believe her eyes.

Encased in the structure of this skirt and jacket, her tall gangly limbs looked statuesque, almost royal. She lifted her chin and noticed how the V of the neckline seemed to elongate her neck and make her look slimmer. Holding her own gaze in the mirror, Ava turned to one side and, arching her back slightly, checked her profile. She had miraculously acquired curves. The rose colour of the tweed was unmistakably feminine and yet it did not look ridiculously out of place on her broad shoulders. It was a wonderful outfit. More importantly, she was wonderful in it.

'I look so different,' she said. She smiled nervously at herself in the mirror.

'You look beautiful,' Nessa said.

'What she looks,' Miss Connolly added, 'is stylish. A sense of style will carry a woman much further than beauty, if she knows how to use it.'

Nessa looked at the designer, wondering if she was being negative about her daughter's appearance, but she seemed not to be. Although she was, indeed, a very stylish woman, Miss Connolly was no great beauty herself.

'Beauty fades with age, Mrs Brogan. Style matures. If a woman has the right clothes with the perfect fit, she will never be without confidence and grace.'

All Ava knew was that, for the first time in her life, she felt beautiful. She had never wanted anything as much in her life.

'We really were hoping for a dress,' Nessa said. 'It's for a wedding, you see. My husband's colleague—'

'I prefer the suit, Mother – please?' Ava pleaded.

'A suit is perfectly acceptable for day wear at a wedding,' Sybil asserted, pulling out a lace blouse from her rack. 'And this will dress it up for evening wear – I assume you have pearls?'

'Of course she has pearls,' Nessa said, anxious to reassert her status, and resigning herself to lending her daughter her own pearls in the interests of fulfilling her husband-finding potential.

Ava was barely listening.

She could not take her eyes off her own reflection. She did not think she was beautiful. Indeed, that would never be the case. But in this suit there was no denying she had something. Style, Miss Connolly had called it, but it was more than that. When Ava Brogan looked at herself in the mirror she saw somebody she recognized. Neither the gawky girl of her childhood, nor the gangly tomboy of her young adulthood – but the person she was always meant to be.

For the first time in her life, Ava looked and felt like a woman.

4

FTER SHE discovered her parents had died, Sheila escaped into the radio, listening to it obsessively, every minute that she could. The joyful twinkling jazz piano of Count Basie, the comedic lyrics of Fats Waller and the harmonic bebop of the Delta Rhythm Boys were able to cheer her up in a way nothing else could. The pleadings of Louis Armstrong spoke to her soul and listening to music was the only time Sheila was able to be herself.

Uncle Samuel deplored swing. When Count Basie or Eddie Condon came on the radio, he would rage and fluster. 'Turn off that rubbish!' he would shout. 'Music is Mahler and Mozart – never forget that, Sheila.'

Samuel hoped Sheila would develop more sophisticated, classical tastes as she grew older but his pompous pronouncements only made her even more determined to pursue her love of modern music. She bought records and hid them in her room. There was no point in trying to explain to her uncle that this was the music that moved her. Not the droning misery of Mahler who reminded her only of her dead family and all she had lost. This was the music that made her feel alive. It was new, exciting. Swing music was who she was now – and that was all that mattered. Classical piano made her recall learning 'Für Elise' on her uncle's knee and Sheila had closed the door on those times. Good or bad, she did not want to remember.

As she grew into a young woman, Sheila fulfilled her family obligations by being a grateful little orphan and a good Jew. Samuel and Anya Klein hoped she would meet a nice boy in school whom she might marry. A doctor, or an accountant, perhaps, not a musician like her father, or a poor professor like Samuel. A good Jewish man with some status and a little money. Sheila deserved a nice husband who could give her a good life, after all the poor child had been through. She went along with their wishes because she was grateful for all they had done for her. At the same time, she could feel something wild smouldering inside her. She knew that, however happy it would make Anya and Samuel, a cosy life in Riverdale was not for her. At nineteen, during her second year of college where she was studying pharmacy, the fire broke out inside her. She went to see Charlie Parker playing at the Three Deuces and that night, in the velvet-red underbelly of New York, Sheila grew up. She sat on a leather banquette in a smoky corner swaying from side to side, a cigarette expertly falling from full scarlet lips, and she felt as if she was at home. Shy of dancing in public, she hid in the corner, watching as couples twisted their hips and swung their partners, pretty skirts swooping and smart boys smiling. Black and white, rich and poor – everybody wanted to dance.

This was where she wanted to be, not in some dusty college.

Sheila's quick academic mind enabled her to fly through her college work at double speed. The rest of the time she spent in the jazz clubs around 52nd Street: Three Deuces, Onyx Club, the Famous Door. She stuck out her degree to keep Anya and Samuel happy, then, as soon as she could, got a job in a diner in the city and left the house in leafy Riverdale.

'Where will you live?' Samuel said. He was sorry she was leaving but Sheila was an adult of twenty. She could go where she liked.

He could see she was aching to get away. She was escaping her past. She needed to do that.

'I'll find somewhere in the city,' she said. 'I'll be back every weekend.'

Anya wept like Sheila was dying. Sheila knew she should feel bad at leaving them but, in reality, she felt relieved, and that just made her feel more guilty.

She took a room in Times Square, above Al's Diner.

Sheila felt at home in Times Square with its huge, Technicolor advertisements urging people to 'Relax with Camel Cigarettes' or improve their lives with Admiral Television Appliances. The transience, the constant moving, was in such sharp contrast to the leafy, closeted environs of Riverdale, yet, for some reason, the crazy pace made her feel at ease. This was a no-man's land, a commercial hub where people came to see a show, eat a meal, or dance their socks off for a few hours before going back to their suburban lives. Times Square offered New Yorkers a brief interlude in their dull lives to be entertained and indulged. Anxious for adventure and escape, Sheila turned that series of sweet, brief interludes into her life.

Sheila soon got bored working in the diner. The daytime hours didn't suit her. So she got herself a job in the Twilight

Ballroom, an old-style dance hall, right across the street. She lived from one work shift to the next, from one man to the other, club-to-club, dance-to-dance – snatching meals when she remembered and going back to her shabby apartment.

Sheila started out waiting tables, then worked behind the bar and eventually, after five years, was promoted to manager. The Twilight had a resident band who stuck to ballroom and swing. It was a good job and it enabled her to live the nocturnal life she enjoyed, but as the years went by, Sheila's heart remained firmly in the jazz scene. Part of her felt that she should be working in the jazz clubs and not some schmaltzy outdated ballroom. However, she also knew that if she worked in the clubs where she socialized, she might go into a hedonistic free fall. Sheila knew how to party but she knew her limitations too. She loved her black musician friends but loving things too much could lead to trouble, so she kept a respectable distance, working hard in the ballrooms then relishing her rare nights off in her precious jazz clubs. Ballrooms and jazz clubs and even the up and coming dinner-dancing venues were worlds apart from one another. Those musicians who worked in the ballrooms were mostly white and classically trained. The self-taught musicians in the jazz/R&B clubs were mostly black. They overlapped, of course. Good musicians were always welcome in both camps, and it wasn't unusual to see a middle-aged white saxophonist in an all-black jazz band or, indeed, a black trombone player in a big band.

However, all of this was about to radically change, and Sheila wanted a piece of it.

Sheila had bought a record the year before called 'Crazy Man Crazy' by a white kid called Bill Haley. The record had a wild beat, and she liked it. So when she heard that this kid from Michigan had just got a regular gig in New Jersey in a dance bar, she decided to go and check him out.

As soon as Sheila walked in the door she could tell this was a country bar. Not her scene at all. Nice girls in pretty dresses with full skirts – boys in Sunday-best shirts and slacks. Not as formal as the ballrooms – but all white. She got a drink and stood at the small bar and watched the crowd. As they waited, Sheila could feel their excitement in the air. But then, she thought, country people always got a bit excited when they were out. Eventually, a bunch of white boys came on stage. The chubby front man had a big smile and a cowlick in his hair. They all wore long, tartan jackets and dicky bows. Pure hick. The singer was carrying a guitar and as he closed his eyes and reached his head back to release the first note, Sheila braced herself for the cowboy yodel. What came out surprised her more than anything else she had ever heard. As the band broke into 'Rock Around the Clock', her hips started to swing.

Sheila was a cautious dancer. In the jazz clubs, she never felt she belonged on the dance floor. She sat, clicking her fingers, tapping her feet, smoking laconically, enjoying the music that way. But with this new, strange rockabilly sound she found her hips were swaying from side to side at a speed that felt fast – too fast – and yet she was compelled to move in a way that felt utterly natural. It was as if the beat had injected her, and everyone else there, with a kind of electricity. Her body seemed to understand what to do in a way it had never done before now. By the time the lead singer roared out 'put your glad rags on', Sheila had grabbed the hand of the nearest stranger, not noticing or caring who he was, and was allowing herself to be swung and twirled around the floor in his expert grip, her feet stamping out the one-two beat as if she were born with it inside her.

Then, as Sheila moved around the floor like a wildcat she realized she had heard this very song being played before. It was a proto-rock song called 'Rock the Joint' that she had as a Jimmy Preston recording. She had always enjoyed the beat of it and yet she had never actually danced to it before. However, the way these hillbilly boys were playing the tune she simply had no choice but to dance. It was like a tribal drum, as if something old and terribly familiar was instructing her to get 'with it'. When the song ended her body was hungry for more and she joined the crowd in baying for Bill and his Comets to play it again, and again. Three times the crowd danced to that tune as if they had never heard it before. While the band took a break, Sheila leaned against the wall, and it hit her like a thunderbolt. This was black music for white kids. These hillbilly kids and their crazy white R&B could change the world.

The next day she went into work and marched straight into Dan's office.

'You have to book this band, Dan,' she said, 'Bill Haley and His Comets. They are calling it rock and roll; it's going to change everything.'

Dan looked across at her, narrowed his eyes and gave a hollow laugh.

'I heard of them, bunch of kids from Michigan. Waste of time. It'll never take off.'

'But…it's like black music for white people, Dan. This is what we've been waiting for. You didn't see the crowd there. They were going nuts.'

Dan shook his head.

'I heard about it. Jumping up and down and going crazy like savages. The kids are going wild – it's a phase. It'll never catch on.'

'Well I think it will!'

Dan smiled at her, although she could sense he was getting irritated.

'I had a meeting with the boys in the band about it last week.'

'Without me?'

'Sheila, darling, I've told you before, leave the music to the experts. As manager, you are in charge of keeping the books straight and making sure the cloakrooms are tidy...'

Sheila would have walked out if she thought she could have got a manager's job anywhere else. If she left the Twilight, she'd be back to square one selling cigarettes in some other dive. How she wished she could be in charge of the whole place. In charge of her own life...

'Me and the boys have been looking into it and, let me tell you, rock and roll ain't never going to hit the mainstream ballrooms and dance halls. Not in New York – not anywhere. The big bands are going nowhere. This rock and roll nonsense is a flash in the pan. Dancing cheek-to-cheek is here to stay. Let the lunatic kids wear themselves out in their living rooms and underground dives, they are not coming in among the respectable folk in the Twilight.'

If Dan McAndrew had been a respectable, churchgoing, God-fearing man, Sheila might have understood his resistance. But he was anything but. He drank like a fish and cheated on his wife. However, he was also funny and charming, so he got away with it. In the years that she had been working for him Sheila had come to care about his business, and a little bit about Dan himself. Sheila knew she was right about bringing in rock and roll. Unfortunately, being a woman meant that she could never be right when it came to a man's business. However, knowing that just made her even more determined to keep trying.

A month later, 'Rock Around the Clock' was all over the TV and radio. Still Dan and the resident band would not change their minds. The old guard would not let down their guard. If they let this reprobate music into their ballrooms, all hell might break loose.

Sheila decided to try and persuade Dan one more time.

At one a.m., after the bar shut up and the club closed for the night, Sheila ran into the ladies' restrooms to get changed out of the pencil skirt, blouse and heels Dan insisted she wear at work. She pulled on pedal pushers, low pumps and polo neck sweater, all black – her off-duty uniform. Briefly, she checked herself in the mirror. Shaking out her bun and pulling her eyebrow-length fringe down, she squinted through it as she quickly slicked a slash of red over her full lips. She barely looked at herself before moving on. Time in front of the mirror was wasted time. Sheila was puzzled by women who spent time fussing over themselves. You couldn't change how you looked any more than you could change who you were. Men said they preferred pretty faces so women spent a lot of time trying to make themselves look prettier for them, but Sheila had sussed out long ago that it was all just a game. Seduction had very little to do with beauty, and everything to do with sex. Sheila wasn't 'easy' for the sake of it. She was discerning about whom she slept with. The guys she had sex with, she liked. Sheila needed affection and the human touch as much as the next woman, but unlike most women, she was not prepared to get married to have it. As soon as she felt a guy was getting to like her too much, getting soft on her, she made sure to blow him off. Sheila did not want to shackle herself to one man. She found the very idea boring and frightening. If she could find a man who was her equal, one who would let her work and be herself, then that would be fine. But if there were guys like that in New York, she never met them. She always made her position clear with all her lovers. No strings. Strictly sex. Most men didn't believe her. They convinced themselves that she must be in love with them and sometimes got very offended when they found out that she had not got the least intention of marrying them. Sometimes men fell in love with her. She broke some hearts but, as long as she gave them a warning shot, Sheila did not feel she was doing anything wrong. Intimacy, and the hurt that went along with it, was beyond her. That was the way she liked it.

When Sheila walked into his office, Dan was slightly taken aback. He had never seen her with her hair down before. She looked a bit wild tonight. Untamed. Angela, his wife, was on holiday in Italy for the month. Angela's family were old mafia. They all met in Naples once a year and Dan was never invited. It bugged him how her brothers were always lording it over him as if they were something special. Tough guys. He could tell they thought his wife was too good for him. Nonetheless, Dan had promised himself he would be good while she was away, this time. Plus Sheila worked for him and that had never played out too well for him in the past. She was on about the rock and roll thing again.

'It's not just about the dancing,' she insisted. 'If we get in on the rock and roll scene we could back our own band. Make records. Make a fortune!'

'We're fine as we are,' he said.

What did Sheila know about business? She was a woman. Albeit a smart one and, he had always suspected, a bit of a firecracker.

'But if you don't move with the times, Dan, we'll get left behind and—'

'I'll tell you what, sweetheart,' Dan said. 'Why don't you try and persuade me over dinner?'

'It's one a.m., Dan. There's nowhere open.'

'This is New York, doll,' he said. 'There is always somewhere open. Besides, I know a place.'

Sheila knew what place he was talking about. His place.

Dan was incorrigible but there was something irresistible about him. It was late but Sheila was wide awake and the adventure of doing something illicit was calling her. Maybe it was time to get to know the devil she already knew a bit better.

'OK,' she said, 'but just dinner.'

'Just dinner,' he said. 'I promise.'

Then he smiled and pulled up his crossed fingers from beneath the desk. She laughed.

5

T HE AFFAIR with Dan lasted four years. If you could call it an affair. It was a casual arrangement based on attraction and need. There was a kind of fondness, by dint of having known each other for as long as they had and working together. The fact that he was married suited Sheila. When she was a kid, Sheila had known that staying at home making soup and rearing children would never be the life she wanted. The affair with Dan bore out that her early instincts then had been right. Although their affair was sporadic, this was the longest 'relationship' she had had with a man. It taught Sheila that she was too selfish, and not cut out for pandering to a man's needs. Both Dan and Sheila knew that she would never be a threat to his marriage. She would have been horrified if he had left Angela.

Sheila was discreet and accommodating. Dan was great in the sack, and always on hand for company while Angela was tied up with her huge, Italian family.

She was not in love with Dan, nor he with her, but there

was a kind of equality that suited her. Having worked with her through ten years, Dan knew her. He knew what she was capable of, what she wanted. There was loyalty and respect there. At least, that's what she had thought until a week ago, when Dan had called her into his office and told her his fiery Italian wife had found out they had slept together. Sheila was horrified.

'Just once,' he said. 'That's all she knows about.'

'How did she...?'

'She got it out of me,' he said. 'She can be very... persuasive.'

Sheila closed her eyes and grimaced. She was sorry that she had betrayed Angela but mostly sorry that she had found out. She had known the woman, if not exactly liked her, for a long time. Angela knew that Dan was a philandering pig. He had slept with every bar girl, every waitress that had ever come through the door of the Twilight. In fact, his wife would have thought it miraculous that Sheila had managed to hold him off for as long as she had. And just once. That wasn't too bad.

'I'm sorry, Dan, that's a bummer.'

'Yeah,' he said. 'So we better, you know?'

'No, totally. I get it.'

That was that. It was back to business and how it had been before. However, when you sleep with a man, even if he is your friend, especially when he is your friend, everything changes.

Today, less than a week later, Dan called her in to say he had brought a new manager in over her head.

'Angela doesn't like us working so closely together. She doesn't mind you tending bar or being around, but not in a management position. I'll keep you on the same wage but...'

Sheila was seething with hurt rage. She looked across at him.

Her boss, her lover looked sheepish, small, scared – but at the same time his eyes were mean and determined. He meant it. He held all the cards.

'You can't fire me because I don't give a rat's ass about your stinking job! I've had enough anyway! I'm outta here!'

'Baby, please – I wasn't trying to fire you I just need...'

But he was trying to fire her. They both knew it. Dan had deliberately brought the new manager in. Sheila Klein was the feistiest, proudest woman he knew. He had known she would walk out.

Sheila stood and, arms folded, glared at him.

She wasn't leaving empty-handed. She didn't even need to say the word 'severance pay'. Dan reached for his cheque-book, and as he looked up sheepishly she just said, 'Make it hurt.' It sickened her to see him so pathetically sorry.

Sheila snatched the cheque out of his hand, and shoved it in her pocket without even checking the amount. Then she turned on her heels and stormed out of Dan's office, slamming the door behind her.

Sheila ran out the stage door on to Times Square and immediately fumbled in her bag for her pack of cigarettes. As she found them, she realized she was still holding a lit one. The long ember nearly fell into her open purse. 'Shit,' she cursed, and threw it on to the ground. She pulled a fresh one out of the pack and shoved it in her mouth. Her hands were still shaking with rage as she shook and flicked the Zippo half a dozen times before getting a flame. Finally, she drew the nicotine down into her lungs and felt herself begin to calm down.

Sheila thought now of all that she had done for that man. All that energy to try and persuade his lazy ass to get with the times? She had actually cared about his business. It made her feel sick at how damned stupid she had been to believe he might think he owed her something for her trouble. Loyalty? Respect? No. They were things men gave to other men in business. Women were for waiting tables. Sure, make the girl a manager, give her a few extra dollars, but respect a woman for doing a man's job? Nah. Never going to happen. And now he was flinging her out on the street like trash?

She threw her cigarette on the ground, lit another, and walked across to her apartment.

Inside, she went straight to the fridge and took out a cold beer. She flipped the lid of the bottle with her teeth then sat on her small bed, looked out the window and thought about what she was going to do next.

Part of Sheila was raging again at the injustice of having worked all of those years and leaving with nothing but some lousy cash. Money was never the point. Sheila knew that she had forgotten more about music than Dan and his ballroom-owning business buddies would ever know. Yet they were the ones who held all the power. She had tried to help Dan make more money by getting hip to the new scene, but he had laughed in her face. And, as she looked across at the sunlight flashing off the lit-up Pepsi sign, Sheila had a thought, as powerful as the revelation that night when she first heard Bill Haley. Rock and roll was here to stay and so was she. To hell with Dan – he had done her a favour. Losing her job at the Twilight was an opportunity. She was over thirty now. A spinster, for sure, but she wasn't ashamed of the fact. Sheila had known from a young age that she couldn't rely on anyone except herself. However, because she had been working for him for nearly ten years, she had come to rely on Dan more than she ought to have done. She didn't love him, and had only slept with him out of comfort because he was there, and she knew him, and couldn't be bothered to try and find a new, more exciting lover. Worse than that, she had become complacent about her work. Her passion for music had become dulled by time and familiarity.

In the ten years since she had left college, Sheila had never really thought about her life, where it was going or what she was doing.

But that, she decided, was all going to change.

Sheila had always wanted to be a music manager. Out there, on the scene – finding new talent, then bringing them along, turning them into stars, making hits and making money.

She was going to take this slap in the face from Dan as the kick she needed to make it work. There wasn't anybody to push her forward, but that meant there was nobody there to hold her back. She'd flown in the face of convention already just by being a single Jewish woman working in a white man's world. She was going to get herself out there, find herself an artist and start making hit records.

If she got to stick one in the gut to Dan McAndrew and his fuddy-duddy ballroom while she was doing it? Well, that would be a bonus.

She made a start the very next day.

Sheila made a list of all the great musicians who she knew were without formal management, or who would be willing to switch to somebody with her kind of fresh ambition. If she could manage a few established jazz musicians, offering them good bookings and better deals on their existing pay, Sheila believed that would give her the basis from which she could seek out and make investment in completely new talent.

She was delighted to see that the list was long, ten to fifteen definite-maybes – she knew a lot more people than she had realized. The list done, she washed her face, took off her bra and lay down for a nap. Seasoned night worker that she was,

Sheila always rested in the afternoons so she would be ready to work hard in the hours when most other people slept.

But this time, she could not sleep. For an hour, she lay there, just staring at the heavy blinds. She noted the slice of sunlight at the sill that settled on the dusty floor like a ray of hope. Sure, she was alone – at thirty-one, Sheila figured that was, more or less, a given now. She had hoped to find love, just like everybody else, but she knew she wasn't most men's idea of romance. She was too tough, too outspoken. Plus, she liked sex for the sake of it, just like a man. Men loved her for that and all of her best friends were men, but they didn't fall in love with her. How could they? She was too much like one of them. Some afternoons, lying alone in her single bed above the diner, Sheila felt sad about that. But not today. Today she was going to put them all aside and follow her dream. Her first love was music, it always had been. Until now she had been flirting from the sidelines; today, she was going to jump right in and join the game. Sheila Klein: Talent Manager. Hell, Sheila Klein – Music Impresario. She was only mad at herself for not doing this years ago, irritated by the part of her that had set her own ambitions aside out of loyalty to Dan and – yes – perhaps a bit of fearful laziness too. Those days were over now. All she had to do was find herself some talent, and if there was one thing New York had in abundance, it was talent. There was nothing to hold Sheila back. Not a man, or a job or responsibilities of any kind. She was as free as a bird to pursue her dream and, hell, was she going to fly.

She leapt out of bed and checked her watch. Four o'clock. Her friend Frankie the Sax had a regular gig playing with a five piece at a dinner club up on Lexington. Frankie was old-school. He had no manager – he worked all the time on word-of-mouth and more or less lived in the places he worked. He'd be up there now in the small club kitchen, eating his main meal of the day with the kitchen staff buzzing all around him. Then he'd march out to the bar and drink a few beers, followed by three whiskey chasers, then slide nice and easy over to the stage where he'd be mellow and smiling before the punters came in for the pre-theatre dinner bookings at six.

Frankie was a great place to start and with that knowledge Sheila felt a kick of excitement in her stomach.

Frankie was in the kitchen of the club, as she expected. His long black coat hung down over the edge of the tall barstool, his porkpie hat was perched on the side of his head, white hairs powdered his temples.

'I don't know if that's such a good idea, honey,' he said. 'There's already too many managers in this town.'

'But I know music, Frankie.'

He laughed and shook his head. 'I know that, girl, but I'm telling you – this town's gone crazy. Everything's changed. Soon as a boy opens his mouth to sing these days, there's a man there wants to make money outta him. My day we played for love and whiskey – if the punters threw you a few bucks – well then we got to eat. Now they got every two-bit kid singing before they can barely talk. There was a kid here; I was bringing him along, slow like. He had some talent but I said, you gotta bide your time, boy, wait until your voice matures, until your soul matures. You know what I mean? He ran outta here in a huff. He had heard about some English kid who was writing songs in a "music factory" downtown. I swear, they producing music in a factory now...' He shook

his head in disbelief before continuing, 'Would you believe
that same kid came back in here last week lording it up in a
Mercedes-Benz? Some man from Decca give him a deal.'

'Who's looking after you these days, Frankie?' she asked.

The wily old charmer shook his head again and laughed
her off.

'I'm too old and ugly for you to manage, honey. Besides,
I don't need no management. I roll along just fine as I am.'

Sheila gave him a peck on the cheek. He helped her put
together her list, but didn't seem too hopeful about anyone
taking her up on her offer.

However, she was undeterred, and spent the following
week diligently trawling all her favourite haunts. She headed
out at six every evening, and visited every club, large and
small, on the island of Manhattan. She talked to every musician, those she knew and those she didn't know. By Friday,
to her disappointment, she realized that Frankie was right.
All the great artists she admired already had management
and all of the new, younger acts that were worth their salt
had already been snapped up.

They were all really enthusiastic for her but nobody wanted
to be managed by a girl with no track record and none of
them knew anyone that was still looking for management.
She talked to just about every musician in town, even the old
jazz-hands, but even they had lost their laid-back edge. Suddenly, music had become all about the money. People had
been buying records for years, but since rock and roll came
along, they were buying a lot more. Music lovers were still
packing the dance halls and they were still listening to music
on the radio, but now, nearly every home in the country had
a record player. This was not simply the 'music business' any
more, it was now the 'recording industry'. There was money

to be made and, when it came to money, New Yorkers didn't hang around. The club owners, the managers, the music producers and the record companies were all in cahoots with each other. It was one big boys' club. There was a party happening and Sheila was not invited. Making money was a serious business and she knew that being a woman meant she would never be taken seriously. She began to see that while she had partied behind the scenes in the jazz and R&B clubs over the years, she had never actually worked in them. She was, after all, little more than a fan. A groupie. If she had left the Twilight all those years ago, when her instincts told her to, when she had first heard Bill Haley, she could have walked into any club and put together her own rock and roll band. But she hadn't had the guts.

But Sheila was determined. For as long as her savings would carry her, she followed every lead, rooted out every possibility. She kept going to the clubs looking for her star. However, as one week turned to two, and three weeks turned to four, she saw a pattern emerge. It seemed that the more she pushed her friends in the music industry, the more the musicians pulled back from her until, politely, backstage became off limits. Nothing was openly said, but it became clear to her that behind the scenes was not an area open to Sheila any more. Curtains began to be drawn, special areas were cordoned off for 'friends' and 'record executives'. All her old friends were suddenly busy, running off to the next gig as soon as she walked in the door. After trailing around her favourite haunts trying to charm a break out of somebody, Sheila became not only disheartened, but puzzled.

Was she imagining it or was there something else going on?

She cornered Frankie again, this time waiting for him in the diner across the road until she saw him heading into the

Cotton Club. He saw her coming and rushed towards the alley and the kitchen door, but she headed him off on the corner.

'What is going on, Frankie?' she said.

'Nothing, honey,' he said, but his voice was flat and he looked, Sheila was surprised to note, frightened.

'Why is everybody avoiding me? Is there something flying about that I don't know about?'

Everybody knew everybody in New York City. Manhattan was an island, the music industry was a family. When you were flying high it was like being at the best party in the world. When things were bad, it could get very small. Sheila could see in Frankie's face that something bad was going on.

Frankie looked behind her to check if they were being seen talking together. There was only one reason people in New York looked around the streets like that. Suddenly, it hit her. Angela – Dan's wife. Angela McAndrew – formerly Angela Balducci of the notorious Mafia clan.

Frankie shook his head. 'I know you didn't mean no harm by it, honey, I know you don't like trouble. But they are bad men, Sheila – you know who I'm talking about?'

Sheila nodded. 'I know who you're talking about.'

Frankie put his arm on her shoulder and said, 'Sweetheart, they are saying some bad things about you right now.' She looked up into his old face, his eyes were kind and rheumy with sadness. His pity was so gentle, paternal almost, that it didn't offend her. She felt like crying. Like she might collapse into his great coat and stay there for a while.

'It's not just the Balducci brothers neither. They got some Irish mob in their pocket, too. Guy called Joe Higgins been sniffing around asking questions. He owns a small club in Hell's Kitchen but he's trying to work himself up into the big time and looking for the Balduccis to back him. I hear he's real mean, Sheila. Maybe it's best if you left town for a while.'

Sheila nodded and smiled, but her heart was breaking. Leave the city? Was she being chased out by Dan's bully-boy in-laws? Was it possible? But the Balducci boys were a bad bunch all right. Sheila looked at the stern, worried face of her old friend and realized with a growing sense of alarm that this was really happening.

If Angela's brothers were going about town warning innocents like Frankie the Sax off her, no wonder she was persona non grata in the clubs.

'Thanks, Frankie,' she said. 'Maybe I'll do that.'

She kissed him and he said, 'You take care now, honey,' before tapping twice on the big steel door and being let in by the janitor. As Sheila watched him go into the kitchen she knew she was saying goodbye, not just to Frankie, but to a part of her life.

As she walked back towards midtown, Sheila let the reality of what she had just learned sink in. Aside from her dream being shattered, she had run out of money and she needed a job. Nobody would take her on as their manager right now.

There was no point in even trying. If Angela's brothers had got to the smaller club owners, then there wasn't a dance hall in Manhattan that would give her a job washing dishes.

She wouldn't give up. She didn't know anything else. But she would have to get out of the city for a while and figure out how she was going to make this work.

Sheila had made a big mistake. She knew that. Dan was the married one but the woman was the one who always paid. It wasn't fair but she would be dumb to think it would be any different. She had screwed the wrong guy, with the wrong wife, from the wrong family and now – she was screwed.

There was no sense in crying over it. She just had to move on. Where and how, she had no idea. The only one place she knew she could go at that moment was the last place she wanted to go.

Back home to her aunt and uncle in leafy Riverdale – the Bronx.

6

ROSE'S BEDROOM was on the first floor and looked out on to the courtyard at the front of the house. It was just short of midday and a small breeze was tickling the tall bamboo plants that sat in huge exotic pots on the cobblestones. A gang of swallows were swooping across towards the gooseberry bushes in her mother's walled garden.

Rose lived with her parents in a large, stone-fronted house about a mile outside Foxford, on the Ballina road. Dr John Hopkins was the general practitioner in the town and tended to the medical needs of the people of Foxford with great kindness and efficiency. He and the local priest owned the only two cars in the small town.

The courtyard was surrounded by a high stone wall covered with ivy. The stone arch led to a narrow public road down which cars rarely passed. From her window Rose could see the small wooden gate, which led to a hilly field, circled by shrubs and trees. It was part of their garden, but semi-wild. A man came to mow it throughout the summer, but otherwise her mother had her hands full with the rose garden and the walled fruit garden and rarely ventured across the road to 'the hill'.

Rose was sitting by the window, painting, with her easel propped up on the wide, deep sill. The weather had cooled in the last few days and there were droplets of condensation on the inside of the glass. Rose was trying to capture the drops of fluid, with their sparkle and shadows, in a charcoal drawing. She looked across to the field and, from behind a bank of hydrangea to the left of the hill, she saw Patrick's hand waving a blue shirt.

Excited, she grabbed her cardigan from the bed, and ran downstairs. 'I'm going out, Mother,' she called into the kitchen.

'Where are you going?' Eleanor called out anxiously.

'Just taking a walk across the fields to do some sketching. I'll be back within the hour.'

Rose was always careful never to stay out longer than she promised in case her mother became suspicious and followed her. They would keep her boarding with the nuns in Crossmolina till she had finished her Matriculation exams at nineteen, then they would decide what was for the best. But Eleanor wondered sometimes if it was right to keep her daughter so cosseted. Rose saw nobody these days and only went out for the walks she took across the fields with her chalks and pencils. She made rough sketches which she would later turn into beautiful watercolours at home.

What Eleanor did not realize was that Rose's notepad was already filled with detailed drawings of flowers ready to show her mother when she got in after a deliciously clandestine hour with Patrick Murphy. Now, Rose sauntered casually from the house, crossed the road and, as soon as she was out of sight, ran over the hill to the bushes at the back of the hill where Patrick was waiting. She was so happy to see him that she simply tumbled into the arms and began kissing him.

'Did you miss me?' she said. The line of her white neck was taut, her face bent back, lips parted, her blonde curls tumbling down her back, eyes sparkling with unashamed joy. Every time he laid eyes on her Patrick was shocked anew by her beauty. More than that, she seemed to understand him. Rose's passion for drawing was as strong as his own love for singing.

'I missed you madly every minute of every hour and well you know it!' he said, laughing.

'I felt like I was going to go mad these last two days – I was furious when my mother told me we were going to Galway for the day. You do realize it has been nearly a full forty-eight hours since I last saw you? I was afraid you would have forgotten all about me.'

'Never! What was your name again?'

Rose punched his arm, reached up and kissed him briefly on the lips then all over his face, pulling him down with unexpected strength on to the ground until the two of them were laughing and rolling around on the warm, soft grass.

Patrick touched her tenderly, tentatively – running his long, browned hands over the bare skin of her neck and her arms, then, finally, slipping back the strap of her cotton sundress, the creamy curve of her shoulder. After the christening touch, he gently kissed each place in turn before kissing her mouth, reaching into her with a hunger that made her whole body ache. She felt passion race through her in a wave – as if she was drowning again and he was the only one who could save her. Rose knotted his fingers with hers then reached their intertwined hands and arms out to their sides. The push and pull of pushing their hands away from their bodies was a dance of discretion; a way of holding each other while stopping themselves from taking the next step. Their young, vital bodies hurt with a yearning but they both knew they could not go too far. While Rose, at only eighteen, was recklessly in love, she knew it was her responsibility, as the girl, to hold herself back from luring her lover into trouble. They were in enough trouble already just seeing each other.

Rose knew that she would never experience a love this strong, this certain ever again. This was the love Hollywood films were made on. The instant passionate knowing you have, one for the other. Rose would do anything she could to protect it.

In the last few weeks she had even withdrawn from her dearest friend, Patrick's sister Sinead, because she was afraid that she would have to confide in her and Sinead might confide in her own parents. The easy-going Murphy family would probably be delighted to see their son happily in love with their daughter's friend, but Rose's parents would be a different matter altogether. Deep in her heart, Rose knew they would not approve. To supplement their small farm, Patrick's father worked in the local woollen mills, and his wife and six children lived in a two-bedroom smallholding with three cows and a handful of sheep and two small fields just outside the town. They were respectable, but they drove a horse and cart and did not own a car. They were not the sort of people the Hopkinses would invite to take tea in their drawing room and they would certainly not allow one of them to marry their precious only daughter.

Rose pushed Patrick back then shook her head quickly from side to side to break the spell. She sat up and straightened her hair then leaned back against the bark of the narrow tree and took out her pad.

Patrick ran his hand in frustration through his thick hair, puffed out a deep breath and let out a short, angry sigh. He lay on the grass in front of her and Rose felt the gaze of his blue eyes on her as she reached into her pocket for a pencil.

'Stop looking at me,' she said. 'I'm the one with the pencil. I'm the one looking at you.'

'You're so beautiful – I could look at you for ever,' he said, and meant it.

'Well don't,' she said smiling. She felt thrilled when he told her she was beautiful. 'Look over there at that tree while I draw your profile.'

Reluctantly, he turned his face, his eyes rolling back towards her.

'Stop,' she said. 'I'm serious, I want a drawing of you.'

In the shadow of the tree, his face relaxed, his deep tan revealing white crow's feet around his eyes. His nose was strong and his browline high, his eyes glinted shards of blue and grey. In that moment Rose could see and feel that Patrick was not simply a young man, but nature itself. He was the earth beneath them and the sky above. As complex and beautiful as a tree or a flower – as significant as a single blade of grass in an endless, lush, green field. While she sketched the lines of his face she tried to capture not simply a likeness of his good looks, but the essence of who he was. Deep, sensitive, artistic. Other girls saw the handsome, dark-haired bad-boy. None of them could know what lay underneath. None of them could know what she knew about him. None of them could feel his spirit the way she could. Rose wanted to define his spirit in a drawing so that she could show him how much she not only loved him but could see him for who he was. If Patrick saw himself how she saw him, if he knew how well she knew what lay inside him – he would love her for ever.

He would never look at another girl. She would be the only one.

Under the dappled sunlight she looked so perfect Patrick could not believe he had found a sweetheart as delicate and beautiful as this girl was. The wind touching the leaves sent dappled flecks of light across her pale skin and the blonde curls tumbled over her shoulders. Patrick watched Rose as her eyes flicked across and then down at the page. Something about the way she was so absorbed in her work, the confident skill and the way her small hand moved across the paper, brought such a stab of love in his heart that he said what he was thinking out loud.

'I love you.'

As the words came out of his mouth he wondered if he should be saying them. Although he could feel that he loved her in his heart, it was the first time he had ever said it to her. Indeed, at twenty-five, it was the first time he had said it to any girl – and he had been with plenty. It was always worth thinking carefully before you gave a girl ideas. Otherwise she might think you wanted to marry her.

Patrick reassured himself that he was only telling the truth. He had meant the words fully when he said them and, oh, but she was beautiful, so beautiful.

He sat up and reached across, gently taking the pencil from her hands. Then he gave a broad smile, before taking her face in his hands and kissing her softly on the lips.

'I love you too,' she said.

Patrick was visibly relieved. It was out now – she loved him back. They loved each other. She was the girl for him – it was settled. They could date now, and all the others would leave him alone. He could take her to the pictures in Ballina and show her off to his friends and family.

Patrick did not question the ease and speed with which she had replied.

'I'll come down and talk to your father,' he said brightly, 'so we can put a stop to all this secretive nonsense and start courting properly.'

He hadn't noticed the way that Rose's hand halted on the page when she heard him say 'I love you', or how she had begun drawing again as she said, 'I love you too'. Neither did he sense that her kiss was not as passionate as he might have imagined it should be after the first declaration of love. When the kiss was over she prodded him playfully in the chest and said in a firm, gentle voice, 'Sit back how you were – I'm not finished drawing you yet.'

She smiled at him, dazzlingly, which he took to mean utter happiness. In fact it masked the fact that Rose did not know quite what to say. The very fact that he had told her that he loved her was, for an older lad like Patrick, tantamount to a marriage proposal. Patrick was not some stupid boy of eighteen, mooning over her. At twenty-five it was time enough for him to get married and if you told a girl you loved them, especially a girl like Rose Hopkins, the doctor's daughter, that was what you meant.

Until now she had assumed that Patrick understood that the secrecy was because her parents would not approve of him, not because her parents would not approve of the fact that they were courting without serious intention of marriage.

She could not hurt his feelings by telling him that her parents would not think that he was good enough for her. Of course he was good enough, he was too good. Rose knew that she would never find anyone who understood her as he did.

Never find anyone who would complete her the way that Patrick did. She had not realized that she had been incomplete without him until that day at the lake when he had swooped her up out of the water and kissed her. Now, she could not go back to being without him. She would only be half of who she was. Rose didn't know why that would be but in the hours she was not with him a terrible ennui descended on her. When she was with Patrick she felt powerful, fulfilled, whole. Just being with him rescued her from herself. They were soulmates, she knew that. Much as her parents loved her and wanted her to be happy, they did not understand her as Patrick did: the life and death nature of her drawing, the passion she felt for nature, but mostly, the all-encompassing love she felt for this man. There was no way that her pragmatic father and anxious, snobbish mother could begin to understand Patrick and Rose's love for each other. Her parents would find a way of putting a stop to the romance if it became public.

'Let's run away,' she said.

As she said it Rose had no idea what she was suggesting. All she knew was that she could not have Patrick going to her parents' house and talking to her father. She could not bear the thought of seeing the disappointment in her father's face or the fear in her mother's eyes when she found out her precious daughter had been 'running about' with 'that Murphy boy'.

'We could go to Dublin: I finish school in a year.' An idea began to take shape. 'You could go ahead of me and get digs and a job. I could go to art college and you could sing. You know you'll never get work singing around here.'

The more she spoke, the more Rose started to believe that it could be true. They could go away and start a life together in the city. It was where they both belonged anyway – the artist and the singer, there was nothing for them around here. They would have to get married, of course. But once it was a fait accompli and her parents saw how happy she was, and that Patrick was a good man, they would come round to the idea. They had already agreed to let her go to college, more or less, so this would be the perfect solution. If she and Patrick started dating here, now, in the small town of Foxford, her parents would disapprove. That would not stop them, of course. Their love was too strong. Nothing would stop them. But nonetheless it would taint the beauty of what they had. If they ran away and got married her parents would have no choice. They would have to continue as normal and, in time, they would come around to loving Patrick too. Rose knew it would all work out. It had to all work out, it was just a delicate situation and she knew she had to be clever about how she would make it all happen.

'It sounds a lot simpler to me to just tell our families that we are doing a serious line...' he said. 'Besides, I hate all this creeping around, putting charcoal stains on your dress so your mother thinks you are drawing flowers – we're not doing anything wrong.'

Rose began to panic.

'My father would be really upset,' she blurted out, 'because you are so much older than me. I am still his little girl and—'

'—he's afraid I'm not going to be a gentleman and that I'll defile you.'

Then he leant across and grabbed her by the waist. 'Maybe he's right about that too, aghrá!' And he tickled her so hard that she dropped her pad, clutching at her skirt with her charcoal-covered hands and squealing with delight.

Patrick settled his body in behind hers, putting his arms around her neck so that they hung, temptingly, in front of her breasts. 'So that's why I should go and talk to him,' he said, kissing her neck and adding, 'I can reassure him, tell him we're serious. Tell him that we're to be…'

Patrick frightened himself, coming so close to saying the word 'married' out loud.

Rose was happy that he had left the word hanging in the air. She turned around and sat, with crossed legs, facing him, patting down her skirt between her legs so that her pants weren't visible, the light cotton tucked into the curve of her thighs.

She said, 'Let's just keep it the way it is for now. I'll be nineteen in a few months and, if they don't push me into the convent in the meantime, we can talk about it then.'

Patrick smiled and nodded. 'Sure,' he said.

In truth, Patrick wasn't ready to get married. To Rose or anyone. He was still waiting to see if his father could get him a job in the Foxford Woollen Mills so that he would have a steady enough income to help him pursue his singing career. Not that he had any idea how he might go about that. All he knew was that he could sing as well as John McCormack and everyone said he was as much of a fine thing as Elvis Presley. He had his regular gig in Ballina town hall playing the Saturday-night dances, which made him a big deal locally. But although his skiffle-playing friends were happy with that, Patrick dreamed of bigger things. The world was changing – Bill Haley and Jerry Lee Lewis had seen to that. In the past year, rock and roll had started to creep into the dance halls around Ireland. Even the priests had been powerless to stop the jiving, jitterbugging revolution. Everyone Patrick met told him that he was so good it was only a matter of time before he was 'discovered' and became a famous singer. Patrick always laughed off the accolades but, deep in his heart, it was what he wanted. At twenty-five he had finally come to realize that it wasn't going to happen for him in Mayo. He had to get himself somewhere – London, Manchester, America, anywhere that he might be discovered. In reality, he had never travelled any further than Galway. His father said he didn't have it in him and Patrick was starting to wonder if perhaps his father was right.

Maybe it was the time just to bite the bullet and move away. Perhaps Rose was right and the move to Dublin wasn't such a bad idea. He could pick up some casual building work, he was a decent enough carpenter when he wanted to be. Although where would they live? How would they live? A lot of lads went to London but he had never managed to scrabble together the fare. The Hopkins family had money. Perhaps her father could loan them the passage over. Although, they'd have to be engaged before he could even ask for anything like that – and if they went to London, or even Dublin, they would have to marry for sure.

Patrick looked at her sideways for a moment and a small feeling of doubt crept into Rose's heart. Perhaps he was changing his mind about the whole thing. Perhaps her reticence about telling her parents had upset him. Had he guessed at the truth? Should she go ahead and tell them, and to hell with the consequences? Then they could run away together. It would be crazy but they loved each other so much, she knew they'd manage somehow. That would be the right thing to do: honour their love. Be brave. Be fearless as lovers should be.

But before she had time to put words to her thoughts, Patrick said, 'We'd best be getting back.'

He helped gather her things as she shook down her skirt, then as he leaned in to kiss her goodbye, Patrick stopped and picked out a daisy head from a tangle of curls on her shoulder.

As he looked at her face he felt overwhelmed by the sheer wonder of how beautiful she was. He desperately wanted to pick her up in his arms then lay her down on the grass, give in to his most base desires and take her, right there in the open country. He knew from her pleading eyes that she would not stop him. In fact, he believed she wanted it too. But she was too young, and they had already taken things far enough. Even if he didn't feel like it, even if it went against every natural desire in his body, Patrick knew he had to be a gentleman.

So he simply smiled, then they kissed and parted under the tree, as they had done a dozen times before.

As she walked back over the hill towards home, Rose felt a sheet of melancholy fall down over her heart, although she could not say why. Their kiss was tender, and sweet but nonetheless it had felt, to Rose, like an ordinary goodbye.

7

ELEANOR HOPKINS was preparing dinner when she looked out the window and saw Rose coming towards the house from the small hill across the road. Her appearance was messy, as usual. Her cotton dress was crumpled, her slim athletic legs, on which she refused to wear stockings, were doubtless spattered with muck where she had trudged through a puddle in her flimsy plimsolls. And, Eleanor noted, her hair was not tied back in a neat bun like her own, but instead it tumbled around her shoulders, probably full of tangles that she would have to try and brush out that evening.

Eleanor tutted to herself disapprovingly but, at the same time, felt a flash of fear. Although Rose was a good girl, with her quiet demeanour and her love of art and her good manners, she had a savage beauty that worried her mother. She looked untethered – wanton. Eleanor had always tried to keep Rose tidy as a child, tying back her hair and containing her growing curves in smart clothes. Now that Rose was eighteen, Eleanor did not have any jurisdiction over her daughter's wild beauty.

She often felt powerless over her adopted child and worried about her growing older in a way she believed she might not have done if she had been her own. Rose did not have Hopkins blood so how she turned out was God's department. Eleanor could only hope He knew what He was doing. Sometimes, anxious Eleanor wished she was more like the ardent rural Catholics. They seemed to get great comfort from their faith, with their whispering confessionals, endless chanting novenas and statue-turning, candle-lighting, medal-kissing rituals. Eleanor was reluctant to leave her daughter's welfare to God alone. She loved her too much. She could barely express her fears for her daughter, even to her husband. He would have said she was being irrational, but he only half knew the truth about his wife's experiences before they met. He would not have wanted to know more, even if she could have told him.

As her daughter neared the house Eleanor thought Rose looked more pensive than usual. These days, she came back from her walks fresh-faced and happier than usual, as if refreshed and invigorated by the combination of open air and creativity. At first, Eleanor had been worried that Rose was sneaking off to see a boy. But, on reflection, she didn't believe her daughter would be that duplicitous, or that she would be afraid to confide in her mother about such things. Eleanor kept her own fears away from Rose. She always kept her voice breezy when she talked about young men, encouraging Rose to get to know that nice Anthony Warren, who had just got a place studying law at Trinity, or Bishop Richard's son, who would be home from Harvard this summer. Middle-class Catholic men from educated homes were thin on the ground, but then, no girl in Mayo was as beautiful and as cultured as Rose Hopkins. Eleanor knew that her daughter would not be stupid enough to throw herself away at some local boy.

In any case, Rose never stayed out later than an hour and always came back with charcoal stains on her fingers and dress. She generally left her sketch pad on the kitchen table and, while she washed her hands in the scullery sink, Eleanor made a point of having a quick flick through. It was always filled with exquisite pictures of flowers and trees. Eleanor fretted about her daughter's ambitions to be an artist and how it would affect her chance of securing a nice boy. The uncertainty brought a tightness to her chest.

'You worry too much about her,' John would say when Eleanor voiced her concerns. 'She's a good girl and it would be a terrible shame to waste that talent. Let her go off to Dublin and see what happens. She has to learn to make her own way in the world.'

When John talked like that, Eleanor knew he did not have the first idea about Rose. She could not say why she felt that her daughter was heading for trouble. Only that her maternal instincts told her Rose, her beautiful Rose, was more sensitive than most. 'Artistic' was how her husband described the raw spirit that seemed to inhabit their daughter: driving her to spend hours alone, drawing. Only Eleanor could see how vulnerable she was. She had none of the practical grounded ways of her friend Sinead. She was winsome, imaginative – not of this world. The idea of her going up to Dublin terrified her mother.

When she came in from her walk today, Rose seemed different, somehow. Her eyebrows were set in a small frown and her lips were tight, as if she was worried about something. She was quieter than usual, and barely greeted her mother as she came in the kitchen door. She was holding her sketch pad and there was charcoal on her skirt.

'Go and wash your hands, darling,' Eleanor said. 'Would you like a sandwich for lunch?'

Rose felt vaguely irritated with her mother. Everyone else in the town had their main meal or 'dinner' at one o'clock, then 'tea' in the evening was bread and jam or a boiled egg. The Hopkins were the only people who had 'lunch' and their dinner in the evening. Her mother said it was because of the hours her father worked, but Rose knew that this 'European' routine was just another way of Eleanor establishing herself as a cut above everyone else. How Rose hated her mother for standing in the way of her love for Patrick. For being such a snob.

'I'm not hungry.'

Eleanor looked devastated, so Rose said, 'I'll just put my sketch pad away then come down for tea.'

Eleanor watched her, clutching her sketches as she walked up the stairs. There was something wrong. Rose was usually very anxious to show her mother the drawings she had done while she was out. Something was not right.

They chatted pleasantly over tea and discussed the upcoming fundraiser for the new church roof. Rose was having some of her small watercolours framed for sale. She brought a selection downstairs so they could decide which ones would be best, but left her pad with her drawings from the day up in her room.

Later that evening, Rose went for a drive with her father. The Catholic bishop was sick and John was called out to the palace. Rose went along so she could sit in the kitchen of the impressively large, if somewhat ugly building, where she would be fed biscuits and gossip by the old housekeeper, just as she had done since she was a child.

And John treasured these outings with his beautiful daughter.

John had adapted better to Rose's maturing than Eleanor had. Their relationship, if anything, had blossomed over the years and when Eleanor saw it she felt a pain and sense of estrangement that somehow she felt powerless to reverse.

As soon as the car pulled out of the drive, Eleanor rushed up to Rose's room, and grabbed her sketchbook from the bureau by the window. She quickly flicked through to the last pages and was relieved to see the usual pictures. There was a sparsely drawn page spotted with poppies, the next had intricate sketches of wildflowers, another page was generously swiped with black charcoal marks identifiable as blades of grass, and then a close-up of a tree trunk that was so extraordinarily detailed Eleanor leaned in to look closer. As she did, she noticed that the page was standing back slightly from the spine. Rose's sketch pads were made of thick, expensive paper. They bought them by post from a supplier in Dublin. Eleanor held the pad close to her face and carefully studied the spine. There was a sliver of black space. The page after the tree trunk had been torn out.

Eleanor checked the dustbin where Rose threw her discarded work. It was empty. She ran downstairs to check the kindling basket where Rose sometimes put her paper waste – also empty. She hared back upstairs and began opening and closing drawers. She searched behind the bureau, lifted the cushions on the window seat and the rug until, finally, she found it, under the bed. A sheet, hurriedly thrown, discarded like lost rubbish. However, the mere fact it had been hidden told Eleanor that it was far from rubbish. It was a secret. When she lifted the page and saw what it contained, her worst fears came to life.

It was a portrait of a devastatingly beautiful young man, his eyes seeming to flicker off the page, gazing out mournfully into the distance. Eleanor recognized him instantly: that useless good-for-nothing, slick-haired gutty-boy Patrick Murphy.

Eleanor put her fist to her mouth and cried out in anger but also in pain. She did not know if she was more afraid of the fact that her daughter was in love, or of the man she was in love with.

Furious, every instinct made her want to march over to the Murphy house and tell the young man to keep his filthy hands off her precious daughter. But Eleanor had enough sense to know that would not work. How many times had she herself been warned as a young woman? It had made no difference to Eleanor and would surely make no difference to her daughter either.

She would have to be smarter than that.

Her hands shaking, Eleanor put the room back into order, carefully placing the picture under the bed in exactly the same position she found it so that Rose would never find out that her mother knew her secret.

Patrick was delighted with himself. Tony had given him a lift into Ballina on the tractor that morning, and he had been in to see the manager of the town hall, Liam Brennan, about securing a regular Saturday-night slot. Liam fancied himself as a music impresario and was bringing in a showband from Athenry the following weekend. He wanted to know if Patrick and the lads could support them.

'Come in an hour earlier than usual. The good news is, we're charging double on the door and so we'll be able to throw a few pounds your way.'

A paid gig. It wasn't much, but it was a start. Patrick was

humming 'Singing the Blues' to himself as Tony dropped him off at the bottom of the lane to the house. As he turned in the gate he stopped singing. There was a car outside the house. That could only mean the priest or the doctor, neither of which, as a rule, brought good news. His mother had been ill last year and had been sent up to Galway for a stay in the hospital. When she came home, nobody exactly knew what had been wrong with her, her being a woman and all, but they had known it was serious because his father had said it was a miracle to have her back at all. When Patrick saw Dr Hopkins's car he instantly feared she might have had a relapse, but then, as he came towards the house he saw his mother at the front door saying goodbye to the doctor, and she looked fine. Another, even more ominous, thought began to form in his head.

Patrick nodded a greeting at the doctor, taking his hands out of the pockets of his blue jeans, trying to look more respectable. He wished he had worn his trousers and jacket into town, but he had wanted to look with-it meeting Liam.

'Patrick,' Dr Hopkins said, nodding at him cheerily.

'Grand day, Doctor,' he said.

'It is that, Patrick – I hope it holds for you.'

Patrick thought to himself, That wasn't so bad. If there was anything wrong the doctor wouldn't be passing the time of day with him like that.

'And you, Doctor, you might take the roof down on the car and give her full tilt one of the days before the summer is out.'

The good doctor laughed and said, 'Indeed!' before tipping his worn trilby and getting into the car.

There, Patrick thought to himself. A grand man. No mention of Rose or anything like that at all. Probably just calling in to check up on Mammy and she looks fine so...

As soon as he got into the house, however, Patrick sensed all was not fine.

His mother's smile, so radiant for the doctor, disappeared the second they were inside. His father was puffing on his pipe at double speed.

'Have you been carrying on with Rose Hopkins?' he said, before Patrick's mother had even closed the door behind them.

Patrick didn't know what to say. He had never been caught out lying like this before. In truth, he had never yet lied – or done anything very much that was worth lying about. His parents were easy-going people. His father had taken him to the pub for his first pint when he was sixteen and, aside from teasing the odd bull over a wall, or, when he was very small, stealing the occasional cigarette, Patrick had no reason to lie to his parents about anything.

He had no reason to lie about this either, except that Rose had not wanted people to know. Or rather, had not wanted her parents to know, for some reason.

'I don't know about carrying on. We've been very careful…' That sounded awful. 'I mean, I've kissed her and that…' Why was he sounding so guilty? 'There's nothing illegal about it – I'm a man of twenty-five and she's eighteen – a woman.'

'She might be of legal age, Patrick, but she is still a girl,' his mother shouted at him. 'The same age as Sinead! Your baby sister!'

Patrick was confused now.

'Sinead's been dating Tommy Fleming since she was sixteen, and he was only a year behind me in school.'

'That's not the point!'

'Well what is the point?'

'The point is, you shouldn't have lied…' his father said, still tut-tutting hard on the pipe.

'I know, Da, I'm sorry, it's just that Rose didn't want people knowing. She wanted it kept secret for a while.'

His father just raised his eyebrows; his mother was flustered.

'Look, son,' she said. 'It's just that you can't go about…' She paused, then seemed to gather herself up into a fury again before saying, 'You can't just go about the place messing around with the doctor's daughter.'

'We weren't messing around – I already told you—'

'I mean – dating the doctor's daughter. You can't go about dating her.'

'Why not?'

His mother looked to his father for support and his father shrugged and looked back at her, raising his eyebrows, then looked Patrick straight in the face and said, 'Because you just can't.'

He looked back at the fire, as if ashamed of the outburst, then released a long stream of smoke from his barely opened lips, before tapping some of the ash on to the stone grate beside him. Slowly, he picked up a snifter from the tobacco tin by his side, and pressed it down into the smouldering bowl. His father only ever relit a finished pipe immediately when there was something wrong.

Patrick knew what was being implied here. He just didn't want to believe it. It wasn't her age that bothered them. It was her social status.

'You think I'm not good enough.'

His father continued to look into the fire.

'It's not that, Patrick,' his mother pleaded. 'Please try to understand.'

Patrick was her eldest child. Her blue-eyed baby boy. A laughing, sweet-talking charmer of a boy, he had been star of the church choir. When his voice broke at fourteen, the priest and organist had been distraught. By sixteen he had developed a deep baritone.

Mary's eldest son had owned her from the day he was born. She adored him. There was not a woman alive good enough for him. But even so, the humiliation of the doctor calling to say that her son had been carrying on with his daughter was terrible. Dr Hopkins had been such a gentleman about it too. Not even saying how wrong it was or anything – just did they know? It was clear, though, that he didn't approve. In all fairness, Mary Murphy thought to herself, how could he approve of his daughter going out with Patrick?

'Oh, I understand all right,' Patrick said, and marched out of the door. He grabbed his bicycle from the front yard without a backward glance and cycled into Foxford. He wasn't going to be told by anyone that he wasn't good enough for their daughter. His family were hard-working, God-fearing, honest people.

Twenty minutes later Patrick walked into the Mayfly, the small hotel in the centre of town. Dr Hopkins looked up from his sandwich and coffee and his face flickered with something like disappointment before setting itself in a grave, but friendly way.

He said, 'Patrick. Won't you sit down. Can I get you a pint?'

'I don't drink,' Patrick said, then realizing how ludicrous that sounded, added, 'During the week,' which was true.

'Tea? Coffee?'

Patrick shook his head. He felt nervous. Perhaps this had not been such a good idea.

John Hopkins's face was benign and comforting, full of concern and kindness, as it was when you went to him as a patient. Suddenly Patrick felt bad for carrying on with his daughter and not telling him about it.

'I know why you are here, Patrick.'

'Dr Hopkins, I'm sorry that we've been sneaking around but—'

'Patrick, it's all right, really.' Patrick was relieved. This was a lot easier than he had thought it was going to be.

'I understand that you love my daughter and want to marry her.' Patrick tried to keep the surprise off his face. He had been expecting some kind of a ticking off.

'And while you are a very fine young man, Patrick, I am just concerned, as any father would be, as your father would be if Sinead was being asked for her hand, as to how you are going to look after her?'

This was way more than Patrick could deal with on the spot. He tried to steady himself and come up with something, anything, to get himself out of, or indeed, into this fix. He wasn't entirely certain what he wanted any more. Did he want to be with Rose and married? Or be with Rose and not married? Had he, indeed, asked Rose to marry him? He was sure he would have remembered if he had. What had Rosie told her father? Had she sent him here to put pressure on Patrick to get married? No. She was the one who had wanted to keep it a secret. This was clearly why. Patrick was certain he loved Rose but how could he say to Dr Hopkins, 'I love your daughter but I am not sure if I want to marry her'?

Or, perhaps, he did want to marry her but, like the good doctor, was unsure how he would keep her? Patrick had had an idea about that too – what was it?

'If I could just know, Patrick, that you had prospects, abroad even, then perhaps we might come to some kind of an arrangement.'

There it was!

'Well, sir...'

'Please call me John.'

'Well, John, I had been thinking about going to London. Perhaps getting something set up over there and then sending for Rose, when she was finished school, of course, and after we were… you know…' John looked at him quizzically until he said, 'married.'

'And you'll need some money to help you set up first?'

The way he said it, straight out like that, made it sound cheap, as if Patrick was begging for money, which he wasn't. Then, the good doctor smiled, his kind, soft features sort of crumpling in on themselves, and Patrick knew he didn't mean anything bad by it.

'I may be able to help you, Patrick,' he said.

Then he leaned over and he patted Patrick's hand, as he had done when he was a child, to comfort him before an injection.

Dr Hopkins had a cousin in New York who owned a large golf course and clubhouse. They held a lot of functions there, weddings, dances, 'that type of thing', he said. John was going to contact his friend and see if he could get Patrick a job there. Of course, he would have to start doing some work in the kitchens and waiting tables, but his friend was very well connected and would surely help him to get on in his singing career.

If things worked out, which of course they would, because John had always known Patrick Murphy to be a bright, intelligent and ambitious young man, Patrick would let John know when he had things set up, then he could send for Rose. John would organize everything from this end. But there was one proviso: Patrick was not to tell Rose he was leaving.

'She will be so upset,' John said, 'and you know what the ladies are like, Patrick. They don't always know what's best for them. Look how she kept you a secret from us.'

It was true. If Rose had been out in the open about their relationship from the beginning, this could have happened ages ago and his parents would have been spared their upset.

Patrick left for Dublin the following week. He wrote Rose a letter explaining everything and saying goodbye. John assured him he would deliver it as soon as possible, and pass on his details in New York.

'She will be upset at first, but you know you're doing the right thing, don't you?'

Patrick explained it all to his parents. His father said nothing. His mother was upset that he was leaving, but told him he was right to take the opportunity when it was handed to him.

As he left the house for Dublin with his small suitcase strapped to the back of his bike, he kissed his mother and said, 'Don't cry, Ma, I'll be back soon. I have to come back anyway, to get my Rose. She'll be mad as hell at me – but she'll know it was something I had to do.' Then he turned to his father. 'A man's gotta do what a man's gotta do, Da – isn't that right?'

His father raised his pipe at him, winked and smiled as his mother wiped her tears away with the hem of her apron.

'Back soon,' he shouted as he wobbled down the drive on his bicycle, 'with my first million!'

If he had turned round in that moment, Patrick would have been hurt to see that neither of his parents looked entirely convinced.

8

THE SUIT was delivered to their home in Yonkers three days before the wedding. Ava hung it on a hook behind her bedroom door then opened the bag. It was as beautiful as she remembered it, but she didn't try it on in case she didn't ever want to take it off again. Ava was afraid the reflection she had seen in Sybil Connolly's Plaza studio might have been a mirage, a fluke of lighting that made her appear better-looking than she was. So she decided to wait until the day of the wedding before putting it on again. In the meantime her mother's years of nagging paid off. Ava decided her new suit needed a new hairstyle to do it justice. She made an appointment with her mother's local hairdresser, Miss Parrish, where she picked out a picture from a magazine of a hairdo similar to Miss Connolly's – a short, ear-length bob. Two hours later, Ava's mousy hair had been dyed a few shades lighter, cut short and set into rollers. As Miss Parrish took Ava out from under the dryer and began to brush out her curls, even the matronly hairdresser was shocked at how different her young client looked. From a gawky lump of a girl to a sophisticated young woman.

'We have found your style at last,' she said, delighted with herself. Then Miss Parrish went to her handbag and took out a compact and well-worn Revlon lipstick. She patted Ava's nose and chin with the powder, applied a slick of pink and said, 'There you are. The prettiest young woman in Yonkers.' She felt a tear come to her eye. Turning ugly ducklings into swans was her calling.

Ava smiled at her own reflection. She could not help it. Everything about her face looked different. Her neck longer, her nose shorter, and her skin creamier. First the suit, and now this. How her life had changed in just two days.

'Thank you,' she said to Miss Parrish. 'I feel like a new woman.'

Ava indeed felt like a different person walking back towards her car. The new Ava. She was the sort of woman who could walk into a shop and buy a new outfit for herself, just like that. Could acquiring this new confidence really be as simple as knowing her own style? It seemed so. Ava flicked her new hair and held her chin high, proud of her tallness and the elegant demeanour it gave her.

She could not wait to get to the wedding to show off her new self.

The following morning the Brogans drove to Our Lady of Dolours Catholic Church in Westchester County to Gloria Dolan's wedding. Nessa was in a bad mood with her husband and he was not sure why. Earlier that morning she had said to him, 'Doesn't Ava look wonderful?'

'Very smart,' he had replied, barely looking up from his paper.

The two women had been fussing around the kitchen

putting on lipstick and readjusting their outfits and he was worried they would be late. On their way out to the car Nessa had taken him to one side and berated him for not making more of a fuss of his daughter's new look.

'Can you not see how she looks so much better?'

'Better than what?' he asked. Ava joined them before she had the chance to tell him off any more, but Nessa gave him the silent treatment all the way to the church.

As they got out of the car Tom finally got the message and awkwardly told Ava, 'You look lovely.'

Ava laughed and said, 'Thanks, Pop,' and winked to let him know she knew Nessa had put him up to it.

Tom was flooded with such love in that moment for his little girl that he said, 'You always look beautiful to me, Ava – you know that, right?'

'I'm your daughter,' she said. 'You're prejudiced.'

But still, it felt good to be told.

After the church service they followed the other cars to the Westchester golf club where the lavish reception was being held. Tom was a member here, although he played seldom. His position as chairperson of the Connaughtman Association kept him busy most weekends. The charitable organization ran a supper club in their local church centre once a month to help support young Irish immigrants. They raised funds and gathered clothes and care parcels to send back home to the impoverished communities, as well as providing support to help them find work and settle in New York. Barely a week went by when Ava and her parents were not at some function or another. Most of these family events were held in the half-dozen Catholic church halls and Irish clubs around the area of Yonkers/Riverdale where they lived. However, this wedding was fancier than most.

The Irish community was tight-knit, so Ava saw plenty of people she knew. One or two of them passed her by, seeming not to recognize her, which delighted her even more. The style was top drawer; all the men wore expensive suits and the women were filling the room with wide new-look skirts, and some in candy-coloured day suits like herself; the older women in hats, the younger women wearing jewelled headbands cut close to their coiffed hair. Ava was delighted that she could match any of them. So was Nessa, who was dressed head to toe in an emerald-green ensemble. She was in her element. Ava knew what was on her mother's mind but, for once, it didn't bother her. In fact she was delighted to see her mother so happy.

As they entered the lobby, Nessa nodded at a passing hat and said out of the side of her mouth, 'There's Kitty and Kevin Flanagan – the crème de la crème,' then seeing her husband was about to remove his jacket hissed, 'Don't even think about it!'

Tom raised his eyes to heaven and headed towards the bar, while Nessa grabbed her daughter's arm and rose up on her toes exclaiming, 'Holy God! Is that Rose Kennedy?' then deflated. 'No. Bridie Connor. Same hair – similar height – still,' she said, taking heart as they walked through the elegantly laid-out lobby with its swirling patterned carpets and Formica side tables, 'with this upmarket crowd I wouldn't be at all surprised.'

They wandered over to the seating plan and Ava saw that she was at a different table to her parents, at the same table as Niall and Dermot Dolan, sons of the judge. Nessa was temporarily dumbstruck with excitement and before she had the chance to open her mouth Ava gave her a look that said, 'not a word'.

Ava knew Niall Dolan from her Thursday nights at the Emerald Ballroom. While he was great fun and they liked each other, like all of the young men she was friendly with, Ava knew he wasn't interested in her romantically.

She had never met his older brother Dermot before, although she had heard about him from her mother's endless gossip of who was (and wasn't) eligible in the Irish community. Dermot was eligible. A lawyer, he had followed in his father's footsteps, graduating with honours in law from Harvard five years before, and his star, as a brilliant young defence attorney in the New York District Attorney's office, was rising. He was known for using his charm and legal skills to great effect when representing the underdog, and had a reputation for compassion as well as a sharp mind. However, he was still single at pushing thirty, which meant he was probably a charmer and an impossibly good-looking womanizer, like his younger brother. The mere thought of sharing a meal with a dashing man who would doubtless dismiss her, would normally have made Ava feel inadequate and sad. However, today was different. Today, Ava was feeling hot-to-trot.

Walking away from her mother, towards her table, Ava could feel her body inside the armour of her outfit; the prickle of the snug lace against her skin, the movement of her buttocks as they brushed against each other in the tight skirt, the broadness of her shoulders against the smallness of her waist – it all made her lift her head and straighten her back with a poise that felt unfamiliar and yet, utterly as it should be. Ava found herself walking with confidence and grace; like a panther in pink. As if the instruction from her frustrated deportment teacher in finishing school had finally sunk in!

She got to the table early and when she saw she was sitting next to Dermot Dolan she reached down to move her place card to another part of the table. She was feeling too good about herself to be ignored by some snooty lawyer. However, she caught the cuff of her silk blouse on the name placeholder. As she went to release it she noticed the white lace of Sybil Connolly's blouse peeping out from under, and the perfectly turned cuff of her pink suit with its three pearl buttons, and she felt a clip of pride again at her beautiful outfit.

'Won't you sit down?' Dermot Dolan appeared next to her. 'It's Ava Brogan, isn't it?' he said. 'I think we've met before.'

Dermot was an ordinary-looking man, not at all like his dashing brother. He was also stout, a few inches shorter than she was, with a large, soft face, full of good humour and warmth. He was certainly not handsome, but he seemed kind, and Ava was relieved. He looked like the sort of man it might be fun to have lunch with.

Ava saw something in his eyes, too, that she had not seen in any man before. A sparkle that said he found her attractive. Inside, she smiled – a broad, triumphant smile. On the outside, however, she fought to keep her face aloof and somewhat imperious. She was in a Grace Kelly suit and she was going to play this ice-princess cool. That was the way to get a man. At least, that was what Myrtle always said. Ava hadn't a clue herself.

'Have we?' she said, raising one eyebrow slightly before sitting down. 'I really can't remember.' He looked crestfallen and Ava felt bad and quickly said, 'Oh yes, I remember you now,' even though she didn't. 'You're a lawyer, aren't you?' For once she was glad of her mother's eligibility briefings.

Dermot pulled her chair out and once he was sitting next to her he let out a large sigh saying, 'Ah – that's better. We're the same height at last!'

Even though she was trying to play it cool, Ava could not

help but let out a loud, impulsive laugh. Immediately she regretted it, thinking he might think she was laughing at him.

'I'm sorry,' she said.

'No need to apologize,' he said. 'Thankfully my ego is as diminutive as my body.' Which made her laugh again.

'You have a beautiful laugh,' he said. Nobody had ever said anything like that to her before. Ava thought it was strange, but also sort of wonderful.

'Would you like a cigarette?' Dermot's younger brother Niall sat down on the other side of her and held out a box of Lucky Strikes. Ava did not especially enjoy smoking, but she took one anyway. Dermot had his lighter ready and clicked it before Niall had the chance to strike a match.

Niall gave Dermot a murderous look. Was it possible her new look had engaged Niall's interest too?

'There's a really fantastic band booked for later, Ava. They'll be coming on after all the old folks have gone to bed – it should be a blast.'

'Fool,' Dermot said. 'Does Ava look like a teenybopper jiver to you? She's a sophisticated lady – a woman of taste, am I right?'

Ava took a drag of her cigarette and smiled at him sideways. She could feel the excitement bubble up through her. Was it really possible that two of the most eligible brothers in the room were fighting for her attention?

'Ava and I know each other, actually,' Niall said. 'We are regular dance partners, isn't that right, Ava?'

Ava smiled and nodded – enigmatically, she hoped. She was enjoying this. How she wished Myrtle was here to witness her debut as a flirt.

'All girls love to dance, Dermot, and if you didn't have two left feet you might know that.'

Dermot blushed, and set his chin defensively at his brother.

'I can waltz,' he said, and then turning to Ava explained, 'That's the only dance a true gentleman needs. It is the dance of romance.'

'Back in the eighteen hundreds maybe,' Niall said, winking at Ava. 'Dermot has broken more bridesmaids' toes than I've done the jitterbug!'

Then another young man butted in from across the table, 'Lots of rock and very little roll – that's what they say about Dermot Dolan!' And another joined in: 'Remember the time you twisted your back pulling Mary Murphy under your legs at Josie Kane's wedding?' The whole table laughed.

Dermot was red-faced with embarrassment and mumbled to her, 'I'm afraid dancing is not my forte.' Ava decided that she definitely liked him. There was something soothing in his gentle manner and the way he was happy to put himself aside. Most men were such boastful bores.

Over lunch Dermot told her all about his life. She knew most of it already from her mother and from general gossip in their social circles. He told her about his volunteer work ministering to the legal needs of the poor in the area. He was proud of his Irish roots and asked how she felt about the Republican cause back home and how they were fighting to get their land back from the English oppressors.

'My father fundraises for Sinn Fein,' she said.

Ava knew a good deal about Irish politics from her father. She read the Irish newspapers as well as the American ones. Dermot seemed impressed that she knew something about both things and kept questioning her. The conversation made her feel clever and important in the way conversations with her father did.

During the speeches, Dermot had to get up and give gifts

to the bridesmaids. His speech was witty and articulate. And as the room filled with laughter she felt a small snap of pride. As he praised the bride's beauty his eyes moved across the room to her. When he came back to the table he rested his hand gently on Ava's as if to apologize for having left her for so long and continued to attend to her, lighting her cigarettes, pouring her coffee and passing her petits fours.

The band came on stage and began to warm up for the bride and groom's first dance.

'I believe the singer is very good,' Dermot said. 'He is recently arrived from Ireland, so I believe.'

'No rock and roll then?' Niall butted in. 'Will I have to wait until later, Ava, before I steer you away from my selfish brother?'

The opening verse of 'Down by the Salley Gardens' came floating across the worn, wooden dance floor and the bride and groom began their first dance.

'Aha,' Dermot said. 'A nice slow start. May I ...?' He stood up and reached for Ava's hand.

'This song is my father's party piece,' she said to Dermot.

'And it's a waltz,' he said. Then clasping her hand added, 'Could it be any more perfect?'

It was Ava's turn to blush. She could barely believe this was happening to her. Being asked up for the first dance, and a waltz! She did not even dare look across the room at her mother. Nessa would have to be hospitalized with sheer joy.

As they joined the wedding party on the dance floor Dermot placed his hand firmly on the small of her back and clutched her right hand awkwardly in his left. Ava's initial thrill waned somewhat when she realized that Dermot was, indeed, a clumsy and disjointed dancer. With a terrific confidence that his skill did not warrant, he clunked her about on the dance floor with a heavy foot, bruising the tips of her toes with almost every step, and driving her off in a straight line away from the dance floor. Ava redirected him firmly just as the singer came and took his place at the front of the stage. Ava could see that he was around her own age. He was wearing a deep green velvet suit. His hair was soft black curls, his eyes – she could see even from here – were a striking blue.

She could not say if his face was handsome or not because he wore an expression of such ecstasy as he sang 'Down by the Salley Gardens' that she could almost feel his emotion sliding over her skin.

The deep, glorious sound of the young man's singing voice affected her so deeply that Ava could feel her legs weakening beneath her, as if she were about to faint. She loosened her back and arms and sank her head on to Dermot's shoulder.

Delighted with the intimate gesture Dermot relaxed his footwork so that the two of them were simply shuffling on the spot in a sideways embrace. He closed his eyes and drank in the perfume of Ava's hair. He distracted himself from the closeness of their bodies, her breasts against his chest, her breath on his neck, by planning how he could capture her affection. Perhaps he would make a statement and take her for lunch during the week to the Law Society Club. That would impress her. It would show Ava, and her family, that he was serious in his intentions.

9

'I DON'T WANT him in Dublin, or even London where he might come back,' Eleanor had said. 'I want him as far away as possible.'

John had persuaded her that New York was the best option because his cousin owned a golf course. 'He can give him a job and we'll be able to keep an eye on him.' Although he had said it to appease her, Eleanor knew that John had wanted to keep an eye on the lad to make sure he was all right. She would have sent him to Australia or South America and let him fend for himself without a second thought. She felt certain, too, that the wretched boy would have just taken the money and gone anyway. Although she was more afraid of him coming back.

John did not say anything directly to her, but she knew he thought she was being too hard on Rose and the lad. If it had been left up to him, Eleanor felt certain that he would have let the romance play out, right there, in front of all their neighbours. He didn't know how these things could come to a sorry end. He had married the first girl he had fallen in love with, which was her. He could never know the pain that bad decisions in love could make when you are young.

John felt guilty, about lying to his daughter as much as about banishing the boy, but Eleanor knew that they were doing the right thing. In time, Rose would forget this silly lad and Eleanor would fix her up with a nice man from a good family. Someone with a profession. A lawyer or, ideally, a young doctor who could join her father in the practice. In the meantime she would indulge Rose by letting her go to art college. She might even rent an apartment in Dublin and join her there so she could keep a close eye. Eleanor intended to keep a very tight rein on Rose until she felt confident that her daughter's future was certain and safe. This business with the Murphy boy had been a warning shot across the bows. They had caught it just in time, it seemed.

It had been almost six months since they had banished Rose's young man to America. A week after he had disappeared Rose was due to go back to boarding school in neighbouring Crossmolina. She refused point-blank to leave Foxford when the summer ended, saying she would prefer to sleep at home and had no interest in the company of the other girls. Her parents knew it was because she was hoping that Patrick would appear under her window one night, and she wanted to be there. As it was her final school exams year, her parents conceded. So John was forced to drive her to and from Sligo each day for her studies. It was an hour's drive there and back, very disruptive for his working day, but he felt so guilty that he conceded. As each day passed, Rose grew more and more silent and withdrawn. It broke John's heart to see her suffer so, and every day he felt an increasing compulsion to confess. But the lie seemed to grow larger, his actions more difficult to explain. As time went on, and she didn't get better, his cruelty was less easy to justify. John felt he had no choice but to try and draw her into jolly conversation, with less and less success until they simply sat in a terrible sad silence, Rose nursing the secret of her broken heart alone, and her father knowing what was happening, that he had caused it, and yet unable to do or say anything about it.

Christmas came and went, but the pining didn't go away.

Rose was listless and sad all the time, with barely the energy to pick at her food before going straight up to her room after dinner. She withdrew from her parents completely. They tried to persuade themselves that she was upstairs drawing, fighting to deny the fact that she was no longer coming downstairs to show them each finished piece as she had done since she was a child. In truth, both of them knew that she was simply sobbing into her pillow after Patrick Murphy. Both of them had expected her to be upset, but as two months turned to four and Rose grew thinner, John became genuinely worried that his daughter was losing her mind. Even Eleanor was beginning to doubt that she had done the right thing.

One evening, after they had made a particularly excruciating effort to please her with a coq au vin dinner and her favourite fresh cream sponge from Clarke's in Ballina, Rose had stumped up to her room immediately afterwards. Her face was stricken with grief. John was heartbroken, watching her slowly climb up the stairs as if her navy school stockings were too heavy for her legs.

As soon as she was out of earshot he turned to his wife and said, 'It's not right, what we are doing, Eleanor. I have to tell her the truth.'

His wife's reaction was so immediate and so strong that it frightened him.

'You will do no such thing.' Her voice was an angry growl. 'You think you know, but you know nothing. She's upset, but she'll get over it. If she carries on with him...' She stopped abruptly and began clearing the plates.

Eleanor was prone to hysterics so John didn't push any further, but he resolved to find a way of talking to Rose over the coming days.

Patrick had been sending letters to Rose, care of John, as they had arranged. As the letters came through, Eleanor had, of course, absolutely insisted that they should not be passed on. So, when Eleanor went to stay with her sister for a few days, John decided to act. He knew his daughter would be angry and upset, but she would see sense, he was sure, and in any case this terrible situation had to end. By the time Eleanor came back from her sister's house, the situation would be sorted out. So, before he called Rose down for her breakfast on this Saturday morning, he went into his office and unlocked the bureau drawer where he kept cash and confidential documents. But, as he reached to pull out the unopened letters from Patrick, the telephone rang. Dr Hopkins ran quickly out of the hall to answer it. His was one of five telephones in Foxford, including the postmistress's and the priest's. If it rang on a Saturday morning, it was probably an emergency.

'Come quickly, Doctor, Enda fell down – he's not breathing.'

Katherine Pryor from just down the road. Enda's second heart attack – he could save him again, but he'd have to act fast. John grabbed his bag from the hallstand and ran out the front door, without even closing it behind him.

When he started up the car, Rose looked out the window and saw him leave.

It was safe to go downstairs.

Weekends were hell these days. She could not stand to be around her parents. Even though they had not known about her relationship with Patrick, some part of her felt that if they had known the cause of her misery they would have been pleased. Possibly even gloated. The mere fact that she could not tell them about this huge, consuming sadness that she felt in losing the great love of her life was enough, in itself, to carve a huge chasm between them. How could they possibly understand the pain she was feeling? It was as if somebody had cut off one of her limbs. She had not known how much a part of her he had become until he had gone.

His family had told her. Sinead had said, quite casually one day, 'Patrick's gone to Dublin. It's all very mysterious. Somebody offered him a job in America and off he went. Just like that!'

'Just like that.' Rose's heart was broken.

She didn't believe it at first. Patrick would never leave her, and if he did, he certainly wouldn't do it without saying goodbye. Without offering some kind of an explanation, a note, something. But there was nothing. Nothing but a big empty hole where love had once lived. And not just love, it seemed now, but hope and her future and all the dreams and ideas she had of them being artists together, out in the world, painting and singing. Two beautiful people in love, ready to set the world alight. Without him, she wasn't beautiful any more. Without Patrick she had no fire, no heart. She was a shell. She wanted to die.

How could her parents possibly understand? Anyone understand? Except him. And yet he was the very person causing all of this. She had loved him, she had trusted him with her heart and also with her soul. And now, in breaking that trust, he had not only broken her heart, but scooped out her soul too. Rose was lost. Bereft. Broken.

However, she was also occasionally hungry. Just never in front of her parents.

So as soon as her father's car took off at speed down the drive, she knew it was an emergency – probably a heart attack. They were the most popular emergencies around here. Her father did love saving lives. The glory of it kept him going, so he would probably be spending half the day driving to the main hospital in Galway and back. With her mother away, that gave Rose a full day on her own in the house. This meant that she could be depressed, but without the pressure of knowing that her parents were watching her. She couldn't enjoy her cake with her parents gazing at her, wondering if her eating was an indication that things were getting better. Which, of course, they weren't.

As Rose came down the stairs she noticed that the front door was open. While she was closing it, she noticed that the study door was wide open too and the drawer on her father's bureau was pulled out. John always kept his desk drawer tightly locked because he often kept a lot of money in there. He banked most of his takings but liked to keep a good deal of cash in the house as well, for paying the gardener, or getting the car fixed – although she often heard her mother complain about it. Rose had an immediate fear that perhaps they had been burgled, and that her father had rushed out in pursuit – before reminding herself that he would hardly have taken the car. Somewhat intrigued, she walked in and laid her hands on the brown leather desktop and, as she did so, she saw an envelope just tucked into the drawer, as if it had been half pulled out when her father was disturbed. Picking it up, she was confused to see it was addressed to her and in a familiar hand. Under it were two more. Her stomach sank and her hands shook as she tore open the first envelope.

My darling Rose,

By now your father would have told you about our wonderful plan to set everything up for our future together.

He has sent me over to America to a cousin of his, a big, important man called Desmond, who runs a golf course, and I'm going to work there for a while until the singing takes off which please God won't be too long. America is the home of rock and roll, Rose, and I'm so happy to be going there as you can imagine! The English lads like Tommy Steele and Cliff Richard, well they're all right but America is where it's all happening! If I am going to be discovered, that's the place to be. Jerry Lee Lewis? Sure, he'll only be trotting after me once I get going! I might be the new Elvis yet! Now, I know what you're thinking, Rose – you're thinking but if he's the new Elvis he'll have all the women screaming after him and there'll be no room for the likes of me! Well you know that will never happen. You are the one for me, my wee Rosie Hopkins. Here I am sitting on an aeroplane, up above in the sky among the clouds – looking down on Ireland which is smaller from up here than you can imagine. I should be off the head with excitement and looking out the window and thinking of all the adventures ahead of me. But all I can think about is you, my darling girl, aghrá. It has been so hard these last few weeks, pretending I didn't want to see you. I hope you got my last note saying I was away up to Dublin for work and that, and you didn't go thinking that I had abandoned you altogether – although you would know me by now that that would never happen. That was the hardest thing of all, not seeing you or being able to tell you where I was going and what I was doing.

But your father knows you the best of all. Better than me even, I'm thinking, and he said you would try to stop me going. But, Rose, my darling Rose, this is the best thing for us, and that is certain. I've nothing to give you back home (except all my love and kisses and more besides!) but in a few short months I'll be able to send home for you, pay back all the money I owe your father for his kindness in sending me here although I know he did it for you, more than for me, because he wants you seen right with a man with prospects, someone you can rely on. That's what I want too, so that's why I came without stopping to say goodbye. I hope you'll forgive me – and I know that you will.

My darling Rosie, it will be so hard to not see you again for a while. And oh! How I have been longing, this long time we've been apart, to wrap my arms around you and feel you breathing into my neck and the joy of knowing your kisses, time and time again, all over my face, and when I am thinking like that, of what I am missing, even though I'm a man, I could surely cry. But I won't cry, because it will seem a short time coming, with all the work I have to do, before we see each other again. You will have your school to finish and your drawings to do, maybe for art school in New York this time. Although there will be no need for you to work when you're married to a rock and roll star!

Write back to me as soon as you can to let me know you're not mad with me (and if you are take it up with your father ha, ha!)

All my love,
For ever and ever.
Only Ever Yours
Patrick

P.S. I wrote a song for you. It's the first song I ever wrote, but that day and you drawing me I thought how you inspire me too.

It's not very good, I'm thinking, but I am sending it anyway. I hope you don't think it's silly. The air I had in mind was 'Treasure of My Heart' as I know you love the air. You made me sing it for you often enough as we sat in the field in front of your house. I'll be closing my eyes and singing this out when I want to bring you to mind. You are never far away in my dreams, aghrá.

On a separate piece of paper, with several crossings out he had written:

IT WAS ONLY EVER YOU

I ask myself are you the one I dream of night and day
Are you the reason why this yearning never goes away
I ask myself are you the one whose face I can't forget
Your name hangs gently on each breeze I still can hear it yet
I ask myself are you the one whose gentle fingertips
Caressed my skin and kissed me like an angel on the lips
I ask myself are you the one who filled me with desire
Are those the eyes that once searched mine and set my soul on
*   fire...*
Could it be true... could it really be you... the one I search for
*   in a song and waited for so long... was it only ever you?*

I tell myself that you're the one who fills my every day
Your name your face your touch your smile... you take my
*   breath away*
I tell myself you are the very reason I exist
And when you look into my eyes your love I can't resist
I tell myself that on each breeze I'll call your name aloud
And wrap you in my arms each night through every stormy cloud
I tell myself that without you my life would fall apart

Each season will roll round again each memory break my heart
And now I know that you're the only one who makes my life
   complete
And when you whisper in my ear... how my heart skips a beat
There's nothing in this world that makes me feel the way I feel
When I'm with you because I know this love I have is real...
Because it's true... it was only ever you... the one I love with all
   my heart... and have done from the start... It was only ever
   you... my love... yes... It was only ever you

Rose stood in her father's study, clutching the letter, her head swirling with conflicting thoughts and emotions. Frantically, she tore open the next letter in the pile. It was dated less than a week later, 'The place where I'm working isn't in the city at all but in the countryside – like at home...' She skimmed it and grabbed the next one dated less than a week later. 'The lads in the kitchen are great craic...' then the next, 'I sang at a wedding last night. I bowled them over. It put me in mind of our own wedding darling girl...' then on until she reached the last one. Dated early in November it read, 'Why won't you write me back my Rose. I am so lonely over here without you. Have you forgotten me entirely?'

Rose let out a sob, then a terrible rage ran through her as she realized her parents had tricked her, lied to her, and banished her beloved to the other side of the world. But despite the fury at her mother, who she knew, somehow, was behind this, and the hard slap of hurt she felt at being betrayed by her father, Rose could feel her heart pumping with happiness. This letter meant that Patrick had not abandoned her after all! He still loved her! He had written a song for her! 'It Was Only Ever You'. He had written, 'Only Ever Yours' on each of her letters. It was right here in her hand. She kissed the paper and tears of joyful relief poured down her face. Then she remembered that the date of his last letter was November. Three months since he had written to her. Surely he had not given up? Surely he could not think that she didn't love him?

There was only one thought in her mind now. Rose had to find Patrick and be with him. There was no time for consideration, no time even for anger or regret. She had to get to Patrick and let him know that she still loved him. Rose reached into the back of the desk where she knew her father kept cash and found two fat lumps of bank notes. She had no idea how much was there, but she was certain it was enough to get her to wherever she wanted to go. In any case, she couldn't think about that now. Then she rummaged across to the top shelf of the bureau where she knew he kept family documents and found her passport.

She rammed the cash, passport and the bunch of Patrick's letters into her deep cardigan pockets and ran up the stairs. Taking down the small suitcase she used for school, she stuffed whatever came to hand in there: a few random items of clothing, her sketch pad and pencils. The case being only half full, she had a small revelation realizing that she didn't need very many things after all. But she did need Patrick.

Before she ran out of the house, Rose realized that her father might be home soon and would try and follow her. So to put him off the scent, she ran into his office, found the key to his bureau drawer, and locked it. She then wrote a short note saying that she had gone for a walk and not to wait about for her. As she left it on the kitchen table she had a jolt of conscience, then reminded herself angrily that her parents had been lying to her in the filthiest way possible for the past month. She had every right to lie right back at them.

As she quickly pulled on her boots, cursing at the laces taking ten precious seconds from her escape time, she checked her watch. If she cycled like the clappers she would make the lunchtime train from Castlebar in just over an hour. It was too risky going from Foxford or even Ballina. If she was seen getting on the train, her father could get word of it then be ahead of her in the car and waiting to meet her when she got off the train in Dublin. This way she could abandon the bike and slide on to the train without ever getting caught.

Only after she was in New York and reunited with her true love would she get in touch with her parents and tell them she was alive.

Then they would be sorry for what they had done.

As her bare legs pumped the bicycle pedals as hard as they could, pebbles and mud dashing up from the dirt lane that led her on to the Swinford road, Rose astonished herself with her own strength. This was what love was: this speed, this strength, this certain, unfailing, single-minded knowing that she was on the way to Patrick. He was her match, her prize, her everything and she determined to find him, and keep him – and never let him go again.

10

AVA AND Dermot began dating. Their first date was, as Dermot had planned, lunch at the Law Society Club. They had a nice time, talking easily and laughing loudly into the dark, dusty dining room. However, Ava was considerably less thrilled than her mother at his choice of location and worried that he was trying to impress her parents more than her. He dropped her back to the house just before five in the afternoon, and there was an awkward moment when they stood on the doorstep before he leaned in to kiss her. This was Ava's first kiss. Breathless with excitement, she closed her eyes and puckered up, only to be rewarded with a perfunctory peck on the cheek, followed by Dermot whispering in her ear, 'Sorry, this isn't a sweet nothing but I think your mother is watching us through the window.'

While her heart sank with disappointment, Ava couldn't help but laugh and said, 'Well why don't you kiss me anyway and give her something to tell her friends about.' He swooped her down and kissed her on the mouth. Although

Dermot's arms felt strong and sturdy, Ava was still nervous that he might drop her on to the wooden porch. In any case, the performance being entirely for her mother's benefit, it did not feel as a proper kiss should and Ava felt somewhat cheated after he left.

The following weekend he took her out for dinner. They went to a very nice Italian restaurant in the city. Ava would have liked to have gone dancing as well, but given Dermot's lack of grace in that department she did not suggest it. Throughout dinner, despite his efforts to talk about her, she insisted on grilling him more thoroughly about his work, which she found fascinating. As far as she could gather, he defended criminals, which she thought was terribly glamorous and exciting, although once he got going, much of his talk was about the intricacies of the law and court procedure and she could barely make head or tail of it.

'I'm sorry,' he said. 'I'm an awful bore when I get going.'

'Not at all,' Ava said. Although, truthfully, she had been a little bored. For the first time in her life, she had the feeling that she had met a man who liked her a great deal, and although she liked him too, an awful lot, she was not quite so sure how she felt about him romantically. Was there something missing that should be there?

If Dermot had been able to see inside Ava's heart, he would have been dreadfully upset, although not entirely surprised. He knew what he was good at, and that was The Law. When he was in court he could be clever and charming. With his law friends and negotiating almost every area of life, he was a titan of a man. But when it came to girls, he fell down. He was able to make them laugh and generally enough girls liked him and enjoyed his company. They just never seemed to fall in love with him. Dermot, with his keen, lawyer's detachment, knew he wasn't good-looking like his brother and he certainly wasn't a good dancer. Also, he wasn't 'dangerous'. Dermot was the sensible option, considerably more popular with girls' mothers than he was with the girls themselves. There was never any shortage of young women interested in him. Nice girls who were keen to do as their mothers told them and try to win over the unremarkable-looking, pragmatic but very successful lawyer who could offer them a good life in exchange for warming his slippers and cooking his suppers, and hanging off his arm at the occasional law-society dress dance. But Dermot wanted to choose for himself. And he chose Ava Brogan.

The fact that Ava was Tom Brogan's daughter had only registered the first time he had seen her, six months previously, at a Connaughtman fundraiser. His attention had been caught first by her laughter. The delightful sound of a woman letting out a broad, raucous guffaw had arrested him from across the room. When he looked across, he saw this fine woman, with her head thrown back, standing head and shoulders above a group of small, delicate, rather silly-looking creatures. He thought she looked magnificent and immediately had a feeling that this was the woman that he wanted to spend the rest of his life with. It was as simple and as complicated as that. He had fallen in love, and he had not the first clue what to do about it. So, lawyer that he was, Dermot thought it through. She was relatively unadorned – no fancy hairdo or jewellery – wearing a dress that seemed nondescript next to the fluff and froth of puffy skirts and the jewellery of her friends. She looked like his sort of girl. The sort of girl who wasn't embarrassed to throw her head back and laugh. Perhaps, as she didn't seem to set great store by glamour, she might not mind a man being somewhat stout and ordinary-looking.

'Who is that tall girl with the loud laugh?' he asked Bridie Flaherty, a rather annoying friend of his mother's who was always trying to pass herself off as Rose Kennedy.

Bridie grimaced. 'Ava Brogan, Tom Brogan's daughter.' Then, assuming he was more offended than interested, added, 'They only had the one, thank God!'

Dermot didn't even hear her. Already he was marching over to Tom, his hand out in that convivial Irishman-about-to-do-business pose, asking for an introduction to 'your charming daughter'.

Ava had held her hand out politely, and said, 'How do you do.' But her voice was flat and uninterested. Of course, asking to be introduced by one of her parents had been a stupid thing to do. So unadventurous. So mundane. The act simply complemented his ordinary appearance. How, Dermot thought, could the cleverest lawyer in New York have done such a pedestrian, obvious thing? Before he even had time to register her total lack of interest, the wretched band struck up. There was a second when Dermot could have grabbed her hand and whisked her on to the floor and shown her what a fun-loving, exciting, downright hilarious, good-time guy he was. He wanted to do it so badly, that he could almost see the action unfolding in front of him. Except – it did not. Dermot could not dance. He had no sense of rhythm and was, in fact, so clumsy and self-conscious that he knew he was not just an uncomfortable partner, but downright off-putting. So Ava rushed on to the dance floor in a frenzy of excitement without him. She was immediately grabbed into a wild, skilful jive by his brother Niall.

When Dermot saw what a great dancer she was, his spirits fell. She was laughing, and thrashing and bursting with joy. His own heart was bursting watching her, but after a few moments of despair, he resolved that he would find a way of getting through to her. He would just have to bide his time and be smart.

So when his parents were making plans for his sister's wedding, Dermot made sure that the Brogans were on the guestlist, and that their daughter was sitting next to him. He had to agree to Niall sitting on the other side of her because he did not want to alert his parents to his plan. He also paid the band to make sure the first three dances were waltzes.

Meeting Ava again at that wedding, and wooing her, had been the greatest night of his life. The fact that she had been more sophisticated, and somewhat more elegant, than he had remembered her just made Dermot feel all the more pleased with himself for having successfully secured a second date. Now he just had to make sure he could keep hold of her long enough to get her to marry him. He had no doubts. Ava Brogan was the girl for him. She was funny and clever and seemed to have the same steady outlook on life as himself. He could not say that she was beautiful, or not beautiful – only that when he looked in her bright, interested face, he understood beauty in a way he had not done before. From that first afternoon, Dermot felt a warm glow of recognition in his heart that told him they were meant to be together.

By the end of their second date, he felt that he might be starting to win Ava over. And, to a certain extent, he was.

The food in the restaurant was excellent, and Ava did love her food. She ordered spaghetti and Dermot watched, delighted, as she scraped up every last piece of the tomato sauce with her bread.

'What?' she said, blushing slightly as she noticed him gazing across at her with his chin in his palm. 'Am I making a show of myself? It's just so delicious.'

'I'm just thinking that's the most satisfying two dollars I've spent in a long time. I love hearing you laugh, and I love watching you eat. Is that strange?'

'Yes,' she said, waving a piece of bread at him. 'Very!'

She shook her head, smiled and kept eating. She noted that she felt as comfortable as if she was eating at home with her own family, and wondered if that was a good thing.

After the meal they drove up to a parking spot he knew. It was half an hour from the city, so she realized that he must have planned it. He took the roof down on his car and they sat and looked down on to the city lights.

Ava sat and waited to be kissed. Properly this time. But first he asked her if she would like a boiled sweet, he had some in the glove compartment. She was so irritated by the suggestion that she nearly exploded, but just then he leaned across and kissed her tenderly on the mouth. It was different from the kiss on her parents' porch. That had, really, just been pretend. This kiss was soft, and sincere and full of feeling. It was not the passionate, earth-shattering experience she had been expecting (and perhaps rather hoping for), but rather a gentle heart-melting. After they had kissed for a while, he took a small rug off the back seat and laid it over her legs, saying, 'To stop the night chill troubling your knees, m'lady.' In actual fact, he needed to cover up her lusciously long legs to keep his desires in check.

On the way back to Yonkers, Ava rested her head on his shoulder. She felt warm, safe and thoroughly happy. She was with a nice man who liked her and had kissed her. Life was good, better than she could have dreamt it would be.

When Dermot dropped her home, he kissed her again, more passionately, with an urgency that suggested he would have liked to go further. Ava felt reassured and flattered by his desire. They made an arrangement to meet again the following weekend. Then midweek for a movie, then the following weekend for dinner again, and another midweek movie.

Six dates in a row meant that they were now officially sweethearts.

On their seventh date, as he was leaving her on the doorstep of her parents' house, Dermot turned back and said, 'Ava, I want you to know that I'm serious about my intentions towards you.'

Ava smiled, and then bowed her head modestly, although in truth she was smiling inside at his formal use of language. 'Thank you, Dermot,' she said. She knew what he was driving at. 'Serious intent' was the precursor to marriage. Her mother would be thrilled. So would her father, even though he was less anxious to see her settled and away from home.

Dermot put his hands on her shoulders and patted them reassuringly.

'You know, this is not a casual affair for me. It is no fling.'

'Oh, kiss me like you mean it!' she said. Then he laughed, and did.

Once inside, Ava thought about Dermot's use of the word 'fling'. She did not feel particularly 'flung', to be honest, and doubted he had ever had a such a thing in his life, although, of course, neither had she. They were not 'flinging' types. And the realization that she was dating a man who was as pragmatic and unromantic as she was made her feel slightly sad, for a moment. Was this, really, what love was like? Even their dates were becoming routine, starting at the same time, and ending in the same way, with a single kiss on her parents' porch.

No question of anything more than a kiss either. Dermot's hands were always firmly on her waist when he kissed her. He was as reserved and controlled as his conservative, Catholic background had taught him. Ava was bound by the same religious and social conventions, but she understood too that such rules were to be broken. If one didn't feel like breaking the rules, what was the point of them at all?

Only Dermot knew how much he truly wanted Ava. How he ended each date deliberately early with a demure kiss in order to spare her the full force of his desire. Only he knew how much he longed for them to be married so he could take her in his arms each night and make a true, natural woman out of her.

'How are you and Dermot getting on?'

When Ava got in after their seventh date, Nessa ambushed her in the kitchen. She had finally cracked. Tom had repeatedly warned her not to say a word, but the tension had got too much for her.

Ever since she had ruined her first kiss, Ava was getting beyond irritated by her mother's meddling.

'He says he has "good intentions" towards me, Mom. I assume that means he wants to marry me.'

'Now, Ava, let's not get ahead of ourselves. It's early days yet. But you seem to like each other and that's the most important thing. Just relax and enjoy being in love.'

Ugh. Typical of her mother to try and use reverse psychology tactics.

'Thank you, Mom. You're full of good advice.'

'You're welcome, darling,' she said with a false calm. 'Sleep tight.'

From the kitchen, Ava saw her mother do a little dance at the bottom of the stairs then leap up them two at a time to tell her father the good news.

But Ava was feeling flat. Was this what falling in love was supposed to feel like? She did enjoy being with Dermot.

He was very funny and kind, and it was lovely to get the attention from a man. She liked going out for dinner, and getting dressed up – but in truth, Ava enjoyed her nights out at the Central Ballroom with Myrtle too. She was beginning to wonder if perhaps it wasn't a very good idea, after all, to fix up with the first man who fancied her.

11

DERMOT PLANNED the proposal as if he was preparing for a case.

He found it hard treading that fine line between respecting Ava as a lady and showing her his true feelings. Coming off all manly wasn't the way to go, but he feared, at times, that his acting the perfect gentleman had made him appear mundane. He knew Ava was intrigued by his connections to the underworld and that she loved it when he told her about some of the criminals he had defended. One of his clients, Joe Higgins, had been nagging him to come and have a night out in his club in Hell's Kitchen. It was a risky option, but Dermot wanted to make this evening memorable. Also, Joe Higgins was a silent partner of the golf club in Westchester, where they had first met, and Dermot had an idea about that too.

Dermot called for Ava at seven p.m., as usual. Ava decided to wear her Sybil Connolly suit.

As he opened the car door for her to get in, Dermot said, 'Oh, you've worn your suit. That's nice.'

Ava immediately felt irritated. Then he looked at her oddly and said, 'It's a strange thing to wear for dinner. Any particular reason for it?'

Sometimes, he could just be so infuriatingly blunt.

'Shall I go and change?' she said. 'I can go put on something more suitable.'

He did not seem to notice the sarcastic tone in her voice but said, 'No, it's fine. Actually, I'm taking you somewhere a bit different tonight. We're going over to the bad end of town. One of my clients has a club there and he's always on at me to visit. It might get a bit rowdy.'

Ava could not help herself from thinking, I certainly hope so.

She had once asked him, 'Don't you feel awful – getting these gangsters off from their crimes?'

'I'm not getting them off, darling. Everyone has a right to be defended properly in court. It's how democracy works. Only the very best, thoroughly moral lawyers get chosen to work with the very worst criminals.'

Ava remembered his saying that and how stupid and a little pompous she had thought it was. Sometimes, it seemed as if Dermot thought he knew it all. Like her father.

Dermot drove the car towards the city. Ava looked out the window at the Hudson glimmering over on her right. As she sank back into the comfortable leather seats of Dermot's Corvette and watched the evening sun dropping down behind the water, she realized how fortunate she was. It was wrong of her to be bored with Dermot. He was a good man. He was respectful and thoughtful and had perfect manners. He opened the car door for her and presented her with small gifts of flowers and chocolates on their dates. If he did want to marry her, she wouldn't find anyone better.

She certainly wouldn't find anyone that would make her parents happier.

They drove through Manhattan and into the area that Ava knew to be Hell's Kitchen. This was where the Irish mob – the Westies – operated. She had been there once or twice over the years, accompanying her father in his charitable work. Nobody ever bothered Tom Brogan down here. He was a solid Irishman, a devout Catholic and had a good name across the whole community – including the criminal fraternity. The Westies did not approve of Tom Brogan's do-gooding any more than he approved of their money-laundering and strong-arming, but they nonetheless maintained a healthy respect for each other.

Tom negotiated with Westie bosses to get fairer rents for Irish tenants, with some success, and tried to win back lost souls, with less success. He had seen how easy it was for young men to come straight off the boat to the Irish-centric village where they knew their muscle and drinking and Irish bravado would be welcome. Within weeks the best of them would fall into bare-knuckle boxing, gambling, or some other such criminal activity. What nobody told them was that you couldn't move on from the Westies. Once you were in, you were in for life. The gangster code was unbreakable. Tom tried to make sure young Irish men arriving in New York stayed as far away from Hell's Kitchen as possible, and to settle them into the more suburban areas of the Bronx. Sometimes it worked, sometimes it didn't.

Dermot drove them down a quiet street in what seemed to be a particularly seedy area. As he opened the car door for her, he said, 'I hope you don't mind slumming it tonight, my darling. There is no need to worry. I've kept the owner out of jail so many times, he owes me. We'll be looked after.'

He handed the keys of his Corvette to a huge, rough-looking man who nodded deferentially. Ava felt a small thrill as she realized that her sweetheart was able to command the same respect from these gangsters as her own father.

Inside the door they walked up a narrow staircase into the nightclub. It was a small, dark, seedy room, already filled with cigarette smoke and the chatter of Irish drinkers. This was a very different part of Irish New York to the dance halls: people didn't come here to dance, they came here to drink and to gamble and, very probably, fight. The stage was backed with silver and green tinsel and a paper shamrock banner. There were heavy green drapes on every window, the carpet was green and even the small tables at the front of the stage were covered in green baize. It was like being in a green womb. Dermot and Ava were shown to a table at the front of the stage and a rather shabby-looking waiter brought them a bottle of champagne.

'Courtesy of the management,' the waiter said and Dermot nodded his approval. Everything was going to plan. The waiter poured the champagne; he wondered if perhaps now was the moment. No. He would hold off. Wait for the romantic surprise he had planned.

'This is nice,' Ava said. In truth it was thrilling to be here. She looked up hopefully at the small dance floor in front of the stage.

'I thought you'd like to come somewhere a bit different,' Dermot said. Then he leaned across and whispered, 'I know how interested you are in my contacts in the criminal fraternity, so I thought you'd like to see what a proper joint looked like. I hope the food is decent.'

Ava smiled and said, 'I doubt it – but it is certainly unusual.' She sipped her champagne and looked around, fascinated.

'How was your week?' Dermot asked.

As he was looking across the table at her Ava thought that perhaps she could talk to him about her doubts. Confide in him that she was worried that things were moving too fast. His eyes looked so concerned, so enquiring, so kind – she felt she could tell Dermot anything. As she was thinking this through, the lights dimmed and a man who was as round as he was tall, wearing a cheap tuxedo, came out on the stage and announced, 'Ladies and gentleman – we have a special guest in for you this evening to get the entertainment started. All the way from the county of Mayo, would you please put your hands together for Mr Paa-trick Murphy!'

This is it, thought Dermot. The moment had come. He watched Ava, waiting for her reaction as he slipped his hand into his pocket to reach for the ring.

There was polite applause as the young man came out on stage. Ava immediately recognized him as the boy from the wedding.

She felt her stomach lurch as he began to sing 'The Rose of Tralee'. Ava knew all the Irish ballads. This particular one meant nothing to her, but the way he sang it... his voice... his face... He drew something out of her she had not known was there. He sang with such passion that it was as if he was reaching inside her and making every part of her sing alongside him. With every word he sang, and every breath he took, Ava felt herself being transported to another place. She did not know this person and yet through his singing she felt as if she knew him absolutely.

Dermot loosened his grip on the small box. He had arranged with Joe for this particular singer to be here tonight. He knew how Ava loved Irish ballads and she had been so impressed with him at the wedding.

'It's the singer from the first day we met,' he said, leaning across. The box was out of his pocket, ready to press into her palm.

'Shhhh,' she said. She closed her eyes, ecstatic. Dermot thought she had never looked more beautiful than in that moment. He got a glimpse of how womanly she was. A promise of what the future might bring. He felt so emotional that he had to gather himself. He put the ring back in his pocket. Now wasn't the time.

As soon as the song ended, Dermot reached for the ring again but just then their host appeared at the table.

'Now here's my favourite lawyer!'

Joe Higgins was wearing a sharp, shiny blue suit with a broad-shouldered jacket and slim, straight trousers. A real spiv. 'And this is the beautiful lady you keep tellin' me about?' He took Ava's hand and, before she had fully extended it to him, kissed it.

'This is Ava,' Dermot said somewhat nervously.

'Ain't you going to introduce me?'

'Ava – this is Joe Higgins, he owns this establishment.'

'And several others.' Joe patted Dermot's shoulder. 'Thanks to this character, who got me out of a tight spot last month. I hope you know your fella is a kind of genius when it comes to getting guys like me off the hook?'

Dermot shifted uncomfortably in his seat. Ava smiled. He was inviting her to ask what kind of a guy he was. She wasn't stupid. She could see straight away he was a gangster. She could also see that Dermot was a little afraid of him. Ava wasn't. Her father had always taught her that if you looked a man straight in the eye and told the truth, the Lord would protect you.

'That singer you had tonight was very good,' she said.

'You think?' Joe gave Dermot a conspiratorial wink. It looked terrible. This evening was not turning out as Dermot had envisioned. Joe took a big cigar out of his pocket and clipped the end of it.

'I dunno, I'm not big into the serious Irish ballads. Give me Sinatra any day.'

'He's got a strong voice,' Ava said. 'I reckon he could do a pretty good Sinatra if he was given the chance. Seems to me all he needs is a break and a decent band behind him.'

Dermot stepped in then. 'Did you notice, Ava, he was the guy my father booked for my sister's wedding?'

'Really?' she lied. 'I hadn't noticed.'

Mention of Judge Dolan's name immediately altered Joe's aspect.

'The judge is a man of great taste. Would you like to meet the kid? I can bring him out to you.'

Ava's heart did a small leap. She looked at Dermot, shrugging as if she did not care one way or the other, but implying with a flash of her eyes that Joe might not like it if they refused his offer.

'That would be grand, Joe, thanks. Me and Ava would be happy to have a drink with him.'

That was the engagement off the table. Maybe as he dropped her off? They could go in and celebrate with her folks? Perhaps God was telling him not to try to be such a romantic klutz. Don't try and be something you're not, Dermot, he said. Be yourself. That's always the best way.

Joe went off and came back with Patrick Murphy. His green velvet suit was gone and he was now wearing a pair of shabby brown trousers and a white shirt that looked in need of pressing.

Ava felt a little sick. He had the same slightly lost,

down-at-heel look of the poor young Irish men her father helped. The stage suit had been borrowed, she now realized.

'These folks want to meet you,' Joe said rather abruptly, then clicking for a waiter to bring over another bottle of champagne he went off, leaving Patrick standing there.

'Won't you sit down?' Ava said. 'It's Patrick, isn't it?'

Patrick sat down, next to Dermot. In his shabby clothes he seemed diminished.

'You are a great singer,' Ava said.

'Thanks,' Patrick replied, then looked down at his hands. He clearly didn't want to be here and Ava was sorry she had called him out. He was completely different from the charismatic figure she had seen on stage. He seemed ordinary and out of place. 'Straight off the boat' was how her father described these boys.

'Where are you from in Ireland?' Ava asked.

'A place called Foxford in County Mayo,' he said. 'It's very small, you'll hardly know it.'

'Is that the place that has the woollen mills?'

His face lit up. 'It is surely.'

'Well would you believe it? This suit I'm wearing is made from fabric woven in Foxford Woollen Mills.'

'Get away out of that,' he said, and he leaned over and touched the arm of her jacket. Ava shivered, despite herself.

Patrick's hand lingered, his fingers stroking the fabric, until Dermot let out a small cough.

'I'm sorry,' he said, but Ava could see from his eyes that he wasn't sorry at all and she felt excitement unfurl deep in her stomach.

'Somebody belonging to me would have woven that tweed – it could even have been my father.'

'What a coincidence,' Ava said. 'I was told by the designer

that this tweed was a match for the wild hedgerow roses of Mayo, the most beautiful roses in the world.'

'They are that surely and more,' he said. 'And if I hadn't moved over to this wretched hole of a country six weeks ago there is a good chance that's where I'd be working myself.'

'You don't like New York then?' Ava asked.

'Let's just say it wasn't what I was led to expect,' he said.

Dermot began to feel uncomfortable. He patted his pocket. The ring was still there.

'Why don't you order Patrick a proper drink, Dermot? That champagne is awful. Patrick, what would you like?'

'I'll have a pint, thank you.'

Dermot's eyes narrowed slightly. A small pellet of rage began to flicker inside him, although he could not say why.

'I thought we were having dinner,' he said.

'Dinner can wait,' Ava said, firmly, matching his stare. 'I'm sure we are both interested in hearing what brought Patrick to America.'

Dermot was not interested. He should be – but he wasn't. Was this lad moving in on his girl? No. That was preposterous.

Over the next twenty minutes or so Patrick told them his story.

How he had been invited over to New York by a contact he had understood was a man of influence in the world of music, but who, in fact, was just the manager of a golf club that occasionally held functions. He was given a job in the kitchen and after a few weeks of pot-washing was finally given the 'opportunity' to sing on stage at a society wedding, where he might be discovered. Or not. That was the wedding they had seen him at. Joe, the boss of this place, had requested he come down here specifically tonight, to sing that ballad. He had no idea why. With no car, it was impossible for him to get into the city. If one of the chefs was coming into town, he was able to get a ride in with them. Otherwise, he was stuck out in Westchester County.

'Where are you living?' Ava asked.

He blushed. For the first time since she had mentioned Foxford he looked uncomfortable again.

'Patrick – where are you living?'

Ava knew that unscrupulous employers exploiting young men from Ireland often put them sleeping on the banquettes of their restaurants. They were paid their fares over from Ireland but once they arrived they found themselves doing manual labour and sleeping in their workplace until their fares were paid back. Her father had explained it was not simply a way of the bosses saving on rent money, it also ensured that the young men stayed under their control. They ended up being henchmen or pot-washers: slaves to their own people. These young men were usually too ashamed to tell their families back home the circumstances they found themselves in and pretended they were doing grand.

Dermot looked at his watch. 'I'm sure Patrick has to be getting back.'

This was an absolute disaster. He felt bad for the boy and everything, but it seemed that his carefully executed plan for romance was built on a human rights violation. If Ava found that out, well – it just didn't bear thinking about. He would sort it out in the coming week. Have a word with Joe and make sure that the boy was found something better in the city. In the meantime he just wanted to get this evening over and done with as quickly as possible.

'And perhaps we should head downtown for something to ea—'

Ava cut him off. 'Are you sleeping in the golf club?'

Patrick nodded. 'Just until I pay back my dues – then I plan to get something better.'

'You are coming home with us,' Ava said.

A look of panic washed over Dermot's face and as Ava reached under the table for her bag and began to stand up, he leaned over and held her wrist.

'Do not make a scene, Ava,' he said. His voice was an angry whisper.

Dermot felt terrible, but he had no choice. He let go of her hand and whispered, as kindly but firmly as he could, 'You don't mess with these people, Ava. They are dangerous gangsters.'

Ava felt suddenly furious.

'Do you mean to tell me that you are going to let this injustice continue because you're afraid of some two-bit hoodlum?'

'He is not some two-bit hoodlum; he is much more powerful than that. Also, he is one of my clients and it will be the height of bad manners to make a fuss in one of his establishments.'

Dermot knew that sounded bad, but he was clutching at straws. Also, it was true. Sort of.

'Bad manners?' Ava snapped. 'Your client – the gangster – is clearly taking advantage of Patrick and goodness knows who else. Making them work for a pittance with not even a proper bed as payment? Well, if you won't help him, my father certainly will. My father,' she said, pointedly, to Patrick, 'is Tom Brogan. He helps young men in your situation all the time. If you go and get your coat I'd be happy to take you home with me now, this very minute, to meet him…'

This was worse than Dermot thought. Not only did he look dreadful in Ava's eyes – but would her father think less of him as well?

Patrick was confused as to what to do for the best. On the one hand he had not met anybody since he came to New York who would help him move on from the situation in which he found himself. On the other hand, this warring young couple did not seem like the best option. The girl was one feisty creature, that was for sure. Nice eyes. She was kind – but a handful all the same. The man, Dermot, was right – Joe was a very nasty piece of work. Patrick had been told as much by his workmates; he would shoot a man, or have him shot, for looking at him sideways. Everyone working out at the golf club and here in this dive in town knew not to upset their boss. Patrick sensed that Dermot would be able to look after himself but he worried about the young woman. Joe didn't like women too much.

'My lift is leaving soon,' Patrick said, 'so I'll go back to the golf club, if that's all the same with you. But it was nice to meet you and thank you for the drink, and your company.'

As he stood up to go Ava felt she had failed him. Had she humiliated or embarrassed him in some way?

'You are a wonderful singer,' she said, 'and if you can ever make it into the Emerald Ballroom in Yonkers, I am there most Saturday nights. I know everyone in there. I can introduce you to some people I know, if you'd like. And remember my father's name is Tom Brogan, 175 York Avenue, Yonkers. We're in the book.'

'Thank you for your kindness, ma'am.' Then he bowed slightly, turned to Dermot and said, 'And thank you for the drink. You and your wife are very kind.'

When he was gone, Dermot smiled nervously at Ava.

'Sorry for losing patience with you,' he said, reaching for her hand. 'Let's just get out of this place and head downtown for some spaghetti?'

Ava smiled back but barely heard him. She realized her heart felt a little broken. Patrick had thought she was Dermot's wife. He had not checked her finger and seen that she was not wearing a wedding ring.

12

NESSA HAD got herself into such a fluster organizing this engagement lunch, she began to wonder how she'd ever cope with organizing the wedding itself. Ava was being utterly useless. She had showed no interest in finding a dress to wear and seemed to feel that the lunch menu and choice of flowers were of no importance. How she was ever going to adapt to being an important lawyer's wife was beyond her mother's comprehension.

'Should we put canapes on the coffee table? Or up here with the corned beef?' she said, balancing a tray of pineapple and cheese cocktail sticks elaborately arranged around a radish centrepiece.

'You're making way too much fuss, Mom. Really – it's not like it's the wedding.'

'It is a dry run,' Nessa insisted. 'It sets the tone.'

'We've already had dinner with the Dolans. Wasn't that enough?'

Dermot had proposed to Ava while dropping her home

from their disastrous date in Hell's Kitchen. They had agreed to hold off on telling their parents, and make an official engagement announcement over dinner in the Law Society Club. Dermot, not wishing to appear fusty or old-fashioned to Ava, secretly approached Tom at work and asked formally for Ava's hand. He told Tom that he understood his beautiful daughter was extremely precious and that he intended to respect and honour her, and their family.

Tom was as happy as any doting father could be, having his daughter taken away by another man, and agreed not to tell Nessa before the 'official' announcement. Both sets of parents had guessed, when they received the invitation, and all were thrilled, except for Dermot's mother Donna, a rather snooty and very beautiful Italian woman with a contessa somewhere in her family background.

Over cigars in the smoking room after their meal, Dermot's father, Judge Dolan, said, 'I was delighted when Dermot told me he had decided to settle down with a nice, sensible Irish girl. So easy for men like us to land up with some pretty, money-grabbing flibbertigibbet.' Tom smarted at the inference that his daughter was not pretty, but he let it go. Ava seemed happy. She had adopted a serene sort of elegance lately, a smarter way of dressing, and seemed to have calmed. Tom was not entirely convinced by this 'new' Ava – he liked his wild dancing, joke-around girl, but he supposed this is what happened to daughters when they matured. You lost them.

They had passed a pleasant evening. Tom liked the judge well enough. He was a good man, and between politics and their philanthropic interests, they had plenty to talk about.

Nessa, on the other hand, had found herself overwhelmed

in such elevated company. Desperate to impress Judge Dolan's wife, she was unable to stop herself from babbling, 'Of course, we think of ourselves as "Educated Irish". I much prefer to read than watch television, even though we have two sets. One of them is colour.'

Nessa was not stupid. She knew she was being gauche but the more magnanimous Donna Dolan appeared in the face of her ignorance, the worse she got. By the end of the evening Nessa was in bits. Not wanting to give up easily, she became determined to create an occasion that would show her family to be suitable for the lofty Dolans. And so she planned an Engagement Luncheon.

'It gives the ladies an opportunity to discuss the wedding arrangements together.'

'It gives you an opportunity to show us off as posh.'

'Nonsense, we are every bit as good as the Dolans. In any case, it's very important that Mrs Dolan and her daughter don't feel left out.'

Ava had already sensed that Donna Dolan had very little interest in her son's wedding. She had been polite enough to Ava on the few occasions they had met. But Ava only had to look at her high cheekbones, her black glossy hair tied up in a perfect elegant chignon and smooth olive skin to see she was disappointed in her son's choice. In fact, Ava did not especially mind if her future mother-in-law did not fully approve of her. What she minded, very much, was her own mother's insistence on seeking out that approval for her.

However, it was too late to worry about that now. The guests had begun to arrive. Nessa had staggered her invitation times so that everyone would be waiting when the Dolan ladies came in.

First was Bridie Flaherty, their neighbour, stalwart of their

local Catholic church – she would add an air of quiet respect-
ability. Then there was Nessa's cousin Kitty, a widow. She
could always be relied upon to turn up in a crisp blouse.
Finally, there was Jean Brogan; Tom's troublesome younger
sister was thirty-five and a spinster, although she insisted on
calling herself single. Jean wore trousers and had a degree.
Nessa did not approve, but thought her sister-in-law's presence would show them off as modern thinkers as PJ and his
wife were intellectuals. Nessa placed her various friends and
relations around the brown shagpile rug in a way that showed
off the Formica surround on the fireplace to its best advantage. Just then the doorbell rang.

Patrick was a month in New York before he finally gave up
on hearing back from Rose.

'The father was trying to get rid of you, man! Any fool
could see that.'

For the first couple of weeks he had believed that Dr Hopkins had made some sort of private arrangement with the
owner so that he would be given an opportunity to sing.
When the big Irish wedding came, Patrick had been assured
that it was his big break. But that very evening he was back
in the kitchen washing dishes.

His fellow dishwasher, Juan, had drawn him into a conversation about his past. Patrick was feeling lonely that night
and told him about Rose. How madly in love she was with
him and how he had come here on the generous patronage
of her father to build a life for them both. Even as he said it
out loud, scrubbing dishes, side by side with this Hispanic lad
from a poor background, he realized he knew how absurd
it sounded.

'You been cheated, man. Man, that's bad. Sending you away like that from yo' true love. And he was acting quick too, getting you on a plane. Plane ride would have cost you rent for a year. He sure was in a hurry to get rid of you.'

Patrick went quiet. In his heart he saw it was true. He had been a fool. A stupid fool.

The next day he packed up his things and cadged a lift into town with one of the kitchen suppliers.

He didn't tell anyone where he was going and he went to the only other place he had an address for: Tom Brogan's. He had the price of a taxi fare from Manhattan out to the Bronx in his pocket, not much more. The house looked very grand, so Patrick brushed down his jacket, stood as straight as he could, and rang the bell.

Nessa opened the door with great flourish and her most charming smile, expecting to see the Dolan women, only to find a young man standing there. He was carrying a bag and had the apologetic look of one of her husband's unfortunates. Young men like this called to the door looking for her husband's help quite often – but today of all days! Tom was not due home for two hours. This was a disaster.

'I'm looking for—'

'I know well who you're looking for and he is not here. He won't be home for two hours – at least.'

The young man looked suitably mortified.

'You'll have to go home and come back later. After six o'clock this evening. He'll be able to see you then.'

He had that haunted expression they all had when they landed on her husband's doorstep. Broken dreams. Desperate pride. She felt bad but really – this timing was very unfortunate.

'Grand so,' the young man said. 'I'll call again later. Thank you, ma'am.'

Nessa looked anxiously up the road to see if there was any sign of the Dolan women. They weren't due for another ten minutes.

The man turned, walked down the steps, and then moved slowly towards the path. It was apparent he had nowhere to go from here. He was going to wait out on the street. Nessa started to panic. He could be loitering around when the Dolans arrived. What would they think of the area if they saw a destitute young man sitting under a tree outside their house? And then – if Tom brought him in later and they were still there? That would look even worse.

'Come back,' she called after him. Signalling wildly for him to follow her around to the back of the house, she let him into the kitchen and gave him a bottle of Coke, a chunk of leftover corned beef, some crackers and Tom's newspaper to keep him occupied.

Daisy, their maid, arrived at the back door just in time to serve the guests. She was in full uniform, but before she had the chance to apologize for being late, Nessa said, 'Thank *God* you're here. Arrange those chips around the onion dip and do not let him *move* out of here until Tom comes home. Ah! The door! That's them...'

Patrick could see that this lady, presumably Tom Brogan's wife, had the same fierce look of his own mother when she was intent on something. The big black woman in uniform now glaring at him was closer in age to his grandmother. He knew better than to cross either of them. For the first time since he had arrived in America, Patrick Murphy felt completely safe.

* * *

Ava picked out a red shift dress and cream jacket ensemble and teamed it with a pair of low cream pumps. It had caught her eye in her local boutique the previous week. Although she had developed an interest in clothes, and in presenting a smarter, more feminine image, she could still not quite bring herself to go into the large department stores on Fifth Avenue. She found the vast corridors of clothes and smarmy showgirls intimidating. In this smaller, friendly shop she was always able to find just one thing that suited her needs. She back-combed her hair at the roots, puffing it up into a wide bob, applied a little pink lipstick, and took a deep breath.

'You can do this,' she said to her reflection in the mirror, then looked back at herself quizzically. Why was she dreading this afternoon? This was a dream come true, surely? Dermot's family were going to become her family. She was about to spend the afternoon talking about dresses and flowers, choosing the hotel where she would have her wedding reception. Her parents would give her anything she wanted in order to see her married to a man who was educated, Irish, charming and from a good family. They would give anything to see her happy. She shook her head at her own silliness and headed downstairs.

'Here she is!' Bridie said, waving a cheesy pineapple stick in her direction.

Everyone turned to look at her. A flutter of panic caught in her chest.

Her Aunt Jean waved across wryly and said, 'Late for your own party in your own house, young Ava? I'm impressed. We'll make a rebel of you yet.'

Ava inspected the gathering. Her mother- and sister-in-law-to-be were seated on either side of the new fireplace, immaculately turned out. Gloria had her handbag neatly settled on her lap and was removing her gloves. Donna was cautiously lifting a glass of champagne to her lips. Daisy was standing in the corner, almost hidden behind the orange velvet curtains, looking extremely uncomfortable in the ridiculous uniform her mother made her wear when she was entertaining. As usual, Nessa had left her with nothing to do except look the part.

This whole charade was for her. This was her engagement party. Ava was getting married.

'Ava! At last.' Her mother's eyes flickered slightly in admonishment.

Cousin Kitty came over, grabbed her shoulders and gave her a big kiss. 'I can't believe you are getting married!' Kitty had been at the onion dip and the smell of her breath, along with the feeling of panic that was now pounding in her chest, made Ava urgently nauseous.

'Would you excuse me for a moment?' she said, and rushed towards the kitchen.

She ran through the swing doors and over to the double sink where she retched loudly. Nothing was coming, so she stood up, took a deep breath and reached for a glass to pour herself some water.

'Are you all right?'

'Jesus!' Ava jumped, dropping the glass.

'Sorry, sorry...' Patrick got down from his spot at the counter where he had been wondering if he should make himself known, and began picking up the broken pieces on the floor.

'Oh – it's you...'

'Patrick,' he said, 'from the club.'

'Ah yes, I...' She had been about to say she remembered him but, for some reason, stopped herself. Her stomach started twisting again. Whatever was the matter with her today? 'Be careful – the glass...'

A drop of red fell on to the grey linoleum. Patrick had not noticed the cut. Instinctively, Ava reached across for his hand. She opened his fist, lifted the shard of glass carefully out of it as a pool of blood gathered in the crease of his palm. She reached for a tea towel and gently closed his hand around it. All the time his eyes, those endlessly deep blue eyes, remained steadily fixed on her face. Ava had never been looked at in that way before. She told herself he was simply trying to be brave, although the cut was shallow. Her hand held his. She tried to make him clench his fist to stem the flow of blood, but it seemed he would not. He did not tense his hand. She did not want to let his hand go.

'What the *hell* is going on in here? I thought I told you not to…'

Speechless with fury at this tableau, Nessa said in an angry whisper, 'Get back out there this instant, young lady, and entertain your guests. *You, boy*…' she said, jabbing her finger into Patrick's face, 'get back up on to that stool where I left you and do not move an inch, or so help me God, I will put you back out on the street and you'll not get near my husband this night!'

Ava was so embarrassed that she did not know how to react. Patrick quickly stood up and did as he was told.

At the door Nessa paused and, seeing her good tea towel in his bloody hand said, 'I'll send Daisy in to look after that and clear up this mess. Lord knows she looks as if she needs something to do…' Then she swept out.

Now it was Ava's turn to be angry.

'How dare she speak to you like that!' she said.

Patrick was smiling, more amused than offended. 'She reminds me of Mam,' he said.

'You must miss your family.'

He smiled, gave a little shrug and said, 'What's the occasion?'

Why was he smiling? With a cut hand in a stranger's house? Could it be her? She didn't dare think such a thing.

'It's my engagement party.'

His smile faltered. 'You had better get back out to your guests, so.'

Ava regretted telling him she was engaged, then remembered that in the club he had thought she and Dermot were married. Then, the fact that she had made note of it at all made her feel uncomfortable. She forced herself to focus on her mother's terrible treatment of Patrick, who had, after all, come to their house, at her invitation, looking for her father's help.

She had an idea. 'Has your hand stopped bleeding?'

He checked his palm. 'Yes.'

'Good,' she said, then she ran to the back door, picked one of her father's smart hats off the coat shelf and threw it across the kitchen at Patrick.

He caught it, laughing. 'What's this for?'

'Put it on.' He did as he was told, cocking the expensive trilby over one eye and striking a Sinatra pose.

'Perfect,' she said. 'Now, follow me...'

'I'm not moving,' he said. 'I've upset your mother enough...'

But Ava grabbed him by his sore hand and dragged him through the kitchen door and out into the drawing room.

'Ladies,' she announced. 'I would like you to meet Mr Patrick Murphy – who I have invited along to entertain us with Irish songs this afternoon.'

Nessa's eyes were flaming saucers of fury. Ava was momentarily delighted with herself then suddenly realized she was still holding Patrick's hand. She let it go with a sweeping flourish, inviting him to take the stage in the centre of the room.

Patrick stood there, trapped in the glare of ten women. For a moment he wondered how he had found himself in this situation. The room was fancier, more opulent, than any he had ever been in before. But the lady of the house was Irish and her crazy daughter meant well in finding him an audience. So, Patrick did what he always did when he was uncertain, or nervous, or simply standing in front of a group of silent people: he opened his mouth and he sang.

'Oh, Peggy Gordon, you are my darling, Come sit ye down upon my knee...'

As soon as the words began to flow out of his mouth, Patrick fell into the powerful trance of the born musician. The women found themselves mesmerized as his voice lifted their spirits and carried them off into the world of Irish romance.

'And tell to me the very reason, why I am slighted so by thee.'

Bridie was transported back to her father's knee at the Irish homestead in Ireland she had left behind over twenty years ago; Kitty remembered the day she had married her late husband; Jean thought of the boy she had loved in college. How many years since she had lost him, pretending she didn't mind being on her own? But most struck of all by this young man was Italian socialite, Donna Dolan. She had never cared much for Irish music; her husband's love for fiddle music over classical violin irritated her. However, this young ballad singer had genuine soul and for the first time in her life she began to understand and enjoy the romance of the John McCormack records her husband was always playing. After a while Donna found she was leaning back in her chair, smiling. As the wine and the music began to mingle, she found herself humming along. What a lovely afternoon she was having. It sure beat making small talk with this slightly common woman and her friends. Nessa, seeing Donna's newly blissful demeanour, calmed down somewhat, although as the afternoon wore on, she began to feel uncomfortable about Ava, who seemed more taken with this young man than she ought to be.

She was very relieved when Tom arrived home earlier than expected.

'What's going on here?' he said.

Patrick was leading the guests through a somewhat raucous rendition of 'Home Boys Home'.

'...and it's home, boys, home' – clap-clap – 'home I'd like to be...' The women had all had a few drinks by now; even Donna was pink-cheeked and clapping along to the chorus.

Tom threw off his hat and joined in – '...home I'd like to be – home far away in me own country...' – until the song was finished, and the older women laughed and patted their hair, and began to gather themselves together.

'Hey – seems I've missed quite a party here...'

Ava went straight over to her father and gave him a hug, saying, 'Pop, this is Patrick – he needs your help.'

'Well now, I don't know about that. This young man looks as if he is doing just fine by himself.'

Patrick walked across the room holding out his hand. 'I'm very pleased to meet you, Mr Brogan. I have heard a great deal about you and your kindness from Ava.'

'I wouldn't believe a word this young lady tells you. She's a desperate blagger altogether!'

'I don't doubt it, sir,' the young man said. His eyes flicked across to Ava and he grinned. Tom saw the way the boy's eyes softened when he looked at his daughter. He also noted the expression of barely contained fury on his wife's face.

'Well, Patrick,' Tom said, putting his arm around the young man's shoulder and taking him off into the kitchen, 'perhaps you and I should go out and see if we can find you a job and let these ladies get on with their party?'

'Thank you, sir,' Patrick said. 'I'll just collect my bag from the kitchen.'

'No need,' Nessa jumped in, nodding for Daisy to hand him his knapsack and jacket, before herding the two of them out to the car.

'Perhaps I should go with you?' Ava said.

Nessa looked as if she might explode, so her husband said, 'No, Ava, you stay here and entertain your guests, my dear.'

This whole wedding thing really was bringing out the very worst in his wife. At the same time it was wisest to go along with her, so he gave her a reassuring nod as he put his arm around the young man and led him out through the front door.

As the door was closing Nessa remembered her manners and called out, 'Thank you for the singing!'

Nessa felt relief that this would be the last they ever saw of that wretched young man.

13

ON THE morning after the party Ava asked her father about Patrick, but he put her off, saying, 'I think it's just best for you to concentrate on your wedding plans, Ava.'

She knew that was because her mother was there, so she tried to talk to him about it again later but he simply said, 'Patrick is in gainful employ and living in the city, you'll be glad to hear,' then went back to his paper.

Her father was always eager to talk about his work and Ava was hurt by this rejection. That aside, she was anxious to know what had happened to her protégé. Where was he working and what was he doing? Bartending or washing dishes? Was he singing? If he told her that, then maybe she might be able to ask her father what he thought of Patrick. He had seemed to like him. What had they talked about in the car that day? Did Patrick ask about her? But the subject was not up for discussion and Ava didn't push it. She knew why Tom didn't want to elaborate and he was right. It was disloyal of her to be

showing any interest in another man. Thinking about Patrick
was the height of silliness. It was wrong. She was engaged to
Dermot and things were all set. Dermot was a good, kind man
and she wanted to marry him. The church was booked for
three months' time and the reception was to be a grand affair
in the Waldorf. She was having her dress made by Sybil Connolly, with her first fitting that very weekend. Almost every
moment of her spare time since the engagement had been
taken up going to see florists, and hat designers, and choosing stationery for the invitations with her mother. Dermot had
been very busy with his work and so they had barely seen
each other since the engagement. He seemed happy to let her
mother, and his, make all the decisions. She didn't mind one
way or the other about the arrangements, and she supposed
this relaxed indifference was a sort of love. Although it felt
like the opposite of passion, not minding one way or the other
was easy. But was an easy life what she should aspire to?

Every now and again Ava could not help but think about
that afternoon. Even if Patrick had wanted to kiss her, perhaps it meant nothing. Boys kissed girls all the time these
days. Dermot had asked her to marry him and she had said
yes. That was the promise she had to keep now.

'You do realize we haven't even been dancing for eight weeks?'
said Myrtle, when Ava called to ask if her friend wanted to
come to the dress fitting with her.

'I'm engaged, Myrtle,' she said. 'Why would I be going
dancing with you? I'm not looking for a man any more.'

'Well I am.'

'Nonsense – you've too many of them after you, that's your
problem.'

'You were never looking for a man anyway,' said Myrtle. 'You just loved dancing…'

'Love dancing…'

'Well it doesn't feel like it – all the gang are asking where you are.'

'Dermot hates dancing,' she said.

'You can say that again,' Myrtle said. 'I danced with him once, at Patsy Kenny's wedding. He took me round and round in one direction, over and over again. It was like carrying a tree trunk from one end of the dance floor to the other. An endurance test – I thought it was never going to end!'

Ava didn't like Myrtle saying what a dreadful dancer her fiancé was. Dermot may well be a klutz on the dance floor, but he was a good man and she didn't like him being laughed at.

'Come on,' Myrtle said, 'you come dancing this Thursday and I'll come to your wedding dress fitting on Saturday, even though I shall be sick with envy.'

'You could click your fingers and have any man you wanted, Myrtle. Not like me…'

'And yet you've ended up with Dermot, and the prize of a fancy lawyer husband.'

Dermot was nice, but he didn't feel like a prize. Ava pushed the thought aside and agreed to meet her friend.

After an hour on the dance floor Ava took a break at the bar, for the slow set. It wasn't like before; this evening it was by choice. It seemed that news of her engagement, as well as her change in style, had transformed the menfolk at the Emerald Ballroom. At least three of her regular dance partners had asked her to save a slow dance for them. One of them had even followed her back to the booth and made a lunge at her ear.

While she quickly put him off, Ava was enjoying the attention, although part of her felt sad that her time as one of the pretty, popular single girls would be coming to an end before it had properly begun.

'Hello, stranger,' Gerry said. 'I hardly knew you with the new style.'

'Thanks,' she said. 'Slumming it tonight?'

Gerry was the manager here and only tended bar on quiet nights or if they were short.

'Training in a new guy – he's on a break. What can I get you? Still on the coffee?'

'Thanks. How's business? No showband in tonight?'

'Cancellation – Big Tom and the lads got caught in Chicago for an extra night – bit of a mix-up with dates.'

'Bad luck. The resident band looks a bit short too.' It felt good to be having this conversation; like coming home.

'Singer has flu. Leo is normally on drums...'

Ava looked towards the stage where a bulky man in a tuxedo was making a very poor job of 'All I Have to do Is Dream'.

'God love him,' Ava said, 'he's doing his best.'

'He makes a reasonable fist of it usually, but I think he has a touch of the flu himself tonight— Ah, here comes the new boy. Excuse me, Ava...'

Wearing the staff uniform, a green waistcoat and bow tie, was Patrick.

Of course he worked here, of course, why had she not thought of that? This was the first place her father brought all new arrivals to look for work. Perhaps he had assumed Ava would have known that and come here looking for him anyway? Ava found herself completely thrown; her head was spinning, her stomach in knots – what had come over her? She needed to gather herself before he saw her.

She quickly turned her head back towards the stage and was about to walk away when she heard him say her name.

'Ava?'

He slid a cup of coffee towards her and smiled.

When he smiled, she smiled back at him – despite herself. The fear was gone in an instant. As soon as he spoke to her everything felt normal again. Everything felt right.

'That's me.'

'Fancy seeing you here,' he said. 'I wrote to your father and thanked him – did he get my letter?'

She shrugged. 'I don't know.'

'I suppose I should have written to you too,' he said. 'After all, you were the one who introduced me to him. You were the one who...'

He wanted to say 'rescued me' but it didn't sound very masculine.

'Oh no,' she said, rather too emphatically, imagining how Nessa would have reacted to her receiving a letter from the young man. 'There was really no need, it was...'

She wanted to say a pleasure, but then thought that might sound suggestive, which was ridiculously Victorian of her, and that made her blush and shake her own head and laugh, then Patrick started laughing with her. Gerry looked down the bar and saw his new young barman flirting with poor, plain Ava. Although she wasn't so plain any more. Wasn't it amazing what a bit of lipstick and a new hairdo could do for a girl?

When the song ended, a rush of customers landed up at Gerry's end of the bar so he called Patrick down to serve them. The band started up with 'Love Me Tender'. Leo, the drummer/singer, coughed loudly into the microphone and he blanched. 'Jesus, but Leo really is brutal tonight. I think we'd be better off going full instrumental tonight – although the girls do love the few words...'

The idea hit Ava like a slap to the head.

'I'm surprised you're letting Leo away with it when you have the best singer in all of County Mayo under your roof tonight.'

'And who would that be then?'

'Your new barman – Patrick. I saw him sing at a wedding a while back.'

'I thought you two looked as if you've met before...'

'Not like that, Gerry! He was really good...'

'Thanks, Ava, but I think I'd better stick with the professionals.'

'Really?' Ava said. 'How long have I been coming here? I know a good singer when I hear one and Patrick is very good.'

'I don't know.' Gerry grimaced. 'The band don't like strangers coming in. I don't want to upset Leo either – good drummers are the hardest to find.'

But Gerry had learned that it was sometimes worth listening to the young ones. In a business like this the crowd could grow old without you even noticing. So he handed her his list and Ava nodded.

'"Rock Around the Clock", "The Galway Shawl", and "The Locomotion" – nothing too complicated there. Sure, he knows them all...'

She could tell she had got Gerry's attention now.

'Leave Leo to me. You give that list to Patrick, and then take over the bar for an hour. I promise he won't let you down.'

Then before he had time to object, Ava ran across the empty dance floor to the front of the stage. All the guys in the resident band loved her. Ava's exuberant dancing got them through the sometimes humdrum business of playing to the same crowd night after night, week after week. As soon as he saw her, even though he was halfway through a song, Leo came to the front of the stage. The dance floor was nearly empty anyway.

After a few seconds, he stood back up, finished the song, and then announced, 'Ladies and gentlemen, we have a very special guest here tonight. You all know our favourite girl, Ava, and she's going to introduce her friend.'

He hauled Ava up the high step to the side of the stage. She was not even nervous addressing the peppering of dancers that was still there. She could not see the seated crowd beyond them over the stage lights.

'Ladies and gentlemen, I'd like to introduce a very special young singer, Patrick Murphy, from County Mayo. You know him from behind the bar here in the Emerald – the best ballroom in New York State...' A cheer went up, and she felt a wave of excitement at how easily the words came flooding out of her, despite never having been on stage before. 'Gerry is behind the bar for the next half-hour so you had better get the drinks in quick. Grab your partners – because our Mayo Man is going to start us off with a rocking jive – "Rock Around the Clock"!'

Once Patrick was on stage, Leo took off his sequin-collared purple jacket and gave it to the young singer before handing him the microphone.

From the bar Gerry watched in amazement. He didn't know what Ava had said to charm his truculent drummer, but she was some player, that was for sure.

Patrick did not have time to think or be nervous. Gerry had simply shoved the list at him, and then pushed him towards the stage. He didn't worry about the slow set, he knew every Irish ballad by heart, but rock and roll was new territory for him. Aside from that one time at the wedding, and once or twice in the Emerald, he had never really performed with a proper band – a big, professional outfit like this – and certainly never to such a big crowd. At that moment, Patrick was not even sure that he knew the words to 'Rock Around the Clock'. Before the panic set hold of him, he felt Ava grip his arm and she looked at him calmly and said, 'You've seen Bill Haley at the cinema – imagine you are him.'

Behind him the band were silent, waiting for his lead. Patrick stood for a moment that felt like for ever, watching as Ava walked to the side of the stage, then he put his head down on his chest, raised both his hands in the air, cocked his left knee up and pointed his toes to the ground and said into the microphone, 'One, two, three o'clock, four o'clock rock' – Leo bashed the drum – 'five, six, seven o'clock, eight o'clock rock' – another bash – 'nine, ten, eleven o'clock, twelve o'clock rock, we're gonna rock' – bash – 'around' – bash – 'the clock tonight…' Then all hell broke loose in the band. The vibrancy, the urgency in Patrick's voice set them alight. They were experienced musicians. They could feel that he had been waiting his twenty-odd years for this moment. They wanted to make the music come alive for him. And they did. Everyone rushed to the dance floor before the song took off. Every booth in the house was vacated, the bar stood empty. The dance floor was a heaving mass of bodies. Patrick sang the three songs on Gerry's list, and when he tried to go off stage the audience stomped the floor with their feet for him to stay. He ended with a slow waltz to 'Danny Boy'.

Ava was waiting for him backstage. She was jumping up and down with excitement.

'You did it!' she shouted. 'You were brilliant. *Brilliant*!'

As she pulled him into a friendly hug, Patrick's legs felt weak under him. Now that the whole thing was over, it was safe to be afraid. He had just entertained a crowd of almost a thousand people in one of the biggest dance halls in the world. Had that really just happened? Was that him they had been clapping for? It had all come upon him so suddenly – and now the girl that had made it happen had her arms around him.

She broke away from the hug and stood in front of him saying, 'Oh, Patrick – I didn't know if you could do it – but you did! You were—'

And then it happened. Patrick wrapped his two big hands around her face, pulled her over to him and kissed her, fully, on the mouth.

She gently broke away, and then laughed nervously.

'Oh,' she said.

He had not meant to offend her. He had just been overcome with gratitude. Realizing his mistake, he quickly drew back. He loved Rose, and perhaps would always love her, in a way. But Rose was not here. She had not written, and perhaps his friend in the golf-club kitchen had been right: her father had simply sent him to America to get rid of him. Even if that was the case, Patrick told himself, if she had wanted to get in touch with him badly enough, she would have found a way. He had fleetingly thought that perhaps Dr Hopkins had intercepted his letters, but, truthfully, Patrick couldn't believe he would be that conniving and cruel. It was far more likely that Rose had simply met somebody else now that he was 'out of the way'. Somebody more 'suitable', in accordance with her parents' wishes. Rose had let him go as surely as her father had banished him. The thought of that had left him lonely, hurt and afraid – but now Ava had come into his life. It seemed to him that in the short time he had been here, he had lived a lifetime. He had come out here, all alone in the big wide world of New York City, and had somehow survived. Which had been, in no small part, due to the kindness of this young woman and her father.

'I'm sorry. I just wanted to say – thank you.'

She smiled. She wasn't offended, after all. Ava's smile was so broad, and her eyes so bright, that Patrick felt he could see everything in the world that mattered in her face.

'No problem,' she said.

He leaned across again to kiss her, properly this time, on the cheek. But as his mouth was only an inch away from her skin, she boldly turned to face him and whispered, 'It was my pleasure.'

14

SHEILA DIDN'T telephone ahead. She didn't want Samuel and Anya making a fuss.

As she put her key in the door she guiltily wondered how long it had been since she had come to visit. Maybe six months? Now she was arriving with a suitcase.

Samuel heard the key in the door and was in the hall. He silently took her case from her and carried it upstairs to her old room. When Anya came down the stairs, a look of excited elation passed between them. Their girl had come home. Hope. Even though they both knew that Sheila arriving at the door like this meant there was a problem, a failure of some sort.

Sheila followed Anya into the kitchen and picked up the blue apron that was still hanging on the back of the kitchen door, as if waiting for her. Together they prepared the potatoes, Sheila peeling and passing to Anya, who cut them into thin slices and laid them in the baking tray.

'So – how is your life?'

'Good,' Sheila said.

'You have a boyfriend? You broke up with him?' Anya asked.

Auntie was always hungry for information and never minced her words. She was a tough old bird, but she seemed smaller, and more stooped since the last time she had been here. She could see love glittering in her aunt's eyes and felt uncomfortable.

'I'm thinking of leaving New York,' she said. 'Going to work somewhere else. I might only be staying for a few nights. Before I decide where I am going to go. What I am going to do…'

Anya's face hardened and they prepared the rest of the meal in silence before going to sit for a while. The drawing room had hardly changed in twenty years. The wind-up gramophone had been replaced with a record player. The old tube radio, however, was still there. Sheila looked at the ancient object, then at her uncle.

I should love it here, she thought. Knowing that Anya and Samuel were living a life filled with love, and contentment and easy domesticity, made her impossibly sad. She had never thought she wanted that life and yet she felt the loss of it when she was with them.

Being back here, like this, homeless and jobless, felt like a personal failing. At the same time, Sheila knew she was strong. She kept reminding herself that this was a temporary setback. She would move to Boston, or Chicago perhaps. Once she moved on she would start again, start a new life, in a different city. She would be anonymous again. Free. In some ways, perhaps, this extended visit was a goodbye to her old life and the start of a completely new one. Who knew when she might see the old couple again.

* * *

After they had eaten their meal, Anya announced she was going to the bakery.

'Cheesecake. My Sheila loves her cheesecake,' she said, touching Sheila's cheek. Her aunt's hands had always felt old to Sheila, but now they seemed gnarled and ancient. She felt a moment of fear at how old her aunt and uncle were getting.

Anya gave her niece's cheek a gentle slap. 'Look at how thin you are! We'll make you fat again. I promised them I would make you fat...'

She trailed off. Anya always found a way of bringing Sheila's parents into the conversation. She knew that Sheila did not like the truth, but she also knew that they had been wrong, back then, to lie about her parents. The truth was always better than a lie, even when it was done to protect somebody. Samuel nodded across the room at her irritably, but Anya was defiant. No matter how painful it was, the truth must be faced.

'You're in trouble?' Samuel asked Sheila as soon as his wife had left the house.

'Nothing I can't handle, but...' She looked to see if he would question her further, but his face was impassive. She felt grateful and simply added, 'I needed to get out of the city.'

'Well,' he said, 'this is not the city, for sure.'

She laughed. He knew how much she hated the cloying suburbia of Riverdale.

'I came to see you too.'

'I know that,' he said. Although he knew no such thing. Samuel wondered, for a moment, if he should apologize for Anya, but decided against it. Samuel believed that pain was something that everyone had to deal with in their own way. Sheila had her own way. He felt sad that she did not include them in her life any more. But he also knew that as guardians, they had to let her go. They were not her parents.

'You lost your job?'

'I quit.'

'You need money?'

'I've got enough to last me a while.'

Samuel walked across to the sideboard and took out a hundred dollars. She shook her head, but he pressed it on her. 'You know you can always come to me for help.' He paused, adding, 'You always have a home here, you know that. Stay as long as you like.'

'I'll pay you back,' she said. As she kissed him, she thought how she would never be able to pay them back for all they had done for her.

Samuel closed his eyes as her lips touched his sagging cheek. Inside, he allowed his heart to call her 'daughter'.

Sheila ate a large slice of cheesecake under Anya's careful watch, smoked a cigarette with Samuel, then said, 'I'm going to take a walk. Don't wait up.'

There was nowhere for her to go out here, but she needed some air, and to escape from the house.

She wandered into Riverdale, with its single row of shops, a hair salon, diner, small boutique and Jewish bakery. She walked past Joyce's Bakery, where Sheila's birthday had been written in a book and the same cake was produced every year, a chocolate and vanilla ring sponge. Philip in the salon hair was nearly as old as Anya now. He used to set her hair into tight curls every Saturday afternoon and had trimmed and set

Sheila's unforgiving frizz straight every six weeks. Walking these streets again plunged Sheila back into her childhood. She knew that this place should make her feel comfortable, happy and secure. But every perfectly trimmed lawn, and clean, painted house in this neat cloistered neighbourhood made her feel trapped and claustrophobic. Riverdale and her aunt and uncle's house made her feel like a child again: a victim of war. Sheila knew she was anything but a victim.

She walked faster away from Riverdale and towards Yonkers. As she reached the end of St Andrews Place she hit the corner of South Broadway. She noticed a large, square building with flashing lights out front and realized she was in the heart of Irish New York. She didn't know this part of town. The Jews and the Irish lived side by side in adjoining suburbs but never paid each other much attention. As soon as Sheila was old enough to escape Riverdale, she had headed straight towards the bright lights and glamour of Manhattan. Other areas in the Bronx were foreign territory for her.

The sign outside the building was flashing green: the Emerald Ballroom. Sheila didn't know much about the Irish but she knew they liked to drink. And she needed a drink.

She paid her dollar at the front door, but didn't bother to check in her coat. She would not be long. The place was thronged. It was a standard dance venue. It could have been the Twilight Ballroom, except it was much busier. This was midweek but it was as packed as if it was Saturday night. The long banquettes at the side were flanked by two big bars. Sheila bought a packet of cigarettes from a plump tray-girl in a hokey uniform emblazoned with shamrocks and went to sit at the bar.

She looked around at the crowd. They were all Irish.

She didn't know how she could tell except that she just could. The men were bigger and broader than usual. The women were plumper and they laughed more. It felt strange sitting in a place like this as a punter. The band was absolutely dreadful. Actually, the band was fine, it was the singer who was truly atrocious. Out of tune in an almost comical way. Service at the bar was dreadful too and as Sheila tried to order herself a whiskey, some kind of a kerfuffle started up and she was unable to get anyone's attention.

Frustrated, she lost patience and got up to leave. She congratulated herself for having left her coat on and was just about to push open the exit door when 'Rock Around the Clock' came on. It was still her favourite number, and she could use some cheering up. She lit a cigarette and stood, twisting on the spot, elbows by her side. The kid singing on stage was doing a good job, and he had a pretty good voice too. That being said, every damn kid in town could sing 'Rock Around the Clock' these days. When that final abrupt cymbal came down at the end, Sheila threw her cigarette butt on the floor, stubbed it out with her heel and pushed open the exit door.

A voice stopped her in her tracks.

The boy on stage had started singing a ballad in the deepest, sweetest baritone she had ever heard. She took her hand from the door and leaned against a pillar. Her knees felt weak. She did not notice what song he was singing, only his voice. It was such a powerful sound, it seemed to enter her body and make her tremble from the inside out. It created an emotion in her that was so powerful and so new she could not say what it was. All she knew was that she had never experienced anything like it before. It was as if somebody had torn open her skin, unzipped her so that her very soul was naked.

She felt utterly exposed. And yet it was not an uncomfortable feeling, but a glorious one.

Crowds had gathered around the stage and a hush came over the place as he sang. Sheila looked around her. It was the women's faces that struck her. They were all, without exception, gazing up at the boy on stage. He was barely through the first verse and yet each female in the room was mesmerized, seduced by the extraordinary baritone emanating from him.

And that's all he was. A boy.

Nice-looking, dark-haired and probably Irish. Not her type, of course, but he was oozing charisma, and talent and stage-charm. She knew he was a newcomer, a nobody. It was probably try-out night, judging by the atrocity that was on before him. He was wearing a cheap jacket that didn't fit right and was holding the microphone like a nervous amateur.

Put all that together and he almost certainly didn't have independent management yet. He would just be a part of the resident band. In which case it would be bad form to contact him directly. He was owned by the club and, if there was one thing she knew about the Irish, it was that they were territorial.

The Irish scene was quite different to the one she had worked in. They called their ballrooms dance halls, instead of ballrooms. It was typical of them to give a hokey name to what was actually a vast empire, owned largely by one man. Iggy Morrow. Sheila had never met him, but very few people on the ballroom circuit had. He was so elusive that some people said he didn't actually exist, but his clubs were so tightly run by a series of managers that it hardly mattered. The Emerald, she figured, was probably one of his.

In any case, Sheila didn't know, or care, who ran this place.

All she knew was that the guy up on stage had some talent. With a voice like that he could conquer the world. Hell, with a voice like that, she could conquer the world. She had to find a way of getting hold of him.

15

GNATIUS 'IGGY' Morrow was something of a legend. Despite rumours to the contrary, he did actually exist. The Irishman owned thirty-three dance halls across Ireland and Britain as well as the US. Other ballroom owners were astonished that he managed to juggle all of these venues. Dance halls, they all knew, were a hands-on business. The owner needed to be on site to make sure that nobody was pilfering from the till or slacking. Iggy's trick for keeping absolute control over his empire was a combination of well-paid, loyal managers and eccentric unpredictability. Nobody in the world knew where Ignatius Morrow was at any given time. One day he could be in Manchester, the next, Boston. Unmarried, he had no fixed abode, keeping hotel suites in his favourite cities and living out of a suitcase. He might swoop down on one of his businesses at any time without warning. This kept his managers on their toes and his staff on red alert at all times. In addition to owning the venues, Iggy also managed and promoted most of the bands that played in them.

He looked after them too. Unlike many of the ruthless managers who kept their bands on a meagre salary and milked everything from record sales to door takings, Iggy shared his good fortune and rewarded his bands with a percentage. He got rich – they got rich.

Everyone knew the rules. Managers had absolute autonomy. If there was a problem, they had to sort it out themselves. But whenever Iggy arrived, everything had to be tip-top, from the ladies' bathrooms to detailed records of bar takings. One night, legend had it, he walked into a dance hall in Liverpool, sacked everyone on the spot, and had the place open again three days later with entirely new staff and management. Nobody knew whether it was because the place was badly run, or because Iggy was keen to make a point. It worked.

Iggy's other obsession was the music. It had to be excellent. All managers had to stick to his rigorous booking schedule for his bands. Showbands were the future of the dance-hall scene, he believed. They could make records as well as draw crowds and the two fed off each other. Iggy kept his resident bands employed, partly out of loyalty, but mostly to fill in the spaces until he had enough showbands to move around his venues permanently. Resident bands were a thing of the past, although a lot of other dance halls kept them on for ease. Iggy was not afraid of a challenge and it kept him on the move.

Apart from the managers and bands, few of Iggy's staff knew what he looked like. At forty, Iggy was tall and thin, with an angular face and an attentive expression that made him appear curiously bird-like. He was not a man that one would pick out for his good looks. However, once you knew who he was, you would never forget him. As a punter in a crowd, he was invisible. As Iggy Morrow, music millionaire, he was memorable. Aware of this, Iggy was protective over his love life. Early marriage to a glamorous but avaricious English bunny-girl in his twenties had cured him of all idealism about romance. Money and business was his mistress. When Iggy needed female company, he could be a gentleman, but essentially, he was a loner. If you didn't know him and you found yourself standing next to him in a bus queue, you might think twice about starting a conversation.

Which was why he was very surprised when the woman standing next to him, near the exit of the Emerald, turned and asked, 'Excuse me – do you know where the manager's office is?'

He looked at her, somewhat taken aback at being spoken to in his own club.

The manager, Gerry, didn't even know he was in yet. This was obvious, because the place was a shambles. Iggy had been horrified to see that gobshite drummer, Leo, murdering 'Love Me Tender'. Now some kid had wandered up from behind the bar and was on stage singing 'Rock Around the Clock'. At least he was doing a decent job of it, the crowd were all up dancing, but hell, he wasn't even wearing proper stage attire. This was just not good enough.

'No idea,' he said adding, rather abruptly. 'What do you want the manager for?'

Sheila smiled inwardly. Her gut was telling her this guy was the manager. No drink? He certainly wasn't on a night out. And only a manager would look that anxious and defensive in a place of entertainment. Although, she thought, he should be defensive given the mess he was making of this place.

'I just wanted to congratulate him on the music tonight.' She took a drag from her cigarette and looked him straight in the eye. 'And the service at the bar was excellent.'

His face hardened. He was mad as hell, and not bothering to hide it either. He looked kind of mean. She liked that. He also looked like he might explode at her any minute and she liked that too. Suddenly, Sheila remembered herself.

She wasn't here to antagonize the manager. She was here to try and cajole a novice singer out of him.

The kid was singing 'Danny Boy'.

'Well,' she said, softening her tone, 'whoever does run this place has certainly got a nose for talent.'

'You think?' Iggy said, absent-mindedly, looking around for Gerry. 'Excuse me,' he said, abruptly. Sheila's eyes narrowed as she watched him walk over to the bar.

So he wasn't the manager after all. Could this possibly be Iggy Morrow himself?

There was only one way to find out. Sheila followed him to the bar, keeping a few feet behind so she couldn't be seen. Sheila had a crazy idea. As she watched the frightened collapse of Gerry, Sheila saw that she was right. They had words; Sheila knew what they were as surely as if she had said them herself.

'Get this sorted then meet me in the office.'

She followed him again, towards the black, felted door that led to a small corridor with two doors marked 'Dressing Room' and 'Office'.

Sheila took a deep breath before knocking. Iggy Morrow. She smiled to herself. This was some turn-up.

'Mr Morrow?'

The door opened so suddenly that she almost punched his nose with her still raised hand. 'Get in here,' he said. 'Who the hell are you? Are you a bloody journalist?'

'No,' she said, surprised to find herself even able to speak in the face of such unprompted fury.

'But then how the hell do you know who I am?'

'I guessed.' Her usual wry, clever caution seemed to have deserted her. He asked questions, she answered them. That was the way this was going.

'What do you mean, you guessed?'

'I saw the way you were talking to the bar manager so I guessed you were the owner of the place and also...' Why was she being so... so... submissive to this odious man?

'Plus you look like the owner.'

She could not imagine a legendary Irish music magnate looking like anything else. He looked powerful. Whatever that looked like. His clothes were modest, this scruffy office even more so. But his face had a cold, determined edge to it. She was in the presence of a man with absolutely nothing to prove and yet she could see in his eyes that somehow he still believed he had everything to fight for.

'If you're not a journalist, then who the hell are you? And what do you want?'

'I want the boy on stage,' Sheila said.

Iggy raised his eyebrows in surprise, and Sheila saw a trace of amusement cross his face.

She allowed herself a small smile.

'I'm a music manager,' she explained. She knew she was pushing it a bit, but hell, she was here now. She may as well go for it. She held out her hand. 'Sheila Klein.'

He took it reluctantly. Sheila had met some strange men in her time but he was one seriously charmless character.

'I am interested in taking him on.'

If she was a music manager, she wasn't a big one because Iggy had never heard of her. Probably just chancing her arm. The business was full of fly-by-nights these days. People trying to make a quick buck off the back of other people's talent.

But he had never seen a woman claiming to be a music manager before. Iggy was curious.

'What's so special about the kid?'

He watched her face closely as she answered and realized that he didn't really care about the lad. He was enjoying looking at her, watching the way her broad, full-lipped mouth pursed before she spoke.

'Well, he's got talent...' she said. Her eyes narrowed as she continued, 'His voice certainly has range, which means he can do rock and roll but he can also own a ballad. He's good-looking, that's a bonus...'

Iggy felt a flicker of jealousy that surprised him. She was hard, she seemed cold, but Iggy felt strangely comforted by her. As if she were a weaker version of himself. Weaker and yet, on some deep level, she frightened him a little.

'There is just something about him that would really add to my stable of talent,' she said, looking him straight in the eye, privately praying that he would not ask her about the other acts.

He didn't, but Iggy knew damn well she was a novice. Only the desperate or the naïve would come knocking on his door like that, talking bullshit about the kid owning a ballad. He had no doubt that she wanted to be a manager and he could also see that she had no idea of what that meant. She thought she was tough but she wasn't.

'So?' she said. 'Are you going to let me take this boy on for you? Or with you? Can we do a deal? What do I have to do to persuade you to talk to me?'

'I'm afraid it's out of the question.'

'But—'

'I'm afraid it my business policy, Miss Klein, not to form partnerships with anyone, and, as you said yourself, the kid has got far too much potential to let go.'

'Who is he?' she asked. 'The kid? What's his name?' He could see she was furious. Those dark eyes were flashing fire at him.

'That is beside the point...'

'You don't even know his name,' she said. 'Some manager you are, Mr... Mr Morrow.'

As an insult it was pretty weak, and inaccurate. It had been stupid of her to come in here and chase down the singer, especially with a man like this. She turned away and said, 'I won't say it was a pleasure meeting you, and the best of luck with your nameless singer. I won't be looking out for him because I expect he'll be disappearing without a trace under your careless hand. Good evening!'

She opened the door to go but to her absolute astonishment, Iggy said, 'Would you join me for supper?' adding, as an afterthought, 'Please?'

She looked at the inscrutable face of a man who was used to getting what he wanted, and found herself considering the offer for one second.

'Mr Morrow,' she said, smiling charmingly at him, 'I'm afraid it is my business policy not to have supper with people that I don't like.'

Then she gave the door a good slam behind her.

16

IT WAS Patrick who finally broke the kiss, saying, 'I'd better get back to work.'

'Of course,' she said. 'Myrtle will be wondering where I am.'

She did not give a jot for Myrtle. She could have stood there kissing him all night. Before they parted, Patrick took her hand and said, 'Thank you.'

She did not know whether he was thanking her for putting him on stage or for the kiss, or perhaps a combination of both. Stupidly, she wished he had said something else. Something that might give her a reason to change her whole life; to give up her fiancé and a secure future for an entirely insecure and barely formed dream.

For the rest of the evening, Ava watched him as he worked the bar under Gerry's watchful eye. She knew he would not be able to escape before the end of his shift, but nonetheless she sat in her regular booth to the left of the dance floor willing him to seek her out again. She refused several dances that night until Myrtle began to suspect something was up.

'Are you OK?'

'I'm fine,' she said, knowing that she didn't sound fine at all.

'I think you're up to something.'

Ava smiled casually, and said unconvincingly, 'What would I be up to?'

Myrtle stared at her and smiled. Ava could not help a small smile back.

'Were you canoodling with that singer backstage?'

'I most certainly was not!'

'I thought so. He's not a bad-looking buck...'

'Seriously, Myrtle, I would never do anything like that.'

Myrtle raised her eyebrows, and then shrugged her shoulders.

It was a small denial, but Ava felt bad lying to her friend. Myrtle kissed lots of boys, but then, she was not engaged to be married. Ava had only ever kissed Dermot. She was more afraid that Myrtle would encourage her than judge her. Ava was afraid of what she might do with her friend's backing.

Myrtle looked up and waved across the floor.

'Oh look – here's your favourite jiver... Hey! Niall!' She nudged Ava. 'Your brother-in-law-to-be – maybe Dermot sent him to keep an eye on you...'

The mention of Dermot's name sent a shiver through Ava.

She picked up her purse and said, 'You're right – there is something wrong with me. I don't feel at all well. I'm going to head home.'

In the days after it happened, Ava kept going over the kiss in her mind. She was angry with herself, barely able to admit that she had, in fact, not just allowed, or even encouraged, but rather had invited Patrick to kiss her. It was a terrible thing to have done. She was engaged to another man, a good man, and the man her family wanted her to marry. It was a terrible sin against her parents and God and even, surely, herself, to be kissed by another man. Not just kissed, but to feel such a fiery passion for him. And yet, no matter how much she prayed and asked God's forgiveness, no matter how angry and upset she imagined her parents would be if she called off her engagement, she could not make herself wish that it hadn't happened.

She was regretful, of course she was, but she was not remorseful. When Patrick Murphy kissed Ava, her whole body had come alive. More than that, she had felt a searing, absolute joy being in his arms. A belonging, a feeling of righteous pleasure that was the opposite of sin. They were meant to be together. For the time they were kissing, behind the stage of the Emerald Ballroom, shielded from the world by a navy velvet curtain, Ava felt as if she was, finally, in the place she had always wanted to be. There was no rhyme or reason for this, why she should want to be making love with a strange-looking Irish boy who tended bar and sang, rather than the kind lawyer to whom she was engaged, but that made the feelings she had for him all the more magical. The truth was, kissing Patrick had felt completely different to kissing Dermot. 'God makes his magic in the heart,' the Irish nun had taught them in convent school, 'and the devil makes his magic in the body.' She had felt the devil's magic when she was with Dermot, sometimes longing that he would touch her more intimately when they kissed. With Patrick her body was on fire and it ached with sweetness, a longing that was close to pain for the rest of that night. However, it was the craving in her heart, the fear that she might never be with him again, that was causing her almost unbearable pain.

For a full week Ava wrestled with herself. She could not sleep and barely ate. On the Thursday afternoon she excused herself from work. She had made several mistakes in an important document she was typing up for her father and he had noticed how preoccupied she seemed. And sad. Unlike herself.

Nessa, too, had noted her daughter's nocturnal wanderings and the loss of her normally hearty appetite that week. Her instinct told her there was something very wrong.

'There is no need to be nervous about the wedding, darling, everything is under control,' she said over dinner.

Ava threw her fork down on her plate and shouted, 'I wish you would just shut up about this stupid wedding,' and ran upstairs to her room.

'Think you might be overdoing it a bit on the arrangements, dear,' Tom said to his wife, but deep down he feared it was more than that.

Alone in her room, Ava felt she could not take another step in her life until she had sorted out the terrible mess that was in her head and her heart.

She knew what she had to do.

She went to her bureau, took out her best notepaper and wrote a short note which she then put into an envelope and addressed. Then she went downstairs, put on her coat and took her father's keys from the hallstand. She would not need to tell him she was taking the car – she hoped she would not be more than an hour.

Her stomach was in knots as she drove along the Hudson Parkway. The sun was sinking behind the dusty trees along the riverbank and the water was glimmering with orange and purple reflections and shadows. Its extravagant beauty made Ava feel all the more ashen inside.

Dermot opened the door, surprised at her unannounced arrival. He gave a big smile and stepped back. Ava stayed on the doorstep. Determined not to humiliate him with explanations or apologies, she took a deep breath and simply pushed out the words, 'I'm calling off the wedding, Dermot, I'm sorry. I just don't love you.'

Dermot felt the whole world collapse beneath him.

'I see.' He nodded. The words just came out automatically. As they did when somebody delivered terrible news at work, and he needed time to gather his thoughts before responding. Except there was no response to this. There was no solution. What came out of his mouth next was as automatic as the last. A type of negotiation to see if the deal was sealed.

'Is there somebody else?'

Ava was wrong-footed. She felt like lying. Dermot was such a good man. A solid man. A good friend. She didn't want to hurt him. But she owed him the truth. As much of the truth as he could stand anyway.

'Yes,' she said, 'there is.'

Of course there is, thought Dermot. He knew who it was too. That young Irish singer, Patrick. The lad was handsome, full of romance. Ava loved music and dancing; it suddenly seemed like the most natural thing in the world that she would want to be with somebody like him, instead of with a stuffy lawyer. Dermot thought of the first time he had seen her jiving wildly at the fundraiser, full of energy and life. And then her face as she had listened to the ballad. He had brought Patrick into her life that evening as a gift to express his love for her, but she had fallen in love with him instead. Dermot's world was shaken to the core, but he could not blame her for it. She was, as some part of him had always known, too free, too beautiful a spirit for a mundane man like him.

It hurt. It hurt more than he could possibly say out loud, but what hurt most of all was that it also made perfect sense.

'I expect it's that young singer Patrick? I could see you were keen.' Perhaps he shouldn't have said that last bit. But Dermot couldn't help himself. He was only human.

The pity and guilt Ava had been feeling disappeared. Not only was Dermot not going to plead or fight for her, but he seemed to know that she was carrying on with Patrick and had done nothing to discourage her!

Furious, she said, 'Well goodbye then!'

On the way home she drove to his parents' house and left the short note of apology she had written in her bedroom, then she went home to face her own parents.

In the time she had been gone they had speculated, and guessed, where she had been and what she was doing. Her mother had sensed Ava's reservations about getting married from the start of her engagement but had put it down to nerves and inexperience with men. Although neither Nessa nor Tom said it out loud, they had both instinctively recognized her fancy for the young Irish lad. Tom had an impulse to confess that he had placed Patrick as barman in the Emerald Ballroom, Ava's favourite dance venue. Nessa was furious.

'You stupid, stupid man – you haven't the brains you were born with! The last thing Ava needs now is a distraction like that. If she breaks off this engagement, Tom, it will be entirely your fault.'

'But if she doesn't love him—'

'Don't be ridiculous. Dermot is a good boy from an excellent family. He will make her happy.'

'Maybe the other lad would make her happy too?'

'Do you know nothing? Look around. This comfort is what Ava is used to. Dermot can give her all this and more.'

'Comfort isn't everything, Nessa.' Tom was worried he might have gone too far but he loved his daughter and it was important he had his say. Tom had really liked Dermot. He was a fine young man and personally, he had found him easy company. He reminded him a lot of himself as a younger man. Dermot was steady, honest and hard-working.

However, he was concerned only for his daughter. Nessa had no such compunction. She was determined to get her way and see her daughter married well.

She roared at him, 'That's easy for you to say. Have you forgotten what life was like before we came here? Four children sleeping top to tail in one bed? Stepping out into the yard littered with cow dung? No running water in the house? No electricity...'

'It wasn't so bad.'

'You have a short memory, Tom Brogan – you couldn't wait to get out of the place.'

'We were happy growing up in Ireland...'

'We are happier now.'

Tom raised his eyebrows.

'I had nothing when you fell in love with me.'

'You had prospects,' she said, 'an education – a middle-class uncle to sponsor you coming here...'

'I made a success of things because I had your support, Nessa – not anybody else's. My labour bought all this but I was only able to do it because of your love...'

'Love!' Nessa spat the word out. 'Love doesn't put food on the table. Love doesn't pay the bills.'

Tom knew it would not only be pointless contradicting her, but hurtful. The Brogan family had a bigger farm than Nessa's family, who were dirt-poor. His own mother had been disappointed when he married Nessa, and although it was never mentioned, Nessa knew it. That was why she worked so hard to elevate herself socially.

'If she breaks off with Dermot she'll never meet somebody else as good as him.' Nessa closed her eyes and breathed in on her panic. 'But we are worrying too soon. She loves him. Everything will be fine.'

Then they heard the front door open, and Ava came into the kitchen.

'I have broken off my engagement to Dermot,' she said and ran out again. Nessa wasted no time chasing her up the stairs.

Ava was already seated at her dressing table, applying make-up and fixing her hair.

'I know where you're going,' Nessa said, 'and I think you're making a very big mistake.'

Ava had suffered enough in the last week wrestling with her conscience; she would not be bullied by her mother.

'I don't love Dermot, Mom. It would be wrong to marry him.'

'And I suppose you think you love this other lad?'

Ava got a fright. 'I don't know what you're talking about – I've arranged to meet Myrtle at the Emerald.'

Nessa softened her voice.

'Don't do this, Ava. Dermot loves you.'

'I don't think he really does, Mom, I—'

'Of course he does. Telephone him now – tell him you've made a mistake. It's pre-wedding nerves. He'll understand. It's not too late.'

Now it was Ava's turn to get angry. 'I am not marrying Dermot. It's done. That's final, you'll just have to get used to it.'

'You'll never meet anyone as good as Dermot…'

'Perhaps I already have.'

But Nessa was ready for her.

'You think this young man loves you, Ava? Really?'

Of course Ava did not know if Patrick loved her. But she was certain, after kissing him, that she did not love Dermot and that she could not marry him. She also knew the only place she had wanted to be the last week was back in Patrick's arms and she owed it to herself to try. To at least see if he felt something of the same for her.

'Just you remember,' Nessa continued, 'that Dermot Dolan was the first boy that ever showed any interest in you.' Her voice was hard and clipped. 'You seem to have forgotten your tremendous good fortune, meeting someone upstanding, someone who could have anyone he wanted and yet he chose you. You could trust a man like that. You could trust him to his word...'

'What is that supposed to mean?' Ava said.

'You are very naïve, Ava,' her mother said. 'Most girls your age have more sense because they have more experience with men. This – Irish boy – this person...'

'Patrick.'

'Whatever – who is to say you can trust him? He comes over here from Ireland, penniless, then he meets you, with your important father, and your comfortable life...'

'What are you saying?'

'I am saying, Ava, that men like that cannot be trusted. They will make you feel as if you are the most beautiful girl in the world but...'

Ava felt a bubble of hurt rise up through her chest.

'But what, Mother? I'm not beautiful, is that what you are trying to say? Because I know that... I know what I look like.'

Nessa held back from comforting her. This was too important. Ava needed to understand what she was giving up.

Who knows what she would be letting herself in for if she ran off with this unknown gouger from Ireland? Nessa was suddenly furious with her husband for dragging all these needy young men into their lives. Nessa knew Patrick's type well. A charmer, with his singing and his black hair and twinkling Irish blue eyes – typical chancer. That whole romantic 'croppy-boy' nonsense was irresistible to the second-generation New York girls, but that didn't fool Nessa for a moment. If her daughter hooked up with him, she would be signing up for a lifetime of poverty. Ava would spend the next fifty years of her life waiting for that waster to come home from the pub. Nessa Brogan hadn't supported her husband while he worked his fingers to the bone making a life in America for her daughter to throw it all away on some foolish notion. The girl was 'in love'. Nessa had been in love a dozen times before she settled on sensible Tom Brogan. She loved her daughter and could not let her make the biggest mistake of her life.

Ava's face was full of defiant anguish as she blurted out, 'I know I am too plain to get a man, Mother, and yet here I am – with two of them after me!'

Nessa did not lose her temper, but took a deep breath, looked Ava steadily in the eye and said, 'That young man is after your money, Ava. You are too naïve to see it, but I've met chancers like him before in Ireland. He has no education and no qualifications—'

'Patrick is not a chancer, he is a singer and you don't need qualifications to sing.'

'I am sorry to say this, truly I am, but you are simply his ticket to an easy life.'

'Well,' Ava said, holding her mother's gaze, 'I don't care if he is after my money, I intend to be with him anyway. I love him that much and there is not a goddamn thing you can do about it. '

Nessa finally lost her temper.

'If you're happy knowing that he's simply after your money,

there is nothing I can do about that. Just don't come crying to me when it all goes wrong!'

'I won't!' Ava shouted as Nessa slammed the door behind her.

Tom heard the shouting from downstairs. He sat at the table with his head in his hands, wondering how two women could cause one man so much trouble.

17

AFTER HER mother had left, Ava fought back the tears and checked her face in the mirror. She had been crying, so her face was blotchy and her eyes were red. She took out her panstick and began the transformation. Eyeliner, mascara, rouge, lipstick – weapons she had recently discovered to help transform her appearance. She quickly smoothed down her bob.

'You are beautiful,' she said to the reflection in the mirror. It felt pointless and slightly mad to be talking to herself in this way but Ava was determined to prove her mother wrong. The feeling she had for Patrick was real. With Dermot, there had been no question of anything 'happening' before they were married. And yet both she and Patrick had been unable to help themselves. Kissing each other in that reckless way that they had was as immediate and natural and inevitable as rain on an April day. You didn't feel that kind of passion towards somebody unless the love was real. She had doubted her feelings for Dermot, but she would not doubt her feelings for

Patrick. She would not. No matter what her parents thought of him, Patrick was the real thing.

Ava opened her wardrobe and picked out her rose suit. It was her talisman now, her lucky-in-love suit.

She teamed it with a tight silk blouse in sky blue.

The tailored outfit was entirely unsuitable for dancing, but then Ava did not intend to do any dancing that night.

She was going in search of an altogether different kind of excitement.

Ava sat to the side of the Emerald's dance floor, in a banquette facing the bar, for almost the whole evening. Men came and asked her to dance but she dismissed them all, waving them away with a cool detachment that was, her regular dance partners observed, most unlike her. Instead, she simply sat smoking, nursing a single coffee, and looking over at Patrick. She did not smile brightly across, signal for his attention or acknowledge him in any particular way. As the evening wore on and she did not move from her spot, Patrick realized that she was waiting for him. Not to see him sing, dance with him, or engage him in conversation. She had come for him. She smoked, and stared, mostly into the middle distance. He had thought a lot about her since their last encounter. To be singing on stage and then to come off and engage in an endless kiss with a beautiful woman had felt like the perfect moment. Patrick had been unable to stop himself imagining she was his darling, Rose. He had believed that he would never kiss another girl that way again. With that urgent feeling in the pit of his stomach, rising up through him, making him feel strong and confident, warm and weak – all at the same time. But as soon as it came the moment passed as the taste of this new girl came to him. Patrick had thrown himself into the kiss with Ava and, in that glorious moment, had felt as true to her as ever he had to Rose.

Ava was his talisman too because when his shift was over, Gerry had come and told him that the owner of the club had been in and heard him sing. 'No promises,' he said, 'but he liked your style and wants to try you out as resident band singer.'

Patrick nearly kissed him.

'Don't get too excited,' he said. 'Same salary and we still need you behind the bar.'

'I won't let you down,' Patrick said.

Ava was the girl that had made that happen for him.

But Patrick also knew that the relationship which had begun with that kiss must end with it too. Ava was engaged. Plus her family were big shots, and even though he was from a good family himself, if he wasn't good enough for Dr Hopkins, he certainly wouldn't be good enough for Ava's family. He knew that Tom Brogan was a decent man, not a snob. However, he had been inside their house and seen the luxury in which Ava had grown up. They had two television sets and carpet on their walls. The Brogans would never accept their daughter taking up with somebody like him.

And yet, here she was. Waiting for him.

The bar closed at one a.m. and Patrick quickly went to the staff area and changed out of his uniform. When he returned, the band was finishing up with the Irish national anthem. As they came down on the last bar, everyone moved towards the wide double doors but Ava remained where she was. As he walked towards her he saw her face blanch as the fluorescent lights came up and she momentarily lost sight of him. By the time Patrick reached her table, 'hello' seemed too small a greeting somehow, so he said nothing. She stubbed out her cigarette and then, unable to hold his eye, simply looked down at her hands. He could see how nervous she was. Without saying a word Patrick simply took her hand. She led him out to her father's car in a corner of the parking lot. When they were both seated she looked at him and smiled, that glorious open smile, and they kissed for the second time. As the parking lot emptied, they moved into the back seat and made love.

Afterwards, Ava was surprised at how little shame she felt. In fact, she felt perfectly wonderful. Liberated. It was as if, for the first time, her body felt wholly alive. All those years of dancing, had, she now realized, merely been her body going out in search of this truth. And now she had found it. This was love. An infinitely bigger and more seductive feeling than the simple camaraderie she had enjoyed with Dermot.

Ava was not a girl any more. She was a woman. And she liked it. Gathering herself, she began searching around for lost buttons, while Patrick found himself half trapped in his own trousers. They laughed at the shocking recklessness of what they had just done.

Looking out on the empty car park, they talked.

They talked about Patrick's dreams of being a singer. He told her about the beautiful town of Foxford, in County Mayo, and his family.

'Mammy and my sisters cried and pleaded with me not to leave them but I knew I had to come. I knew I had to make it in America...'

He didn't mention Rose or Dr Hopkins and Ava didn't ask how he got the money for his flight. Patrick was relieved about that but then realized why she hadn't. Rich people didn't worry about things like that. He told her, then, in great detail about his boss in the golf club, embellishing his antics to make himself sound slightly heroic.

'I told him, "I will not work another day in this lousy place" – and I walked straight out the door without looking behind.'

Even though Ava knew he had effectively run away, and that it had been her introduction to her father that had saved him, Ava told herself he was just showing off, which was what men did when they were trying to impress you. Some men. Her father rarely showed off and neither did Dermot but then neither of them had been that bothered about impressing her. As Patrick talked, Ava looked at the dusting of hair under his open shirt, his firm square chin toughened with the day's stubble, his glittering blue eyes, his fine head of black curls, and she wanted to reach over and sink her fingers into them again, and tear back his head and engage him in a savage kiss. He was magnificent and he had been the first man to make proper love to her. He was her hero now. There was no going back.

'I know now I can be a big singer,' he said.

'You were wonderful,' she said.

He smiled and stopped short of thanking her. He had thanked her already. She knew how grateful he was. He did not want to diminish himself in her eyes.

'I know I can be a big star,' he said, 'and I won't stop trying until I get there.'

'I don't doubt it,' she said, smiling.

Patrick was so excited that he could have talked all night about himself. Making love was wonderful, but the thing he had missed most about Rose was having someone to share his dream with. Now he had met somebody else. He put the thought of Rose to the back of his mind and reminded himself that Ava was different. Not a girl like Rose, but a mature woman. Sure, hadn't they just gone the whole way? He had never gone that far with Rose. Rose was just a girl. A woman was what he needed now.

'What about you, Ava?' he asked. 'What do you dream of?'

Ava had never thought about dreams in that way. She loved life itself, not dreaming about it. Life was life and dreams were dreams. She enjoyed dancing, but had never been foolish enough to imagine she could make a life out of it. She had always hoped for marriage and children but being engaged to Dermot had never felt like a dream come true. It felt like the fulfilment of an expectation.

Of course, like all women, Ava had dreamt of romance. Of being held in the arms of an impossibly handsome man and told she was beautiful, even though she knew she wasn't in real life. It was this knowledge that made her the practical girl she was. Having dreams of being beautiful and experiencing romance would only lead to pain. And yet, here she was, being romanced by the most handsome charismatic young man in the whole of New York.

'Nothing really,' she said, 'except this evening feels unreal somehow, don't you think? As if we were in a dream?'

Ava immediately regretted saying it. She felt foolish. Immediately she wished for him to tell her that she was beautiful, that this was a dream come true for him. He hadn't a clue what she was talking about but as he saw her face fall, he quickly said, 'It is surely.'

Ava tried not to look disappointed and changed the subject.

'So how do you suppose you are going to become a famous singer?'

Patrick thought he detected a slight barb in her voice but then he looked at her sweet face and he knew that couldn't be the case.

'I shall just charm all the ladies of New York in the way that I have charmed you,' he said.

'Is that so? And it will be as easy as that?'

'Well,' he said, 'perhaps I will need some help, aghrá...' and he leaned over and kissed her again.

They drove around the city all night. Parking in different places; kissing, talking, making love.

When Ava got home that morning she found her parents sitting in the kitchen waiting for her. There was nothing either of them could say. They knew where she had been and who she had been with. They did not need to ask what she had been doing all night. She was not their little girl any more. They had known the time would come, one day, that she would leave them. Nessa had hoped that she would simply pass her on to another good family, into an easy, domestic life that she could share with her. Tom had only the father's hope that his little girl would never grow up at all.

Ava and Patrick continued to see each other. Shortly after that night, Ava moved out of home into a small apartment in the Upper East Side of the city. It was small and poky but near her father's office, where she continued to work. Tom bought her a second-hand car, and arranged a driving test for Patrick, greasing the right palms to ensure he passed it. On the day she moved out, Tom also took a day off work and helped her move in her things. Nessa had not spoken to Ava since their confrontation. However, she did leave a box of crockery and kitchen utensils at the back door. As her father lifted the box into the boot of his car Ava asked him, 'Will Mom ever come round, do you think? I love Patrick and I know I did the right thing in breaking it off with Dermot. Do you think I did the right thing, Da?'

'Now, Ava – you know there's not a man in the world good enough for my favourite girl.'

'Even Dermot Dolan?'

'Even Dermot Dolan.' He smiled warmly at her. 'Your mother will come around, one day, although I can't say when. She's stubborn – like you.'

After Ava left that evening, Dermot stood in his hallway, unable to move for what seemed like ages. Time stood still. Even though he had intuited her affection for another man, even though he understood her reasons for ditching him for somebody more exciting, the shock was terrible. Not so much that she had left him for another man, more the shock of what she had left him with. Which felt like nothing. Of course, he had always hoped that one day, he would find a wife. But he had never been prepared to compromise. He wanted to share his life with a woman, not simply take on a glorified housekeeper, which, as far as he could see, was what marriage meant to many of his successful lawyer friends. Dermot compromised a great deal in his work, defending gangsters who were sometimes guilty of the crimes he got them off on. He had to pretend to like people he despised. He never wanted to do that at home. He could have got married a dozen times over. He knew that as soon as news of his break-up with Ava became public the cream of respectable Irish motherhood would be throwing their daughters at him again. But he didn't want to compromise. He loved Ava. He had been disbelieving that she might love him back. But not so disbelieving that he had been prepared for her to leave him. When they had got engaged, Dermot had thought that his life had come together so wholly, he had taken his eye off the ball. Was there anything he could have done to have stopped her from running off in this way?

His thoughts were interrupted when the theme tune for *Search for Tomorrow* came on the TV. He wandered in to the living room to switch it off and as his hands reached towards it he wondered if this would be the week that Dick finally got together with Jane. He smiled to himself. It was Ava's favourite TV show. He had only bought this set to keep up with her. It was the best TV money could buy. It was going to go into their home together.

Dermot turned the knob and watched the picture disappear into a tiny white dot. As the screen went black, he sat down on his settee, put his head into his hands and cried.

18

AFTER THAT first night, Ava was very careful. She travelled across town to find a drugstore where nobody knew her and stocked up on contraception. It was embarrassing introducing the biscuit-coloured balloons into her relationship with Patrick, certainly not romantic in any way. But Ava knew how important it was that she did not get pregnant. Not until they had decided what was for the best.

Patrick kept his room in the apartment he shared with six other lads. It belonged to his boss and the rent was negligible as long as you were working for him. The boss was Ava's father's business acquaintance, Ignatius Morrow. He had seen Patrick singing the night she got him on stage, and was so impressed, Patrick said, he had promised to make him a star. It was great news, but it also meant a longer day, as rehearsals were in the afternoons and went right up until his night shift in the bar began. However, Patrick spent every spare moment he had with Ava.

Ava loved him. Or rather, she was a passionate and

voracious lover. Since that first full night together, Ava felt as if the floodgates had been opened. She was hungry for Patrick in a way she used to be hungry for dancing. She would get home from work every night and prepare the house, and herself, for his arrival after the evening work shift. More often she would be half asleep in bed, and feel him crawl in next to her. Already naked, his hands would seek her out in the darkness. After they had made love she would get up and pull back the curtain, and under the blue lights of the city she would trace the fine features of his face with her fingers and wonder how she had come to be making love to a boy so handsome and sweet.

There was a boyish innocence about Patrick that enchanted her. He was so different from the confident, pragmatic men that she knew. She felt he needed her to look after him and that made her feel wanted.

Two months after they had established this comfortable routine, Ava took sick.

She woke up one morning feeling nauseous and headachy. She vomited, something which she never did. Shocked, she stayed in bed for the day and found that she was fine later that evening. Patrick came round as usual and they made love. She got up before him, as she always did, but as she was applying her make-up, she vomited again.

Morning sickness.

Ava was not stupid, but she was so terrified that she tried to push it to the back of her mind and soldiered on. It was another three days before she went to the doctor. By that time the sensible, pragmatic side of Ava had already counted ten weeks back to that first night in the back of her parents' car. The other, wishful, optimistic side of her burst into tears when the doctor told her.

Ava and Patrick married within days.

Her parents did not object. This was, after all, the only way forward and at least she was getting married. Nessa had come to feel that this new Ava was a complete stranger to her. She had visions of Ava becoming one of those renegade 'beatnik' girls she read about in the magazines. She might decide to live in sin and have the baby out of wedlock. Where would they be then! When news of her pregnancy and impending marriage threatened to unhinge her, Tom pointed out that they should be grateful that Ava was not running wild. Patrick, too, was a Catholic, and so, in some part, his decision to marry Ava had been made the night he made love to her in the back of her father's car. You didn't go all the way with a girl like Ava and then abandon her.

When she told him she was pregnant, Patrick was not as upset as he imagined he would be. In some ways, he was relieved. He had held off on asking Ava to marry him because he felt he was still engaged to Rose. Perhaps, he had been thinking, he should make more of an effort to contact her, break it off properly, even though he felt certain it was over from her side too, otherwise she would have found a way of getting in touch. He thought about telephoning Rose from the office at work. He felt sure they would allow him to do it if he explained it was a family emergency. But then, he would have to find her telephone number. He supposed he could ring the exchange in Foxford and asked to be put through, but then they would know who he was – and it all seemed so very confusing.

The moment Ava told him she was pregnant the problem of breaking off with Rose seemed to go away. His answer had been given to him.

The very next day, he asked Gerry for an advance on his

wages then took the afternoon off and shopped around the city until he found a ring he could afford. It was plain gold from a discounted and seconds jewellery shop. She smiled quietly as he placed it on her engagement finger.

'Are you sure?' she said.

'Yes,' he said. 'I have never been more sure of anything in my live-long life.'

She looked into his eyes and it seemed as if he meant it.

On their way to City Hall, Ava and Patrick passed through Columbus Park. They were early and sat for a moment on a bench. There was a small group of hipster students sitting on the grass. One of them had a guitar and another was singing, all under a cloud of pot smoke as Patrick lit his own cigarette.

Ava looked down at her legs, encased in tan tights, crossed at the knees, barely covered with the skirt of the cream woollen dress she had bought for the occasion. Patrick was wearing a suit he had borrowed from one of his friends at work. It was navy and slightly too long on the leg. Ava had made the decision to get married without her family there. Patrick had not written to tell his family about the wedding. 'They are so far away,' he said, 'my mother would fret. I will write after we are settled.' Ava was hurt that he didn't want to share the news, but when she pushed him on it, saying that she would arrange a telephone conversation, he put her off, quite abruptly. She didn't question him further. Perhaps there was some estrangement she didn't know about. She knew so little about Patrick's life. Although she knew all that she needed to know, which was that she was madly in love with him. And, if Patrick could not have his family there to support him, she decided to do without her parents. However, Ava did feel sad that she was taking this step without them. Seeing the hipsters cheered her up. People like that didn't worry about marriage or doing the right thing. Soon people would not bother getting married at all. Not that Ava would have wanted that. She loved Patrick and they were having a baby together. That was what you did when you felt strongly enough about somebody to make a baby with them. You married them. You pledged to spend the rest of your life with them. That was God's will.

One of the couples began making love, right there, under the tree. Kissing with a messy, wet passion, their hands exploring, crawling all over each other's bodies. The man's hand shoved under the girl's blouse and began kneading her breasts. Ava felt a sudden shiver of shame and embarrassment. She looked at Patrick, panicking at the thought that he had seen it too. He said nothing, only turned to her and said, 'We had better be making a move.' He took her hand then raised her fingers to his lips and kissed them.

This wasn't ideal. The baby, the shotgun wedding – any of it.

But in that kiss, as with every kiss Patrick gave her, Ava felt everything in her world come right again.

19

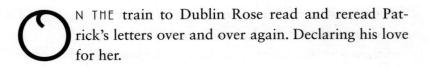N THE train to Dublin Rose read and reread Patrick's letters over and over again. Declaring his love for her.

My darling girl, you cannot imagine how hard it is for me not to be able to hold you in my arms. How I miss your face and the touch of your small hands upon me.

Begging her to get in touch.

I cannot understand why you have not written up to now. I can only imagine that you are busy with your studies. Please write to me and tell me you have forgiven me for leaving you behind.

Innocently recalling the machinations of his escape:

My mother had an awful job trying to find my birth certificate! Your father was great though – he made a phone call and got me a passport in double quick time. He could have sent me across on the boat like my grandfather, but he paid the full price of an aeroplane ticket. He is a generous man, Rose, make no mistake. A good man. I know this has been difficult for you, having me gone, but it is for the best. Thank your father again and tell him I will pay him back in full although he knows that we are both gentlemen and I won't let him down.

His family knew as well. Had they all plotted to keep them apart? No. They were nice people. It was her own parents that were behind this nasty trick. Rose's fingers tightened around the letters and her heart hardened with fury. Part of her wondered how Patrick could have been so stupid not to see what was going on. It seemed so obvious to her now, but then she thought how could she have been so stupid? She knew what a snob her mother was and how her father played man-of-the-people, but really was as much a snob as her mother. But this? Even she could not quite believe that they would go to these lengths to stand in the way of love. Who had told them? How had they found out? It didn't matter now. It was all over. She would never speak to them again. She would go to America and find Patrick and be with him, for ever. She was finished with her parents.

Rose looked out of the window at the passing countryside. It was a flat day, but the grey sky against nature's colours only served to make them appear brighter: the green grass of the grazing fields, the copper moss of the bogs and the messy yellow gorse that lined the train tracks. On another day, in another life, Rose would have snatched up her pad and started drawing. Not today. Today, the lacy outlines of the trees against the sky, the hares hopping across the fields, the whitewashed cottages dotted across the Mayo landscape like little rays of hope and home, were all invisible to her. There was nothing she wanted to do until she saw Patrick's face again.

She took the drawing of him out of her bag, and unrolled it to remind herself of what he looked like. She remembered pulling the drawing out from its hiding place between the floorboards, and realizing that her mother must have found it. Perhaps the first day she had drawn it, before she had time to hide it properly. That was how all this had started. Well, she determined, her parents wouldn't find her out so easily again.

Rose and her family had flown to London on a surprise trip the year before. Rather than book their flights by phone and risk his wife and daughter receiving them by post, spoiling the surprise, John had simply said they were staying in Dublin. After a night in the Shelbourne he had walked them down to the Irish Travel Agency on D'Olier Street and paid for the tickets in cash. They had issued them straight away, and it had been so thrilling going to the airport and on to her first flight. The three of them had been so excited, travelling by air for the first time. 'All you need to go anywhere in the world these days,' her father had told her, 'is a spirit of adventure, a passport and a ticket!' Once they had returned her father noted to her, with interest, that they were thinking of bringing a 'visa' system in to America for travellers, 'but it's a long way off yet', he had said. When the flights to New York from Dublin had launched the year before Tom had also pointed them out in the paper with the idea that they all might go on a family holiday there. Well, now she was going. On her own. Without them!

When the train arrived in Heuston Station, Rose went to the bathroom and changed into a smart dress and jacket, stockings and shoes. She tied up her hair into a tidy top-knot and applied some lipstick to make herself look older. In the cubicle she counted out the money she had stolen from her father. There was nearly six hundred pounds. She was shocked to find so much. It was an absolute fortune. Perhaps even a year's salary. She blushed and thought of how scandalized her parents would be to find she had taken such a huge sum. Then she thought of how much money her father must have spent sending her lover away to America, and her resolve hardened again. Rose took a taxi from the station down to D'Olier Street, went into the travel agency and bought a ticket for the following day. She had wanted to travel that day but the girl in the office, not much older than herself, had explained that the first flight out was in the morning.

'You'll need to give them the name and address of the people you are staying with in New York. It's very straight-forward,' she said. 'Once you have an airline ticket and a passport, there's no fuss. As long as you're not planning on getting work...'

The girl looked at her keenly, but Rose smiled and assured her she was only going on a short holiday. It was her intention to get a job and stay there for ever, with Patrick, but she would never be allowed on the plane if she said that, so she gave Patrick's name and the address of the golf club where he worked. Even if they bothered following it up, which she doubted, Rose knew that Patrick would sort everything out. The most important thing was to find him.

At the travel agent's suggestion, Rose stayed overnight in a small boarding house off O'Connell Street. She barely slept a wink, ploughing through the landlady's copies of Irish *Tatler* magazines in the dusty downstairs lounge, trying to keep herself distracted. Every inch of her body was simply fizzing to get on the plane.

The following morning, she took a taxi out to the airport. She went over to the Aer Lingus check-in desk and presented her passport and ticket to the ground hostess.

The woman looked her up and down. Moira had been working for Aer Lingus for ten years, and this route had only been opened a few months ago. This girl did not look like the typical transatlantic passenger. Only the very wealthy could afford to fly anywhere, let alone New York. To Moira's seasoned eyes, this young woman did not look rich. Plus, her passport said she was barely eighteen. Moira thought she had better check with her boss.

'Excuse me for a moment, miss.'

In the back office she found the new ground-staff boss, an Englishman called Mr Simpkins.

'Sorry to disturb your lunch, Mr Simpkins, but there's a girl out here that seems rather young to be travelling alone.'

'Is she eighteen?'

'Yes.'

'Is her passport in order?'

'It seems to be but—'

Percy Simpkins had only been in Ireland for a few weeks working the new transatlantic route. He did not like having his lunch interrupted.

'Can you not deal with it?'

'Well, I'd rather you checked her in.'

Moira was nearly thirty and one of the older ground hostesses. She was less easy to boss about.

Percy put his sandwich back on his plate, irritably placing his napkin down on top of it.

The young woman at the front desk had her back to him. He assessed her briefly, thinking that her jacket looked a little crushed. He was about to give Moira an approving nod when the girl turned. Her extraordinary beauty hit him so hard that he stepped back slightly. With her hair pulled back, the young woman had a gloriously striking face. High cheekbones, blue eyes glimmering out at him, she smiled and asked: 'Is there a problem?' Mr Simpkins decided she could only be from the highest European aristocratic stock.

'None at all, miss, just checking that your passport is in order.'

'Is everything all right?'

Rose gave him her best smile and Percy's jaw dropped at the sheer, Hollywood dazzle emanating from her.

'Just fine, miss. Where would you like to sit?'

He handed Rose a boarding card and her passport whilst not taking his eyes off her face.

'Have a good flight,' he said, regretfully, as he watched the slim, elegant figure walk away from the desk towards the departures gate.

It was not until Percy Simpkins was back at his desk eating his lunch that it occurred to him how strange it was that the young woman was travelling with only hand luggage.

When they sat down, the air hostesses handed everyone three picture postcards with their drinks. The first had a photograph of a jumbo jet on it, the second an illustration of the interior of the plane, the third a picture of the food they could expect to eat, arranged neatly on a little white tray. Rose put the three cards straight into her bag. She would not be writing to her parents and she would be seeing Patrick in person soon enough. The flight itself was very long, bumpy and quite frightening. The man sitting next to her vomited into a small paper bag for much of the journey.

Rose was exhausted, and managed to sleep a little on the flight. For the last couple of hours before they landed she revved up, not just with the knowledge that she would soon be seeing Patrick, but also with the excitement of simply being on this crazy adventure. Soon she would be in America! She was there for the sole purpose of seeing her lover; without him she would have no reason to go there. She took out his last letter and checked the address, repeating it to herself – Westchester Lakeside Golf Club, 500 Ridgeway – over and over again until the destination was seared into her mind. It sounded like a simple enough place to find. What a surprise he would get when she walked in the door! She couldn't wait!

They landed in Newark airport early in the morning. Rose changed her Irish money at the bureau and found she had less than fifty dollars left. The flight had cost a fortune. She wondered how far fifty dollars would get her in America. She had no idea about American money. She had little enough idea about Irish money. Her parents paid for everything.

She bought a map in the airport and looked up the address of the golf club in Westchester County but she could not find it on the map. She had no idea what the nearest train station was and decided that the easiest way to get there was probably by taxi. Even though her father had a car, she and her mother would often call a taxi to take them up to Galway for the day.

The taxi driver was black. Of course, she had seen black people in the movies – *Gone with the Wind* was her favourite film and the church sent money across to the priests who were working in Africa – but Rose had never actually met a black person before.

She sat in the back of the yellow taxi and told him the address.

'That's a long way, miss,' he said. 'It will cost you ten dollars, maybe more on the meter.'

That seemed to be a lot of money but Rose didn't mind. Even if Patrick wasn't there, she would wait for him until he came in. Then he would look after her.

'That's fine,' she said.

In the city the traffic got bad and the cab driver looked in the mirror to get the measure of his passenger. He was curious: it was a long drive to Westchester and the radio was bust. She was one pretty thing, but she wasn't a typical airport fare. For a start she was too young. Who travelled on an airplane at that age? She had no luggage, so maybe she had just been out there seeing someone off? In any case, there was something in her eyes, in the way she was gazing out that window, at the suburban clapperboard houses, the roadside diners and shabby motels, as if she'd never seen nothing like them in her life. He caught her sneaking sideways glances at him in the mirror. And not those kind of glances either. It was like she had never seen a black man before.

'Where you from, lady?' he asked.

'Ireland,' she said.

'You just fly in this morning?'

'Yes,' she said – and then it all came tumbling out. The dreamy boyfriend. The cruel parents. Stealing the money, running away. Donnie wished he hadn't asked.

'The flight was a lot more expensive than I thought it would be.' Then she got worried that Donnie might think she didn't have enough to pay the taxi. 'But don't worry, I've fifty dollars left, plenty to cover the taxi fare!'

Jesus! This kid was going around asking to get mugged!

'And are you sure your boyfriend still works in this golf club? He knows you are coming, right?'

The girl snapped, 'Of course' in a way that suggested she was not at all sure, then resolutely looked out the window, indicating that the conversation was over.

Donnie had a bad feeling about this kid but his wife was expecting their third child any day now and he needed all the fares he could get. The last thing he needed was a runaway ingénue in the back of his cab causing trouble.

Westchester was way out of the city. It seemed to Rose that they were heading for the middle of nowhere. They had driven for half an hour along broad roads that were wider and longer than any road had a right to be. Everything here seemed bigger. The cars, the vast hills with mountains beyond them. Even the trees seemed somehow taller and more leafy, more voluminous, than the trees at home in Ireland. There were sprawling buildings on the side of the roads with huge signs like 'MOTEL' and 'DINER' above them. Rose was beginning to feel overwhelmed when they turned into a long driveway, past an empty security hut, and into an open space covered in manicured hillocks dotted with little flags, stretching out on either side of the neat road as far as the eye could see. As they pulled up to the large, square building, with its white pillars and stucco carvings, she began to feel a little overwhelmed.

'Would you like me to wait for you?' Donnie asked.

'No thank you,' she said. 'I'll be fine.'

Rose had not liked the driver's earlier inference that perhaps Patrick had run away. In truth, she had been more frightened than annoyed by it. The black man asking all those questions had made her feel uncomfortable. Ill at ease. She wasn't sure if it was him or the questions themselves that unnerved her.

What would she do if Patrick wasn't here? Rose decided that was out of the question. She would have faith. In Patrick, and in herself for coming here to find him. If her parents had had faith in Patrick, and her, none of this would be happening. Although strangely, she was kind of glad it was. This was some adventure she was on. When she saw her love again, this lonely leg of it would be over, and they could begin the great adventure of their life together.

She took a ten-dollar bill out of her purse and handed it to Donnie. She barely stopped to thank him or to wonder about whether she should give him a tip. She just ran, almost skipping in through the grand front door of the clubhouse.

There was a large reception desk with an older gentleman in a smart blazer behind it. He eyed her suspiciously as she came across and said, in her best accent, 'Good morning. I am here to see Mr Patrick Murphy.'

'Certainly, miss. I'm afraid I don't recognize the name. Is he a new member here?'

Rose blushed. She was not ashamed. There was nothing to be ashamed of.

'No,' she said. 'He works here.'

'I see,' said the man. He had an English accent, and looked at her imperiously. Rose found her voice shaking as she said, 'In the kitchen.' Then, remembering why she was here, firmly added, 'If you just show me the way to the kitchen area I can find him myself.'

The man smiled. 'I'm afraid that won't be possible, miss. The clubhouse and the kitchens are all gentlemen only. If you would wait here for a few moments I will go and enquire after... Mr Murphy.'

'Thank you,' she said. Rose sat down on a leather chair and waited. She was shaking with nerves. The reason for her whole journey was this moment. The moment when he would walk out and see her. What would they do? Where would they go? Would he be able to kiss her, right here, in this strange, posh male-only place? Or would she wait here until he had finished his shift? Would the two of them go dancing out into the evening, then maybe call a taxi? Rose closed her eyes and tried to imagine how their reunion would unfold. With a rising sense of panic she realized that she could not envisage it.

The man seemed to come back just a few seconds later and she stood up.

'I'm afraid,' he said, 'that Mr Patrick Murphy no longer works here.'

Rose tried to sound steady.

'I see,' she said. 'Do you have any idea where he went?'

'None at all, I'm afraid.' The old man looked genuinely concerned. 'I asked around and, while one or two of the staff knew him, they said he left in rather a hurry and didn't give any forwarding details.'

That was no surprise, the old man thought, the way these Irish gangsters treated the kitchen staff. And now this pretty young thing was looking for one of them, probably all the way from Ireland. The poor Irish really were such savages. Still, nothing he could do. This was a very expensive private club. No women or blacks allowed in the building, and that was that. He wouldn't have let her in the door at all if she hadn't moved so damn fast.

'I'm so sorry,' he said, 'but I really am going to have to ask you to leave. We have a party due in from the course any moment now...'

He vaguely hoped she had a taxi waiting but, hell, that wasn't his problem. The clubhouse was his domain. If she was caught wandering about outside, that was gate security's problem. They should never have let a woman in in the first place.

Rose stepped out into the blistering sunlight. Patrick was not here. Where was he? He was gone? How would she find him? She was in a daze, absent-mindedly holding her bag, and took two steps before the magnitude of it began to hit her. She was in New York. Alone. Patrick wasn't here. She had to find him – but how? She had lost him. She would never find him. The tears came before a mixture of shock, exhaustion and hunger made her legs collapse and she fell. Before she hit the ground she felt herself being scooped up again by two strong arms around her waist.

Donnie pulled her up on to her feet and half walked her into his cab.

As he arranged her on the back seat she said, 'You're still here?'

'Yes,' Donnie said. 'I'm still here.'

He knew the girl was trouble but he couldn't abandon her without knowing she was safe. Donnie was a good Christian and never left a fare unless he knew they were safe. God was always watching.

20

'SHE IS not staying here!'

Donnie's wife Marisa was standing in the small kitchen next to the living room in their two-bedroom apartment on the top floor of the Harlem brownstone.

'Quiet down, honey – she can hear you.'

Marisa had her hands on her hips. She took one of them off to point accusingly at him, then wagged it in the general direction of the pretty white girl Donnie had brought home in his taxi not an hour before. He'd expected her to feed the kid. Marisa found enough food and just enough courtesy to give the stranger lunch but she was not having her stay under their roof. They had two small kids and another one on the way. No matter how good a Christian her husband was, no matter what their pastor said or Jesus himself said, Marisa had only just managed to move one useless cousin-in-law off their couch after a six-month homeless stint. She was not bringing another waif in under her roof. Not even a clean, pretty one. Hell, especially not a clean, pretty one!

'I don't care if she can hear me,' she said, bringing her voice down to an angry whisper. 'I told you before, Donnie, you can't go bringing home every bum that gets into your cab…'

'Aw, come on, baby. That girl ain't no bum.'

That was the wrong thing to say. Marisa looked fit to explode.

'I'm taking the kids to the store. I want her gone by five.'

'Where will she go?'

'Not my problem…' And before he could object, added, 'And not yours either!'

Marisa went into the room to collect the two children, and found them watching, transfixed, as the girl, Rose, sketched on a pad.

Marisa felt even more agitated. She had so little to give her children these days, this third pregnancy had hit her hard. It did her heart good to see them happy.

Flossie, aged three said, 'Mom, come and look.'

Marisa felt a stab of irritation but went to look at the drawing. It was a beautiful sketch of the small bunch of weeds and wildflowers, which Flossie had picked in the park that morning and Marisa had put into a jam jar. Tears came to her eyes. Everything made her cry these days. Half the time she didn't even know she was doing it. After this child, no more. No matter what the pastor dictated, or how much Donnie objected, she was getting contraception fitted and that was that!

'That's very good,' she said, brushing away her tears quickly and reaching for Flossie.

'Leave the children here with me if you like,' Rose said. 'I do so appreciate you bringing me into your home when…'

When what? She had been abandoned? Lost the lover she had come here to find? Was fearful she might never find him again? Rose needed to gather herself, to think about what her next step might be, but found there was such a fierce panic pounding through her that it was all she could do to keep herself from throwing herself out of Donnie's taxi at a stop sign then running aimlessly around the unknown streets screaming 'Patrick!'

In the end, she had steadied herself by concentrating solely on what was in front of her. Rose had always used drawing to calm herself down, and the first step in drawing was looking. Looking out of the window at the vast city, with its tall, looming buildings and teeming streets seemed too overwhelming. So as Donnie talked, Rose scrutinized the back of his cab, the polished screen between the cab and driver, the advertisement for hair colourant on the back of his seat, the worn, leather seats. When they got to his apartment, she was in such a daze she barely took in her surroundings. After a sandwich and some strong coffee, she began to feel a little more settled, but it was the two small children that grounded her. She took out her sketch pad to entertain them, and as she drew, she began to feel more like herself.

As her mind settled she began to think logically, for the first time since she had found Patrick's letters. Everything had happened in such a whirlwind and she had been so intent on getting here, that she could now see she had been caught up in a kind of madness. She supposed that's what they meant when they said 'madly in love'.

Patrick would not have told her he was leaving his job because he had had no reply to his letters. He might well think that she had jilted him. Her father had organized Patrick's job on the golf course. However, if Patrick had left there under a cloud, leaving no forwarding details, there was nothing to be gained going down that route. And besides, she was still so angry with her parents she did not want to contact them.

New York was a huge city but Rose knew that there was an Irish community here. It couldn't be that hard to find him. Patrick, as a true Irishman, would be with other Irishmen. With other men from County Mayo, if at all possible – people from Foxford. What she needed to do now was find out where the people from County Mayo gathered in New York City. She also needed to stay calm and spend the few pounds she had left carefully. This taxi driver and his wife were the only people that were standing between her and those tough-looking streets. Donnie was a kind man but Marisa looked cross.

'Well,' Rose said now, 'I do so appreciate your inviting me into your home. You are surely very kind Christian people, and your children are,' she looked down at the two babies and smiled genuinely, 'so beautiful.'

Donnie was due out on another shift and Marisa had been planning to kick the girl out with him as soon as he got back. She looked at Rose and her two children and thought how nice it would be to have an afternoon to herself.

'Well,' she said. 'If you don't mind?'

Marisa touched the heads of both her children and beckoned Donnie out into the hallway.

'On the way to your shift call into Pastor Wiggins. He'll know what to do. Tell him to call around after supper and if she stays here she sleeps on the couch and pays like a hotel, understand?'

Donnie nodded.

As soon as Marisa left, Donnie told Rose she could stay the night and that he was going to talk to his pastor.

'Are you Catholic?' she asked.

'Methodist,' he said, 'but we're all Christians.' He seemed like he was taking it as an insult.

'Oh no,' she said, 'I just meant that if he was a Catholic priest, he might be able to help me find Patrick.'

She sure was stuck on finding her man. Donnie knew that, of course, every woman needed a man, but he had a bad feeling about this guy. Such a sweet little thing she was, to be let down by him just disappearing on her like that.

'You might ask your pastor if he knows any Irish Catholic priests?'

Pastor Wiggins, an ancient black man with white hair, was curious to find himself being called upon to help a middle-class white Irish girl. Not pregnant, or beat-up – just that she was chasing some boyfriend over from Ireland on an aeroplane, if you don't mind, then had run out of money just in time to take charity from a poor black family.

The streets of Harlem were alive with needy families and if Donnie and Marisa Jones had not been such kind good people, he would not have bothered making the calls he did.

He took Donnie into his office and made a call to Father Moran, who was based in the parish adjacent to Harlem, that took in parts of Hell's Kitchen. He worked the 'poor Irish' shift, which was tough, but not as tough as Harlem. 'Poor Irish' were better than political Irish. But they were still white. And Catholic. The men maintained the veneer of professional friendship, but they were in fierce spiritual competition with one another.

'One of my congregation just took in a girl from Ireland, straight off the plane...'

'An aeroplane? Not the boat?'

'I know. Stole the money from her parents to get here and now she's stuck here with this family who can barely feed themselves. She doesn't know a soul. Straight out of a convent. I wouldn't call except that this family have enough troubles…'

Wiggins was getting the upper hand.

Never let it be said that the Irish didn't look after their own. A convent-educated Irish girl taking charity from poor black Christians in Harlem? He never heard of such a thing!

'Where is she from?'

'Ireland.'

Moran signed loudly. Now it was his turn to show Wiggins what Christianity was all about – Irish Catholic style.

'Where in Ireland? Have you a county? A town even?'

Wiggins conferred with Donnie.

'Oxford? Near a place called Mea-yowh?'

'Foxford, County Mayo. Give me the family's address. I'll get on to the Connaughtman's Association. I can't promise to have her out of there by tonight, but certainly we will get someone to collect her first thing in the morning. Of course, we'll remunerate the family for their trouble.'

When Marisa returned with the groceries, Rose helped her unpack and prepare a chicken and rice supper. After they had eaten Rose offered to look after the children again while Marisa went to visit her sister. Being with the children meant she did not have to explain herself, or stress about Donnie coming home with news. The children forced her simply to be in the moment with them, drawing or playing.

After she had put them both to bed, Rose went to her purse and took out three dollar bills. She tucked them in behind the wooden crucifix on the mantelpiece and said a silent, but heartfelt prayer that she would find Patrick.

At that very moment, across Harlem, Father Moran got on the phone to Tom Brogan.

21

AVA STARTED to 'show' early on in her pregnancy, partly because she quickly started to gain weight. She was happy to give up work in her father's office and concentrate on making the perfect home for her and Patrick and the new baby. Although her pregnancy was unexpected, she quickly became very excited at the idea of becoming a mother. An only child herself, it felt as if very soon her family would be complete. Although her parents offered to buy her a home, they decided that they would stay in Ava's small apartment which they were managing to pay for themselves. It was not pride so much as the feeling that, in some way, she had still let her parents down. She had a husband, and soon she would have a child. In a way, that was all her parents had ever wanted for her. Perhaps, also, it was all she had ever hoped for herself. And yet when she was with her parents she felt as if her relationship still fell under the shadow of the circumstances in which it had started.

The nursery was little more than a box room, a large

cupboard. She and Patrick had chosen the paint together in a hardware store around the corner from the house. For weeks, now, the paint pot had been sitting at the door waiting for Patrick to get a day off. Since the opportunity to sing had opened out for him at work, he had been working nearly all the time. Ava missed having him around, and with the baby coming, and the ongoing awkwardness with her parents, sometimes she felt lonely.

However, she knew how important Patrick's singing career was to him so she said nothing. Ava went ahead and picked out fabric for curtains and a quilt, a sky-blue cotton with small ducklings on it. She understood that men were not interested in such things, but nonetheless she wanted there to be a sense of occasion and excitement about the baby's coming. Perhaps because its conception had been unplanned it was all the more important to make plans now.

On this particular day, Patrick promised he would stay at home and paint the room.

He told Gerry that on no account would he come in early for rehearsals. He and the wife were going to spend the day together decorating the nursery and, later in the afternoon, go to the hardware store and buy wood and other materials for him to make a crib. In the evening, he had promised Ava that he would take her out to their local bistro for a spaghetti dinner.

The day before, he had come into the bedroom and found her trying on a dress for the occasion. She was struggling to get her arms into it. 'I'm getting so fat,' she complained. 'I have nothing to wear.'

As he attempted to zip it up, Patrick did experience a moment of alarm at how much bigger she had got in just a few weeks since the wedding. However, he had the good sense not to comment upon it, and reassured her as he helped tug her arms free.

'It doesn't matter what you wear, after all. It's only Tony's and they won't mind if you don't look fancy.'

She smiled. Patrick thought she looked a bit sad. Ava didn't always seem as happy as a new bride and pregnant mother should be. He worried that it was his fault. He worked long hours and while he wished he could spend more time with Ava, the truth was, when he was up on stage singing, even just in rehearsals, he was happier than anywhere else. Sometimes he stayed behind after rehearsals to practise on his own. He would put on a record player to the side of the stage and sing along to Elvis, mimicking his microphone holds, hip movements and practising his own passionate crooning face, which Gerry had told him 'sent the women crazy!' Some afternoons he became so lost in the music that the hours just slipped by him and he would forget to go home before his evening shift began. He worried, sometimes, that he was a bad husband. Although Ava never nagged him or criticized the amount of time he spent at work, Patrick often sensed that she was disappointed in him. This should have made him come home more but he reasoned that the harder he worked the quicker he would become a big star, and once that happened everything would be all right. They would have enough money to buy a nice house in the suburbs near her parents. Then she would be happy with her baby and her nice kitchen and all the things she was used to. In the meantime, he had to try and keep her sweet in the best way that he could. By telling her that he loved her and that everything would be all right.

'I still love you, darling, and besides, you'll lose the weight after you've had the baby.'

Ava wondered sometimes how Patrick could say such hurtful things without even knowing it.

The next day, Ava woke late. Patrick had already been to the bakery and she could smell fresh coffee brewing on the stove. She smiled to herself. Life was perfect after all. She tugged on her robe, went out to the kitchen and pulled him back to bed, laughing.

After they had made love, Ava realized it had been over two weeks since they had woken up together, and she wanted to lie on in bed, but Patrick was determined to get working on the nursery.

They both dressed in their working clothes, without even showering. While Patrick began preparing the bedroom for painting, Ava set up her sewing machine on the kitchen table and got to work on the curtains and coverlet.

She put on the radio. There was a repeat of a Jack Benny comedy show, *The Drive-In Movie*. She had listened to the bespectacled comedian every week, as a child, with her father. The comedian even reminded her slightly of him. She turned up the radio and said to Patrick, 'Listen to this – you'll love it! He's hilarious!'

Patrick pretended to listen. He was struggling to cover the carpet with the old sheet, having already spattered it with yellow paint. In truth, he was not a delicate house painter. The only painting he had ever done was in the cottage in Foxford, which was roughly whitewashed, inside and out. This room had skirting boards and picture rails and a carpet, which all had to be avoided. Angelo, the building superintendent, had offered to do the job for them for a small fee and he wished he had taken him up on it. Ava would be furious about the carpet, as any right-minded woman would be.

'Listen to this bit...' Patrick heard Ava call through from the kitchen.

'Oh, boss, you're not counting Tuesday night, are you?'

'Why not?'

'That's when I had my appendix taken out.'

'What's the difference, you didn't get home till three in the morning!'

As he anxiously dabbed at the fallen paint spots on the carpet, Patrick laughed as loud as he could, but it sounded fake.

Ava could tell he wasn't enjoying the show, and why should he? Patrick was Irish, after all. There was no reason why he should 'get' American humour. She turned the dial to music radio and Perry Como's voice came booming out.

She could feel Patrick's mood lighten through the half-opened door.

'You know,' he called out, 'I'm thinking of working "Catch A Falling Star" into Friday's set.'

'I think you should,' Ava shouted back. 'It's a great song and you would do a great job of it.'

'Will I sing it now for you?' he said, appearing at the door.

He had paint all over his face. Such a cheeky, handsome face. Ava laughed.

'Instead of painting?'

'As well as. I've nearly finished...'

'Let me see...' She got up but he stood in front of the door and closed it.

'Later,' he said, holding the brush up to his mouth like a microphone.

As he sang the first notes, the phone rang. Ava went over to it, laughing.

It was Gerry from the Emerald.

Her heart sank.

Patrick took the phone.

'You know I'm having a day off, Gerry – there is not a hope of me coming in today.' Then, winking across, he added, 'I have important business here with my wife—' Before he finished the sentence Gerry interrupted him. Patrick's face lit up, his eyes glittering with excitement. 'Sure, sure,' he said, before putting the phone down.

'I'm really sorry, Ava,' he said. She could tell from his tone that he wasn't sorry at all. 'It's just that this is a really big one. Something amazing has happened.'

Ava looked at him. She was angry but hid it. What could it possibly be that was more important than this? She couldn't say it out loud because whatever it was he clearly thought it was more important.

'Iggy Morrow called. He's on his way in and he wants to see me.'

'What about?' said Ava.

'I've no idea,' Patrick said. 'But he's the big boss man, and when he wants to see you…'

'If you want to see Mr Morrow, my father can just call him up.'

She was making him feel stupid. Her father was a big boss man too. It was her way of showing him her family were important. More important than him. Well, Ava didn't work there. She didn't know how elusive Iggy Morrow was, what kind of an important man he was. Her father might be important but he wasn't a music mogul. If Morrow wanted to see him, right now, then that's where he needed to be.

He didn't need to explain himself to anyone. He didn't need to explain himself to a wife who thought she was better than he was.

Patrick walked past her into the shower without saying anything.

Ava's anger melted away into a small pocket of despair at having upset him.

While Patrick washed and put on his good suit, Ava had a quiet, petulant cry in the kitchen as she finished hemming the curtains.

When he came out, Patrick came over and stood in front of her looking contrite.

'I'm sorry,' he said. 'I have to go. I'll call in to Angelo and send him up to finish the painting.' He kissed her on the top of her head and added, 'I'll be back as soon as I can.'

After he had gone, Ava turned off the radio and walked into the half-painted room. In the empty flat a terrible feeling of loneliness opened up inside her. She tried to remember that she was not alone, there was a baby growing inside her, but she could not get a sense of it.

After a few moments, Angelo called to the door. He was a swarthy Italian workman in his mid-forties who lived in the basement apartment with his wife and four children. Although he was about the same age as her own father, he always had a slight twinkle in his eye.

'How is my favourite Irish lady?' he said. 'Your husband, the big singing star, has left me to paint the baby's room.'

'Thank you, Angelo,' she said smiling.

She gave him coffee, and made him a sandwich for lunch so he wouldn't trouble his wife, who was still nursing their youngest.

As they sat at the table, she noticed a change in his attitude towards her. Normally she could rely upon Angelo to be openly flirtatious, offering up some lascivious remark with a wink and a smile. Today, his voice was flat and his warm eyes indifferent. Perhaps he had had a row with Maria, or lost a night's sleep with the baby. However, Ava read his dispassion as a personal slight. That was how it was when you were pregnant: even the most kind and good-humoured of men weren't interested in you any more.

'Maria says you must call down and she will tell you everything you need to know about babies,' Angelo said. 'How long have you got left?'

She didn't want to tell him she was not yet four months along. She felt so big and dowdy already.

'Soon,' she said. The birth was months away and she felt like a fool making such a fuss about having the nursery painted so early.

When Angelo had gone, Ava hung up the curtains and stood for a moment in the yellow room. Patrick had promised to make a crib, but she was beginning to wonder if it would ever happen. Everything was set up for their perfect life together and yet she felt as if there was something missing. She was lonely, and, in truth, also a little bored. Perhaps she should have stayed on at work? Although working while you were pregnant was widely thought to be unseemly. She should have enough here to keep her busy if Patrick was coming home every evening for dinner. But without a husband to look after, what was a wife to do? In Yonkers Ava had been involved in the church, with her mother, fundraising for poor families back home in Ireland. Since moving to Manhattan, she had been attending St Patrick's cathedral every Sunday. However, the cathedral was a large institution in itself, with an established committee, and it felt somewhat intimidating to start a relationship with them, especially in her current condition. She could get involved in the Catholic Connaught Woman's Association. As Tom Brogan's daughter she could pick and choose the district and role she wanted to play, but Ava was slightly afraid of the gossip that might ensue. The Brogans were mid-level Irish royalty and she had no doubts that her break-up with Dermot had spread through the grapevine already. Her marriage to Patrick had been very fast, and it would take only one smart Irish biddy to add up the weeks until the baby came for them to be dining out on her family's disgrace for years. It was better for her to keep a low profile, at least until after the baby came and things had settled with her parents.

In the meantime, she had to find something to do to keep herself busy – starting with this afternoon. The apartment was spick and span, and she was darned if she would go to the trouble of preparing a meal for Patrick. If he was not back in time to take her out for her spaghetti dinner, he could starve!

Ava wandered into her bedroom and looked at the clothes she had been trying on the night before, scattered across the wardrobe door and chair. Most of them didn't fit her, but even though Ava knew she would lose the weight after the baby was born, part of her just wanted to throw them all away. These were the clothes she had bought and worn before she had met Patrick. She was a different woman now, in a new life. The pedal pushers and sweaters she had worn dancing, all those dresses her mother had made her buy that she had never liked, the very sight of them irritated her. Perhaps it was time to let them go, and with them, her past. Remembering her work with her mother, and the clothes parcels they sent through the church across to Ireland, she decided to parcel them up and find a way of approaching her mother with them.

Opening her packed closet, Ava took a deep breath and began to plough through her clothes. She sifted out the items that no longer fitted her and put them into a pile on her bed.

Holding up each one, she noted sadly that most of them had been bought in preparation for being the lawyer's wife, during her courtship with Dermot. The smart navy cotton dress and jacket suit she had worn to meet his parents for the first time. The silk, pussy-bow blouse she wore on their third date. She only wore it once, regretting the high neck one evening as she had tried to unbutton herself to lure him into a more passionate kiss. The red shift dress she had worn to her engagement party and finally, her Sybil Connolly rose suit.

Ava stood in front of her dressing table mirror and held it up in front of her. It seemed like it belonged to another woman.

She thought about how much her life had changed in just a few months, how much her body had changed. She looked across at herself and almost jolted at the look of fear in her eyes. It was the prospect of how much more change she knew there was to come with this baby.

In that moment, despite being married to a man she loved, despite carrying the baby that she very much wanted, Ava felt overwhelmed by her own life.

22

IGGY COULD not get Sheila Klein out of his head.

As soon as she left the building he went out to the bar and gave Gerry a roasting. Gerry was convinced he was about to be fired. But in the end the only instructions Iggy gave him were to give the kid a regular slot with the house band three days a week and, 'Get him a decent stage suit, for Christsake!'

As his manager was sheepishly heading out the door, Iggy barked, 'What's his name?'

Gerry looked confused.

'The kid! The kid! What's his name?'

'Er – Patrick Murphy,' Gerry said. His boss's behaviour, and sudden patronage of Patrick on the strength of that frankly accidental performance, was puzzling. Iggy was a difficult boss in that he was exacting. But he was pretty easy to read.

Gerry could see he was off form, but he had no idea by how much.

During the next hour Iggy tried to go through the books, but the whole time he felt restless, as if something was missing.

He decided to go back out into the club to see if that Jewish chick had hung around. He was sure that she hadn't, but still, he thought he'd go out and check anyway. He wandered around, even going back to the place by the door where she had first approached him. Of course, she wasn't there. She had stormed out.

He went back to his office and opened the books again. Ingoings and outgoings, deliveries and overheads. Bar takings were up on last month, door takings were down on the last six-month period... Oh! To hell with it! He threw the books aside – who cared about them anyway? That chick had got the last word on him. And some cheek she had coming in here, to his club, pretending to be some kind of a bigshot manager when he knew everyone in town. She was a nobody, but she had knocked him back. Iggy didn't get knocked back by anyone. Not for a long time. Not by anyone who knew who he was.

He had asked her out to supper and she had said 'no'. The hell with her...

Iggy picked up the phone and rang old Hymie Baldwin across town. Hymie owned the Spotlight Ballroom in the East Village, where Iggy had cut his teeth behind the bar as a fifteen-year-old roughneck straight off the boat from Ireland.

'Work for a Jew if you can,' a man on the boat across had advised him. 'Work hard and they'll pay you properly. Only work for your own when you don't need something.' Iggy had learned everything he knew in business working for Jewish bosses. It was, he knew, what made him such a success. He wasn't afraid of upsetting his own. He wasn't beholden to anyone, or afraid of anyone. Wherever he was, Iggy remained an outsider and he liked it like that.

Now he asked his old friend straight out, 'Do you know a broad called Sheila Klein? Calls herself a music manager.'

'Ouch,' Hymie said. 'She worked for Dan McAndrew at the Twilight. Did more than work for him, too. His wife, Angela, is one of the Balduccis. I heard they were pretty mad. I was kind of hoping she might turn up here, looking for a job. She was one hell of a manager, by all accounts. More than that lazy, womanizing shyster deserved, anyway. But with those Italian gorillas after her, I'm guessing she skipped town. Why the interest? You looking for staff?'

'I'm always looking for staff, old man.'

They exchanged a few more words before Iggy put the phone down.

He was disappointed. Dan McAndrew was exactly the sort of lazy, louche character he despised. Ignatius Morrow was certainly not interested in his leftovers. Even if he were, he reasoned, women were enough trouble on their own, without the Mafia after them. Plus, Miss Klein had skipped town. So, that was that.

Except that Iggy had an itch now and he couldn't let go until it was scratched.

The next day he went to Boston to check on his establishment there. He rang round. Nobody had heard of Sheila Klein. From there he went to Chicago, and made a few more calls. Again – nobody had heard of her. Cincinnati, Fort Worth, St Louis – no one in any of the clubs in any of the cities where he operated had known of a dark-haired Jewish broad in her thirties come in looking for work. Furthermore, word was spreading that Iggy Morrow was losing it. Ringing around competitors, chinwagging and asking questions? Every stop, Iggy told himself he was being a fool. What the hell was he doing looking for this woman? He didn't even know her. Somehow, she had got right under his skin.

As the weeks passed and his enquiries led to nothing, Iggy

began to worry that something had happened to her. In a whiskey snooze on his regular long-haul flight to London, Iggy had a nightmare the Balducci brothers had found her. They were following her through the streets of Willesden in north-west London, and he was chasing after them, but, no matter how fast he ran, he couldn't catch up to their slow, menacing swagger. He woke up calling out her name. The air hostess, Linda, brought him over a blanket and coffee.

'Who's Sheila?' she said, teasing him.

He decided enough was enough. He visited Manchester, Liverpool and Cork on that trip. Returning to New York from Dublin he made a conscious decision to stop looking. He would not ring Hymie or other club owners to see if Sheila had turned back up on home soil. Enough was enough. She was just some woman, and if she was in trouble it was nothing to do with him.

There was one sure way to scratch the itch she had given him, but Iggy didn't call any of his girlfriends on that trip. He just didn't have the will for his usual enjoyable but ultimately pointless encounters. Next time around, next trip, he told himself. Or perhaps, he thought, I am just getting too old. Too old for all the travel and the cheap sex. Maybe, he worried, I am losing my mind altogether, chasing around after some woman I don't even know.

His flight came in early and Iggy decided to head straight to Yonkers for breakfast in Katie's, his favourite diner, before going across to the Emerald. It was closer to Riverdale than Yonkers, but he could use the walk. When he was done there he would head across to the club, get all his paperwork done before noon, then go back to his hotel, sleep and be ready for his flight to Boston the next morning.

The diner was busy, but that was no great surprise. It was a

great place, popular with the Irish crowd. There were proper
Irish rashers and sausages shipped in from home, and brown
bread like 'your mother used to make'.

Not that Iggy had grown up eating rashers and sausages,
or indeed had a mother to make brown bread for him. Home
was a Christian Brothers orphanage, whose brutality ended
when he ran away at thirteen to work in Dublin and save for
the boat ticket to his American dream. Iggy reinvented the
truth by re-creating the vision of Ireland for the Irish abroad,
and the Irish at home too. And in doing so he was able to
invent a pretty fiction for himself with the finest rashers and
sausages and strong tea, never coffee, in a Yonkers diner.

'The usual, Katie,' he said to the woman at the counter. She
gave him a mug and he sat down in his favourite booth with
a copy of the *New York Times*. A waitress came over with the
coffee jug as he put his hand over the mug – she splashed it
with boiling coffee.

'Ouch!' he said and looked up at her angrily.

A somewhat defiant pair of dark eyes looked straight into
his, and a broad mouth twisted in very slight but nonetheless
unmistakably amused recognition.

'I'm sorry,' she said. She didn't look sorry. And she wasn't.

Sheila had hoped never to see the creep Morrow again,
although she had also known that in taking a job in an Irish
diner, on a die-hard Irishman's patch, was not exactly the best
way of avoiding him.

She had needed the money and this gig was a last resort. It
was near home and she had nowhere else to go. The knock-
back from Iggy that night had thrown her, and she had
decided to sit tight and try and save enough money to get
herself to another city to start a new life. In truth, though, she
didn't feel like running anywhere.

So she took this job, but Sheila hated waiting tables and frankly, she was lousy at it. People might forgive a young waitress for spilling coffee, but they expected a kind of home-spun charm from older servers, and Sheila was pretty short on that. The dim and dusty world of New York nightlife was what she knew. Over and over she told herself that if she could have that ten minutes in front of Iggy Morrow back again, she would offer her services. Hell, pulling pints or selling cigarettes in an Irish dance hall was better than this.

So, here he was.

Still, they had parted on bad terms and Sheila didn't do apologies – empty or otherwise.

'It's you,' he said.

'You want some ice for that hand?' she asked, without making a move to help him.

'No it's fine,' he said. Then, remembering himself, said, 'It's Miss...?'

'Klein. Sheila Klein.'

Iggy felt pleased with himself. As if he had somehow clawed back some of the self-respect he lost while chasing around after her. At least she had no idea he had been looking.

Sheila shuffled from foot to foot.

'Hey, lady! Where's my coffee?' a fat regular called from across the room.

She arched her eyebrows at Iggy in an embarrassed apology and went off to serve the other customer.

Iggy watched her as she worked. Her skinny black pants with a matching black sweater made her body look even narrower than he remembered. Her hair was slung casually into a ponytail at the nape of her neck and her back was so straight as she walked across the room, it looked like she might snap in half. She seemed full of more energy than her thin body could contain.

Although she said little, and moved carefully, Iggy could sense something glittering beneath the surface of her reserve. An anger. A hunger. As his gaze carefully followed her he alarmed himself with the thought that she might walk out the door of this establishment at any moment and he might never see her again.

Katie brought over his breakfast herself.

'New girl,' he said.

'Worst waitress I ever had. Charmless. I'm doing a favour for her family.'

'She's local?'

'Nice old Jewish couple, the Kleins, German. She grew up with them. Her family died in the war.'

So this is where she was from. She hadn't moved far out of town, but, as he knew himself, the Bronx was a million miles away from Manhattan if you were looking for somebody. Iggy looked across at her again, refilling the coffee pot behind the counter. He felt a silly disappointment that she had not stuck around in the area for him.

He went up to the counter to pay. Katie had left Sheila to deal with him.

She came over with his check. He wasn't interested in her. She'd blown it. Guys like him didn't go around giving people second chances, even when they didn't know that they wanted one.

So she was absolutely astonished when the great Iggy Morrow handed over two dollars and said, 'You want a job?'

She wanted to lean over and hug him. But hugging wasn't her style and so, instead, she found herself saying, 'A job doing what?'

Her lower lip was trembling. Iggy could sense the tension in her voice and see her eyes lose some of their determined hardness. She was desperate. She needed work, the Mafia were after her, she'd be a lucky woman if he offered her a job, even selling cigarettes or working in the cloakroom. Would she go out to dinner with him now? he wondered. He knew she would, but he didn't know if she would want to. And he wanted her to want him.

In that moment he knew that, while she was keeping up the tough façade, she would take anything on offer.

In that moment Iggy knew that he had complete control over Sheila Klein.

'I would like you to come and manage Patrick Murphy for me. You were right. The kid's got talent, but I don't have time to bring him on.'

Inside, Sheila was screaming. Was this happening? Was this guy for real? She kept her face as impassive as she could and narrowed her eyes. Persuading herself they looked as hard as concrete, she said, 'Fifty-fifty – straight down the line.'

Jesus, Iggy thought to himself, what am I taking on here...

'Sixty-forty – and I pay his salary. Best I can do. Take it or leave it.'

She made him wait for five beats, then nodded. 'You've got a deal, Mr Morrow.'

Iggy went straight back to his hotel, told them to keep his room for an extra two days and cancelled his flight to Boston.

23

ROSE PASSED a very pleasant evening with Donnie and Marisa Jones. Especially when she learned that Donnie had arranged for the local Irish Catholic priest to introduce her to an Irish gentleman the next day who might be able to help her find Patrick. Given a choice, she would have called on him that very evening, but basic good manners required that she stay with this nice family for one night, at least, as she had arranged – leaving money for them that she sensed, more than saw, they probably needed.

'I feel so lucky,' she said, when Donnie got back from his shift and told her about the priest.

'New York's not so big as all that,' he said, 'when you are churchgoing people. Ministers and priests in this city know just about everyone.'

'Time for bed,' Marisa said, scooping up the baby from Donnie's lap.

'Can the white lady draw me another picture?' she cried.

Marisa smiled apologetically.

'The white lady is called Rose – and no, she can't draw you another picture. Goodness knows you've worked our guest hard enough today!' Marisa felt bad taking money off the girl now that she had grown used to her.

It was immediately clear that this blonde, delicate-looking creature came from money. Those pearls were real. But this chick was also tougher than she looked. Stealing from her parents and chasing all the way across the world looking for her man. Marisa knew tough. Her mom had raised Marisa and her older brother, Christopher, by herself, holding down three jobs. Marisa went out working in a hair salon at fourteen, and between them she and her mother sacrificed everything to put Christopher through art school.

While Donnie put the baby to bed, Marisa went around the room tidying, carefully picking up the dozen or so drawings that her children had been pestering out of Rose. One was of the youngest child. Plump cheeks and sparkling eyes, her features captured perfectly, her nut-brown skin shaded in soft charcoal smudges.

'You're good,' she said.

'Thank you,' said Rose. She knew she was good. Praise meant very little to her.

'You been to school?'

'Art school? No. Not yet.'

'Why not?'

Rose felt a little irritated.

'I haven't had a chance yet. I only just left regular school. My parents were going to... Well, you see I'm over here now...'

Chasing after some damn-fool man, Marisa thought. 'My brother was in art school.'

'He's an artist?'

Rose didn't care, she was just being polite.

'Kind of. My mom and I paid for his studies, we never thought we'd see our money back but... now he has a really good job in an advertising agency.'

'That's nice.'

Was there any point in even talking to this girl? She was so caught up with finding this guy. However, Marisa hated to see talent go to waste.

'It's just he uses a lot of illustrators and you seem really good.'

'Thank you,' said Rose. She wasn't sure what Marisa was driving at. A job? But that hardly seemed likely. She hadn't even finished school.

'Once I find Patrick I'm sure everything will be fine.'

Marisa smiled, tightly. Rich white people. They really were different.

'Well, you know where I am,' she said.

'Yes,' said Rose. Even though she did not have the first clue where she was at all.

The following morning Father Moran came to collect her in his black Ford car. She thanked the Joneses and as she was getting into the car, Marisa handed her a piece of paper with their address on it. Rose stuffed the note carelessly into her coat pocket, trying to keep herself in check as the old priest drove slowly across the bridge out of the city into the suburbs of the Bronx.

The priest was not only old but rather grumpy. As soon as he drove off he began to question Rose about why she was here and what on earth she thought she was doing leaving Foxford and demanded to know where she got the money for an aeroplane ticket.

'My father gave it to me,' she lied. 'He's a doctor.'

Rose shuddered as she realized she sounded exactly like her mother. 'Doctor's daughter' gave her an elevation in status that could, if not excuse her behaviour, then at least might soften the priest's attitude.

'And you came here chasing after a man, I suppose?'

'My fiancé,' she pronounced, 'is working in New York. I came to surprise him, but now it seems he left his previous employment. It's just a question of finding out where he is gone.'

Father Moran shook his head.

'And what is this fine fellow's name?'

'Patrick,' she said.

'An Irishman in New York called Patrick? Goodness me, I never heard of such a thing.'

She really did not like this priest. However, he was the only person she knew right now that would be able to help her.

'Patrick Murphy.'

'Well, that narrows it right down. There are hundreds of thousands of Irishmen in New York. It was very irresponsible of you to come looking for one of them without making proper arrangements. And now, do you see, you are putting all of us out. '

A terrible despair crept over Rose. Perhaps the priest was right and she would never find Patrick after all. What would she do? How would she survive?

She went very quiet and when the priest glanced across at her, he saw tears pouring out of her large blue eyes and down her creamy cheeks. He was immediately sorry to have upset her. It was just that sex and all that nonsense led to such trouble between people, and there were so many other things to be concerned about, people suffering genuine hardships, that it was hard not to lose patience sometimes.

The girl could not have been more than seventeen or eighteen, not much more than a child really. Perhaps he was being too hard on her. After all, she was a long way from home, and she obviously came from an educated class of people.

'There there,' he said. 'Tom Brogan is a very good man. He is chairman of the Connaughtman's Association, so if your… fiancé… is still here in New York, there is a good chance he'll help you find him.'

Rose wiped away her tears and gave him a glittering smile.

'Thank you, Father,' she said in a heart-melting tone that made him wish everyone would address him with such devout reverence.

Rose stared out the window, feeling fearful and worried that she had come all this way for nothing. Worse was the idea that she might go home without seeing Patrick.

This place felt so strange, so foreign. Everything looked so new, so modern. Even new houses in Ireland looked old. Everything in Ireland was touched by history, personal or political. Everyone knew where everyone else was from. If you tried to build a new house, or a new life, the past would always catch up with you. Over here, the past meant nothing. Perhaps she meant nothing to Patrick any more. The thought terrified her more than the idea that she might never see him again.

After what seemed like an age, driving endlessly through neat, swept streets with polished gardens, they came to a wide road and pulled up outside a rather grand house.

Father Moran lifted her bag out of the car and a nice man, about the same age as her father, wearing horn-rimmed spectacles and a benign expression, greeted them at the door.

'This is Rose,' the priest said. 'She has managed to find herself alone in New York, and I was hoping you'd be able to help her out.'

'Hello, Rose,' the man said. 'We'll see what we can do for you. Won't you come in, Father?'

'No, no, Tom – thank you. I have urgent business to attend to...' Truthfully, he had had enough of this rather mournful young woman's company and was anxious to get back to the city and the good cooking and jolly ramblings of his comely Kerry housekeeper.

Tom took Rose straight into the kitchen. It was a Saturday and Nessa was in the city shopping. The house had not been the same without Ava, and while they both missed her dreadfully, Nessa was still disappointed and upset over her marriage. Tom had hoped Ava would have called in to see him at work sometimes, but even if she had, it would have felt disloyal of him to meet her without Nessa.

It was nice to be in the company of a young woman again. Although it was very unusual for a young Irish woman to arrive in New York and not immediately go into the care of employers and/or family. The young men were the ones that came here speculating for work and found themselves getting into trouble.

He made her tea, and within a few moments they were talking about where she was from, although not the full circumstances of what had brought her here. After the priest's unsympathetic reaction, Rose was nervous about confiding too much in strangers. These people could help her to find Patrick, but she was also entirely dependent on them. She was in a strange place without her parents there to look after her. She needed for this kind man to like her, so she moderated her story. She told him that she had always dreamed of coming to New York. 'And what do your parents make of it?' he asked. How could she begin to explain? So she just tightened her lips, and looked across at him with her big, blue eyes and let him draw his own conclusions. Some part of Rose knew that Tom would assume her parents had committed sins against her that were too harsh to be spoken but she *was* still angry with them. Rose justified the assumptions that would be made by her coy silence by telling herself that her parents had acted cruelly and unreasonably. When Tom asked where she got the money to come, she told him the truth and said she had stolen it from her parents. She then said that she knew it was wrong and she hoped that one day they would forgive her. She just wanted to have an independent life. That last part was a lie, but she wanted this kind man to like her. She needed his help.

Tom flinched. Ava had an independent life now. A life independent of them, anyway. Tom did not press Rose as to precisely how her parents had been cruel to her but experience in these matters told him it must have been severe enough for one so young, and clearly so delicate, to have run to the other side of the world to escape. He knew, too, that cruelty was not the preserve of the poor, and that snobbery often let psychopaths from the privileged class go unpunished. Her parents, probably her father, must be truly despicable.

'I have a friend in New York I would like to find,' she said. 'His name is Patrick.'

Tom smiled. She was such a sweet thing. 'I'm afraid every Irishman in New York is called Patrick, my dear. Even me, occasionally,' he said.

'Patrick Murphy,' she said. 'We were engaged. Well. Sort of.'

A small cloud wandered into Tom's mind.

'Again,' he said, 'Patrick Murphy is a very common name.'

It was unusual that his new son-in-law (it still felt unnatural calling him that) was from the same part of the world as this girl and his name was Patrick. However, both were common and if, by some remote chance, they did know each other, the last thing his daughter needed was more complications in her already very fraught situation. So Tom pushed any idea of further investigation to the back of his mind and concentrated on where to place this needy young woman.

He could see that she had never worked behind a bar and would not be fit for cleaning bathrooms or waitressing with her rarefied background. In all honesty, he had not got a clue what to do with her. She needed to be advised and looked after by women. Maybe pointed towards a secretarial course of some kind. For the time being, however, the best place for this innocent young woman was, clearly, with the nuns at St Agnes on the Upper West Side. Tom took Rose out to his car, lifted her unopened bag into the trunk and, as he settled her into the front seat of the Lincoln, apologized at the swiftness with which she was on the road again.

'Where are we going?' she asked.

'Back to the city again, I'm afraid.' Honestly, he thought, Father Moran didn't have the brains he was born with. The priest could have organized all of this himself.

'I think you'd be best off with the nuns, dear. Don't worry, they are not all old fuddy-duddies. The sisters at St Agnes are all quite young and very kind. They'll help you get a job and fix you up with an apartment in due course.'

Rose felt quite sick. She had not travelled all of this way to live with nuns. She could do that at home.

'So you don't know anyone called Patrick Murphy?' she said again.

Tom felt irritated by the question.

'No,' he said, quite firmly, 'I don't.'

Rose looked out the window at the wide roads, the lattice bridges, thousands of cars and people. Patrick was out there somewhere but she was as close to finding him as she had been at home in Mayo. With a rising sense of panic and dread the magnitude of where she was and what she had done began to hit her.

She was broke and utterly alone in big bad New York City. Worse than that, now she was going to live among nuns.

24

THE KID was sitting on the edge of the stage with his legs dangling down in front of him. He was wearing a suit and his hair was slightly frizzy as if it had been freshly washed. He was handsome, but he needed to look a whole lot slicker than this if Sheila was going to do anything with him.

She had been home to change out of her work clothes before coming back to the Emerald. She had put on a fresh uniform of black pants and polo neck sweater, but made herself look smarter by backcombing her hair into a high ponytail, applying some eyeliner and lipstick, then throwing a smart trench coat over the top. Gerry, the lousy manager, had opened the door for her and said that Iggy was in the office and she could call in on him later, when she was done.

Holding out her hand as she walked across the room, Sheila now said, 'Hello, Patrick, I'm Sheila, your new manager. I am so excited that we're going to be working together.'

When Gerry had told Patrick the news that Iggy had hired a manager for him and he was to come straight over and meet them, Patrick had not been expecting a woman. He didn't know that women were music managers. Perhaps they were like secretaries and Iggy didn't think he was important or good enough to have a male manager yet. Patrick was disappointed but immediately decided it didn't matter. A few weeks ago Iggy Morrow had noticed him, and now he was making an investment in him.

The boy was gawping at her with his mouth slightly open. It made him look somewhat gormless. Had he never seen a woman before? With those good looks, she doubted that was the case. He really was a distractingly pretty boy. Anyway, she didn't need him to be bright, and she didn't need him to like her, she just needed him to look gorgeous and sing. She had remembered his moody good looks, but she needed reminding of the voice.

She said, 'So, Patrick, let's get straight down to business, shall we? Why don't you run me through your repertoire.'

'Now?'

Sheila smiled. The very brittle 'management' smile she reserved for shoddy cleaners and lazy barmen.

'Is there a problem, Patrick?'

'Well, it's just that my wife is pregnant and I said I'd take the day off.'

A wife? Sheila's heart sank. The number-one rule for aspiring young pop stars was 'no wife, no girlfriends'. You belong to your screaming fans. Iggy had kept that one quiet from her.

'And yet,' she said firmly, 'here you are.'

'Yes well, Gerry said that Mr Morrow asked if I could come in and meet you, and now I've met you, so...'

Patrick's new manager pursed her lips, her dark eyes glowering with a barely veiled threat. The expression brought to mind Patrick's Aunt Biddy, when she had walked into a pub back home and caught him breaking his confirmation pledge. The silence seemed to last for ever until she finally said, 'Patrick.'

'Sorry,' he said.

'Shall we get started?'

'Of course.' What else could he say?

For the next three hours Sheila put Patrick through his paces.

He had the raw material, but there were plenty of pretty boys out there who could sing. Sheila knew she had a lot of work to do to get Patrick on track to stardom.

First, she made him run through every song he knew, unaccompanied.

Patrick felt very uncomfortable at first. He had got used to singing in front of an audience, and although he often practised on his own, this woman stood squarely at the front of the stage with an imperious expression on her face. It was most off-putting.

For the first two songs, he was so nervous he kept stopping, forgetting the words, hitting bum notes. He moved on to one of his best ladykiller tunes, 'Only You', but ended up so off tune that he thought he might cry. He then moved on to a couple of Irish ballads that he had been singing since he was a child and knew completely off by heart. Sheila seemed particularly uninterested in them, checking her nails and chain-smoking with obvious boredom.

During his rendition of 'The Galway Shawl' she walked across to the bar and poured herself a whiskey. Patrick found himself so addled and insulted that he stopped singing.

'Why have you stopped?' she said.

'You don't seem to be enjoying it,' he said.

She took a long drag of her cigarette and blew it out in his direction.

'It's not about me enjoying it, Patrick. It's about both of us figuring out where your strengths lie. Keep singing to the end of that song.'

Patrick was feeling frustrated. He had never had such a dreadful, unappreciative audience, and it was shattering his confidence.

'What's the point if the audience doesn't like it?'

'I am not your audience, Patrick,' she said, 'I am your manager. Don't ever forget that. No, I do not like those schmaltzy Irish ballads, although I'm sure they make lots of Irish ladies go weak at the knees. However, unless I've listened to you sing every damn line, I can't be sure that I'm not missing something…'

He didn't have the first clue what she was talking about. Neither did she really.

'Look,' she said, inviting him to sit down on the stage next to her. 'You are a good-looking kid and you can sing. Now that you have a nice regular gig here, you can call yourself a professional singer. That's a lot. That's more than a lot of kids get.'

Patrick nodded and tried to look sage. Inside he was thrilled. He was a professional singer!

'But it's not enough for me.' She lit a fresh cigarette from the old one, which she stubbed out on the stage.

'Let me tell you something, Patrick. You're my only client. Just you. Nobody else. I saw something in you a few weeks ago and I hounded Iggy Morrow to let me manage you.'

Patrick didn't know whether to be pleased or not. He thought he was Mr Morrow's charge. He was the one paying his salary.

'Mr Morrow may be paying your salary, Patrick, but believe me, I am calling the shots here.'

This woman was scary, it was like she could read his mind.

'So what I need to do now is take that little special some- thing I saw in you, nurture it, make it grow until it is big. Really big. So big, that everyone in this country knows who you are. Elvis big. Jerry Lee big. There's a lot of copycats out there, and right now you're one of them. You've got the Elvis moves but here's some news for you...'

Patrick flushed.

'You are not Elvis, Patrick, and you know why?'

Patrick shook his head politely. He felt a bit sick.

'You are not Elvis because you are not different. Elvis was different. Bill Haley was different...'

Patrick shifted around uncomfortably. He wished to hell he had just sung all the songs like she had asked him to do.

'... Little Richard? Different. When I heard you sing a few weeks ago, on this stage, I thought I saw something, some little spark, that might set you apart. Something that could make you different too. Something that could make you big. But what I'm getting from you right now, Patrick, is run-of- the-mill. Are you with me?'

'Yes,' he said. He could feel tears building up in the back of his eyes. He swallowed hard.

'What I'm getting is regular, dumb-ass, white Irish-boy bullshit. Is that who you are? Just some regular fool kid who happens to be able to sing good?'

'No, ma'am.'

'Good. Because I don't need that. I need a star. Could that be you?'

'Yes, ma'am, it could.'

'I want to you sing every single song that you know how to sing, as best as you can, to me, just me, right here, right now, so that I can figure out what is special and different enough about you that I can use to help make you into the kind of star that I need to get on my books so that every bullshit man in the music management business will take me seriously. Are you going to do that for me?'

This woman was truly crazy and he was going to do every single thing that she said.

'Yes, ma'am, I most certainly am.'

For the next two hours she cajoled and coached him through every song he knew and some he didn't. They played every record in the place and she put him through his dance and microphone moves, making him sway, and throw his mike from hand to hand a thousand times until it was as natural to him as gunslinging to the seasoned cowboy.

She instructed him on just the right way to tilt his head and where to set his eyes to get that gazing into the distance mooning about his true-love-ways look. She taught him to loosen his hips so that he owned his 'Elvis', and made him drop the raised-lip snarl so that he didn't look derivative.

By the time Sheila sent him home sweating and exhausted, Patrick felt he was just getting into his stride. He had worked harder than he had ever worked in his entire life, even when pulling in the hay on the farm during the hottest summer days, and yet it felt liberating to be told what to do. He was honing his craft, and he would have stayed all night inching through each improvement. Sheila, however, was glad to send him home so she could regroup. The kid had everything: talent, looks, willingness and ability to learn. What he lacked was an edge. Every act needed an edge, and Sheila was not sure that Patrick truly had one.

'Send my apologies to your wife,' she said, as he was leaving.

'Ava would love to meet you,' he said. 'Perhaps you will come round for a meal soon.'

'Perhaps,' she said, although they both knew she was just being polite.

The wife thing was not good. Fans liked their stars single. Sheila would have to figure out a way around that one too. Iggy had given her the opportunity to work with Patrick but, although Sheila sensed something special about him, for the life of her she could not get it out of him that afternoon. He was good, but 'good' wasn't good enough. She would have to work with him a lot more before he was ready for her to bring out into the world. Until she had a recording contract, Patrick couldn't earn any money for her outside the salary Iggy was paying him to sing in his venues.

Iggy had worked that out too.

He had a plan: Gerry clearly couldn't manage his place on his own so he would put Sheila in as joint manager.

However, it was tricky because Iggy had a policy of not putting women he fancied on his payroll.

And he fancied Sheila.

There was no getting around it. Around six o'clock he went into the manager's restrooms to have a shower and change into a fresh shirt. As he stood in front of the mirror patting after-shave on his freshly shaved cheeks, he thought to himself how hollow and haggard he looked. Beady eyes glared back at him, accusingly. Even though he was a self-assured man, certain about almost everything he said and did, Iggy always looked perplexed and slightly annoyed. It was one of the great injustices. He was not handsome. He never had been and while it had bothered him as a boy, when he started making money it stop bothering him at all. Women liked money and power. They liked looks and talent too, but Iggy's money and power put him on a level playing field with his handsome young acts. The problem was not that women didn't find him attractive, the problem was that Iggy didn't always trust their intentions. So, while he found a lot of the women he knew sexually attractive, they were simply not interesting enough for him to want to spend time with them outside the bedroom.

Sheila was different, and as Iggy was preparing himself for the evening he could only hope he might be spending in her company, he could feel a hint of fear creeping into his heart. He had never been in a position where he felt nervous before seeing a woman. He worried that he might become diminished if he allowed himself to fall in love with her. He had cancelled his travel arrangements to Boston the following day. His whole month's schedule had been compromised because of a woman. This was not good. And yet, Iggy knew he had to follow it through. The fact that she had turned up like that, after he had been looking for her, was a sign that fate already had him in her grip. A smart man knew when the wind was too strong to fight. Sometimes, in life as in business, Iggy thought, as he tightened the knot on his silk tie, and grin-checked his teeth in the mirror, you had to let yourself get blown around a bit, just to see where you landed up. The true test of a man was where you would take it from there.

Sheila's spirits fell when she walked into the office and saw Iggy perched on the side of the desk, freshly shaved, in a three-piece suit. One look at him was all it took to tell her Mr Morrow was planning to take it all the way this evening. Dinner and a nice hotel. It would be a nice hotel because he was rich. But that really was not the point.

Sheila was exhausted after working so hard all afternoon with Patrick, and now her boss wanted to sleep with her. Not simply wanted to. He intended to. There was no other possible explanation for the deliberate way he was standing, cigar in hand, trying to make himself look as powerful and important as possible.

'Things went well with Patrick?'

The formality was gone now. It was straight down to business. Sheila liked that, at least.

'Very well,' she said. 'I think we'll work well together.'

'How would you feel about joint-managing the place with Gerry? As you can see, he's a bit overwhelmed. He could use a helping hand.'

Sheila was less insulted than disappointed at how predictable he was. Having him turn up like that and then offering her the job of managing Patrick had turned her life upside down in a day and set her on a path which had felt, until a few seconds beforehand, like an unforeseen adventure. Now the sense of adventure had been replaced with the dull inevitability of sex. Sheila was not a romantic soul. Often, if the opportunity to sleep with someone came up, she was happy enough to run with it. She thought that Iggy was an interesting and attractive man, but never before had Sheila felt offended by the idea of having sex with somebody.

'Two jobs in one day, Mr Morrow. You're a very generous man.'

'I rang around town and I've heard you're a good manager. I'm no fool.'

'Neither am I…'

She let that hang in the air for a few minutes but he didn't flinch. If he had been ringing around asking questions then he knew about the Balducci brothers. He also knew that she had slept with her last boss.

'How come you're all dressed up?' she said, raising her chin at him.

It was his turn to flush, although he made pretty certain he didn't show it. Jesus, but she wasn't making this easy. Whatever 'this' was. Iggy decided to play it straight. That was always the best hand to play in business if you were not sure.

'I was going to ask you out to dinner and if it went well, back to my hotel.'

His eye was unflinching. His gaze was steady and remained cool, and yet she felt it sear through her like white heat.

'Pretty fancy suit for dinner.'

'Was planning a pretty fancy dinner.'

She opened her palms and looked down at her outfit.

'I'm not dressed for dinner.'

'It doesn't matter.'

Sheila didn't know if he meant 'It doesn't matter what you're wearing' or 'It doesn't matter because I don't care that much'. She couldn't read him, and suddenly the distinction mattered.

'What doesn't matter?'

Iggy took a deep breath. Sometimes you had to take a risk.

'It doesn't matter what you wear and it doesn't matter if we don't go out to dinner.'

Nobody had ever been that straight up with Sheila before. Nobody had ever been that straightforward, that honest in their intention. She didn't know what it meant, and she didn't care what it meant either.

She just walked straight across the room, took the cigar out of his hand, stubbed it out on the polished mahogany desk then kissed him. Iggy stood, steady but utterly powerless as she pulled her sweater over her head. She clambered up on his desk and whispered, her voice heavy with desire, 'You don't own me.' Knowing as she said it, in some part of her, that it wasn't true.

25

THE CONVENT was in a large old house in the Upper West Side. It was clean and warm and the nuns were friendly and many of them were quite young. The building itself was jolly, for a religious institution, with fancy wallpaper as a backdrop for all the religious statues. The girls slept in dormitories, with a tall locker each where they could hang a small number of clothes. There was a curfew of ten p.m., but apart from that, and a short morning mass at eight a.m., the girls could come and go as they pleased. Rose was put to work cleaning and cooking in the convent itself. For the first few weeks, it was decided, the nuns would get the measure of what her capabilities were before they tried to get her a job out in 'the real world'. Tom had told the mother superior, Sister Augustine, that Rose was escaping 'an unnamed abuse' at the hands of her parents, back home in Ireland. The nun did not prod for more information. These things were best left unspoken. Propriety would be recovered, in time, through prayer, good food, hard work and kindness. Sister Augustine put Rose in a small dormitory with two other Irish girls: Eileen from Cork and Una from Connemara. Eileen was twenty-three, and at secretarial school. She had been unable to find either a husband or a job in Ireland so she had been packed off here to New York to live with an ancient aunt who had died while she was en route by boat. The nuns had offered to sponsor her secretarial training and she would pay them back after she started working. Una was still recovering after giving up a baby for adoption at another convent, where she had been so brutally treated that kindly Sister Augustine had taken her in.

Her room-mates were good fun and she liked them but Rose was not in the humour for making friends.

'So, what brought you to New York?'

It was the first question they asked, but Rose felt too foolish to say why she was here, so she smiled and said, 'A new start, you know?' She felt lost. Everyone here knew where they were going. Even poor Una had dreams of training in a hair salon as soon as she felt well enough to re-enter the world. Rose had no plans. Her plan had been to find Patrick and live happily ever after. It had failed. Now what? There was nothing. Just a void. So, she just kept her head down and did as the nuns told her. Rose was happy for them to tell her what to do because she felt broken. Lost. She had no spirit left in her. Sister Augustine had a soft spot for the beautiful girl who looked so much like the film star. Grace Kelly was a good Catholic and, even if this young girl did not seem particularly devout, she looked the part at least, even though she did not feel Rose belonged in New York. Rose decided to simply sleepwalk through her chores and try her very best to forget about Patrick Murphy until something else presented itself. Although she did not have much confidence that anything would. Without Patrick, her life was over.

A few days after her arrival at the convent, Rose went back to her room after her morning chores were finished to find Una and Eileen plotting a night out.

'They won't be on stage until nine, and sure we have to be back here by ten. It'll take us an hour to get home from Yonkers. We can't do it!'

'How about if we get a taxi?'

'That takes nearly as long,' Una complained.

'You're "in" with Sister Augustine, Rose. Ask her for a special dispensation.'

'What for?'

'Urgh – you are so not with-it, Rose,' said Eileen, thrusting a leaflet into her hand. 'The Dolly Butler Band are playing the Emerald in Yonkers on Saturday. They are the biggest thing back home in Cork – I have to be there...'

But Rose wasn't listening. She was staring down at the leaflet as if she had just seen a ghost. On the left-hand corner of the page, in the black-and-white picture of smiling Dolly sitting in the middle in front of her all-male seven-piece band in their smart sweaters, was a small picture of Patrick. His hair was different, set into a quiff like Elvis, but it could not be anyone but him. Next to it the caption said, 'Supported by the Emerald's popular resident singer, Patrick Murphy.'

Rose was beside herself and it took every inch of energy she had to maintain her composure. Although she was fit to explode with excitement, she didn't want to share her personal business with these strangers.

'What is a resident singer?' she asked, keeping her voice as light as she could.

Una snatched the leaflet off her.

'Patrick Murphy – he's a dish, all right. Resident singer means he is there all the time.'

'You mean during the day as well?' Rose said.

Una looked at her sideways; their new room-mate was a strange fish.

'Actually, I think he probably is. Doesn't Patrick work behind the bar there sometimes, Eileen?'

'Never mind that – Rose, will you clear Saturday curfew with Sister Augustine?'

'I'll do it now,' Rose said, flying from the room, grabbing her purse and jacket as she left.

She didn't go and see Sister Augustine. She ran straight out the door and grabbed a taxi for the Emerald in Yonkers.

The place was all locked up, and she banged and banged and banged on the door until, finally, a man came and answered it.

'I need to see Patrick Murphy,' she said.

'Who are you?' Gerry asked. A mad fan? Lucky Patrick. She was a looker. Anyway, he couldn't let her in. Iggy and Sheila were in conference with Patrick, and Gerry had been put under strict instructions to keep everyone out of their way for the afternoon.

'I'm a friend from home. I need to see him urgently.'

That was another poster of Patrick up outside the door. It was him! It was really him! And now he was a big singer, and she had found him, and everything would be as it should be! Rose could hardly believe this was happening.

'Afraid he's not here. Have you tried him at home?'

Gerry was sure Ava would be back at their apartment. Great girl, Ava. Patrick was one lucky guy. She would entertain this girl for Patrick. No better woman.

'I left his address in my other purse,' she lied, scrabbling for a scrap of paper and a pen in her bag. 'Could you give it to me again?'

Gerry jotted down Patrick's apartment details and Rose hopped straight back in another taxi into town. All these taxis, all this money. It didn't matter a damn any more.

Soon they would be together and he would hold her in his arms and everything would be all right again.

26

PATRICK WAS on a high when he got home from the Emerald that evening. He had learned so much about himself as a performer during the afternoon. Those few hours in the company of Sheila had been more productive than all the weeks he had been singing on stage and, indeed, the twenty-five years he had been singing before that, thinking he knew what it was all about. He knew nothing. But he didn't mind one bit because Sheila was going to show him how to do it right. Sheila was going to make him a star. It was late, but there was still time to take Ava out for that spaghetti dinner. She would be angry with him for staying away for so long, but once he started to tell her about the day he had had, and all the wonderful things that were ahead for him, and, of course, them, she would certainly forgive him.

As soon as he got in, Patrick ran straight into the bathroom and put the shower on. Back out in the hall he started to strip off his clothes so that by the time he was in the kitchen, his shirt was on the floor behind him, and he was already pulling his vest over his head, saying, 'I know, I know I'm late, Ava, but I've got so much news. You would not believe the day I've had but I can just tell you that everything is going to start happening for us now. All the dreams we ever had are about to come true…'

He had unbuckled his belt and was scrunching his vest up into a ball for the laundry basket when he walked into the kitchen and saw her. It took everything in his power to stop himself from letting out a yelp of shock and shouting out her name. For a second, although it felt like an hour, Patrick just stood there, unable to move. The sun-kissed-blonde hair, the piercing blue eyes looking across at him, pleading. Rose. From Foxford. Sitting in his kitchen, talking with Ava. Could this really be happening? It was like he was in some kind of a weird nightmare. And yet, she *was* here. The questions how and why could barely form themselves out of the intrusion of her just being here. Even so, Patrick could feel his body begging him to go across the room and embrace her. He kept his arms firmly by his side and tried to hold his face as naturally as possible.

'Darling,' Ava said, smiling at first, and then laughing at the ridiculousness of her husband, accidentally stripping in front of another woman. He would be so embarrassed, especially when he saw it was somebody from home.

Ava and Rose had become great friends in just a few hours. At first, Ava had been taken aback by this breathtakingly beautiful young woman arriving at her door saying that she knew her husband. Her nervous manner had made Ava feel uncomfortable. However, she was only in Rose's company for a few moments when she realized there was nothing for her to fear. Rose had such a delicate, open face and her manner was so gentle and sweet, so lady-like, that Ava instantly took to her.

Rose had not known Patrick very well, she assured Ava. She had led such a sheltered life – it was more that Patrick's name was known to her as a young man from her village who had gone to New York.

'I just wanted to meet someone from home. Not having any family here. I am staying in a convent.'

Rose was keen to wait until Patrick got back from work. Ava explained she was in the middle of some chores and asked if she would like to help her sort through some clothes for a charity package. It was so nice to have another woman to talk to. These days, Ava saw very little of Myrtle, who had a job and spent her evenings and weekends in the Emerald. Ava got the feeling that Myrtle was annoyed that her plain friend had got married before she did. There was not a hint of that kind of nastiness from Rose. She was a real lady. All charm and smiles as she helped Ava pick out the clothes to keep until after her pregnancy. She was particularly taken with Ava's Sybil Connolly suit and discussed the Foxford Woollen Mills tweed with her at great length. She reassured Ava that she would fit back into the suit after her pregnancy, and helped her pick out other clothes that would be suitable to send back to Ireland.

'How do you send them?' Rose asked.

'I don't know,' she said. 'My mother organizes it.'

As soon as she said it, Ava realised she sounded rather pathetic, especially to this brave young woman who had travelled across the world to rescue a new life. Ava determined, in that moment, that she would write to her mother and ask advice about where to send the package. An olive branch. Life was too short.

After they had sorted out the clothes and discussed Ava's plans for the nursery and the baby, the young women prepared supper together and waited for Patrick to come home. And here he was. Although he looked somewhat discombobulated.

'Of course, you know Rose?'

'Oh yes. Hello,' he managed to say.

Patrick could not have been more thrown. Immediately, he checked Ava's face for signs of anger or upset. How much had Rose told her about them? Ava looked quite happy so it couldn't have been much. More importantly, what the hell was Rose doing here?

Ava was disappointed that he seemed unimpressed to the point of being rude. Really, he was so caught up with work all the time, he could think of nothing else.

'Rose has come to stay with us for a while...'

'Good – erm...'

Ava was so embarrassed by her husband's behaviour she couldn't even look at Rose. Sometimes she wondered if she would not have been better off marrying a gentleman, someone with proper manners. Dermot flashed into her head and Ava quickly reminded herself that you could teach a man good manners but passion was something that could not be learned.

'You remember Rose? Of course you do!' Ava kept her voice sunny.

'Yes' was all he could manage.

Throughout the meal Patrick's strange, dark mood continued. Ava was secretly fuming, trying to draw conversation out of him on the subject of his new manager and work but with little success. Ava was mortified. She liked Rose and Patrick was making things positively uncomfortable. He might not have known her well, but Rose was the first person who knew Patrick from Ireland that she had met, including his family.

After they had eaten supper, Ava decided to go across to the ice cream parlour to get some dessert. Perhaps if Patrick was left alone with Rose for a few moments, he might find his manners!

As soon as Ava was gone, Patrick turned on Rose.

'What the hell are you doing here?'

Rose immediately burst into tears. This was not how she had imagined their reunion would be. She had come all the way across the world, only to find that the love of her life had married somebody else. That was bad enough, but it might almost have been accepted for the disastrous mishap that it was. In the hours that had passed since she got this terrible news, as she was nodding to his wife, talking about charity clothes and being as brilliant an actress as she could be, covering her horror with charm and polite chitchat, Rose had thought of every possible scenario to justify his betraying her. He must have been lonely and believed that she didn't love him any more. But when his first words to her were so cruel and cold, Rose could not bear it. It simply wasn't possible that she had come all this way for nothing. It wasn't possible that Patrick did not love her any more. It was unthinkable.

'I came to find you.'

Patrick had suspected that to be the case but, even so, he was frightened. He didn't even ask how she had got there or whether her parents knew where she was. All he could think of, right now, was that Ava could not find out.

'Well, now you have found me. You can't stay here. It's out of the question. Ava does not know that we were sweethearts…'

'I haven't told her.'

'Good.' He stopped short of saying thank you.

'It was my parents, Patrick. My father tricked me, he tricked both of us. I didn't get your letters, I found them in my father's desk and as soon as I found them I came straight away. I thought you didn't love me any more...'

'I don't love you any more.'

Rose took a sharp intake of breath. It was as if she had been stabbed. She looked at his face. He had to love her. He must be lying. For a terrible moment she imagined that perhaps she was just believing that to save herself the pain of having chased across the world on a whim for a man she thought loved her. If he didn't love her then she was the greatest fool that ever lived. If he didn't love her, it was so much more than the humiliation and the hurt. Patrick was everything to her. If Patrick didn't love her everything would be gone. Life would not be worth living.

'I'm with Ava now. We're married.'

Patrick was as white as a sheet and his gaze was flitting around the room.

He was lying. Rose felt a thin veil of relief.

'Say it again,' she said. 'Look me in the eye and tell me again that you don't love me.'

He looked at her – pitiful, pleading.

'I don't need to say it again. I love Ava. I married Ava...'

If he stayed hard and tough Rose would go away. He wanted her to go away, although now that she was here, sitting in front of him, in the flesh, his beautiful, delicate Rose, close enough to him to reach out and touch her hair and feel the soft lips at the end of his thumb, Patrick was no longer sure of anything.

'You have to leave,' he said. 'You must see how impossible this is.'

He had thought he would never see her again. He had,

perhaps, hoped that would be the case. Her father had sent him to America to keep them away from each other. He understood that now. In some small part of himself, Patrick feared that perhaps that had been the case all along. Perhaps, in some hidden part of himself, he had traded his love of Rose for the opportunity to come to America. Now, when everything was working out so well, his past had turned up to punish him.

Ava opened the door, abruptly, and they both started slightly.

'How have you two been getting along?'

Ava stood looking puzzled at them both until Rose said, 'Just fine.'

Patrick smiled, his best, most convincing stage smile. This was a nightmare, but if he didn't play along, he feared Rose would tell Ava everything. Aside from the fact that he had been in love with Rose, Patrick knew that the way in which he had abandoned her might upset kind-hearted Ava more. Even if he had thought to tell her the truth, the moment he saw Rose in their house, the lie had begun and now he had no choice but to follow it through.

'Although,' Rose added, 'I do not want to be a burden on you.'

'Why, there is no burden at all,' said Ava. 'Is there, Patrick?'

'No,' he said. Everything out of his mouth now was a lie. Curse Rose. What was she playing at? Where would this end?

'No, thank you, I'll stay at the convent, but if I could just get a job,' Rose said, 'something small, anywhere. I suppose, in a way, I'm being selfish.' She added, 'I have not seen anything since I got here and I would just love to work somewhere that I might see a bit of the New York life I've heard so much about.'

Rose knew, in some part of herself, that she was being cruel, manipulating Ava's good nature in this way. She was, truly, a lovely woman. It was not her fault that Patrick did not love her, could never love Ava, the way he loved her. This was something Ava had got caught up in. Something she could never understand. Rose felt bad for her. Worse, she felt bad lying and wheedling to get her own way. But what choice did she have? Patrick was, after all, the love of her life. After talking with Ava it was clear that she had not stolen him from her. Rose was confident that Ava had not even known she existed. That, in itself, gave Rose some comfort. The fact that Patrick had lied to Ava, and never explained to her about their love, their engagement, was testament that she must still mean something to him. The fact that Ava was pregnant made it even worse. But Rose knew that her love was pure and true. Great passion meant great sacrifices. And the passion Rose shared with Patrick was not the ordinary love of everyday life. It was something so much bigger than marriage. They were soulmates. Nothing could part them. Not her parents, not the great Atlantic Ocean, not even marriage to another woman – however nice she was. They were meant to be together. And even if Patrick did not have the courage to face that right now, in time he would.

'I've got an idea,' Ava said, taking up her guest's cue. 'Patrick, why don't you take Rose into work with you tomorrow? You can collect her from the convent, I'll call Gerry now. I'm sure he'll be able to find some small job for her.'

'I don't want to be any trouble,' Rose said.

'It's no trouble at all, is it, Patrick?' Ava said, looking at him firmly.

He really was being insufferably childish. Ava could not

imagine why he was behaving so badly, but while she was irritated by his taciturn manners, she was, at least, comforted by the fact that he obviously did not have any particular ghrá for this beautiful girl from back home.

27

'AGAIN!'

Patrick had sung 'It's Only Make Believe' half a dozen times, and he still could not get it right.

Sheila had decided that, like Conway Twitty who had made the song a hit, Patrick's voice was best suited to contemporary ballads. His being Irish, he had a country twang. However, she was anxious to get away from the Irish ballads and pure country – she would never get a hit out of that. 'It's Only Make Believe' was, she felt, the perfect song for him. But it was also Conway Twitty's song, and Patrick was performing just like a poor version of somebody else today. No matter what she gave him to sing, he seemed to turn it into a dirge. His voice was as strong as ever but his eyes were completely dead. There was no life in him, no passion. The voice was passable, but he was an unconvincing performer. Sheila was starting to get annoyed. She didn't need a copycat, she needed an original star, but Patrick was letting them both down with these lacklustre performances.

As his voice reached for the crescendo, Sheila waved her
cigarette at him.

'Stop, Patrick. You sound awful. I don't know what's
wrong with you today...'

'I'm sorry, Sheila.'

At least he knew something was wrong himself.

'Would anyone like some coffee? It's just finished brewing.'

It was that irritating Irish girl again. She was a kid from
Patrick's hometown. Some kind of a runaway. Patrick and
the girl had come in with his wife, a plain-looking woman
who, although friendly enough, kept insisting that her father
was some Irish big shot who knew Iggy. That irritated Sheila
far more than it impressed her, but she took on their sad case
anyway. For no other reason than she thought her pretty face
about the place might put a bit of life into Patrick. Having her
young star married with a child on the way was an unnatural
state of affairs for an aspiring pop singer. Girls and drugs and
parties were what made great rock and roll singers. Not nagging wives and weeping children. However, it was clear that
this girl was madly in love with him. Every time Sheila turned
around she was there offering coffee or lazily wiping down
a booth, while gazing up at him with a sometimes frightening intensity. Frankly, the girl seemed a bit nuts. Sheila had
hoped she might provide an adoring audience. However, it
seemed more likely that the simpering admiration was putting Patrick off his singing rather than adding to it. She had
thought she should probably get rid of her, but at the same
time it was important that Patrick learned how to sing the
same, whatever else is going on in his life. The kid needed
to man up and not let his life being run by a bossy wife or
the lovelorn attention of a pretty girl. He had to get used to
singing to crazy fans if he was going to be a star. Although

by his performance today, that was seeming less likely than ever.

Sheila really needed Patrick to become a star.

In the past couple of weeks she had begun to feel unnerved by her situation. Here she was, again, managing a club and sleeping with her boss. Iggy wasn't married, although he was so distant and secretive he could just as well be and nobody would ever know it. He was, when he was around, an attentive and caring lover. He gave her small gifts, although they were never insulting (underwear) or extravagant (jewellery she would never wear), as many of Dan's gifts had been. He was careful in his manner too, and Sheila understood his reticence as respect. There were certainly no insistent professions of love as there had been from Dan and she was grateful for that. Sheila hated being lied to more than anything else, but this meant that she had a tendency to believe men when they told her they loved her; the alternative – that they were lying to please her – being too dreadful to contemplate. Sheila had believed Dan was in love with her, and that silly belief had prolonged the affair, making it more than it should ever have been. Now, here she was in the same situation again. Iggy was as straightforward and honest a person as herself; she trusted that. However, he was pathologically secretive, and that was, in itself, a kind of lying. Nobody knew where Iggy would be from week to week. She knew that was how he ran his business and how he kept control of his empire, but nonetheless, Sheila felt uncomfortable always living on the edge of his life. Iggy himself admitted that it was a 'strange way to live', but he could see nothing wrong with it. Indeed, Sheila had always lived life on her own unconventional terms. However, they were her terms as part of her life. Living on the edge of somebody else's was a completely different matter. From day to day, Sheila did not know where her lover was or when he would be back in New York again. She was being sucked into his footloose, routineless way of living and she didn't like it. This uncertainty had led her to stay with her aunt and uncle in Riverdale for the time being. They did not ask about her comings and goings. Auntie made up cold plates for her supper and left them in the Frigidaire for whenever she might be around. They did not know she had a lover, and the nights that she spent in hotels with Iggy they put down to late working hours. They were so grateful for the time that they had with her that, although every week Sheila intended to leave and find her own apartment again, somehow she returned to the comfort of sharing some semblance of a domestic life – standing at the sink washing out somebody else's cup, listening to the radio with her uncle – however fleeting it might turn out to be.

In addition to that, she did not want to tie herself down financially to rental lease when she had no idea how long she would be around. She knew, already, that history was repeating itself and that she did not intend to stay managing the Emerald and being Iggy Morrow's mistress indefinitely. As soon as Patrick's career was up and running and he had a recording contract she would be able to leave and start expanding her portfolio. However, she had to find him a hit record first, and songwriters weren't cheap. She didn't want to have to charm that money out of Iggy; not, indeed, that charming anything out of Iggy was possible, but if she didn't come up with something soon, her dreams would start to disintegrate again. And Sheila could feel she was close, so close to success now, she wasn't going to let it go again.

'Let's wrap it up for the day, Patrick,' she said, ignoring Rose. Then, more to punish him than anything else, added,

'I'm sure Patrick could use a coffee, sweetheart. You guys go ahead. If Gerry needs me, I'm in the office.'

Sheila went into the office then nearly jumped out of her skin when Iggy suddenly appeared standing next to the filing cabinet as she shut the door.

'Christ! What the hell are you doing in here?!'

The curse came out before she even knew what she was saying. Iggy laughed. He loved when this happened. It was the closest he came to having fun in his job. Once people had been working for him for a while they got used to his sudden appearances, and that took the amusement out of it.

'This is not funny,' she said. 'I could have had a heart attack.'

'Well, you didn't,' he said, putting his arms around her waist and pulling her into him, 'although your heart is beating kind of fast. Just let me check in here ...' He placed his hand gently on her breast.

Sheila's eyes fluttered closed, and she leaned back, unable to help herself. No matter what time of the day or night he suddenly appeared like this, she always wanted him.

She made herself pull away.

'I'm busy. If you can turn up like this to check up on me, you can't expect me to drop my pants every time you come into the room.'

Iggy flinched. He hated when she referred to work and 'them' in the same sentence. It made what they had seem cheap. And it wasn't cheap. Not to him. Iggy had never been in this situation before. Sleeping with somebody that worked for him. He made a point of never doing it. Sheila was an exception. She had been an exception since that first night, he knew that now. Although he did not like to admit it, Iggy was in love. All the signs were there. When they were alone in

a room together all he could think about was making love to
her. Everything she said, even the banal, everyday business of
their work together, was fascinating or amusing just because
it was Sheila saying it. When she cursed him, he laughed.
When she berated or belittled him, he couldn't feel angry.
Instead, it felt like a knife in his chest. She weakened him,
and in her company sometimes he felt powerless. At the same
time, however hard she appeared, some nights after they had
made love, when she could be persuaded to spend the night
with him in his hotel, he would watch her sleeping and his
breath would catch at how delicate and vulnerable and warm
she was. In life, Sheila was feisty, a livewire. In her sleep, and
in some of the quieter, gentle moments in their lovemaking,
Iggy sensed a tenderness, a sensitivity he found too compel-
ling to name. Sheila was, in her lithe figure and her hidden
spirit, he believed, like a child-woman. She was tough and it
was no game, he knew she was no pushover, he could not pull
the wool over her eyes in business or in their private life, and
nor would he attempt to. However, on some level he knew
that she needed looking after. For the first time in his life,
Iggy felt that was something he wanted to do. But he mis-
trusted that instinct and pushed it to one side. Partly because
he knew she would never concede, and partly because the
idea of loving someone that much, being tied to somebody
else's life, somebody else's needs, was beyond him.

While Iggy counted the days until he would see Sheila again,
he was grateful for the incessant travelling because it enabled
him to keep control over himself. If he gave in to his feelings,
he would have spent every day and every night in her company and let his great empire crumble to the ground. The fact
that he could never let that happen was, he believed, his saving
grace. To allow such romantic instincts would be dangerous,

particularly with a woman like Sheila, so independent, so cool, so reserved, so very much like himself. He knew what level of detachment he was capable of and he believed she was capable of the same. However, when he was with her, he found he was unable to help himself from wanting more. Not more sex and more amusement, but more of the thing he could never admit to wanting: the intimacy of love.

'I thought we might eat in the city tonight?'

Sheila was furious. Furious at him for creeping up on her like that, furious at herself for her impulsive, shocked reaction which made her seem foolish, but mostly furious with the irrational impulse she was now feeling, to simply grab Iggy by the collar, kiss him, then make love to him in the office in the middle of a working day.

'Well – I can't tonight,' she said coolly. 'I'm busy.'

She could tell by the look on his face that he didn't believe her. She had half a mind to lie and tell him she was seeing another man. He would believe that. Sheila knew she had that much power over him at least.

'I promised to have dinner with my aunt and uncle.'

For the first time in her life, Sheila was aware of using her family as a kind of trophy. Iggy had no family. He had told her about his life in the orphanage. She had never confided in him about her parents and brother. How could she? She had never spoken about anyone. And yet, here she was, triumphantly proclaiming what little family she did have. What was this impulse to be cruel that he brought out in her? We are both orphans, but at least I have some family.

'Why don't we bring them with us? I would love to meet them.'

As soon as he had said the words, Iggy knew that he had gone too far.

Sheila blushed and coughed. She seemed as awkward as it was possible for a person of her cool demeanour to be. Her smile was apologetic, pained.

'I don't think that's such a good idea. Do you?' she said.

At once, it seemed like a dreadful, hurtful thing to say to him. At the same time, she did not see what else she could possibly say. The idea of her lover meeting her family, her precious aunt and uncle, was anathema to her. He must have known, as much as he seemed to know her at all, that she was not the marrying kind. She had never brought anyone home to meet them before, and to do so would be making a statement so broad, so sweeping, she could not possibly justify it.

Iggy felt the knock-back as a kick of rejection.

'I suppose not,' he said. He was back on the sports pitch of the orphanage, in the sidelines of the football game, nursing a bloody leg, waiting for the jeering in the changing rooms. He left there promising himself he would never be slapped around again. And yet here he was, having his heart and his ego bruised by this woman. Letting her do it because, underneath it all, he believed she was as sweet as he was.

As he turned his back on her, pretending to tackle the papers on his desk, he hoped it was true.

'How is Patrick going along?' he asked without looking at her.

'To be honest,' she said, 'I think he would be better if he was working with some new material.'

'Original material?' Iggy said, his eyes resolutely on his paperwork.

'Yes,' she said. 'He's got real potential. I'd love to try and get a recording contract.'

I bet you would, thought Iggy. Then the pair of you would

fly out of here in five minutes. He resolved to get proper contracts drawn up on his next trip to Boston to see his lawyers.

'Well,' he said, ready to look up at her now, 'when the audience out there get sick of hearing every song in the hit parade, here and in Ireland, come back and have a talk with me then.'

He was angry and she had bruised his ego, Sheila knew that. All the same, she was annoyed that he rejected her suggestion so quickly, and annoyed with herself for not being more coy and manipulative in her timing.

Iggy began fiddling around with his paperwork again and as Sheila left, saying, 'I'll see you later,' he barely grunted a reply, and did not look up from his desk, although he did hear her mutter, 'If you're still here...' She closed the door rather sharply behind her.

Heading back into the ballroom, Sheila paused at the door for a cigarette. As she was lighting it her attention was caught by a heated argument that appeared to be happening at the side of the stage. It was Patrick and his simpering fan. Fascinated and not wishing to be seen, she lowered her cigarette and eavesdropped.

'You said you loved me!' the girl shouted at him.

'Shhh – somebody will hear us!'

Too late, somebody already has, thought Sheila to herself, smiling.

She stood stock-still, so she wouldn't get caught in her hiding place.

'I don't care who hears me, Patrick. I love you and I know you love me! We can make it work.'

Silly girl, thought Sheila. Still, the kid was a dark horse after all. She didn't know he had it in him. Although he was handling it very poorly. He seemed very agitated. The colour in his cheeks rising, his hands opening and closing as if hoping to release his anger.

'How many times do I have to tell you, I am married to Ava now. We have a child on the way. Things have changed. This is going nowhere.'

'I know it's a terrible situation, Patrick. You know your marriage was a mistake. At least if you can admit it we can move on. Nothing is impossible. We can work it all out—'

'There is no "we"! You have to stop talking like this. It's over. Please, Rose, stop acting crazy!'

The girl was enraged now. 'What about this?' she screamed at him. She waved a sheet of paper in his face, and then started to read from it.

'"There's nothing in this world that makes me feel the way I feel—"'

'Stop it! Stop it, I'm telling you…'

'"When I'm with you because I know this love I have is real…"'

He reached out to grab the page from her. Tears were streaming down the girl's face. This is all too dramatic, thought Sheila. Two children having a lovers' tiff. It all seemed rather overblown and silly to her. In fact, she began to wish it would end, so she could come out of her hiding place and light her cigarette.

'I suppose none of this means anything to you, I suppose I never meant anything to you…' Then she scrunched up the piece of paper and threw it dramatically aside. 'Perhaps it was all lies, Patrick. Maybe it was always just your plan to get to America. Maybe you just tricked my father into giving you money and were delighted to get away from me? Is that how it is?'

Patrick closed his eyes in frustration, seeming to gather himself for a few seconds before opening them again. And when he did, from her hiding place it seemed to Sheila that he was looking straight at her, although, in fact, he was looking straight through her. Back into a past when it was just the two of them, kissing, in a field.

'You know that's not true, Rose. You know how much you meant to me.'

In the young singer's eyes Sheila saw a passionate pleading look. If only he could put on that look when he's singing, she thought.

'Then there *is* hope for us, Patrick.'

Sheila raised her eyes to heaven. If this nonsense didn't come to an end soon she have to go out and stop it herself.

'No, Rose,' he said again, storming off with the crazy pretty girl in close pursuit.

Sheila came out from behind the curtain, shaking her head in a mixture of amusement and frustration at what she had just seen. Patrick really was a hopeless case. For such a good-looking, talented and ambitious kid, he was still such an ingénu. If he was going to sleep round on his wife, well, he needed to learn to lie a bit better than he was doing. And not just to his wife, but his lover too.

She lit her cigarette and walked across to where they had been standing to pick up the piece of trash that Rose had thoughtlessly thrown on the floor. She looked around quickly before opening the crumpled page, to amuse herself by reading the love letter that seemed to have caused all this trouble.

Immediately, she saw that it was not a love letter, but a handwritten poem. Her eyes quickly scanned the words.

It was a love song.

Sheila smiled, carefully folded the paper and put it in her pocket.

At last, she had struck gold.

28

A COUPLE OF days after Rose came into their lives, Ava had received a reply from her mother in the post. It was a mass card, presumably to pray for the recovery of her sullied soul, getting pregnant before marriage etc. However, Ava was nonetheless glad to get the peace offering. In the past week Ava had become aware that there was a life growing inside her. She was only just beginning to show, but she had begun to feel that she was pregnant, and not simply fat. The awareness that she would be a mother soon made her conscious of her own mother's love for her, and Ava felt softer towards her. And she began to understand that Nessa's anger had been based only on the worry, fear and betrayal she would no doubt someday feel as a parent.

The letter contained a formal introduction to an Irish priest in Manhattan with whom Nessa had volunteered her to do some charitable work. Her own priest had told her that Father Moran, who worked in Hell's Kitchen, was looking for a respectable woman to help coordinate a 'Parcels to Ireland' programme. Nessa had suggested Ava as she had some volunteering experience in their own Yonkers parish. Also, she was her 'father's daughter' when it came to such things. Reading between the lines, Ava felt the note itself was acknowledgement that she was now living an independent life. If Nessa did not wholly delight in her marriage, she was, perhaps, coming to accept it. The note was also a not very subtle assurance that the continuance of Ava's good Catholic habits would help bridge any gaps in her mother's approval.

The church was in the heart of Hell's Kitchen. The last time Ava had been to this part of town was with Dermot, the night he had proposed. The night she had first met Patrick. She brushed the thought aside as she pulled the car up and parked it on the sidewalk at the bottom of the church steps, so that she would not have far to carry her heavy bags of clothes. She felt curiously independent and brave coming to this part of town on her own. However, the experience of helping Patrick's friend Rose get on her feet with a job in the Emerald had made Ava see that, like her father, her mission in life was to make herself useful to other people. Ava had taken it upon herself to contact Gerry at the club and ask if he could get Rose a job. He had said they were always in need of reliable Irish girls and had passed the message on to his new boss, and Patrick's new manager, Sheila, who had given Rose a few hours cleaning during the day, and occasional work covering the cloakrooms. The next visit she made was to Sister Augustine to see if Rose could be allowed to come home late on certain evenings, if her new job required it. The nun was very accommodating, and impressed with the pragmatic, pregnant young woman, especially when she learned she was Tom Brogan's daughter. When she told Ava that it was her father who had brought Rose to the convent in the first place, Ava was taken aback. Had he not known that Rose was a friend of Patrick's? The nun also explained, on the quiet, that it had been some 'awful' experience with her father that had sent the girl chasing halfway across the world to escape them. Ava could not imagine what that terrible thing would be, but the information just made her feel even more warmly towards the young woman. It made Ava feel even more fortunate to be in the position she was in. She was married to a good man with a baby on the way. Although their life was modest, they loved each other. Despite Patrick's great aspirations for fame, Ava did not feel she needed much more than they already had, except perhaps more of her husband's time. Although, she determined, if she were to spend her own time more usefully, doing good deeds, she might miss his company less. One had to make sacrifices in life and getting pregnant out of wedlock had been a dreadful sin. So, it seemed only right that Ava should make amends by helping people who were less fortunate than herself. Helping Rose had given her a small start and today, volunteering for the church, could be the beginning of a new, positive phase in her life.

The church was quiet for a Saturday, with a dozen or so people occupying the pew opposite the confessionals. Ava was irritated with herself for not having remembered Saturday-morning confessions would probably be underway at this time. She really had been very remiss in her religion of late. The feeling of sadness flooded over her briefly as she thought how far she had fallen from her faith in the past few months. However, she reminded herself she was here now to make amends to God, her church, her parents and herself.

She wondered if Patrick felt the same way. She had noticed
him moving away from her in the bed lately. She was hurt,
but she could understand it. Her body had changed and no
man would want to make love to a woman knowing there
was a child inside them. She still had the same urges surg-
ing through her body despite the fact that she was pregnant.
If anything, they were stronger than ever. That, Ava now
believed, was God's gentle way of punishing her for not keeping a check on her passions. So, she didn't bother Patrick, had
a cold shower every morning and had now resolved to be the
best person she could possibly be.

Knowing that Father Moran would be in a hurry, Ava left
her two heavy bags at the door and hurried up to the sacristy
to catch him before confessions began.

Dermot was having a wretched morning. First of all, he had
been unable to find a clean shirt. His ironing service had not
delivered the day before, so he had been forced to wear yesterday's crumpled and slightly stained one. This was just one
of many small domestic disasters that he had been having of
late. Work had been busy and he had not had time to do all
the chores that, if he were a proper man, he would have a wife
doing for him. Dermot did not mind doing his own laundry
and, as a matter of fact, he was rather a good cook. However,
at the age of thirty, he felt the failure of his bachelor status
more sharply now than ever before. Before he met Ava, Dermot had been resigned, if not entirely satisfied, to being on his
own. There had been a rhythm about keeping the apartment
tidy, a routine in putting the trash out, going to the grocery
store, leaving money out for the cleaning woman. However,
the very moment he and Ava got engaged, with the promise of

marriage, Dermot allowed his entire domestic routine to fall apart. No woman wants to be married to a fuss-budget of a man. A decent woman will want a man she can take in hand. So instinctively Dermot began to let his domestic life go to pot. It seemed the right thing to do. Even though the engagement went on for only a matter of weeks, he had been unable to recover his meticulous, organized home life. Ava had been the love of his life. Losing her had meant losing everything. If his life went back to the way he was before he met her, to the man he was before he met her, surely that would make the loss even greater because it would be as though she had never happened.

Better to have loved and lost – and all that.

In his scruffy shirt Dermot had to go down to Hell's Kitchen on what he had been led to believe was a straightforward document-signing mission. When he got there he found that Joe Higgins had arranged a meeting with one of the Balducci brothers. Some business about some woman who had slept with somebody's husband. Dermot had been dragged in to 'mediate' the situation, which was gangster code for 'if we do something really terrible can you get us off?'

Dermot had spent his morning listening and nodding sagely as some of New York's most terrifying gangsters set before him convoluted scenarios of premeditated violence: 'If a guy were to… say… lose his footing and accidentally fall into a large hole…' 'If a guy were to accidentally shoot himself in the knee – and say there was another guy in the car with him when it happened…', and trying to find a way of responding that would not result in him playing centre stage in one such scenario.

All of this in yesterday's shirt.

By the time he got out of there, Dermot was so stressed

there was no way he could get into his car and drive. He walked around the block a couple of times, but he was more nervous of running into one of his clients, a highly likely scenario in this end of town, so he decided to pop into the church. He was not a good practising Catholic: Christmas, weddings, keeping his mother happy was about the strength of it. But occasionally, when he was passing, he popped into this church. It was a peaceful place to come during a crazy day and he always managed to clear his head when he came here.

Dermot sat on the end of a pew near the back of the church then closed his eyes and let himself sink into the incense-scented silence. Peace. At last.

When he opened his eyes, however, he got such a fright that he nearly jumped out of his skin.

Something more terrifying than any gangster scenario that he could possibly imagine.

It was Ava. She was walking directly towards him.

Dermot froze. He had not seen Ava since that night she ditched him. He knew she had married that singer, after becoming 'disgracefully' pregnant, as his mother described. Dermot had been beyond hurt. He knew he had to deal with it and, being part of the same Irish community, would certainly have to face her again one day in the future. But not today. He was not ready. He was not prepared. He was wearing yesterday's shirt.

She had not noticed him so he would have to act quickly. Dermot leapt to his feet and ran to the nearest hiding place. The confessional box.

Father Moran said goodbye to the lovely young woman, who turned out to be Tom Brogan's daughter. She really was a charming thing. The ladies that worked in his parish were a very tight-knit, older gang and she would be a real addition. A breath of fresh air. There was something, however, troubling him about their meeting, which he could not quite put his finger on. He was musing on that as he sat down in the box. First penitent in would be Bridie Flaherty. She was always first on a Saturday. Bridie would have been here since nine, doing the stations and firing out a few decades of the rosary. With a bit of luck she might have murdered her husband this week to make up for the years of sinless Saturdays she had made him endure. He engaged in his preparations, a good scratch followed by a pre-confession hearty cough and nose-blowing ritual. Bridie always gave him a few seconds before she came in.

'Bless me, Father . . .' said a low man's voice.

'Jesus Christ!'

The Irish priest made a habit of never swearing, unless he was drunk. Certainly never in a place of such holiness as a confessional.

'You are not supposed to be in here,' he boomed. 'Get out and wait your turn!'

Bridie heard him and was delighted. She, along with the other penitents, had been horrified to see the young man leaping into the confessional. They assumed he was, at least, a murderer looking for urgent penance.

Dermot was mortified but, at the same time, he wasn't going out there to face Ava. Especially not under this new, embarrassing circumstance.

'. . . for I have sinned.'

'You most certainly have . . . now get—' But Dermot was going nowhere.

'It has been ten years since my last confession.'

'Humpf,' Father Moran said. 'Clearly.'

Now that he had started, the priest had no choice but to let him continue. Anyway, he consoled himself, a break from Bridie couldn't be a bad thing. Men of his age in suits in this area often brought in great confessions. Sex and drugs and the odd maiming – occasionally a murder. No priest really liked to hear of terrible crimes against God and man happening on one's doorstep but at least, Father Moran thought, it gave one a sense of purpose. The devout Bridie Flahertys of this world were two a penny but a good gangster could really turn a Saturday morning confession around.

Unfortunately, this was not one of those men.

Once Dermot started saying the confessional prayers, he found that the floodgates opened and it all came pouring out. Father Moran got the whole story. About how he was in love with this girl, and how he had been so happy, and then he had asked her to marry him, and she had said 'yes!'. Oh joy! But then she had let him down by falling in love with somebody else, needless to say, a cad – a no-good singer called Patrick Murphy who deflowered her (he said, haltingly) – and now she was pregnant and married to this Murphy but he was still in love with her himself and what was he going to do?

Patrick Murphy? Hadn't Tom Brogan's girl mentioned that name to him earlier? Good heavens! Ava was married to Patrick Murphy and this young man was in love with her too. Father Brogan wondered who he was. He would ask Bridie later. Now then, that was a nice piece of gossip to pick up on a Saturday morning. But he felt certain there was something else. Something about that name, Patrick Murphy, that he couldn't quite remember. He had thought it earlier when Ava had mentioned it to him. There was some connection he wasn't quite making. Ava had said there was a girl newly arrived in the city and she might get involved in the parcels to Ireland. From Mayo...

'What should I do, Father? What do you advise?'

Oh God. He was still here.

'I am not here to advise, only to give penance. Say two Our Fathers, a decade of the rosary and a Glory Be.'

When the young man didn't get out, Father Moran realized he was stalling because he was afraid of running into Ava. He could be here all day!

'What I suggest you do, young man, is get a firm grip on yourself. Stop sitting around moping, get out there and find yourself another woman. There are plenty of fine young women in all the dance halls in New York and once you get out among them you will find that one is much the same as the other.'

'I can't dance.'

Even to Dermot's ears it sounded pathetic. The priest sighed deeply. This lovelorn idiot was really trying his patience.

'Well go and take some lessons then. Young Ava Brogan is married now and that is all there is to it. Now hop out of this box and give somebody else a turn.'

When Dermot didn't get up he barked, 'She has left the building!'

Dermot got up to leave so quickly he banged his head on the way out. A line of old ladies glowered at him so murderously that he didn't even kneel down to say his penance.

Back outside, when the cruel snap of daylight hit him, Dermot realized he was furious. This was why he had stopped coming to mass, this Irish-American nonsense where everybody knew everybody else's business. It was worse than any gossiping small town in Ireland.

His heart was broken and nobody cared. Not even, no, especially not, his priest.

Dermot decided to go home to sit in his apartment and feel sorry for himself for the rest of the day. But first he would head up to Saks on Fifth Avenue to buy himself a dozen new shirts.

29

SHEILA WENT to the Lexington club where Frankie the Sax worked and managed to catch him on the kitchen phone.

'Who was that kid you said got some other kid to write that tune? Turned up in a Benz, got signed to Decca?'

'I hope you ain't still in town, girl?'

'I'm staying with my folks. Out of town. In Riverdale.'

'Riverdale? Nice. I didn't even know you had folks.'

Sheila didn't know if Frankie had family either. She was guessing there weren't too many of them if he did. That was the way the scene was. They were each other's family, except there were no questions and no commitments. That was how she liked it. Freedom. Now she was living with her aunt and uncle and embroiled in some kind of a strange scene with Ignatius. The quicker she got Patrick's show on the road and got enough money to move on, the better.

'His singing name was Johnny Blue – I don't know who the writer was. Some English kid, I think he said. The song did

OK but not as good as Johnny hoped. I think he had to give the car back. As far as I know, he's still gigging. You can catch him at Mo's on a Wednesday.'

'You got a number for him?'

Frankie laughed. 'I ain't even got a phone, sugar. Got no place to put one neither. Call Mo. He'll put you in touch.'

Sheila thanked him. Was she crazy doing all this? Frankie's tone certainly implied she was. But Sheila could feel her break was coming. She had to keep going.

It took a few calls before she eventually tracked down the songwriter. He was a kid called Malcolm English who worked out of a music factory in Chelsea. It was a large loft space where half a dozen young guys all worked and lived together. They spent their days writing music and jamming, and their nights partying and fooling around. They were hipsters, rebels. Some of them were trying to break into the music industry, others were already out of it, disillusioned with the big business.

There were any number of well-known songwriters that Sheila knew she could approach, but they were all expensive and she doubted any of them would be happy to work with another man's lyrics.

'Man, this is schmaltzy stuff,' Malcolm said when she handed him a piece of paper where she had freshly typed Patrick's poem. 'Did you write this?'

Sheila stood in front of him in full skinny black beatnik gear, her dark eyes glaring at him from behind her long fringe.

'Do I look like I wrote it?' she growled.

'I guess not,' he said sunnily in his London accent. He smiled to himself as he realized she was trying to intimidate him. Malcolm didn't even know what intimidate meant. He was twenty-four and the world was at his feet. He had

already written half a dozen hit songs in the UK before deciding he didn't want to be part of the music establishment and
splitting for America to start again. The world was changing.
A cat could move from one place to another – all he needed
was cash. Malcolm chose who he worked with and when.
He certainly didn't usually work with other people's lyrics
but he liked this woman. She was kind of cool for an old bird.

'The kid that wrote this has a lot of passion, but I need to
get it out of him. Can you help me?'

Malcolm liked a challenge.

'You want a ballad?'

'No. I want *the* ballad. I want the best, most painful, most
passionate ballad anyone has ever goddam written. I want
something that will make every single woman in the world
fall in love with this guy.'

'It'll cost you...'

'... and I want it for free.'

'You're kidding, right?'

Now Malcom was intimidated. Hell, he was scared. This
woman was sitting on the edge of his desk and now he knew
she wasn't cool after all, but crazy.

'Look,' she said, offering him a cigarette. He took it, shaking his head slowly. 'You're good, I know that. If I had a
load of money I would give it to you to write the music for
this song. But then, I would be crazy not to, right?' Now the
woman was admitting she was crazy. 'But listen to this, Malcolm. If the song's a hit, I stand to make a fortune. I should go
and steal the money to give to you to write this song for me
so that every penny that it makes belongs to me. That's how
the record companies do it, right?' Malcolm nodded. 'So
how about this. You write a song, with these lyrics, with no fee.
Then, I give you a contract saying you have fifty per cent of the

copyright, and as such you get fifty per cent of all record sales. Does that sound reasonable?'

From experience Malcolm knew that music managers and record labels were making a fortune out of his work. He got paid a one-off fee, albeit a very good one, but by the time his songs were marching up the hit parade, he had already spent the money. He had hoped the system in America might be different, but it seemed it was just the same. This woman was clearly interested in operating outside the system. She was one of them.

A week later, Malcolm delivered the song.

Sheila could read music but Patrick could not so Sheila arranged for Malcolm to stay for one rehearsal to work through it on the piano with the singer.

She had called both of the young men into the Emerald for a rehearsal at three in the afternoon, making sure that Malcolm would arrive twenty minutes before Patrick so that she had a chance to look at the song and give it her approval. The band would join them for a full rehearsal at six when the doors of the Emerald officially opened for business. The dancing crowd didn't start coming in earnest for at least two hours after that, and the band didn't really consider themselves 'onstage' to their audience until eight.

Malcolm handed Sheila the sheet music and she scanned it, humming along on the first read. He was impressed that she grasped the notation so quickly. Even more impressed when she sat down at the piano and, falteringly, played it. 'I like it,' was all she said. Malcolm gathered from her demeanour that that was high praise. Then she stood up and gestured him to take her place just as Patrick arrived.

Sheila could not imagine two young men who were both the same age and probably equally musically talented and yet were so very different. Patrick, with his Irish good looks, so earnest and passionate, wearing his heart on his sleeve; Malcolm had that sneering, slightly cynical edge, but was as earnest and devoted when it came to making music.

'Patrick, this is Malcolm,' she said. 'He's one of Britain's best songwriters and I got him to write you a song. Hopefully, a hit song.'

'Cool,' said Patrick. He tried to look pleased. He was trying to look pleased for everyone these days: Ava, Sheila, Rose. God! Rose! What the hell was he going to do about Rose? That thought had been occupying his every waking moment and Patrick was finding the strain of living a lie terrible. Things were becoming unbearable with Ava. He felt guilty and trapped all the time. He hated Rose for doing this to him. Worst of all, Sheila was not happy with him. Their last session had not gone well, and he was beginning to believe she might get rid of him. He could not blame her if she did. She wanted him to sing with passion but Patrick felt all stodgy inside. Singing had always made him feel free, as if it was a release. But since Rose had come back into his life everything inside had become clogged up with all the lies and guilt and confusion. Sheila had commissioned a song for him but all he could feel was this fear he would not be able to sing it.

She handed him the sheet. He glanced at it briefly and said apologetically, 'I can't read music.'

'Listen to Malcolm sing it, and look at the notes while he does – you'll pick it up.'

Malcolm played a brief intro and as he began to sing, the words *It Was Only Ever You* burned up at Patrick from the sheet. What was this? His poem to Rose?

'Where did you get this?' he wailed at Sheila.

'I found it on the floor after you had a row with your girl-friend,' she said dismissively.

Malcolm looked over, worried.

'Carry on playing,' she said, nodding at him.

'I won't sing it!' shouted Patrick. He felt on the verge of tears. Was this some kind of a terrible joke? 'You have no right…'

Sheila's lips tightened and she held out her hand, signalling Malcolm to stop playing.

'I have every right,' she said. 'I am your manager. You entered into a contract with me to sing any song that I gave you and do whatever I thought was necessary to get you on the ladder to being a star. So far all you have given me is Irish schmaltz. We had an agreement, Patrick – I do the thinking and you do the singing. I don't care how embarrassed you are right now, how humiliated you feel. I do not care how much of a mess your love life is in. All I care about is what you sing and how you sing it. So either you sing me this song the very best you can or you walk out that door, right now, and I will find me another Patrick Murphy.'

Patrick's face was burning. He felt like walking out, he really did. But he also knew he had come this far and if he turned back there would be nothing waiting for him. This was the end of the line. Pleasing Sheila was his only hope.

And so, after Malcolm had sung through 'It Was Only Ever You' and begun playing the intro again, Patrick opened his mouth and he sang. He was so embarrassed, the first line came out in a whisper.

'Louder,' Sheila said.

He pushed the sound out from his chest.

'Louder, I said!'

He threw his voice into the words. Had he really written them? O God, on the plane. Rose had thrown them back at him…

'Louder! LOUDER! Jesus, Patrick, where is your voice? GIVE ME YOUR VOICE!'

Patrick felt like punching her for all this badgering. This was just the worst thing that had ever happened to him. He hated her more than anything in the whole world. As Patrick was singing the words he thought how much he hated her, so he sang as loud and as hard as he possibly could. Then, when the song hit its towering crescendo, he missed the note, and it came out in an angry squawk. He sounded terrible.

When the song was finished, Sheila stopped pacing, looked up at him and smiled.

'That was good,' she said.

'It sounded terrible,' Patrick said. Had she lost her mind?

'Of course it sounded terrible. But the performance had emotion, and that's all I care about. Now we've just got to teach you to sing it as well.'

Despite his anger and humiliation, Patrick felt something fall into place. He did not know what that something was, only that he had something to reach for.

And reach he did.

For the next three hours solid he sang the song over and over and over again.

Sheila roared at him: 'Higher!' 'Lower!' 'Faster!' 'Slower!' 'More feeling!' 'Put your heart into it!' 'Rubbish!' 'Start again!'

She interrupted and criticized and pleaded with him until he felt his throat dry up and Malcolm over on the piano thought his hands would drop off. The composer was now so sick of the song it made him regret ever having written it.

And still Sheila shouted, 'Again! Not there yet.'

Then, as the afternoon wore on and the band were given their sheet music and began to join them, her tone softened. 'Nearly there.' 'One more time.' 'Good performance' and 'We're close to it now.'

Finally, at six thirty, Patrick gave her what she had been waiting for.

Each note was perfect but it was the passionate innocence in his delivery that gave the song its uniqueness. The thing that would make the song a hit, its singer a star, and its manager, finally, a success. As Patrick reached for the high notes in the penultimate stanza, the final 'you' of 'It Was Only Ever You', the one that all those hours ago he had thought was impossible, Sheila closed her eyes and felt the notes reverberate through her entire body. This was music. This was what it could do to you. She opened her eyes and looked at him, her young star, and noticed that the passion that had been lacking even just a few hours ago was miraculously returned, and in greater measure than she could possibly have imagined. Marvelling at how he was able to drum up such emotion looking out into an empty room, she followed his eyes.

There, standing in the direct line of his gaze, was the pretty young blonde girl, Rose.

He was singing to her, and she was sobbing her heart out.

The club was virtually empty, apart from a half-dozen regulars who had come in for the early bird cocktails, and the luxury of practising their dance moves on an empty dance floor as the band rehearsed. Such a small crowd was all but invisible to the performers and staff who were used to seeing large crowds. To them, with only a half dozen regulars scattered across the vast room, the room was more or less empty. A smattering of committed dancers would hardly notice the young singer kissing the bargirl.

Unfortunately, one of those regulars was paying them a good deal of attention. Myrtle had come early on a promise to perfect her jitterbug with a hopeful young man she had been dancing with the past three Thursdays in a row. Quite used to seeing her friend's husband Patrick on stage, she was stopped in her tracks by the beautiful song he was singing.

'It was only ever you...' he crooned across the room, gazing off behind her to some imagined true love. Even though he was her friend's husband, not for the first time Myrtle felt herself go weak at the knees. When Patrick sang, he really was an absolute dreamboat. Although, offstage, she found him to be a bit of a sap, this was the dreamiest dreamboat song she had ever heard him singing. She was quite carried away with herself and when he had finished she waved across at him. As he climbed down from the stage Myrtle was fully expecting him to come across to her and exchange a few pleasantries. Instead, he walked, as if in a trance, straight past her to the spot where he had been looking as he sang. Myrtle turned around and saw that blonde hussy, Rose. She had always suspected the tart had designs on her friend's husband. If Myrtle was married to a man like Patrick she certainly wouldn't be encouraging him to have pretty, female 'friends from home'. Ava would never suspect such a thing could happen, of course. She was too good. Everyone thought Ava was terrible leaving Dermot and going off with Patrick and getting pregnant, but Myrtle had known Ava all her life and understood that she wouldn't have done something like that unless she was truly, madly in love. Patrick had seduced her into getting carried away with herself. It had been out of character, and she probably would have been better off marrying Dermot. They were certainly more suited. But then, Myrtle reasoned, what girl doesn't want a love so romantic, so powerful that she gets carried away? That was what happened to her friend and now she was being punished; her worse nightmares were coming to pass. Sweet, stupid Ava had entertained that girl Rose, becoming friends with her, and now she was kissing her husband. Kissing him! As if it were the most natural, beautiful thing in the world. The same way, no doubt, he had kissed her. Myrtle was boiling. She lit a cigarette and stood, glaring at them, willing them to turn around and see her. What a fright they would get.

Except they did not turn around. They were too lost in their kiss. Lost to the world. Myrtle could not have been more hurt and angry for her friend, but seeing them, standing there, locked in each other's arms, Rose's delicate blonde face leaning up towards Patrick's willing mouth, her small hands desperately clutching his shoulders, his long arms wrapped around her body at the waist, recklessly, openly kissing in front of everyone, Myrtle had to admit it: they did look terribly in love.

30

AVA HAD not been feeling well all morning. She had been sick after her breakfast, and when the nausea had abated it was replaced with a nasty cramp that came and went.

Knowing that if she went to the doctor he would tell her she should probably go to the hospital and get checked out, Ava reassured herself that this was simply a return of her earlier sickness and decided to go ahead with her plans anyway.

This was a very big day for Ava. Father Moran had sent out a circular with the previous week's church news sheet asking all of the ladies of the parish to bring in clothes for the Parcels to Ireland project, along with names and addresses of people in their parishes back home for them to apply to have the clothes sent to.

This was the first time that Ava would be meeting many of the ladies from the parish. She knew from experience with her mother that the older more established ladies of the parish did not always welcome new faces. Especially not a younger one who might be seen to be taking over their territory. Ava didn't mind this. She rather enjoyed the idea of buttering up and charming the old guard. Ava got on with most women. This was, she knew, because she was not pretty enough for the younger women to feel threatened and she also had a sensible way about her that the older women liked. However, by now, everybody in the Irish Catholic community would know about her shotgun marriage. Ava felt nervous about facing them, in spite of telling herself she was married now and so had nothing to be ashamed off. Giving a good first impression was important if she wanted to overcome their prejudice.

Deciding what to wear was the big thing. Ava had quickly sewn herself up a smock dress the night before, from some expensive cream wool she had bought on sale. It was a simple, unfussy garment, but it sat neatly over her small, but growing bump. If only she had something nicer than a plain cardigan to cover her arms. Looking in her closet for inspiration, Ava saw the rose suit. It was out of the question, of course, but the pink weave was a perfect match for the cream dress. She tentatively reached for the jacket, then, taking a deep breath, tried to fit one of her arms through the sleeves. It was a tight squeeze. She could barely bend her arms at the elbow, and, of course, there was not a hope of closing it, but even left open, it set off the cream dress and made it look special. It transformed her from a dumpy pregnant woman into an important, dynamic church lady.

The suit had transformed her life once before, and now it was doing it again. Ava smiled as she ran out the door and headed for the church.

* * *

The church ladies loved her straight away. They all knew
Tom and Nessa Brogan, by reputation at least, and the fact
that this respectable couple's daughter had fallen somewhat,
before redeeming herself through a speedy marriage and a
desire to do good works, made her all the more adorable to
them. Ava was under the impression that Father Moran had
given one or two of them a firm talking-to beforehand, but if
it made her job easier, so much the better.

Ava's job was to gather and coordinate all of the clothes
and put them into piles that were of equal value. There were,
as she knew there would be, objections.

'I would like to make sure that that yellow jacket reaches
my cousin in Kilkelly.'

'This bag here simply must reach Cork in the next month. It
contains a dress for my grandniece's first Holy Communion.'

'My brother is a farmer and if we don't make sure he wears
a respectable suit for market day, he'll never get a wife.'

'Ladies, ladies,' Ava commanded them. 'Can I just remind
you all that these clothes are intended for the most needy?
And while I understand that we all want to look after our
families back home, we really must be mindful of spreading
our privilege equally.'

They nodded at her wisdom, as she assured them that the
programme would give them the opportunity to do their own
personal packages as well as charity ones. She remembered
her mother once telling her: 'Half the time they just want to
get together with other women, show off the clothes they can
afford to give away and talk about their families back home.
It's as much of a charity to the women giving the parcels as
those receiving them.'

By late afternoon there were thirty parcels ready for dis-
patch. Ava had eaten nothing all day, despite there being a

table laid out with a tea urn and an impressive array of sand-
wiches and cakes. She had taken a mouthful of tea earlier but
was unable to keep it down. The cramps had been coming
and going, but Ava found when she was busy and distracted
she could ignore them better than if she was at home.

However, around five o'clock she got a wave of pain that
forced her to sit down. The ladies immediately gathered
around her in a concerned group but she pleaded with them
to leave her alone for a few minutes to gather herself. Pregnancy was a funny business, so they left her alone.

She held her head down for a few minutes and breathed
into the pain. It was so intense she felt like crying out but
she did not want to make a fuss that would draw attention
to herself. So she kept her eyes closed and breathed until
the pain subsided. When she looked up again she saw Myrtle walking across the room towards her. What a wonderful
surprise! Had she come to join the parish? Ava didn't care.
She had come at just the right moment when she was feeling
vulnerable in front of a group of strangers she was anxious
to impress. If she was sick her old friend would find a way
to get her out of there while maintaining her dignity. Myrtle looked determined, sweeping through the other women,
as they wondered who this assertive gatecrasher was, assuming she must be something to do with their charismatic new
leader. For a moment Ava wondered herself how Myrtle, with
her rescuing demeanour, had known she was sick.

'I need to talk to you, Ava,' she said, plonking herself down
beside her. She stayed quiet for a few seconds, with her eyes
lowered, wringing her hands. Ava realized she was not here
for her, after all, but had some problem of her own she wanted
to share. She felt the bite of resentful disappointment. Then
Myrtle looked straight into her eyes and grabbed her hands.

'I don't know how to tell you this, I have been going over and over it wondering if there is a way I can not tell you – but you're my oldest friend and you have to know the truth. And I am the only one that can tell you...'

Ava felt a knot tighten in her stomach. She did not know if it was fear of what Myrtle was about to tell her or the baby-wind cramps she had been experiencing all day. The threat of a pain was so intense, she felt as if her head was in a guillotine waiting for the blade to drop.

'... but yesterday when I was... Oh, hell – I'll just come out with it – I saw Patrick making love with Rose.'

What happened next was so shocking that Myrtle and the ladies would not be the better of it for years to come.

Demure, stoic Ava threw her head back and let out a scream so bloodcurdling and terrible that it reverberated through the sacristy and up the centre of the silent church like an invasion of demons.

At the same time, a gush of blood came pouring out of her, running down her legs, and spreading in a violent, crimson puddle on the linoleum floor. As Ava slumped forward in a faint, her shocked friend caught her body, shouting, 'Quick! Somebody call an ambulance.'

When Ava woke up she was in a hospital bed. Myrtle was holding her hand, looking both concerned and frightened. Ava remembered the reason she was here like a bludgeon across her head.

'The baby?' she managed to say, although she knew the answer. Myrtle shook her head. There were tears streaming down her face. Ava, despite her situation, felt she should comfort her.

'This is my fault,' Myrtle said. 'I should never have told you.'

'It would have happened anyway,' Ava said. 'I had been having pains all morning.'

She should have gone to the doctor. They might have saved the baby. This was her fault. The business with Patrick and Rose, she did not want to think about that now. She couldn't. It was too painful.

'I called your parents,' Myrtle said, 'they are on their way. Do you want me to call…'

Myrtle couldn't even say his name out loud.

Ava shook her head, then closed her eyes tightly and let her bitter tears burst out of the corners. As her old friend held her hand, Ava sobbed quietly into her growing grief and waited for her parents to arrive to take her home.

31

'OH DEAR, oh dear – this really is the most unholy mess,' Father Moran lamented. And he wasn't simply referring to the bloodstains on his new linoleum floor.

Breda, one of the more eagle-eared ladies, had been arranging a plate of flapjacks behind where Ava was resting and had heard her friend tell her about her husband's indiscretion just before the miscarriage took place.

A rather zealous old-school Catholic, the lady believed it some form of divine intervention.

'The Lord works in mysterious ways,' she said to her priest, sagely.

'He certainly does,' said Father Moran. Although his withering look implied he wondered how the Lord expected him to tolerate such superstitious nonsense from some of his less erudite parishioners.

The poor girl. He wondered if there was anything he could do for her.

'That Patrick Murphy,' he heard one of the women say. 'Carrying on with some girl from home right under her nose. And out there on the stage at the Emerald every week as if butter wouldn't melt.'

Something began whirring in the old priest's memory.

'What's the girl's name?' Father Moran asked, before catching himself engaging in idle gossip.

'Rose,' Breda said, delighted to not have to pretend she had not been listening closely. 'She definitely said, "Patrick and Rose" – then the dreadful thing happened. The blood! The screaming! Goodness me but I shall never forget it! The Lord works in mysterious...'

There it was now. The full story. That wicked girl that he had picked up in Harlem had deliberately come over here to take away lovely Ava Brogan's husband. The lad himself was hardly to blame. Sure, what could he do about it? Once a siren like that set her sights on an ordinary man, he would not be able to help himself. Ordinary men were different from the likes of himself who were destined for a higher order of behaviour. Even so, Father Moran had seen many a cleric fall prey to the seductions of a wicked girl. It was important for all men to be vigilant. The girl might have been forgiven if she had simply been seduced. But she had obviously come here on a premeditated mission. Father Moran felt somewhat guilty that he had not made the connection before now. He might have stopped this from happening if he had done so. It was hard to think now what to do for the best. In any case, he should give Tom Brogan a call and see if there was anything he could do to help the family.

* * *

Kissing Rose last night had been a mistake. He had not meant for it to happen, but while he was singing, Patrick had found himself overcome with emotion. He got caught up in the words of his song as if they were really true. And it wasn't hard, because they had been true, once. He remembered how he had felt when he first wrote them, the desolate unhappiness he had felt leaving his true love behind. 'Feel the words' Sheila had said, and that was what he did. So, when he saw Rose standing in front of him, weeping with love for him, he understood for the first time the heartbreak he had caused her. In singing the words 'it was only ever you' he was genuinely pleading for her forgiveness and understanding. Coupled with this sadness was the elation that he knew he was singing better, and truer than he ever had done in his life before. When he walked across the room to kiss Rose he was in a trance of his own making. It was as if his own heart had drugged him. While they were kissing, he was carried back to the fields of Foxford and it was as if there was no one else in the room. No one else in the world. It felt as if they had never been parted. It felt so natural that it could not be wrong.

'Do you really think this is a good idea, Patrick?'

Sheila had sneaked across the room and asked the question right into his ear with mocking pragmatism. It was over. The spell was broken.

He quickly broke away and went to the bar. When Rose tried to get him on his own again later that evening in the club, he avoided her.

Patrick was angry with himself for having given in to his old feelings. What had he done? What had he been thinking? Not only was he married to Ava, but he was not in love with Rose. Not any more. Over the past few weeks Rose had been making his life hell. Following him around at work, constantly trying to get him alone so she could persuade him to come back to her. He had held firm, but now, it seemed he had ruined everything in that stupid moment of weakness. Patrick had allowed himself to get carried back to who he once was, who they once were together. He was not that boy any more. He was a married man, soon-to-be father and a successful singer. Once enough money started coming through he would send what he owed back to Rose's father and ask him to come and take her back to Ireland so she would stop causing trouble for other people.

Patrick left the Emerald early to go home and get changed before the evening shift. They had been rehearsing 'It Was Only Ever You' all day and Sheila had given him the evening off. 'I don't need you until about ten tonight, Patrick. We'll just warm up your voice with a couple of numbers, and put the new single out to the audience. But I don't want you to overdo it. I want you on top form from now until we break you out.'

'Yes, ma'am,' he said. She gave a swipe to tell him not to be cheeky. Sometimes Patrick wished he could just tell Sheila what was going on with him. She was, in her own way, kind and he did feel that, singing aside, she cared about him. But he knew Sheila didn't like hassle, and right now, that's what his whole life felt like.

As he opened the door of the flat Patrick concentrated on how much he had been looking forward to seeing Ava all day. She would be back from her church work by now and they would have a couple of precious hours alone together.

But when he opened the door and walked into the bedroom, where he thought he heard her, Myrtle was in there. She had one of Ava's suitcases on the bed and was filling it with clothes.

'What's going on?' Patrick asked.

Myrtle didn't even look up at him but continued folding and throwing clothes into the suitcase in a rather violent, pointed way.

'What does it look like? I am packing a bag for Ava.'

'What's the matter? Where is she?'

Myrtle stopped and looked at him. For a second he saw the terrible look of pity cross her face. Then, seeming to think better of it, she bared her teeth at him and said, 'What the hell do you care? Philandering bastard.'

That could only mean one thing. She'd seen them. She'd seen him kissing Rose.

'I can explain—'

Myrtle shook her head and carried on with the packing.

Maybe she hadn't told Ava yet?

'Myrtle, please. It was a terrible one-off mistake. I've been under a lot of pressure – Ava would be heartbroken…'

'Huh!' she exclaimed in a sharp huff. 'She's a lot more than heartbroken, Patrick, *she* is broken. She is in the hospital…'

'The hospital?' Patrick stared at her in shock. What did she mean?

'Yes, Patrick! The hospital! Congratulations for ruining her life…'

'Which hospital? I have to get there now – is she all right?'

Myrtle looked at Patrick and his face was a mess. It was contorted, horrified. This was not how she had expected him to react. She took a deep breath and for the second time that day delivered ruinous news.

'She lost the baby…'

'Jesus Christ no.' Seeming to lose the strength in his legs he sat on the side of the bed. The baby? He had not really thought about the baby that much since Ava got pregnant.

It was really her concern, her joy. He just went along with it. But now, suddenly, this thing, this person that he had not even come to know in any way, was gone. Why did he feel it with the shock of death when it had not even been properly alive to him? How must Ava be feeling? He had to see her, right away. He had to put his arms around her and tell her everything would be all right.

He stood up. 'Come on,' he said, 'let's go.' He knew he had to act fast but everything seemed vague, abstract, as if none of this were truly happening. 'I'll drive us to the hospital...'

'Patrick, sit down,' said Myrtle. He was in shock. This was terrible. She wanted to hate him, for her friend, but she couldn't. He was broken. And if there was anything more pitiful in the world than a broken man, Myrtle did not know what that thing was.

She put her hands on his lap as she had done with his wife earlier.

'Ava knows about you and Rose.'

'You told her?' he said. He could feel a bulb of anger open in his stomach. Then he remembered the baby was gone – their baby – and the bulb rotted away to nothing.

'I told her,' she said. This was the bravest Myrtle had ever been in her life. Twice in one day. She wished, more than anything, then, that she had kept her mouth shut about Rose. Patrick loved Ava, that was clear to her now. He was eaten up. What had she done?

'Look. She doesn't want to see you right now. Her parents have arranged to collect her from the hospital. I am going directly out to the Bronx with her bag. I will tell her how upset you are and how sorry you are and perhaps you can call tomorrow and go and see her then?'

'I'm coming with you now,' he said, standing up. 'I have to see her, Myrtle. Please, you must help me. I promise, if you can just tell her to see me, I can make all of this right.'

Even though, in his heart, in this moment, he could not feel that was true, if he was able to get Ava and say it to her then perhaps everything could be made right again.

'Please, help me,' he said, again.

Myrtle had no choice. She finished packing the case and let Patrick drive her out to the Bronx.

They drove quickly and in silence. Patrick did not ask any details. He did not want to know. He was still in shock. All he wanted was to see Ava. He would hold her in his arms and let her pour everything out on to him. He would explain about Rose, tell her everything. He would say he was sorry over and over and over again, and he would keep saying it until she gave in. He would tell her the truth and she would forgive him. He would make everything all right again.

Tom Brogan met them at the front gate.

When Myrtle had told him she would go back to the apartment to get Ava's clothes, he had thought this might happen.

He was not long off the phone to Father Moran, who explained about Rose. Patrick and she had been engaged in Ireland. He had promised to marry her, to send for her when he was on his feet. Instead, the rogue had married his daughter. Doubtless, as his wife had always suspected, for money and gain.

Who knows, but perhaps Patrick and his girlfriend had always planned to run off together when they had the money to do so. Tom Brogan barely cared what they had been planning to do. He was just horrified to have allowed his daughter to be part of such a treacherous manipulation. Tom Brogan was not a man given to fury. He was liberal and

forgiving. He was always willing, perhaps too willing sometimes, to give the benefit of the doubt. This was not one of
those times. Tom Brogan had no doubt whatsoever that Patrick and Rose had lied to his family and hurt his daughter,
immeasurably. His wife believed that the news of Patrick's
betrayal had brought on Ava's miscarriage. Perhaps she was
being dramatic, but it pained him to think that, in insisting
that Ava's relationship with Patrick was ill-advised, Nessa had
been right.

Tom felt that he had failed in his duties as Ava's father.
He had failed to protect her from a bad marriage, and from a
bad man. Not only that, he had been responsible for putting
the cuckoo into her nest.

The only thing left that he could do for her now was to
make sure that she never saw Patrick Murphy ever again.

He marched down the drive, and taking the case from
Myrtle said, 'Go straight up to the house, Myrtle. I want a
word with...' Patrick's name crumbled in his mouth, 'him.'

The moment she was out of earshot Patrick started
babbling.

'I am so sorry, Mr Brogan. I know this is all my fault. Is
Ava all right? I need to go and see her. I need to explain everything to her. I need to.'

Tom Brogan could not remember ever having been so angry
in his life as he held his palm up in front of the young man's
chest to stop him walking on. He was not touching him, and
was afraid if the young man stepped forward, he could not be
responsible for his actions.

'I do not care what you need. I do not care what you want
to do. You leave my daughter alone, you hear? You are never
to see her again. Go back to your poisonous girlfriend and
look for some sympathy, you will find none here.'

'Mr Brogan, please, I need to see Ava. Our baby...'

When he mentioned the baby, Tom saw red. He closed his hands into two fists and cocked his head sideways in an angry stare. In that moment, Tom Brogan could have been one of the gangsters he so despised.

'I'm warning you, boy – if you take one step further on to my property I will call the cops. Do you understand me?'

He looked at Patrick in a way that left him in no doubt that he meant what he said. The kind eyes of the man that helped had disappeared and been replaced with the burning fury of betrayal.

Patrick nodded that he understood and turned back.

He stumbled more than walked the few steps to his car. His hands and legs were shaking so hard he did not think he would be able to drive. But Tom Brogan was standing watching him go. Patrick drove the car to the end of the road, then, still shaking, pulled his vehicle up on to the sidewalk.

There he sat, quietly, waiting for the tears to come.

When they came Patrick felt his soul had been turned inside out. He cried for his baby, for his lost wife, for the family he had left behind in Ireland. For an hour he was just a man, sitting in a car on his own, crying his heart out. Nobody troubled him, and when he was all cried out, Patrick started his car again, and drove around the city until he was nearly out of gas. He did not know where to go. He knew that he could not face going back to the apartment. The mere thought of sitting in their home, being surrounded by their life, was too much to bear. Then he remembered. He was an Irishman and what did Irishmen do when their lives fell apart? They drowned their sorrows. So Patrick started the car again and headed for the Emerald.

Meanwhile, back in the Bronx, Tom Brogan was sitting in

the kitchen. Nessa was upstairs, sitting by Ava's side. Their daughter had barely said a word since she came home. 'She's in shock,' Nessa said.

All that anger had disappeared from his wife, melted away the minute she saw her frail, traumatized daughter come through the door. Nessa had lost two babies before their precious 'keeper' Ava came along. Nobody was better equipped to look after a grieving mother.

Tom felt helpless as his wife prepared tea and toast, filled a hot water bottle and went to sit in uncharacteristic silence by their daughter's bed for the rest of the night.

'She has had the baby keeping her company day and night for four months,' Nessa said. 'She shouldn't be left alone.'

'I'll sit with her,' Tom said.

'No,' said Nessa, 'let me.'

This was women's business and he was banished. There was nothing he could do but sit around feeling utterly helpless. Tom was a helper. Not being able to do anything to help his daughter, or indeed his wife at this time, was excruciating.

But it was as if, in the serenity of her new, understanding self, his wife had handed him her petty grievances about Patrick and their daughter marrying beneath herself. As Tom poured himself a whiskey, he found himself unable to let go of the unjust way this young couple had treated his daughter.

With a sense of resolve he picked up the phone and a few minutes later he was speaking to Mary Geraghty in the post office in Foxford, County Mayo, Ireland.

'Could you put me through to Dr John Hopkins?' he said.

An American accent. She'd not heard that voice before. Maybe it was something to do with the daughter?

'May I say who's calling please?' she said brightly.

'No,' said Tom, 'you may not.'

Despite himself, and the awful nature of his call, Tom Brogan could not help a small smile. Things back home in Ireland never changed.

32

'THEY FOUND her! She's safe! Oh, thank God – thank God!'

Eleanor Hopkins was beside herself. Over the last few months Eleanor had been shattered with the disappearance of their daughter. On a number of occasions, her hysteria had risen to such levels that John feared he might have to admit her to Castlebar mental hospital. He tried to quell her fears as best he could with assurances that he himself had come to believe.

When Rose had first disappeared they were both shocked and worried. Shocked that she had stolen the money from them and worried that she would not be able to manage on her own in the big wide world. John knew that she had found Patrick's letters and assumed that she had gone to New York, and doubtless had found him. Whether it was a wise decision or not, he had not confided this to his wife. He set before her prettier scenarios. That their daughter had gone to Dublin, or London perhaps. That she had taken plenty of money and would get in touch when she felt that they might have for-given her for stealing from them. It could be a year or more, he assured her. 'Rose is a big girl, she can look after herself very well,' he said.

'She is a *child*,' Eleanor screamed at him. 'What kind of a father are you that you won't go and find her...'

What kind of a father indeed, John thought.

If he had not interfered in Rose's life the way he had none of this would have happened. His daughter and her young man had fallen in love. In all likelihood, if they had been left alone, they would have fallen out of love, as young couples often do. If they had got married, they might have fallen out of love when it was too late; either way, it was fool-ish to interfere with fate and meddle in other people's lives in that way. Even if they were your only child. Even if you were only trying to do what was best for them. People had to do what was best for themselves. John knew that now.

'My girl, my darling girl! Now you can go and get her and bring her home. Pack your bag right away and you can go and stay in Dublin until the next flight out. She could be home in a few days! This is wonderful news.'

'I'm not going to get her, Eleanor. She is alive, that's all we need to know. If Rose wants to come home, then she can call us and make arrangements to do that. I will even send her money, if she needs it. It's up to her now.'

Eleanor went white. This could only mean one thing.

'Merciful hour, John – she hasn't married him, has she?'

John lost patience. Of all the terrible things that could have happened to their daughter, alone, in New York, all Eleanor cared about was that she may have married 'beneath her-self'. In actual fact, as that very decent man on the phone had made clear, Rose had acted beneath anything either of them could have imagined possible of her. She had stolen from them, destroyed a marriage and created a level of distress and hurt in a respectable, good family. Truthfully, John had no desire to see his daughter. He was glad she was safe. But, for the time being, until an apology was forthcoming, that was enough.

'No, Eleanor – Rose has not married Patrick Murphy.'

He didn't even want to tell his wife what Rose had done. He was afraid her reaction might throw him further into despair.

'Thank goodness. Well then, there is no reason for her not to come home.'

'She is leading her own life over there. When she is ready she will call us.'

'Did that man give you a telephone number for her?'

'Yes he did but—'

'Give it to me at once.'

John stepped aside and nodded at the pad next to the phone where he had written down the number of the convent where Rose was staying.

Eleanor grandly picked up the receiver and asked to be put through to the exchange.

Inside, she was shaking at the idea that her daughter might not want to come home, as Tom said. What would she do then? These past few months had been occupied utterly with her daughter's disappearance. She had forced the information about her stealing money out of John, after believing that the child had been abducted from the house. At least she knew she had the gumption to go, although she had not imagined in her wildest dreams that she had followed that young vagabond to America.

'Putting you through,' said Mary Geraghty. Eleanor closed

her eyes in preparation for speaking to her daughter, saying a quick prayer that Mary would not listen in.

It was not Rose that picked up the phone but some American girl.

'Can I please speak to Rose Hopkins?' Eleanor asked in her posh, telephone voice.

'She's not here,' said the girl rudely.

'Ah – this is her mother. Can you tell me when she should be back, please?'

'Never – I hope...' Insufferable rudeness, but then, they were American.

'Can you at least tell me where she has gone?'

'I have no idea – but to hell, I hope. Congratulations on raising a prize bitch, lady,' then she hung up the phone.

Eleanor had lost her again. She looked across at her husband, her face collapsed in disbelief and despair.

Perhaps, John thought, it was time to tell Eleanor a few home truths about her precious daughter.

Rose got off work early. She knew that Patrick was planning to spend the afternoon at home before coming back in for his evening shift. Perhaps, if she arrived unexpectedly, there would be an opportunity for them to be alone together again. They needed to talk about things, make plans. They needed to talk about the kiss.

Rose started to believe that Patrick did not love her after all. He was married to Ava, and Rose, despite herself, could see what Patrick saw in her. Ava was a warm, kind woman, as kind and sweet a person as Rose could imagine anyone being. As Ava befriended her, part of Rose wanted to believe it would be possible for them to be close. But, no matter how hard Rose told herself it was the right thing, the sensible thing, the decent, and eventually, the *only* thing to do – she simply could not let go of her feelings for Patrick. Her love for him was embedded too deeply in her. Although, she wondered, surely this was not what love was all about? All this chasing around? All this lying? When Patrick said he loved Ava and not her, in her heart Rose simply could not believe that was true. However, she did believe it was possible, that he loved both of them. And that being the case, then as he was married to Ava, Rose knew that she should do the decent thing and let them be.

But then he had kissed her and everything changed again. How could he not love her when he wrote that song?

Rose had just arrived for the evening shift and was putting on her uniform when she heard him. She could scarcely believe her ears. After they had had that fight and she had thought it was all over. But he must have picked up the sheet of paper that she had thrown on the ground and written music to the lyrics. Now he was singing those words he had written for her: 'It Was Only Ever You'. His message could not have been clearer if he had written above the stage in ten-foot letters, 'I still love you, Rose Hopkins'.

As she walked through the club towards the centre of the dance floor and stood in front of him, he sang directly to her. There was no mistaking his feeling, his love, his longing. Everything she had been through in the past few months; stealing the money from her parents; chasing across the world, persisting in her love for him, even when he pushed her away; the guilt of deceiving his wife after Ava had been so kind to her; all of those terrible things faded away to nothing when he walked across the room and held her in his arms and kissed her.

He had, of course, chased her off afterwards. This was a very complicated situation and she knew that Patrick would want to do the right thing. Perhaps that was staying with Ava, after all. But even if that was the case, Rose owed it to herself, and him, to acknowledge their grand passion. In her darkest, most selfish moments, Rose determined that if she could get him on his own and kiss him again, she would make him see that their love was strong enough to get them through whatever was coming down the line. That their passion was strong enough, deep enough, to sacrifice a marriage for.

When she got back to her room in the convent, she found Rose's friend, Myrtle, sitting on her bed. Myrtle came quite often to the Emerald and had made a point of introducing herself when Rose first started working there, although she had had very little to do with her since. Rose sensed Myrtle didn't like her, and the expression on her face now suggested she hadn't changed her mind.

'Hello,' Rose said, trying to keep her voice light, 'what are you doing here?'

'The question is surely,' Myrtle replied, 'what are *you* doing here? Oh yes, that's right – stealing my friend's husband and causing her to have a miscarriage.'

Rose gasped.

'Ava lost the baby?'

'... and her husband, thanks to you.' This was terrible, shocking news.

'Where is she?' Rose asked.

Myrtle stubbed out her cigarette and looked across at her with a nasty sneer.

'Not that you care but she is at home in the arms of her loving family. And before you ask – Patrick is with her sobbing his guts out. It seems you have ruined his life as well as hers.'

'I don't know what you mean,' said Rose. She felt sick. All these lies were bunching up inside her, poisoning her.

'Of course you do. I saw that pathetic show you put on at the club. That kiss.'

'You told Ava?'

'So what if I did,' said Myrtle. She had felt guilt gnawing at her ever since breaking the bad news, but justified it by insisting to herself that it was all Rose's fault.

'It wasn't a proper kiss anyway, I could see that right away. It was all for show. Us pretty girls all know how easy it is to seduce a man into kissing you. But it doesn't mean anything. I could see right away that Patrick was playing with you. He is completely different with Ava, you can see how much he cares for her. Besides, Sheila told me she had encouraged him to do it. She was trying it out as part of the act. Make the girls swoon.'

Myrtle wasn't as good at lying as Rose was, but she was learning fast.

Rose felt a wave of nausea. Her head was spinning. Could it be true that Patrick had been playing with her? Could it be true that he loved Ava and not her? That his kiss was all part of the act?

'But still,' Myrtle continued, 'I found it quite disgusting. And so did Ava, and so, by the way, did her family, especially after all they have done for you.'

Rose was burning with shame.

'I also saved you the trouble and filled in your room-mates, Una and Eileen, nice girls – I know them from the Emerald. Oh yes. Everybody knows what a slut you are now. Also Sister Augustine who, as you can imagine, was *thoroughly* appalled.'

Myrtle stood up and reached down beside the locker and

picked up the bag Rose had travelled to America with, and handed it across to her.

'I assumed this was your grubby little case so I have filled it with your grubby little clothes and you can run away back to Ireland to your mammy and daddy, who, by the way, also know where you are and what you've been up to. Tom Brogan filled them in on all the nasty things you've been getting up to since you arrived in New York.'

Rose stood there in shock. She did not know if she would be able to move her feet.

Myrtle shook the bag at her.

'Are you taking this or would you like me to kick you out with nothing?'

Rose reached across and took the bag. She felt she should say something, 'Goodbye' or 'I'm sorry', but there were too many people to say sorry to and the goodbyes ran too deep.

Myrtle walked her down the front steps of the convent and watched her until she had cleared the block. Where would she go? The only other place she knew was the Emerald, but humiliation would be waiting for her there too. She stood under the awning of the apartment block and looked up and down the busy sidewalk. People rushing about, busy in their lives. Men in hats rushing to and from work, women pushing buggies towards the park, old ladies wheeling buggies full of shopping. Everyone in New York had a life. She had been clinging on to somebody else's, trying to steal another woman's husband, another woman's life. Rose checked her purse. She found one five-dollar bill. As she rifled through looking for another, she pulled out the slip of paper that the taxi driver's wife, Marisa, had given her when she first came here.

Rose had nowhere else to go, so she hailed a cab and asked the driver to take her to the address in Harlem.

33

ATRICK SAT in the bar of the Emerald and drank himself into a stupor for nearly three full days, under
Gerry's watchful eye. The bar manager put him in
a quiet corner at the end of the bar then filled him to the
brim with drink, listening, as much as his work would allow,
as the young singer's pain came roaring out of him. Tear-
ful regrets about the beautiful family he had left behind in
County Mayo, and the simple life he should have followed,
taking a job in the Foxford Woollen Mills like his father. Then
his own stupidity in losing his wife, and when it came to the
baby, he would become crippled with a regret so heartbreaking that, once or twice, Gerry simply handed him the whiskey
bottle and let him take it from the neck. When he was done
crying, Patrick would rant and rave, ruing the day he had laid
eyes on that wicked blonde temptress, Rose Hopkins, cursing
her snobbish parents from the high-heaven. When he became
too rowdy and began to upset the other customers, Gerry
would call one of the doormen to help bring him down to

the cellar where they would lock him in a stockroom to cool off. His fellow Irishmen set up a bed with blankets and cushions and brought him down food and coffee until, sobbing and regretful, he would go back upstairs to start again. Sheila was horrified with the ritual, but Gerry explained that it was important for Patrick to 'drink it out'. It was like lancing a boil, Gerry explained. 'Otherwise, it'll fester. And once an Irishman starts to fester, you'll never get him back the same way again.'

After three days, it was over. Patrick took his breakfast and coffee and did not go back to the bar. His hands were shaking and his head felt as if there were a dozen goblins in there, hammering. He was, in some ways, grateful for the physical hardship because it took from the emotional pain that the drink had masked, but not cured. In his dedicated grief, Patrick had, at least, come to understand with absolute certainty that his marriage to Ava was over. Her family had never fully approved of him in the first place, and, after what had happened, there would be no going back. Rose had ruined his life. He had ruined his own life then by allowing his pathetic heart to lure him into kissing her. The reality was, he was on his own in New York. All he had now was his career. Although, without somebody to share it with, that hardly seemed to matter any more.

'How dare you contact the Decca scout about the kid? He rang me earlier about some deal you are trying to fix up. Who sanctioned you to get a song written for him?'

When Iggy had asked Sheila to meet him in his office, this was not what she had been expecting.

Sheila had put out her cigarette at the door and unbuttoned

the top button of her new black shirt in preparation for the assignation. Iggy had been away for nearly six days, visiting his properties in Ireland and Britain, so this trip had been longer than most. She had missed him, and she knew he had missed her. Within an hour of getting back into New York her lover always took the opportunity to show her just how much. Usually prefaced by a stern invite to meet him 'in the office'.

Except now he was giving her a telling-off? Not a sexy telling-off either – a real one.

Who sanctioned the song? Was he kidding? She knew that little bum from Decca wasn't used to dealing with women. The fact that he had called Iggy at all was humiliation enough, without Iggy not standing up for her and telling him where to get off.

'Nobody sanctioned the song. The kid wrote the words and I got some other kid to write the music...' As he opened his mouth to object, she filled it with the words, 'for free.'

'Nobody works for free.'

'OK – I gave him a percentage of record sales.'

Iggy put his head in his hands before looking up at her. His face was angrier than it should have been. Maybe he had had a bad flight.

Actually, it had been a great flight, and one of his favourite Aer Lingus hostesses, Belinda, had given him the number of her hotel room. He would not take her up on the offer, but it had briefly irked him that he shouldn't, or rather couldn't, even if he had wanted to. The truth was, he didn't want any woman apart from Sheila. That alone gave her a power over him that made him feel uncomfortable. Iggy had no idea if Sheila felt the same way, but she acted sometimes like she could take him or leave him. The way that air hostess threw herself at him, she knew he was the boss. A man needed to be in charge of his own destiny but, in his intense feelings of fondness towards Sheila, and his growing dependency on seeing her, Iggy could feel his destiny slipping away from him.

He needed to show her who was boss. Thankfully, she had given him the perfect opportunity to do so.

'So, tell me, how are we expected to get a record deal if you're giving away sales percentage to some songwriter?'

'We own half the song because Patrick wrote the words.'

'So now you are going to tell me that Patrick owns half the song and the songwriter owns the other half. What do we get out of it?'

'A percentage.'

It occurred to Sheila that maybe she had acted too hastily. After all, Iggy had a lot more experience in this field. He was managing and touring acts, many of whom had record deals, but she had wanted to do this on her own. She had wanted to prove to herself that she could do it alone. She certainly needed to prove to him that she was her own woman. Taking help from a man like that could lead to him walking all over you. At least losing her freedom. Just standing here, Sheila thought, is a loss of freedom in itself. He didn't care about Patrick's career, she knew that. He just wanted a piece of the action so he could keep her beholden to him. Well, that wasn't going to work.

Once she had Patrick launched, a record deal secured, 'It Was Only Ever You' in the charts – she was out of here. And no man was ever going to tell her what to do again. Iggy could go to hell.

'A percentage of nothing, Sheila, is not a percentage. The only percentage you can take to a record company to make them listen is a hundred. Artist on a salary, writer on a fee.

When they play a venue, it's a different story – but when it comes to recording that's still the way it's done.'

'Well I think it's fair.'

Sheila could not quite believe that she had said something so lame. But she had.

'Fair?' Iggy was looking at her, his eyebrows raised in amusement, waiting for what she was going to say next.

'Look – the kid that wrote the music to this song has already bagged seven hit singles in the UK. He's a smart kid, he's done the math, and he's sick of working for fees. No matter how high they are he knows he's getting ripped off. You know it's the song that can make or break an artist. You can put out a good band with an average song and they'll do OK. You get a good artist and give him a great song, you can make some serious money. Sooner or later the writers will come round to hanging on to their copyright. And when they do? We've already set our own bar and built up a stable of material. There's a lot of average out there, Iggy, but if you want the very best – you've got to pay.'

Iggy thought about it. Damn but she was making sense.

'And this guy is good?'

'The best. And he's fresh off the boat from England and ready to deal.'

'The song?'

'It's a heartbreaker. A real gut-wrenching ballad. It will make Patrick a star. It will change everything.'

Iggy looked at her intensely. She was so hard to read. A fat ball of smoke from her cigarette drifted up towards her eyes. They were, he noticed, glittering. Ambition? Intent? Desire? Love even? For him? Patrick? He couldn't tell and that bothered him. When the pretty air hostess had batted her glittering eyes at him, he had known exactly what was on her mind.

'I will call my man at Decca and try to rescue the deal.'

That sentence, Sheila decided, summed up everything that she found offensive about the world in general, the music industry in particular and, as a man and an individual, Ignatius Morrow. 'My man', 'rescue', and not her deal but 'the deal'. No matter what she did, he would want a part of it. As long as she was here, under his roof, he was calling the shots. He was the same as every other guy she had ever worked for. Possibly worse. The fact that she had feelings for him was certainly making it worse.

'Great,' she said. 'Thanks.'

There was a pause before he asked, 'See you later?'

Without missing a beat she said, 'Not tonight, I'm afraid.'

He raised his eyebrows in surprise.

'Other plans?'

'Yes,' she said. Then gave him a sharp, curt smile and left the room.

She had no plans. She never had any plans that didn't involve him any more. She had to pull back and stop being at his beck and call. She had to start clawing back some control over her own life.

Sheila went back out into the ballroom to look for Patrick. He should be there now. It was a big night tonight with the scout coming in. She wanted to get in a few rounds of 'It Was Only Ever You' to make sure Patrick was on top form. Maybe the little blonde might come and stand in front of him again – that was some performance she drew out of him before.

When she got there she found him sitting on the edge of the stage. His body was as stiff as a board and he was rocking gently backwards and forwards. Something was very badly wrong. As soon as he saw Sheila he began blabbing, sucking in air between the words to stop himself from sobbing.

'I've messed up so badly Sheila. I've got nobody left...'

Then, unable to stop himself, he began to wail like a child. Sheila tried patting him on the back but she was lighting a cigarette in a hurricane. A dead baby and a thwarted, absconded wife was a lot to deal with, even for a soft kid like this one. For a second Sheila wished she'd come down on the blonde home-wrecker, but she guessed it wouldn't have made much of a difference in the scheme of things. At least he had stopped drinking.

'I've got nowhere to live! I've got nowhere to go!'

'We will fix you up. Don't worry, everything is going to be all right.'

'I can't sing tonight. Please don't make me sing. Don't make me sing that song...'

Sheila reached for a cigarette and realized she already had one in her mouth. She lit the fresh one and gave it to him.

'OK,' she said. 'Just wait here.'

She was not equipped to deal with this emotional stuff, but she knew she had to look after her boy.

Sheila ran to the office, banged on the door and entered before getting a call. Iggy was on the phone.

She ignored that fact and said, 'Patrick is having a crisis. His wife left him. He has been out in the bar, drunk, for three days, so I'm taking him home to the folks with me for a proper meal. Can you call *your* man (she couldn't resist it) in Decca and put him off until I get this sorted.'

Before he had a chance to respond, Sheila was gone.

Dropping everything for pretty Patrick? Bringing him home? Sheila had never invited him to meet her family. In their warmer moments he had dropped hints about home-cooked meals and never having had his own family. She always found a way of ignoring him, adeptly pushing the suggestions aside in that cool way she had.

She was pouring everything into the kid, and nothing into him these days. She was using him, just hanging around to get her act on the road. She was the same as all the other women, after his money and his power; she was using it to do something else. Sheila thought she was so smart. She thought she was better at hiding it than most women, but she wasn't.

To hell with her, Iggy thought. He threw down his cigar, then picked up the phone and called Belinda the air hostess.

34

S HEILA DID not call ahead to warn her auntie there would be an extra person for dinner.

Anya was so excited when she saw Sheila come up to the front gate with Patrick she began shouting, 'Samuel! Samuel! Sheila has a man with her. Quick! Hurry, put on a tie.'

As she ran to the door, removing her apron as she went, she raised her eyes and hands to heaven and thanked God that there was a fine piece of brisket that had been braising in her oven since that morning. It had been intended to last them the week and now God had sent Sheila a man to eat it with them!

She opened the door, grinning from ear to ear and holding out her hands to embrace them both.

'This is Patrick, Auntie,' Sheila said, opening her eyes widely to tell her to calm down. Patrick held out his hand. 'Good evening, Mrs Klein. I'm so pleased to meet you.'

He was very young and, Anya was disappointed to hear from his accent, Irish. Still. He was a man.

'I hope you like brisket?'

'I don't believe I've ever had it before,' he said, 'but I'm sure it'll be delicious if it was cooked by you.'

Such lovely manners! The Irish weren't so bad. The boys loved their mothers, like the Jews.

Sheila was pleased to see that Patrick's spirits had lifted. Although Auntie's attention was excruciating, it was amusing and she would calm down once she was told who he was.

The moment the old lady greeted him, for the first time since he had come to New York, Patrick felt at home. The small, suburban house, with its chintzy net curtains, profusion of ornaments and soft, dark carpets was very different from the bare cottage he grew up in, but he recognized the warm welcome and the instant hospitality. The troubles of his day were forgotten and he was overcome by a feeling of gratitude for being taken to such a safe place. Samuel came out and instantly understood who he was from what Sheila had told him about her business.

'So? You're going to marry my niece?' he said, holding his hand out.

'Samuel!' Anya scolded him. 'I'm so sorry,' she apologized to Patrick. If he carried on like this, Sam would chase him away and Sheila would never get a husband.

'Patrick is my singer,' Sheila said, laughing. 'The one I was telling you about?'

Anya waved her hands in the air and walked into the kitchen. Again, they were talking about things she didn't understand. Another small humiliation. What did it matter if he sang? He was a man!

Sheila could see she was upset and followed her into the kitchen as Samuel brought Patrick into the drawing room to see his records.

Auntie was hunched, her frail arms lifting the huge pot out

of the oven. 'I'm sorry, Auntie. Patrick and I are just friends. He is having problems in his marriage so I brought him home for some brisket. That's all.'

'He is married?' Anya said.

'Yes,' Sheila said firmly. Then, sensing her aunt's disappointment she asked, 'Why do you want me to get married so much? Why is it so important? Am I not enough for you as I am?'

Auntie put down her pot and snapped angrily, 'How can you say such a thing? You are more than enough. You know you are everything to me and your uncle.'

Sheila smiled.

'Then why with The Husband, The Husband all the time? It's so old-fashioned!'

Anya was not stupid. She knew when she was being teased. She turned to her niece and put her hands around her face, her long, knurled fingers framing Sheila's sallow cheeks. Those dark eyes, heavy, knitted brows. She looked so worried all the time. It was the same since she was a child. Auntie wanted, in that moment, to tell her everything. How she had seen her niece so lonely for her family from the moment she got here. That she and Samuel had tried to make up for her loss but they knew they would never be enough. That, despite what she said, and how hard she tried to hide it, Auntie knew that Sheila was sad and did not want to be alone. A husband was not so important as family, but when you have no family, and if she and Samuel died, which they would soon, Sheila would have nobody in the world. Selfishly, Auntie did not want to die leaving the child she loved completely alone in the world. But she could not say all that. So, she looked into Sheila's eyes and said, with as much sincerity as she could, 'Every good Jewish girl needs a husband.'

'But I'm not a good Jewish girl, Auntie.'

Auntie gave her a playful slap on the cheek and told her to peel some potatoes.

While the potatoes were cooking, Samuel introduced Patrick to Mahler (to little effect) and Sheila persuaded Patrick to sing the first two verses of 'It's Now or Never' to show her uncle how her fortune would be made (to even less effect). However, Samuel was delighted with the company. This was the first person Sheila had brought into the house since she was a child.

Patrick helped the women lay the table, but just as Samuel was saying grace, the doorbell rang.

Even though he was the boss, Joe Higgins had decided to do this house call and sort out the Jewish broad himself, for a number of reasons. First of all, he felt bad because Dermot had let him down at the meeting with the Balduccis. His lawyer had not given his questions the gravitas they deserved. At one point, Dermot had contradicted Joe and said that this was not a legal matter 'in any sense I can get involved in'. He had also questioned Joe's motivation in making forensic distinctions between 'manslaughter' and 'murder', questioning his moral stance. Joe was a good Catholic. He went to mass every Sunday and confession once, sometimes twice every month. He did not like having his morality questioned. Bottom line was that Dermot had made him look like an idiot in front of Antonio Balducci. However, he could not afford to lose Dermot, he was the best defence lawyer in town. So, he persuaded Antonio to let him handle this important family matter. 'You don't want to be – pardon the expression, Antonio – shitting on your own doorstep.'

It wasn't a big job. Antonio just needed to assure his sister that the woman was scared and wouldn't be back. He didn't need to kill her or anything. Just scare her, and if that didn't work, give her a slap.

The Italians agreed because they felt this was an Irish matter too. Their brother-in-law, Dan McAndrew, was half-Irish. If he knew Joe Higgins was involved he would get a nice fright, and that might help the lowlife keep his wandering dick tucked away a bit better. Then he might stop upsetting their sister who, in turn, was driving them crazy. Wasting their time when they had more important business to attend to. They had 'spoken to' every damn club owner and scared her out of the city, but the Bronx wasn't far enough away for Angela. She was one vindictive bitch, their sister, but the Balduccis weren't going to have the broad murdered for her. It was too risky. Joe Higgins saying he would deal with it was ideal.

Joe had one other motivation. Iggy Morrow. Iggy was an Irish businessman, like himself. But despite having reached out to him several times over the years, Iggy had always ignored him. Joe didn't like that. It made him look small. Now, he had learned that some kid that had washed dishes in his golf club was working for Iggy. The kid was being groomed for stardom by, guess who? This Sheila bitch. Information had come out through the meeting with the Balduccis, which was very embarrassing for him, as they had assumed that Morrow was in his pocket. It was time for Iggy Morrow to be sent a message.

Joe got into the car where Aiden, his right-hand henchman, had been watching the house for the past couple of hours.

'Only the old couple in there. Then a woman arrived about an hour ago. She had Patrick Murphy with her.'

'Who the hell is Patrick Murphy?'

'The singer! He sings at the Emerald every week. He's fantastic. They're calling him the Irish Elvis. All the old stuff, but he can rock and roll too. The ladies...'

Joe gave him a murderous look and he shut up. He forgot they weren't allowed to go to the Emerald.

Joe didn't bring his gun in with him. He didn't want to be tempted.

'You wait here,' he said to Aiden.

'You don't want me to come with you?' He sounded disappointed. He had been kind of excited about meeting Patrick Murphy.

Joe figured he might end up just talking. He was a reasonable man. But then, if the bird was feisty, and he figured she was, she might make him angry. Then he might lose his temper. A lot of men, Aiden among them, were squeamish about hitting women. Joe didn't like to make a habit of it either, but sometimes, if they drove you to it, there was no other way to get your point across.

The street was quiet, too many neighbours for his liking, so Joe walked quickly across the road and tapped on the door impatiently. An old man answered the door.

'Good evening,' Joe said. 'May I come in?'

Then he stepped in, shoving the old man to one side slightly and closing the door behind him.

'Who are you?' the old man said. He was bristling. Best to ignore him. Ah – here they were. Dan McAndrew's bit and the dishwasher who thought he was somebody. Joe recognized him. He had smartened himself up for Iggy Morrow. The adrenalin was pumping through Joe now. This bit was what he enjoyed the most. Confusion. It was like introducing yourself to guests at a party they didn't even know they were invited to.

'I am so sorry for the intrusion. I just didn't want to be standing around in front of the neighbours, you know? This is kind of a delicate matter.'

'What do you want?' said the old man. His voice was shaking. Joe could tell right away he was as weak as a woman, and as for 'Elvis'...

'I am sorry, sir. My name is Joe Higgins and I have come here to have a chat with a lady called Sheila. I'm guessing that's you, my dear.'

The woman looked across at him defiantly. Joe smiled, sharply.

She should look scared. She wasn't a respectful woman.

'I have come to relay a message from Angela Balducci, although you may know her as Mrs McAndrew. You really want me to say it in front of your father, dear?'

'Go to hell!' she said.

Joe didn't need more of an invitation. He pushed the old man away, so he fell down, then began to lay into 'Elvis', who was foolishly standing in front of the woman. The kid managed to throw out one protective thump, giving Joe a nasty clip to the side of his mouth which really hurt, but it barely gave him pause as he laid Iggy Morrow's 'star' to the ground and began kicking him. He was about to set his foot down on pretty boy's face when he was assaulted with a pungent smell of meat, then whole world went black.

The moment Anya heard the fear and confusion in her husband's voice on answering the door to this stranger, she knew there was trouble, and watched the drama unfold from the dining-room door. When the man began to hit Patrick she did not pause. She picked up the hot brisket from the dining-room table where she had just laid it, then took the five steps it took to get into the hall, stepped over her husband and slammed the cast-iron pot into the side of Joe Higgins's head.

There was brisket everywhere.

For a few minutes they stood there in shock. They thought perhaps he was dead.

'We should call the police,' Samuel said.

'Don't,' Patrick said. 'Joe Higgins is a gangster and you don't want to get involved.'

He looked out the window and saw Aiden, Joe's henchman whom he knew from the golf club, sitting in the car across the road. He signalled across for him to come.

'Jesus Mary and Joseph,' he said, when he saw his boss unconscious and covered in hot beef. 'He won't be happy about this.'

'Good,' said Anya. 'Tell him I am seventy-eight years old and he can come back for more any time he likes.'

Aiden smiled and apologized for the trouble before throwing his boss over his shoulder and carrying him out to the car. He thought about going back to get Patrick's autograph but decided against it. Another time.

When he had left, Anya and Samuel fell into each other's arms, too stunned by what had just happened to even ask questions. Sheila was sitting at the bottom of the stairs. She had collapsed there in shock as Joe landed his first blow on Patrick. She had sat there, helplessly watching the violence unfold. Sheila had imagined herself the sort of person who would have fought back. But the guttural grunts of kicks and fists being administered, the spitting vicious anger of the attack and then finally, as Auntie slammed the heavy pot down on the gangster's head, the way he had fallen to the floor and the shocked look on his face, had affected her in an entirely unexpected way. As the first blow was struck, something inside Sheila began to unfold and she was overcome with a feeling she recognized but had buried all of her life. Terrors she had written down in her dreams, the unspoken-of horrors that had befallen her family, unseen but clearly imagined. Those fears had been folded and folded and folded away into some dark recess in her soul. In the years since she had learned of their death, whenever they threatened to emerge, Sheila would throw a blanket of cynicism and insouciance over them to keep them hidden, from herself and anyone else. Then, as she watched Joe Higgins's face in the second when he believed death had grabbed him, the curtain had lifted. Her darkest thoughts began to unfold and flutter chaotically like black butterflies. Now, the gangster was gone and her family were safe.

But the fear was still there.

Patrick sat down beside her, put his arm around her and kissed her hair. It was as instinctive as his stepping in front of her as he saw Joe coming towards her. He had wanted to protect her. And as Patrick went down with the second punch, he had felt nothing for himself, only fear for Sheila's safety. Then Anya felled his attacker and Patrick got to his feet, and the first thing he felt he needed to do was embrace Sheila.

Sheila gasped, and shocked by the intimate gesture, flinched. Patrick tightened his grip, then put his broad hand over the shaking fingers on her lap and said, 'It's all right, Sheila. You're safe now.'

He realized, then, how much this woman had come to mean to him. How much she had helped and nurtured him. How much she meant to him.

Sheila looked up at Patrick and, for a moment, she saw her brother's face as it might be now. An earnest young man, endlessly hopeful, but, in this moment, full of concerned tenderness.

Sheila's face crumpled and seventeen years' hard-held tears came pouring out of her. The black butterflies were stilled and in their place was an almost overwhelming feeling of love.

35

VA'S RECOVERY from her late miscarriage was long and hard won. However, it was not as long and hard as it would have been without her mother's unstinting support. For three weeks Ava stayed in bed. The doctors had said there was nothing physically wrong with her and that she was more than ready to get up, but only her mother understood her seeming lack of motivation. The baby was gone, her husband was gone, she had nothing to live for. Nessa knew from her own experience that the devastating effects of losing a baby were rarely given the attention they deserved. The focus was always on trying again for a new baby. Ava did not want to go back into her marriage. Not yet, at least. Nessa remained silent. In truth, she had lost any of her opinions on the subject, good or bad. She had lost her fervour about controlling Ava's future. Instead she remained focused on getting her through each day, keeping her calm and as at ease as possible. With daily care Nessa pulled Ava out of the despair and depression she would have certainly fallen into had she been left alone.

Tom was distressed and panicking at his daughter's tardiness in getting herself 'back to normal'. He was still angry with himself for the way he believed he had let her down. Nessa defended her daughter's unwillingness to rush her recovery, ministered to her every day, bringing her up food and ensuring that she ate, just a little. During the brief times she was out of the room herself she left her distracting magazines and books which, for the first couple of weeks Ava did not look at, but then gradually came around to.

As three weeks stretched to four, Nessa called Myrtle, warning her not to make any mention of Patrick or Rose, unless she was prompted. Myrtle brought make-up and rollers and candy with her and said, 'You look a fright!' when she walked into the room, and pretended that everything was normal. She stayed overnight, as they had done when they were children. By the following day, Ava was ready to get up and go downstairs.

Myrtle stayed that second night, and they put on 'Rock Around the Clock' and danced around the living room.

Ava was pretending to be happy, but she was grateful to find she now had enough strength to pretend.

The baby was gone and nobody could bring it back.

She would always be sad about that, but she knew, too, that life would go on. Ava was glad to find the will to live again, even though she thought it had been lost to her.

'Will you ever come out dancing with me again?' Myrtle asked. 'I'm still looking for a husband, even if you're not. Of course, we don't have to go to the Emerald...'

It was a clumsy prompt for Ava to talk about Patrick's betrayal with Rose. She wasn't ready, and felt she might never want to talk about it at all. It felt like an old wound she did not want to pick over. Her handsome husband had been making love to a beautiful girl who had the kind of film-star beauty she could never hope to aspire to. Now, it transpired, he had been engaged to Rose when he married Ava. Patrick had, she was certain now, simply used her to get along in America. Her mother had been right. It had never been true love. Vanity had tricked her into believing she was the kind of girl he could fall in love with, but she wasn't. She was plain old Ava, as she had always been. For a period of time she had thought she was, if not beautiful, then at least attractive. Dermot had certainly thought so. She had been thinking about him a lot these past few weeks. Wondering how her life would have been if she had never fallen in love with Patrick and had stayed with him. They would be married now, and living comfortably near her parents, no doubt. She might even be pregnant.

The problem was, of course, she didn't love Dermot. She had thought she loved him and she might have been happy, but then Patrick had come along, swept her away and shown her what true love was all about. Dermot paled in comparison with the passion she felt for Patrick. Not, indeed, that Dermot would come near her ever again after the sluttish, cruel way she had behaved towards him. Just thinking about it made her shudder. If Myrtle had her way she would spend the rest of her life raking over the dramas of the past, relishing every ghastly moment.

Myrtle gave her a look that said, 'Trust me. You've had long enough.'

'I don't know if I ever want to go dancing again,' Ava said. 'Honestly? I don't know what I want any more.'

Myrtle grabbed her hand and squeezed it. 'Don't worry, Ava, you'll get another one.'

Ava did not know whether she meant baby or husband and

she didn't want to ask. Myrtle had meant both, but she didn't want to push it either. Ava wasn't ready. So, she leant across the sofa, switched on the TV and the two of them escaped into an episode of *Father Knows Best*.

Nessa, who had left the kitchen door open, listened in to the two friends. Above the canned audience laughter, as clear as if it were the only voice in the room, Nessa heard Ava laugh. A little tear ran down her cheek. She could tell, from the tone of her voice, that her precious daughter was, finally, on the mend.

The following week Myrtle was volunteering at Quinn's Ballroom Dancing School in Yonkers. Once a month there were 'men only' evenings where the more atrocious of her students could step on the toes of hardy volunteers of the opposite sex. The humiliation for a man-who-couldn't-dance was that the volunteers were generally women on the edge of spinsterhood, resigned to seeking out the fresh blood of a bachelor who had neither the courage nor the ability to hit the dance halls yet. This was Myrtle's first time. She already felt desperate enough without seeing somebody she knew.

'Dermot Dolan,' she shouted brightly across the room. 'What are you doing here?'

Dermot put on his best criminal lawyer smile but Myrtle could tell he was not one bit happy to see her either.

'I am learning to dance, Myrtle. Well, trying anyway!'

After that awful time in the confessional, Dermot had decided that the ill-mannered priest was right, after all. It was time for him to get back out there and find himself a wife. Knowing that his two left feet were holding him back from entering the only place where a man might meet a woman these days, the cursed dance hall, he signed up for lessons. Dermot was embarrassed to see Myrtle but she was equally embarrassed to see him.

Breaking the ice with happy exuberance was, Myrtle decided, the best way to approach it for both of them.

'I'll take this one,' she shouted across to Mary Quinn, marching over to him. Then she draped her hands over his shoulders for the opening waltz and added, 'Unless you're already taken?'

Dermot shook his head and laughed. He had always liked Myrtle.

The music started and they shuffled around a bit, he assiduously letting her lead so he could avoid her feet.

'God, you really have not got the hang of this yet, have you?'

'No,' he said. Then he laughed, and she laughed and, for a moment, Dermot thought how nice her hair smelt and wondered...

'How is Ava?'

It just came out of his mouth. He had not been going to say anything. Ava was the reason his heart had taken an unpleasant dip when he saw Myrtle, and yet he was compelled to ask.

'Ah.' Myrtle was surprised to find herself feeling a little disappointed. After all, a man was a man, and just recently she had come to wonder how important it was if he could dance or not. Dermot was nice. Certainly, Ava would have been better off if she had stayed with him instead of letting herself get carried away with a handsome cad. It had given Myrtle pause about her own preferences.

'So, you've not heard?'

'No,' Dermot said. Oh, why had he been so stupid and asked that question? Now she was going to tell him about Ava and her wonderful life. He didn't want to hear it.

Myrtle paused. She could tell Dermot the whole nasty story. About Rose trying to steal Patrick and showing the whole marriage to have been a sham. He could tell him about Ava's 'women's problem' that men were so squeamish about: how she had collapsed in the church, spilling blood everywhere, losing the baby, then had lain in bed, depressed and miserable for nearly a month, even when the doctors said, officially, there was nothing wrong with her.

If she told him all that, he might be glad to be away from the whole sorry mess. He might be happy to settle for a nice, cheerful, pretty, sensible girl who would teach him to dance. But then again, Dermot's brother Niall was still single...

'She broke up with Patrick. The marriage is over. Didn't work out.'

'Really?' Dermot's heart soared. What about the baby? Had she had it? He didn't care. It didn't matter. Maybe there was hope. Why that fool Patrick had left her did not occur to him. How any man could leave such a wonderful woman was beyond him. Surely, this meant there was a chance, again, for him? Perhaps – but it was too much to hope for – some residual feelings for Dermot may have contributed to the marriage not working. He could barely contain himself with excitement, but kept his voice light and steady as he asked, 'Is she still in the city?' He looked up and took his eyes from his feet.

'Ouch!'

'Sorry.'

'No. She's been back home with Tom and Nessa for nearly six weeks now.'

That wasn't long off two months. Was it too early to call on her? Was two months a respectful amount of time after a break-up? Would she still be interested? Despite his reservations, Dermot knew that he had to go and see her. It would be embarrassing, potentially humiliating for him, but he had to find out if he was still in with a chance.

In the meantime, Myrtle had made her own mind up about something else.

Volunteering at Mrs Quinn's was not for her. Not even in pursuit of a suitable husband like Dermot. Niall was way better-looking than his brother. And he didn't step on toes!

'Ah, Dermot.'

Tom's heart sank when he saw the smartly dressed man standing on his front doorstep, his nervous smile almost entirely concealed by a huge bouquet of pink roses.

His daughter had just seen off one disastrous romance and now here was another one, seemingly determined to turn their family tragedy into the plot of a Jane Austen novel. Tom wished everyone would all go the hell away and leave his family alone. He just wanted things to be back the way they were before, when it was the three of them. Before his daughter had met Dermot Dolan or Patrick Murphy. He knew it was stupid, and untenable, but things were so much simpler and happier when he was the only man in Ava's life. Was that such a terrible thing for a father to want for his daughter? To be able to protect her for ever? To have her wit and good humour all to himself?

He stepped aside, saying, 'You had better come in.'

'Thank you, Tom.'

He smiled, nervously.

Stupid fool. If Dermot had been enough of a man to hold on to his daughter in the first place, instead of letting her chase off after that gutty-boy, none of this would have happened. The only saving grace in this scenario was that Nessa was out shopping, so would not get to do the 'Mrs Bennet' act which had got them into all this mess in the first place.

'Ava?' he called out to the kitchen. 'You've got a visitor.' He nodded at Dermot's flowers and said, 'I assume they're for Ava?'

'Ah now, they're not really your colour.'

Tom smiled, despite himself.

Ava got a terrible shock when she saw Dermot standing in the hall. She had thought it was Myrtle and had not even bothered taking off her apron. He looked so smart in his blazer and slacks. More handsome, less rounded than she remembered him. His eyes were sparkling in that slightly amused way he had. Although they had always sparkled when he looked at her. 'I'd get these in water quickly, if I were you,' he said, handing over the flowers. 'Your father thought they were for him.'

As she took the roses from him, he turned to her father again and said, 'Sorry, Tom, next time, I'll bring you a cigar.'

He really was a wit! Ava felt like laughing out loud, but she didn't want to give him the wrong idea. Was it possible he was still in love with her? After all she had put him through? She dipped her face in the flowers and in the moment of sniffing their divine, sweet scent she felt – there was only one word for it – happy! Such an ordinary feeling, once, but of late, it had become extraordinary.

'OK, very funny.' Tom was a lot more amused than he was letting on as he pottered out into the kitchen. He had forgotten how much he liked Dermot. He just hoped there wasn't more trouble ahead.

'You look well,' Dermot said.

Ava smiled, self-consciously. She looked a mess but again, she knew he could not see it. She had not even dressed properly. She was wearing no make-up and an old dressing gown over slacks and a light sweater. She could not think of anything to say that would not raise his hopes. Everything she wanted to say, a joke about his shiny buttons, a quip on how he was 'wearing his hair' (even though it was thinning), or even a comment on how well he was looking himself, might slide them back into the comfortable familiarity of how they had once been. How were you supposed to be with a man you had cruelly dumped? A man who had the right to gloat over your misfortune, and yet, in his kind face, she could see so clearly that was not the case. Dermot, sensing her awkwardness, stepped in.

'I was just passing...'

Ava held up the roses and smiled at him.

Dermot's heart ached, just looking at her.

She looked so beautiful to him. He didn't care if she was wearing a dressing gown and her hair looked as if she hadn't brushed it for a few days. She looked like a queen to him. His queen.

'Ah yes. The flowers. I found them on the sidewalk on my way in... They must've fallen out of a florist van.'

Ava laughed.

'You know how careless delivery men are.'

She was grinning now. Her face lit up like a beacon when she did that.

'Look,' he said, 'I heard you were back home and—'

'It's OK,' she said. And, to her surprise, Ava realized that it was.

'Can I take you out to lunch?' he said. 'It doesn't have to be anywhere fancy...'

'Now?'

'Well, if it's...'

She put him out of his misery.

'Great,' she said. 'Let me run upstairs and get changed.'

She left the flowers on the hall table. Tom came back out and picked them up.

'Ah – I get to put them in a vase at least.'

Dermot smiled. He felt he should be saying something to Tom, explain himself somehow. He just wasn't sure what that was. He broke the silence anyway by saying, 'Ava is upstairs getting changed…'

Tom was staring at him intently.

'…I am taking her out…'

Too intently.

'To lunch…'

Then Tom said it. What he had been bottling up for weeks. 'Ava is very delicate right now. If you hurt her…'

'I understand—'

Dermot knew what he was trying to say and wanted to spare him, but Tom would not be interrupted.

'If you hurt her, so help me God, I don't know what I'll do.'

Tom's face was tight with contained rage. Dermot recognized the feeling because he also channelled his masculine anger through the filter of reason. It was how respectable men did things.

'I would never hurt Ava,' Dermot assured him. He would have added more about how he felt about the likes of Patrick Murphy and how he would welcome the opportunity to protect Ava from such men in the future, but she came down the stairs.

They drove as far as Getty Square and had lunch in a diner. Nowhere fancy, just somewhere impersonal and cheap where they were not likely to run into anybody they knew. They talked as easily as they had always done. No mention of Patrick, or lost babies. Dermot told her about his disastrous meeting with Joe Higgins and the Balducci brothers, and Ava was horrified, and impressed, but mostly – amused. She had forgotten how much Dermot made her laugh. What he lacked on the dance floor or in dashing good looks, he more than made up for in personality.

'Actually, I've got a confession,' he said. He took a chance and told her about nearly running into her and hiding in the confessional box. He made it sound so funny that Ava actually wept with laughter, although he didn't tell her about confessing his love for her to the priest. That would have been too much and he needed to hang on to some semblance of dignity.

Once or twice during the lunch Ava felt her hand wanting to creep across the table and take his. She was grateful that he did not reach out in the same way. It would have been too much. But, at the same time, she felt perhaps, if he had it might have felt as if they had never been apart.

After they had eaten and Dermot had settled with the waitress, Ava said, 'Shall we go for a stroll? I've hardly been out of the house for weeks.'

Dermot felt ludicrously happy. He was trying to keep himself in check but his spirit was soaring. This afternoon was going better than he could have ever expected. She was as warm and loving towards him as she ever had been. And, he believed, he had cheered her up and made her happy. Making Ava happy gave him more joy than anything else. Could it possibly be that they were starting again?

As they walked, Ava took his arm. As he felt her hand settle on the crook of his elbow he reached down and rested his own hand on top of it. She did not move away.

They walked in companionable silence, not taking much notice of what was going on around them. Dermot was lost in a reverie of romantic love. He was afraid, in fact, to open his mouth in case he said something foolish like 'Shall we get married?' or 'I love you' and of course it was way too early for that. Dignity was the thing now. Dignity and respect... and then Ava stopped walking.

Dermot rejoined the world and his heart gave a jolt when he saw where they were.

They were standing outside the Emerald dance hall and in front of them was a huge poster advertising, 'Patrick Murphy sings his debut single, "It Was Only Ever You". Saturday, 8pm.'

Dermot began to panic. Ava seemed paralysed. Her hand loosened on the base of his bicep.

Dermot did not know what to say. Did she expect him to say something? There were any number of barbed comments forming in the back of his mind, the most obvious of which was to simply mutter the expletive 'bastard!'

But he was too much of a gentleman to do that. So he simply put his hand over Ava's again, and picked up the stroll. He kept the talk going with silly chit-chat but inside his head he was saying, 'You stupid idiot! You led her straight to him! Stupid, stupid idiot.'

They went back to the car and Dermot drove her home.

The spell had been broken but then, as she was getting out, Ava turned, looked him in the eye and said, with all sincerity, 'Thank you for a lovely afternoon, Dermot. It was really good to see you.'

'Maybe we can do it again?' he said.

She looked at him, seeming to pause, then said, 'Maybe sometime, Dermot. I'm glad we are friends, but...'

'I understand,' he said. Then he smiled, said, 'Goodnight,' and pulled the door shut.

He had given her his heart and, for the second time, she had broken it.

'But'. Dermot knew exactly what that meant. But you are not handsome. But you are not exciting. But you are too nice. Too funny. I love you *but* I am in love with somebody else. Let's just be friends.

All the way back to the city Dermot worked himself up into a rage. He knew he could make Ava happy, but if she was going to persist with being 'in love' with this cad, well then, he was going to have to do something about it.

He had had enough. There were going to be no more 'buts' for Dermot Dolan.

It was time to man up and take action. Dermot ran up the stairs to his apartment and grabbed the phone book from the hall table. He found the number he was looking for and dialled.

A woman's voice answered.

'Is that Myrtle Milligan?'

'Yes.'

'Myrtle – this is Dermot Dolan. I need your help.'

36

ROSE PUT the finishing touches to her illustration. It was a lavish party table with platters of vol-au-vents and steaming apple pies laid out on a gingham tablecloth with the logo 'Molly's Party Platters' emblazoned across the top in copperplate typescript. She was still learning to measure out the stencils, but it looked even to her.

She straightened the A1 sheet on her drawing board and waited while Christopher, her boss, the creative director in Gimble Advertising, checked it over.

Man, this girl was good. In just two months she had picked up the basic rules of advertising design, in addition to being able to draw, always to the brief and close to perfection.

When his sister Marisa had rung Christopher and asked him if he could find a job for some Irish girl she knew, he was sceptical. She did not have an art education or any art training, but Marisa rarely asked him for anything, even though he knew she and Donnie were hard up, so he couldn't say no. The pretty, blonde, demure creature, clearly middle-class, was very different from what he had been expecting. But Christopher took his sister's word that she was 'needy' and put her to making coffee and buying in lunches for the art studio. The kid got lucky on her fourth day in the job. The studio was snowed under with deadlines when a last-minute pitch for a new brand of cigarette came in from the sales team. Chris had no one else, and decided to give her a try-out. It turned out he was the lucky one. Rose had a rare talent for drawing. Less than an hour after he gave her the brief she came back with a life-like drawing of a Hollywood doyenne, smoking with such style that the client bought it straight away. From day one, Christopher had found Rose to be the most efficient, accurate artist he had ever worked with. She was his shining star. Unlike many of the brilliant illustrators who earned a fortune in advertising, Rose was not arrogant or demanding. She was not only an excellent employee but a popular member of the team. The men were all a little bit in love with her, and, because she was so young and innocent to the ways of the big city, the women all felt protective of her. Rose had a bright, friendly way about her, doing the secretaries' jobs for them and always anxious to be helpful and cooperative. She now shared an apartment with two of the secretaries on the Upper East Side. As a fine artist, Rose's salary had already outstripped that of Christopher's brother-in-law Donnie. He felt bad about that, but he had to pay her union rates for the job she was doing. Marisa told him that Rose called around to them every week, without fail, with gifts for the children and themselves. Marisa would not take any money off Chris, so he was thinking of recruiting Rose in his efforts to get his sister set up in a hair salon as soon as this next baby was born. He was beginning to consider her a friend.

'Looks great, Rose,' he said now, leaning into the picture and marvelling at the detail. 'I'd like you to come into the client meeting after lunch.'

Rose loved her work. Christopher telling her what to draw all day long, and having to produce drawings to a deadline, was the perfect job for her. Not least because it offered her constant distraction. Rose needed distraction more than anything else.

'You're my lucky charm, Rose,' Chris said. 'Go out for lunch and I'll see you in the boardroom at two.'

Rose smiled sunnily and said, 'See you then!'

She knew she had been lucky. A whole life in New York. In just two months she was settled into a great job and an apartment in the city. She was making new friends and a whole world was opening up to her.

However, Rose felt that if she was charmed, it was by the devil. She had intended to run away from all the bad things she had done in the past few months. From stealing the money from her parents and leaving them to go out of their mind with worry about her. Impulsively chasing across the world to find Patrick and determinedly pursuing him even though he was now married to somebody else. Lying to Ava and encouraging him in the deceit was the worst of all. She might have been the cause of the loss of that baby, she had certainly been the cause of a broken marriage.

From the vantage point of her new, lucky life, Rose could see the hardship and pain that she had caused. Not only could she see it, she could feel it now. Every day, not one minute went past when Rose was not filled with regret at the intense, determined madness that had overtaken her in her pursuit of Patrick Murphy. Because that was all it was. Madness. When they said 'madly in love' was that what they meant?

She had come to the taxi driver's home in Harlem in a very different mood from the one she had left it in. Almost immediately she confessed to Marisa the terrible things she had done since she had left them. Marisa had not thrown her out on the street, but offered a kind, sympathetic ear and contacted her brother.

The ease with which Rose had fallen into this new life, and seemingly been forgiven for her sins, far from making life easier for her, was making it harder. Aside from the time when she was lost in her work, she felt guilty all the time. A sick dread clung to her conscience. The inescapable knowledge that she was, despite her pretty looks and polite ways, a bad person. Rose hated herself for what she had done and was beginning to hate herself for the person she was because of it. Everybody liked her, but that was because they thought she was a nice person. Only she knew that she was not a nice person. She was a bad person masquerading as sweet. She was a fake and she knew it.

As soon as Rose had begun her new job, she had written to her parents. She had kept it brief, apologized for all the worry she had caused them, and promised to pay back all of the money she had stolen.

She received a letter shortly afterwards from her father, apologizing himself for having chased Patrick away. He assured Rose that while he had forgiven her, he was still trying to persuade her mother that it was a good idea for Rose to stay in New York for a while. Her mother was still very anxious that she come home and missed her terribly.

Reading between the lines, Rose understood that her mother was suffering from depression. She knew that if she was not entirely the cause of it, the disappearance had certainly been a catalyst.

Short of returning home, there was nothing she could do to comfort her parents. She also knew that if she did return home, there would be no comfort for her.

In the meantime, she had to try and enjoy this new life, despite the terrible things she had done to Patrick and Ava. She knew that apologizing to them would not be as simple as it had been with her parents. She had caused a lot of pain and it was better for her to leave them alone to deal with it. To try and offload it on to them would be a selfish act. At the same time, she wanted to try and find a way of living with it, of living with herself, with more comfort.

The offices had been so busy lately that she decided to get out on her own, get some fresh air and try to clear her head. There was a corner café that she liked two blocks from the office, midtown towards Hell's Kitchen. She took a window seat and ordered herself a salt beef sandwich on rye bread and a coffee. Rose gazed out the window, watching the world go by, feeling a little sad at how separate she felt from it all.

As the waitress laid down her coffee she paused with her hand on the cup and looked off into the middle distance as a song came on the radio.

I ask myself are you the one I dream of night and day
Are you the reason why this yearning never goes away…

'Turn that up, Freddie!' she shouted out.

The music became louder, as the waitress sauntered to the next table, slowed down by the romantic, crooning voice:

I ask myself are you the one whose face I can't forget
Your name hangs gently on each breeze I still can hear it yet

Rosie felt her stomach turn inside out. It was Patrick, singing that song. Their song. The song he had written for her, telling her, 'It was only ever you.'

She threw some dollars on the counter and ran out. It had been a terrible shock, hearing his voice like that. What did it mean? She had known that his manager had been planning to release it as a record, but it seemed inconceivable that it had actually happened. Emotion pumped through her, fear, excitement, shame, shock, but underneath all of them emerged the untrammelled thrill of having been loved by him; of being the woman he had written those words for. It was wrong, so wrong, but she could not help it. Would this cursed feeling ever go away? The feeling of being in love with somebody who cannot love you back.

Rose found she had been wandering aimlessly in the opposite direction to the office. Afraid she might be lost, she stopped to check where she was, and saw she was standing outside a church. She had not been to mass since she had come to New York. She stood for a moment, looking up at the imposing building, its ornate steeple reaching up into the grey, Manhattan skyline, competing with the office buildings either side of it, and thought that perhaps her loss of religion had contributed to her wayward behaviour. She had not given a thought to the right or the wrong thing to do in her pursuit of love. She had been too single-minded, too passionate. Perhaps if she talked to a priest and confessed her sins, Rose might get some relief.

She had forty minutes before she had to be back at the meeting at two, so she climbed up the steps. Inside, the church seemed much bigger and grander than on the outside. She immediately regretted the idea of finding a priest and making her confession in such a large, intimidating place.

Then, walking towards her, she saw a familiar face. She struggled to remember who it was before finally recognizing him as the priest who had taken her out to the Bronx. A friend of Donnie and Marisa. Father...? She smiled and walked slowly towards him, desperately trying to remember his name.

He remembered her, though, and marching determinedly towards her he barked, 'I hope you're here to do a confession, young lady.'

Rose started. How did he know? She remembered, he knew Tom Hogan – but it was too late to turn back. He had her in his sights.

'After all the trouble you caused. You should be ashamed of yourself...'

Rose did feel ashamed of herself. She was about to tell him as much when he continued.

'...coming over here, chasing after some man you think you're in love with. I have never heard of such nonsense...'

As he continued, Rose said, 'I'm sorry. I'm sorry, Father...'

Perhaps it was because of the way that she had found herself saying 'Father', even though she was simply addressing a priest, but Rose was taken back to that moment in her father's study where she had seen the letters that Patrick had written her. The letters that her father had hidden. The words of 'It Was Only Ever You' that she had heard earlier in the café. And Rose realized she wasn't sorry for having followed Patrick to New York. She was sorry about what had happened since she got here. And she was sorry that her parents had been worried, she was sorry that she had pursued Patrick when he had not wanted her to, she was sorry that she had kissed him when she had known he was married to somebody else. She was sorry that she hadn't simply told Ava the truth and then walked away, and she was deeply, deeply sorry for having betrayed a nice woman who had been nothing but kind to her.

However, when she looked into the face of the angry old priest, Rose realized that she was not sorry for having loved. She would not apologize for having been true to her heart, and she never would.

37

SITTING ON the stairs of her aunt and uncle's house in Riverdale, Sheila clung to Patrick. She was so raw and emotional that, for a moment, she thought she had fallen in love with him. Then, the shock passed and, as she saw the faces of her aunt and uncle she realized that the love she felt was the all-encompassing love she had felt as a child. The love of life itself and everyone around her. Standing in their hall, shattered with shock, the old couple looked into the face of their niece and immediately recognized that something significant had happened to her. The light in her that Hitler had extinguished was back. It was as intangible and mysterious as love itself. As the couple embraced her after the ordeal, they both felt it in the softened commitment of her arms around them and heard it in a barely discernible mellowing of her voice. Anya saw it first: the child had returned to Sheila's dark, once impervious eyes. The transformation felt as instant and as shocking to Anya as hitting the man's skull with the pot. Why such a terrible event should have had such a positive, transforming effect none of them could guess. Except that an old, sharp edge that had been twenty years in the making had been hit with a hammer and a soft curve left in its place.

Over the coming weeks Sheila polished that curve by encouraging and nurturing Patrick's talent.

Nothing developed between them, except for, on her part at least, a warm sense of sisterhood and mentorship. However, her caring for Patrick did go some way to filling the gap Iggy had left behind.

Her lover had pulled away from her. They had not slept together in weeks and Iggy's attitude towards her had reverted to a respectful employer–employee arrangement. No confrontation took place, just a quietly created distance separated them physically, and emotionally. Professionally, they remained in close touch. Sheila felt that Iggy had come to respect her way of doing things. Under her management, the Emerald was making more money than ever, and he had relinquished all control over Patrick's career and was letting her get on with it. Iggy resumed his rigorous travelling schedule. As he spent more and more time away, into that space emerged an assumption, with Sheila, that it was over. Once, in the office, she had picked up the phone to a woman. An air hostess, the girl had been keen to tell her. It hurt. But Sheila, for all her new vulnerability, could not give in to it. She had to keep herself moving forward, more now than ever. So she focused on her career and channelled that hurt into Patrick.

Iggy had allocated Sheila a budget to spend in whatever way she saw fit. The usual way of doing things for a manager was to engage the interest of a producer and then let them deal with the record company. Sheila had decided that she wanted to retain as much control as possible. Iggy, having set up the recording deal, allowed Sheila to go directly to the record company, setting herself up as producer, even though she had no track record. Sheila approached Malcolm, the songwriter, and asked if he had a young producer in his coterie who might be looking for a break. Declan was a year older than Malcolm, Irish, a technical music buff, bursting with talent and zero cash.

Sheila hired them the biggest, best studio in New York for the day.

'I want big!' she told Declan. 'A big, big sound. When the chorus comes, I want it to be like an avalanche of music. Like Mount Everest collapsing…'

Sheila filled the studio with musicians. They brought in the resident band, and bumped them up to a half-orchestra with some of Malcolm's rock and roll buddies, and Sheila's old friend Frankie and his friends provided some extra wind. She even invited Iggy along so he could see where his money was being spent.

She didn't expect Iggy to come, but he did. She did not notice him arrive and when she did spot him, sitting in his unobtrusive way at the back of the room, watching them all from a distance, Sheila felt a shot of pity for him. He seemed so out of place, so formal, in his straight-from-the-airport suit. She nodded at him and he nodded back, solemnly. He seemed sad and she longed to go over and talk to him. But she pushed the longing aside, reminding herself that they were no longer lovers, or even friends – simply business associates. She had work to do and he was here to make sure that she did it. She was determined not to have him distract her. However, when she looked around for him an hour later, and saw the grey office seat left empty, her heart sank.

Patrick, in contrast, was in his element. He had the song nailed. Every inch the star, he knew every line so well that, at one point, Sheila caught him singing it backwards to try and impress one of the guitarists.

Sheila told him that she needed him to put his heart and soul into every single take. As the day progressed, he did not let her down, as she strove to get the very best recording.

Past lunchtime and into the evening, Sheila cajoled the tired musicians into yet another take as Declan layered the sounds on the complicated deck. The young producer was in his element, sliding and pressing all the knobs and buttons, waving instructions and smoking frantically as coffee cups and bottles of beer gathered all around the edges of his deck. With the intensity of a true composer he altered treble and bass, building and building the sound until the ballad fell gently into heartbreaking, cavernous valleys and rose up in yearning crescendos. As Declan managed the sound, Sheila made Patrick reach, reach, reach for those high notes. She wanted so much emotion in this recording that it would draw tears from a stone.

By six o'clock, everyone believed that the song was in the bag. Except Sheila.

'I've got a half-dozen usable takes here, Sheila, at least two outstanding ones. We're done,' Declan said.

'One more time,' she pleaded.

She felt there was some small thing missing. She could not put her finger on it but she was sure she could get to it, if they would just try one more time.

Tired and hungry, everyone went for one last shot at it.

Sheila sat down, for the first time that day, next to Declan at the producer's bench. She leaned back and closed her eyes, allowing herself to get lost in Patrick's voice.

As his smooth baritone caressed each word, Sheila felt as if she was hearing the lyrics for the first time.

I ask myself are you the one who filled me with desire
Are those the eyes that once searched mine and set my soul on fire

Then, when he came to the crescendo, 'it was only ever you' Sheila suddenly felt it. The feeling she had been waiting for. It was as if her heart had been punctured, and whatever was inside released. A truth came flooding out of her. It was beautiful, certain and yet terrifying, because she had been neither wanting nor expecting to feel it. She loved Iggy. That strange, remote man was her other half, after all. The only man that could ever truly understand her. She had never met another like him and she knew she never would again.

She realized, too, that she had known she loved him all along but had been afraid to face up to it. Because, running alongside the certainty that she loved him ran the knowledge that he was utterly unavailable to her. He would, could, never love her back in the same way. Iggy was a lone wolf. He had never promised her anything different. He had got involved with her because she had been as cold, as hard as he was. When she had started to get close, he had backed off. Now that her heart was open, she could never be with him.

As the band came down on the last note, Sheila wiped away her tears. Everyone assumed she was crying for the song.

'It's a wrap, boys,' she said, clapping. 'Well done – we've got a hit on our hands!'

Sheila seemed happy, smiling and smacking everyone on the back and congratulating them. Inside, though, a bleak feeling had taken hold. Once 'It Was Only Ever You' hit the charts, it would be time for Sheila to move away. Joe Higgins would be back, as he had promised, and to stay any longer would be to put her family and Patrick in jeopardy. Patrick was on the road now. He did not need her any more, not in the same intense way he had needed her up to now. In any case, the kid was becoming way too dependent on her. He needed to stand on his own two feet. She was his manager, not his mother, and the quicker he came to terms with that the better.

More importantly, Sheila still had enough pride not to hang around New York yearning for a lover who did not want her.

Iggy had been hoping to get in and out of the Emerald within the hour. He had one or two things to tie up with Gerry before leaving on a more extended trip.

He needed some time away to think things through.

That day in the recording studio had opened his eyes to just what a great businesswoman Sheila was. Her handling of Patrick's career had really impressed him. She was, much like himself, a trailblazer, arranging this recording of 'It Was Only Ever You' in a completely different way from any that had been done before. Later that evening, the record would launch at the Emerald. Patrick would sing in New York while the single itself would be played simultaneously in each of Morrow's clubs across America, Ireland and Britain. They had been advertising it for weeks and each club would be packed with punters ready to spread the word. As soon as the record had been cut, Sheila had gone out there and bribed all the right DJs to give it airtime. Most of her upfront money had gone into ensuring the right DJs were in her pocket. Iggy had never had the stomach for paying people off, but Sheila had no such qualms. Decca would make a number of the records available in each venue for sale on the night. Sheila had brokered the deal. Record shops were up in arms at the bold move, but she asked Iggy to assure them they would not be making a habit of selling records in this way again. It was a promotional tactic. A way of getting Patrick's name out there in an aggressive, one-shot manner that would lead to greater sales down the line.

Iggy admired Sheila. She was not like anyone else he had ever met. She was creative and dynamic and she got things done. He even thought her to be a lot like himself, but when he saw her in the studio that day, the way that she handled the musicians, and her devotion to Patrick, he realized she was more than him. Sheila was an unknown entity to him. He felt she was extraordinary but there was an edge to her that he felt he didn't know. Could, maybe, never know, and the not knowing made him feel uncomfortable.

To Iggy, discomfort was the opposite of love. He knew that unsettled feeling from his boyhood. Not knowing where you are going or what you should be doing. It was a feeling he had been chasing away all of his life with his meticulous scheduling and his secretive ways, keeping everything so close to his chest that nobody else could get in. Iggy had organized his life so that he remained always separated from other people. He kept himself safe in his quiet isolation. The safety of solitude. Now this uncomfortable feeling was back. Sheila had brought a disquiet, an uncertainty with her.

He admired her, he wanted to be with her. But not if it meant losing himself in the process.

'Did you hear the news?' Gerry said as he walked into the office.

Iggy was in bad form this evening. You could tell from the cold way that he had nodded at him as if to say, 'In my office, now.' He had not even bothered to take his coat off.

Gerry guessed the reason for his bad mood, and his pro-longed disappearance. The boss and Sheila had been having an affair. Iggy had wanted to cool it for a while, so he had made himself scarce. Gerry couldn't really understand what the big deal was. As far as he could see, Iggy and Sheila were as strange as each other. They were a match made in heaven! Maybe if he got married he might be less of a strange fish. Hell, he might even get happy and cut back on the miserable, poker-faced arse act.

'What news?' he said, only half listening. He could not even pretend to be interested in gossip.

'Joe Higgins called around to Sheila's family home and came the heavy. He was acting for the Balduccis, stupid eejit. Anyway, he gave Patrick an awful pelt on the cheek...' Then, seeing Iggy's extraordinary expression of terror and fury, quickly added, 'Sheila's auntie threw a pot of roast beef at him and laid him out. Made quite a mess, it seems. Aiden was in here last night and said Joe is still mad as hell...'

'Why didn't you call me?' Iggy said, although he knew the answer already. Nobody had his number. If something bad happened, or if somebody got into trouble, the managers had autonomy to deal with it themselves. Iggy had no attachments to anyone or anything. Business was just business.

Until now.

Joe Higgins was surprised to see Iggy Morrow turning up in his club. Surprised but secretly pleased. He had doubtless come to plead for his girlfriend. Joe had taken a fall that night, that was true. It had taken him a little time to recover from the nasty gash on his cheek, but more time from the rumours that he had been felled by corned beef in the hands of a seventy-year-old woman. Joe laughed it off, but it wasn't over. Nobody humiliated him like that. The Jewish broad was still around and Joe had plans to send somebody else down to Riverdale to get rid of her once and for all. However, he had to hand-pick them. Aiden and his lads didn't do old people and women, but there were a few guys out there that were less discerning about their clientele.

Just the sight of Iggy Morrow being all manners to his doormen made the fact that his plans had not yet taken shape all the sweeter.

'Mr Morrow,' he said, walking towards him holding out his hand. 'It's a pleasure to see you.'

Iggy paused before raising his right hand. Joe noticed his reluctance and it really got his blood up. This guy had always got on his nerves. He just couldn't make him out. He was a successful guy and Joe could respect that. But he was too straight, if there was such a thing; at least, if he was bent, Joe didn't know about it, and that made him feel uncomfortable. Joe could not help feeling that Ignatius Morrow looked down his nose at him. Plus, nobody knew anything about him, where he was from or who his people were. It just wasn't how things were done. It just wasn't... Irish. He was a man of mystery. Joe figured that was probably a construct. Maybe Morrow just kept out of everybody's way because he was a coward.

'We need to talk,' Iggy said.

'Let's go into my office,' Joe said. 'It's out the back.'

As he guided his guest through the bar with a flourish, Joe noticed Iggy looking around, his lips curling at the abundantly green decor. He made a mental note to get it changed. At the same time, he had half a mind to call a couple of the guys into the meeting to help bring down the great Ignatius Morrow and show him who was boss. Morrow was a powerful man. He could probably pay to get people whacked but he didn't go in for violence. If he did, Joe would have heard about it. He was shorter than him, Joe happily observed. He didn't know what all the fuss was about. Joe could show him a few moves of his own. As they walked through the bar he drew some pictures in his head of how it might go. Joe would get things started with polite chat, explain about the Balduccis and reason with him. Morrow would probably get all uppity with him, Joe would seem to let it go, then you would have to pull a gun. He wouldn't even have to touch Iggy. He was a straight guy, and with guys like that all you needed was a gun in your hand and the kind of face that said you had the intention to use it. He would be frightened out of his wits!

Joe was allowing himself the indulgence of how it was going to be as he turned the handle on his office door. But before it was fully open, Iggy had grabbed Joe's arm and twisted it until he was lying on the floor of his office, face down. Iggy was sitting on his back and had something sharp trained at the corner of Joe's neck.

'I am not going to waste my time reasoning with you, Joe. If you ever come near any of my staff, ever again, I will personally kill you. But I'm guessing that you don't believe me, so I'm going to cut off your ear now just to make my point.'

'No, no, no!' Joe cried out.

He had been threatened enough times in his life to know when somebody meant what he said. Morrow had the cool voice of the guy who means business. He wasn't a hothead like Joe. He was one of the others. The really crazy ones. The ones you avoided. Shit.

'I hear you, I hear you!' Joe pleaded.

'The problem is, I don't believe you're a man of your word,' Morrow continued, not moving the knife an inch, 'so I'm just wondering if I should go ahead and do it anyway...'

'Please, please don't cut me. I swear I'll stay away from the whore and the kid. I promise.'

'Good,' Iggy said, putting the knife back in his pocket.

As he moved his knees from the small of Joe's back, the gangster heard a deafening crippling crack and screamed out in pain.

'That's for calling Sheila a whore,' Ignatius said as he broke Joe's arm at the elbow.

As Aiden ran to his boss's rescue Iggy added, '... and upsetting her family.' Then, as he walked out the door, 'Although I understand the old lady can look after herself quite well.'

He was shaking so hard when he came out of Joe's club that he could not trust himself to drive his own car and had to hail a taxi.

He was not shaking for fear of what he had just done, but the fear of what he was about to do. Even though he knew that it was the right thing to do, the only thing to do, his fear of failure was greater than it had ever been.

Iggy had not been afraid since he was a small boy. That was because he never wanted anything badly enough to be afraid of not getting it. He had a lot of money, but it meant nothing to him. If it all went in the morning he knew he would be fine with that. The great empire he had built up was simply a way of keeping control over his place in the world. It was as much to do with the lifestyle of moving from office to office, country to country, place to place, people to people – keeping separate – as it was to do with a sense of satisfaction of all he had 'achieved'.

Iggy knew that he could achieve anything he set his mind to, and with all his money and success, he could have

anything he wanted. The one thing, the only thing Iggy Morrow believed was beyond him, that had eluded him, was love.
All his life, ever since he was a little orphan boy, Iggy had
wanted a family. Sheila was as close as he had ever got to one
in forty years. As he said to the taxi driver, 'Third and Mill
Street, Riverdale,' the address he had memorized since their
first night together, Iggy still believed it was beyond him, but
he owed it to himself to try.

As the taxi drove up the leafy streets Iggy could feel his
fear rising. All these comfortable houses, filled with comfortable families, eating their meals at the same time every
night, watching TV together, leading small, ordinary lives.
It was another world to him. And as the taxi drove deeper into
suburbia, on every street corner he thought about telling the
driver to turn back. Finally they pulled up outside the house.

'Is this it?' the driver asked.

'I don't know,' he replied, but he got out and threw twenty
dollars at him anyway.

The taxi driver decided to wait. The guy was a generous
tipper and he might want to be brought back to the city if it
was the wrong place.

Anya opened the door and started slightly. She had been
expecting Ruth from the bakery who had promised she would
drop by with the cheesecake. The sight of a strange man at
her door threw her, especially when he said, 'Is Sheila there?'

Immediately, Sheila appeared behind her. As he stepped
inside, Iggy noticed two large cases in the hallway.

'Yours?' he said to Sheila.

She nodded, awkwardly. What was Iggy doing here?

She had decided to quit town before tonight. The big launch
would be high profile, and she didn't want the wrong people
hearing about her being the manager. She was going to take

a leaf out of Iggy's book and stay out of the limelight. She'd written Patrick a letter explaining as much to him, because she knew that he would try and persuade her to be there. Possibly even try to protect her if there was trouble. And that wouldn't do his career any good. Once she was out of the way, Patrick and her family would be safe.

'I just called to let you know,' Iggy said, 'that Joe Higgins won't be bothering you any more.'

She believed him. Iggy was a force to be reckoned with. Way more powerful than Joe Higgins, but all the same she would never have asked for his help. Who had told him?

'So you can put those bags away and come back to work.'

Work. That was all this was.

'I'm not coming back,' she said. 'I always said I would move on, and it's time.'

'I see,' Iggy said, but he didn't move. He couldn't. There was something that he felt he wanted to say but whatever that something was it had eluded him completely. Or rather, it was so terrifying he could not even put words to it.

Anya was standing near the kitchen door. Utterly enraptured with the scenario, she was keeping as still as she could so that Sheila would not notice her eavesdropping. Sheila saw Iggy's eyes move shyly across her, turned around and said, 'Auntie!'

The old lady jumped and Iggy, despite the grave situation he found himself in, laughed.

He leaned past Sheila and held out his hand. 'You must be Sheila's Aunt Anya? She's told me so much about you.'

She virtually ran towards him to take his hand.

'You're the big boss man, so nice to meet you,' she said, almost genuflecting. 'Why don't you come in and have some tea? I am expecting a cheesecake delivery at any moment.'

He smiled again and said, 'That would be delightful.'

'My husband is out at present, but he should be back at any moment and—'

'Auntie!' Sheila said. 'Please, I need to talk with – Mr Morrow.'

It was painful having him there, standing in her hallway, just as she was about to leave. It was difficult enough leaving Auntie and Uncle. She had not been planning to say goodbye to him as well.

'Mrs Klein, Anya,' Iggy said, 'I would love some tea but first, I have something I need to ask Sheila...'

Sheila turned and gave Anya a wide-eyed stare that said, 'You see?' and as she did her aunt's jaw dropped open and she pulled her hands up to her mouth in a shocked gasp.

When Sheila turned around again, Ignatius Morrow was kneeling in front of her.

'Sheila Klein,' he said, 'would you do me the honour of becoming my wife?'

For a moment, Sheila stood there, unable to believe what she was seeing. Initially, she actually believed that this was some kind of dreadful joke he was making in front of her little old Jewish aunt.

Then she looked at his face. His expression was grave and slightly cross, as it always was, but kneeling, looking up at her, there was not a hint of scepticism in his eyes. Only a tender pleading. Iggy wasn't simply asking her to marry him, he was begging her to love him.

She leant down, pulled him up to his feet and glared at Anya until she went away.

'You don't need to marry me, Iggy,' she said. 'I love you, anyway.'

'Then you'll stay?' he said.

'Yes,' she said. 'I'll stay.'

And they kissed, both knowing that Anya was watching from the kitchen door.

'Will we go back to the Emerald?' he said. 'It's your big night.'

'Maybe later,' she said. 'Patrick can fend for himself for a few hours at least. I think we should stay here and eat cheesecake.'

So that's what they did.

38

AVA HAD been unsettled and had barely slept since her afternoon out with Dermot, a week ago. Nessa was beginning to worry that her daughter was sliding back into the listlessness.

In fact, quite the opposite was happening. Ava was thinking about getting her life back on track, and what her next step ought to be.

Seeing Patrick's poster outside the Emerald had jolted her back down to earth. Not that Dermot's attentions had her floating on a pink cloud, but she had been enjoying his company. The intrusion of seeing her husband's smiling, handsome face on that huge poster had immediately given her pause about the wisdom of gadding about with her ex-fiancé.

She saw that Patrick was releasing his first record later that week. So, his dream of being a famous singer was finally coming to fruition and Ava knew she had been an important part of that. How must he be feeling now? she asked herself. Just as everything was coming together for him, his marriage ended and he lost a baby. Ava had not even said goodbye to him, left a note or anything. She had been hurt by what he had done, the terrible betrayal, the way in which she had found out about it and the subsequent terrible loss of the baby, which she had managed to get through without his support.

She began to see that it was not entirely his fault, either. He had come to the house but her father had chased him away. Perhaps if Tom had let Patrick into the house that day, and they had talked, all of this would be behind them now.

Rose was out of the picture. She had left town. When Myrtle had told Ava about how she had confronted Rose, Ava had been quite upset. She felt quite sorry for the girl. After all, the only crime she had committed was loving Patrick and following him to America. She knew that Myrtle was only acting out of loyalty and kindness to her, but there was something humiliating about her husband's lover being banished on her behalf. There was no doubt that Patrick had loved Rose once, enough to get engaged to her. But then, Ava remembered, she had been engaged to Dermot and had left him for Patrick. If Rose and Patrick truly loved each other nothing would keep them apart. Certainly not a threat from Myrtle.

But, whatever he had done, Patrick was still her husband. He had made a mistake, one mistake, albeit a very serious one. But, underneath it all, he was a good man, and Ava knew he would have been suffering. Patrick had always told her that he could never be a success without her. And now that his dream was coming true, the very foundation on which it was built had crumbled. He must be feeling dreadful. Ava, for all the pain she still felt at his having betrayed her, still felt a deep loyalty to the love they had shared and to the baby they had made and then lost. They were married. Surely that meant they should stick together, no matter what?

All of this was swirling in a confusing soup of conflicting thoughts and emotions in her head as she sat down for breakfast that morning.

Nessa put the cornflakes packet in front of her and asked, 'When are you going to see Dermot again?'

You could tell from her voice that she had been clinging on to the question since their afternoon out, a week ago.

'Really, Ava, he is such a nice man.'

Ava felt like screaming at her but instead she just nodded and said, 'I know.'

There was no point in trying to explain any of her thoughts to her mother. In any case, Nessa was right, Dermot was a very nice man. But then, he always had been. He had just never been quite 'enough' somehow. That was something that she could never hope to make her mother understand. In truth, Ava struggled to understand it herself.

In any case, Ava had a feeling that Dermot would always be there, but if she wanted to hold on to Patrick, and their marriage, she would have to act fast.

Whatever the future held for them, Ava knew that she should be there for him on his important night. She would simply go along as a member of the audience. Maybe they would talk. Or maybe he would just see that she was there to support him. Whether they would be able to put the past behind them and reunite was a matter for later. However, Ava knew she had to at least try to make it work.

'Anyway, I'm going out tonight,' she said to Nessa. She did not tell her where or who with and Nessa had the good sense not to ask. Although, as she stood at the sink facing out the kitchen window, she beamed heartily, believing it was Dermot. Wait until she told Tom!

Ava telephoned Myrtle while her mother was out of earshot

to see if she would come along as her partner in crime. She did not mention Patrick, just that she would like to go dancing at the Emerald. If Myrtle told her that it was Patrick's gig, something she would surely know about, Ava would try and persuade her it didn't matter. But, she didn't.

'I'm busy tonight,' she said.

'A date?' Ava asked. If Myrtle met a man now and left her, Ava did not know what she would do.

'Maybe,' Myrtle said mysteriously, then quickly rang off saying, 'Got to go, I have a crazy day!'

Ava tried to keep her head straight for the rest of the day. To her parents' astonishment, she took a train into the city for the first time since her recovery began, and walked round the stores looking for an outfit to wear that night. However, she was so filled with nervous excitement, she could not find anything and took the subway back to Yonkers, where she went to a local salon, getting her hair styled and her nails manicured. In the early evening, she opened her wardrobe to find something to wear. By this time, she was irritated with how she was feeling at the prospect of seeing Patrick again. It was a very different kind of excitement to the lusty nervousness of when they had first met. This stomach-churning was closer to dread than passion. She was not thinking of seeing him with any particular joy in her heart. She only knew that she should be there, and that, if she ended up being on show as Patrick's wife, she should, at least, look her very best. Not simply for him, but more to prove something to herself.

Opening her wardrobe she flicked through endless mediocre, casual ensembles, flinching as her freshly painted fingernails brushed the maternity dresses. Then, she came to it. The rose suit.

She had lost a great deal of weight in the last few weeks. Would it fit her?

She quickly took it out and tried it on. The zip on the skirt ran up like butter. Every button on the jacket closed snugly across her breasts.

Nervously, Ava looked at herself in the mirror. She saw the elegant young woman who had surprised her, a year ago, in front of Sybil Connolly's Plaza suite mirror. Except that her transformation was no longer simply in the suit. It had been earned through a year of love and loss. Life was written on her face, now, and it had made her beautiful.

She drove down to South Broadway and parked outside the Emerald.

Even though it was early there was already a long queue. Taking a deep breath, Ava marched to the top of the queue, as she had done in the old days. Gerry happened to be at the door. His eyebrows raised slightly in surprise. 'Ava. Good to see you,' was all he said, before ushering her in himself.

'You going backstage?' he asked, gently.

'Not tonight,' she replied, and he sat her at a booth near the stage, instructing one of the bar staff to bring across the red VIP rope and wait on her all evening.

Ava appreciated his recognizing her status, but his respect-fulness also made her feel a little sad. This did not feel like her life. Aside from that one night when she had got Patrick up on stage, she had never been a part of his work. He had said that she was his rock, but, in reality, Patrick had done it all by himself. His manager, Sheila, had been the one to encourage and support him. Ava certainly did not resent her for it. She had never had any real interest in the music, beyond dancing to it and enjoying it, just the same as everybody else. She was his audience. No more, no less. In a small, shocking moment she wondered if she had been the inspiration for this record that Sheila had arranged for him. 'It Was Only Ever You'. Surely not. It had never been only Ava. In some part of her, she had always known that. She had always known that she was not the first girl he had been in love with. That was why she had never asked. If she had he might have told her that he was in love with Rose. And although Patrick had been the first man she had gone all the way with, Dermot had been the first man she kissed. If she had married Dermot, before she met Patrick, he would have been the only man she might have known her whole life. And that, even though it was wrong, might have driven Ava half-mad with wondering what might have been...

The compère came out and introduced the resident band. Patrick would be on stage at eight o'clock, less than half an hour away. The place was really filling up fast, and, as the band struck up Bill Haley's Saturday-night anthem, 'Rip It Up!' couples began flooding on to the dance floor. The air was electric with the start of the weekend and everyone was letting off steam. Ava was sitting there, demure with her cigarette and a just-delivered martini, with no intention of dancing. She watched on as guys threw girls over their shoulders, spinning them around, with feet going heel-to-toe faster than was feasible. This had once been her world, but tonight, all that felt like a lifetime ago.

'Wee-ell I got me a date and I won't be late...'

As the song took off Ava's friend Myrtle came into view. She was ripping it up like crazy, right in the middle of the floor with some guy who Ava assumed must be her new mystery man.

* * *

Dermot had begged Myrtle not to make him jive. After his frantic phone call where he had asked Myrtle to come and teach him, once and for all, how to dance, Dermot had immediately regretted the decision.

He never felt more of a bumbling fool than when he was on the dance floor. The baggy, long-line suits, coupled with his complete lack of coordination made Dermot look, and feel, like the greatest idiot that had ever drawn breath. Dermot was at his best in a courtroom, and an old-fashioned three-piece suit like his father, pontificating cleverly. However, Ava was never likely to see him in that light. And if she did, it was unlikely to impress her. He had tried, and failed, so far, to win Ava's heart and, out of desperation, imagined that learning to dance might do the trick. However, he now realized a few lessons wasn't going to fix his broken heart. And, in any case, he had been attending Mrs Quinn's dance classes for months now, and he still had two left feet. He was beyond help.

However, to the indomitable dancer Myrtle, nobody was beyond help when it came to romance.

So, on the phone that day, she did a deal.

'I will teach you to dance and fix you up with Ava if you put in a word for me with your brother.'

Niall, that little tearaway – what would she want with him? 'Fine,' he said. 'I'll put you in his path.'

'And your mother?'

Myrtle knew from Ava that Mrs Dolan was a hard nut to crack.

'I'll tell her you are a real lady from an excellent family.'

'Which I am.'

'Of course you are.'

'We have a deal. See you tomorrow at your place, six p.m. I assume you have a record player?'

'Of course!' Although his records were mostly Mahler.

'I'll bring the records. Roll back the sofa and don't be late.'

In their first session, she laid out the ground rules.

'Rule one: do everything I say. Rule two: listen closely to the music. Rule three: keep going no matter what.'

For the next two hours Myrtle dragged, cajoled, persuaded and prodded Dermot around his living room. Dermot was a nice guy. She liked him. She was glad that he loved Ava and she was sure that, if she could just fire a little jazz into him, she could get Ava to love him back. But when it came to being fun, of which dancing was the top qualification, he was a washout. Finally, after a lacklustre cha-cha, she sat him down, looked him straight in the eye and called him out.

'Do you love Ava?'

'Why?' he said.

'Don't look at me all embarrassed. If you don't know by now then...'

'She is beautiful...'

'And?'

'She's smart, and funny. She makes me laugh...'

As he was talking Dermot began to feel as if Ava was there, in the room with them. 'She is full of energy and life...' God he loved her, 'and she is just about the most capable woman I know...' It was all true. How he wanted her back! He had to win her back!

'Yes, Dermot, she is all that and she loves to dance. So, if you want her back, you are going to have to step up to the plate, loverman. Because Ava is not going to settle for some lousy grey lawyer who is as stiff as a board. Is that you, Dermot?'

'No, it's not!'

'Can we do this, Dermot?'

'Yes!' He was going to jive his way back into Ava's heart if it was the last thing he did!

Myrtle stood up and put on 'Rock Around the Clock' for the umpteenth time.

'And remember – it's only a bloody dance. Don't let it get the better of you. Now. Let's try it one more time. With some feeling, yes?'

As Ava watched Myrtle giving her all on the dance floor, getting stuck into 'Rip It Up!' she felt a twinge of regret that those days seemed to be behind her. She did not quite know how that had happened. Only that the carefree impulse to jump on to the dance floor and let herself go had left her. She had become so distracted by her passion for Patrick that dancing had seemed childish somehow. It was who she had been before she met these men. It was no longer part of her life, and she felt that, more keenly than ever, sitting separate from the crowd in her private booth. Alone, struggling to recover from the aftermath of her broken marriage. Dancing was something you did when you were happy, did not have a care in the world. Perhaps she would be happy one day. As Ava was thinking these thoughts, her eyes fixed on Myrtle.

She was wearing a beautiful sky-blue blouse tucked into a black skirt, which hugged her curves, and a pair of stilettos. It set off her slim figure perfectly and she was dancing very elegantly, and without her usual wild abandon. Nonetheless, her face was glittering with joy, and she seemed very pleased with herself indeed. He must be a very special guy, Ava thought, if he is eliciting this kind of effort from flirtatious Myrtle. As they spun around in a restrained, but perfectly timed turn,

Ava strained her eyes to get a look at him. As he came into focus she was astonished to see that it was Dermot.

That was not what she had been expecting. Dermot? Dancing? He wasn't the best dancer in the room, but he wasn't the worst either. When did this happen? Could Dermot really be Myrtle's mystery date? It certainly looked like it. She was beaming like the cat that got the cream. Dermot was a free man, he could date whomever he liked. But Myrtle? Everyone knew she was desperate to find a husband— Wait – was Ava jealous? As she watched the couple weave in and out, their arms sliding seamlessly over each other's body, smiling, jumping about, having fun, Ava felt a stab of sadness for all she had lost. Then something happened. The band hit a particular part of the song that she loved. Ava felt the music tingling through her feet, then moving up her legs, filling her chest, her arms, every inch of her body until she got up from her seat and began walking towards the couple. As she walked, Ava felt the beat slamming through her, driving her on. 'I'm gonna rip it up...' There was only one thing on her mind: This is my dance, this is my man and, as she pushed Myrtle aside and slid seamlessly into a side swing, This is my life and to hell with the world. I'm gonna shake it up!

Dermot was surprised and almost lost his step when Ava butted in. He had practised every move of this dance meticulously with Myrtle and wasn't sure he could carry it off with anyone else. But Ava was so determined, so glorious in her smiling, smooth energy, that all he wanted was to keep her there, with him. Dermot found he was able to stay one step ahead of her, pre-empting her moves, being the steady presence guiding and leading her into looking good in her favourite place, the dance floor. It seemed that this was what made Ava happy, and Dermot loved making her happy.

When the jive ended, the band moved on to a slow waltz. Ava was utterly distracted by the adrenalin that was still pumping through her. The delight of dancing again. The thrill of it being with Dermot. She paused, briefly remembering that she was here to see Patrick, but then Dermot put his arms around her and pulled her into a tight, chest-hugging waltz hold. Patrick had never held her like that, with such firm determination. Then, without giving her time to breathe, Dermot leaned in close to her and whispered in a voice that was deeper, more masterful that she remembered it being.

'There is no other woman in the world like you, Ava. You are the only one for me and you always will be. Please. Let me make you happy.'

Dermot knew he should stop there but, uncertain he had fully got his point across, he decided to drum his message home with a quote he had recently come across, although he was not sure where from. 'Ava, my darling – you know that "it was only ever you" I could love. Will you give me another chance?'

Ava's stomach did a sideways turn. Dermot was setting himself up in direct competition with Patrick. Using the title of her husband's song to woo her. What an outrageously confident thing to do. No wonder he was considered one of the best lawyers in the country! She was impossibly torn. On the one hand was Patrick, with whom she was passionately in love, and on the other was stalwart Dermot, although, it seemed, that had all changed. In fact, standing here in Dermot's arms, with the heat of the jive still pumping through her, Ava could feel the same powerful stirrings Patrick had brought out in her. Plus, Dermot said Ava was the 'only one' but she saw the way Myrtle had been gripping him during that jive. Imagine if Dermot ended up with Myrtle Milligan.

Her mother would go half mad. Then, Ava realized with something of an emotional jolt, so would she.

She had to act fast.

She brought her voice down to a breathy whisper, and leaned into his ear and asked, 'Have you got your car outside, Dermot?'

Taken aback, and somewhat disappointed at the change of subject, he answered, 'Yes.'

'Good,' she said, reaching for his hand, 'because I want you to take me for a drive.'

Dermot was delighted that Ava wanted to leave with him, alone, and not stay on to hear her wretched husband sing his silly song, whatever it was. However, he was slightly confused about the car. Where was it she wanted to go? What on earth could she mean by 'drive'? Not... Oh now, surely not. How could he even dare think of anything so unseemly of Ava? Not that he had never thought about it but... No, it simply wasn't possible.

Ava dragged her new lover silently across the dance floor and out of the Emerald. She smiled to herself as she thought about the thrills that were ahead of them that night and how shocked Myrtle would be to think what she was up to, especially after she had set her sights on him.

She did not know that Myrtle was with Dermot's brother Niall in a corner booth, engaged in a determined kiss.

39

P ATRICK HAD never been more nervous in his life. There
was about an hour to go until he was due on stage
and he had just read the note that Sheila had left in his
dressing room.

It said she was leaving town for a while and would be
basing herself in Boston, 'for the next few months, at least,
maybe longer'. She would be forwarding her phone number within the next two days, and, in the meantime, his gig
schedule was all set through Mr Morrow's venues, and Iggy's
secretary would be in touch to firm up any queries.

Patrick could not believe that Sheila had abandoned him
in this way. How could he manage without her? He had no
wife to look after him, no family to fall back on. Over the
past few weeks Sheila had become everything to him. If she
were younger, he might even have fallen in love with her. That
evening, when he had taken a fall for her, he had thought that
perhaps he already had. However, he knew that the warm feelings he had towards her were more gratitude than anything

else. Without the help she had given him since he got here, he would be nothing. He owed her as much as, if not more than, he owed Ava.

He looked up at his mirror where Sheila had pinned the words of 'It Was Only Ever You'. He felt a sting of regret for Rose but quickly pushed thoughts of her aside. That was what he always did. He had sung the song so many times now that he had almost forgotten why he had written it. Almost.

He picked up the Max Factor panstick and dabbed a little over his skin as Sheila had taught him to do, covering up any small blemishes on his face. Then he picked up the Brylcreem and comb and began to set his hair into a quiff. There was a time when, looking in the mirror like this, he would have felt secretly proud of how handsome he was. Perhaps, even, thrown himself a charming smile, trying it on for the audience. But tonight he was not in the mood. When he looked in the mirror all he saw was the empty room behind him. A space that should be filled with a wife or a lover. To lose both of those things in one year had been careless and stupid of him. Now, his manager had abandoned him as well. He struggled to hold his hand steady to put the last strand of his quiff in place, his big blue eyes staring angrily back at him. They were glittering with fear. He would not be able to do this tonight. Not alone. He needed someone else there to bolster him, to egg him on. Sheila had been the last one who could offer him the support he needed to get on stage. This was the biggest night of his life, he could not go through it alone.

Through the heavy walls Patrick heard the thump of the visiting showband starting up. He couldn't sit there any longer fizzing with nerves. He had already drunk the two beers that had been left backstage for him and he needed another. He could try to sneak over to the bar, as he would do on a normal night, but this was his big debut and it would be bad form for him to be seen out front with the punters. Patrick decided to go to the heavy fire door that led from the office area to the dance hall. He could try and get the attention of one of the waitresses. Staff were trained to make sure the door was closed at all times, so if it was ajar somebody would notice him peering out. As he looked through the door, he half expected to see Sheila flying around the room in her black hipster garb, bossing people about. However, even if she had been, the huge room was so thronged with people he would have been hard pushed to find her. It was early for it to be so crowded, even for a Saturday night. With a rising wave of nausea Patrick remembered that all of these people were there to see him. He was shaking and badly needed another drink to calm his nerves. He narrowed his eyes and searched the crowd until he saw Gerry serving somebody at a booth. Waving frantically, his eyes moved to the booth itself and with a shocked jolt he saw Ava sitting there. He could hardly believe it. Had she come to see him? Was it possible? Why else would she be there? Again, Patrick waved frantically at Gerry, trying to get his attention, but Gerry walked away without seeing him. Patrick was considering sneaking over to her himself when Ava got up from the booth and moved across to the dance floor. Where was she going? He couldn't see from where he was, and he could not follow her into the crowd, so Patrick ran backstage to look through the side curtain from where he would get a bird's-eye view of the whole floor.

A small ray of hope opened inside him at the thought that, despite everything, perhaps his wife was returning to him. Perhaps he would not be alone this evening, after all. But then, as he looked out, Patrick saw that Ava was dancing a wild jive with some man. He vaguely recognized him, but could not say who he was. As the jive stopped and the music slowed down to a waltz, Patrick said a small prayer that Ava would move away from the dance floor to come and find him. But she didn't. As they waltzed, the man's arms wrapped around Ava. Ava was smiling as she leant into the man's ear and said something. Hot tears poured down Patrick's cheeks as the man's face came into view and he saw it was Ava's ex-fiancé. The man she had jilted to be with him. He had known that she was gone to him before tonight, but this seemed like a special, cruel reminder of all he had lost. After a few moments, Ava and her partner left, hand in hand.

Patrick felt all the old hurt flooding through him. Weakening him, poisoning his desire to sing. He had known that Ava did not love him any more, but the fact that he had hoped, made him feel impossibly sad. Nobody loved him. He had taken everybody's love and ruined it. Abandoning Rose, betraying Ava and finally, he knew, clinging to Sheila like a child – needing more than she was willing to give.

Patrick wanted to run away, out the door, back on to the streets of New York, down to the docks and on to a boat back to Ireland. Back to his Saturday-night gigs in Ballina town hall, squabbling with his siblings over the leg of the Sunday chicken, gathering hay with his father, and those secret summer assignations with sweet, blonde Rose. He began to cry at the very thought of how his life had failed him, and he was just calculating if he had enough money to make a run for it when he heard Sheila's voice in his head: 'Stop crying, Patrick! You're streaking that panstick. Just get out there and sing.'

Patrick wiped his hands across his face just as he heard Gerry bash his door shouting, 'You're on!'

There was still time. He could run past Gerry, through the back exit and leave it all behind.

Walking back to the office that afternoon Rose knew that she had to see Patrick again. She could not move on with her own life until she had resolved what had passed between them. She was no longer certain if she truly loved him any more. She only knew that the madness that had taken her recently had left her, and that she needed to apologize to Patrick for all that she had done.

The client meeting went well, but Rose was unable to get the need to see Patrick out of her head. Since hearing that song on the radio earlier, it was as if he was calling to her.

The image of Patrick, as he had been to her once, kept floating into her mind. His jet-black curls falling into his eyes, singing her some sweet love song as they lay on the grass at the back of her parents' field. Those sharp blue eyes softening with desire, as he pulled her up to the surface of the lake that day. Rose did not need to be rescued any more. In the past two months she had learned to rescue herself, but she felt terrible about all that had happened in the past few months, and needed to, somehow, make amends. As much as she had pursued him before, Rose now felt the need to see Patrick to apologize, face to face, for all of the hurt she had caused him, and Ava. Only then would she be free to get on with her life properly. Perhaps, she thought, Patrick too needed her to set him free? Whatever the case, it was time to, literally, face the music.

Rose finished work at six and got straight on the subway to Yonkers. In all likelihood, Patrick would have moved on from the Emerald Ballroom by now. Certainly, if he had a record on the radio he would be hitting the big time. However, wherever he was, and whatever he was doing, the Emerald would be the best place to start her search.

'Come on, Patrick.'

Gerry had been warned by Sheila that Patrick might get a fit of nerves. Without Patrick knowing it, Gerry had kept a close eye on him all evening. There was no way Gerry was going to give his charge more than two drinks or bring his estranged wife over to cause him a load of emotional upset before going on stage. Aside from anything else, Sheila would kill him if tonight didn't run smoothly. Gerry felt bad for betraying her when he told Iggy about the Joe Higgins incident. He felt sure that was what had chased her out of town on what should have been her big night, as well as Patrick's. It was up to him to make sure that kid got on stage and sang like a pro.

So, when there was no sign of Patrick, Gerry did what he thought Sheila would have done. He opened the door, grabbed Patrick by the arm and dragged him up on to the stage, literally giving him a sharp kick on the behind to propel him in front of the band.

Patrick had no time to question if he wanted to be here. The band had played the opening bars and he had to start singing. As he held the microphone to his mouth, he was aware of the audience, hundreds of people looking up at him, expecting something brilliant. Expecting entertainment, emotion, the evoking of love. 'It Was Only Ever You' was coming out of him automatically. He had sung it so many times before that as soon as the music came on he would start singing, despite himself. He crooned and moved the microphone backwards and forwards and swayed and made all of the right movements. But he wasn't feeling it. As he went through the motions Patrick was actually glad that Sheila was not there to see him giving such a lacklustre performance. Halfway through the first verse he remembered Sheila once advising him to, 'find a pretty girl in the audience and sing the song for her'.

So, Patrick looked out into the crowd.

There, like a vision – and Patrick believed that it was only a vision – in the middle of the dance floor, stood Rose Hopkins.

Could it be true... could it really be you... the one I search for in a song and waited for so long... was it only ever you?

As he sang to his 'vision' of Rose, Patrick began to feel the power of his voice. He remembered the first day he had fallen in love with the doctor's daughter and how his song had stopped a bull from charging. His voice had saved a life and started a love story so great it had crossed an ocean.

Then, as he sang the words, 'I tell myself you are the very reason I exist', Patrick realized the whole truth of his life lay in that sentence he had written. It was not about Rose, after all. He did not need Rose or Ava or even Sheila to make him sing. He had been singing before he met any of them and he would be singing long after every lover, wife or manager had ever left him.

Music was his first love. It was 'only ever' about the music. Music had been the lover that had ruined his life. The promise of a career had lured him away from Rose. The stability and security he needed to build that career had been given to him by Ava. Sheila had elevated him from singer to star. Of all of them, Sheila understood him the best. He was an artist. His art would always come before human love. 'It's the way you're made,' Sheila had once told him. 'Put the music first, life later,' had always been her advice.

Patrick had only known one other person like that in his life. Someone who could get so lost in their work, so lost in their art, that it was as if nobody else existed. Somebody who seemed heedless of the feelings of others when in pursuit of something they loved.

That person was Rose. The song was not about the love he had for Rose, but the thing they shared in common – their love of music and art.

As the song rose in a crashing crescendo,

Because it's true… it was only ever you… the one I love with all my heart… and have done from the start…

Patrick kept his eye on the beautiful blonde vision, although it was not until the song came to its soft, teasing, close,

It was only ever you… my love… yes… It was only ever you

that he realized she was real. It was, actually, Rose standing there, in the flesh. The last time he had seen her in that spot he had walked across the empty room, kissed her and brought his life to an end.

Yet, he was still here, and so was she. Along with nearly a thousand other people, all screaming for him.

Patrick barely saw them as he hopped down from the side of the stage and walked towards Rose. The crowd surged around him so that he became trapped, the people pawing at his chest, congratulating him, girls telling them they loved him, everyone begging for his attention. Patrick panicked as he found that he could not move. He was drowning in adulation.

Then he saw Rose's white-blonde hair emerge through the sea of faces, like a beacon rising to the surface of a stormy ocean.

She reached in and grabbed his hand, and Patrick knew he was saved.

HISTORICAL NOTE
FROM AUTHOR

For the post depression years up to JFK's visit to Ireland in
1963, it was possible for the Irish to enter America with a
passport and an assurance there would be a person to meet
them at the other end. They did this in their droves until,
in the early 1960s, Ireland's Taoiseach (Prime Minister) Sean
Lemass asked President John F Kennedy not to give Ireland
an allotment of US visas in an attempt to stop the brain drain
in Ireland. This led to the introduction of a rigorously policed
visa system that remains to this day.

ᗩCKNOWLEDGEMENTS

Thank you to Judd Ruane for his invaluable research on the showband scene.

Helen Falconer for use of her big brain.

Ella Griffin for daily writing support.

Joe Queenan of Foxford Woollen Mills for research.

Elaine Tighe for writing the lyrics for 'It Was Only Ever You' and wonderful Tommy Fleming for bringing the song to life and recording it.

My assistant Danielle, on hand always, brilliant as ever.

My student Frederique Bresson for her sterling work.

Brendan Hoban for swift replies to 'priest queries'.

My mother Moira for her cheerleading and unconditional love.

My husband Niall, for his endless tolerance and respect.

My sons Leo and Tommo – for giving me the reason to work.

My agent Marianne Gunn O'Connor and Pat Lynch for their faith and constancy.

Amanda Ridout and her Head of Zeus team: Nia, Liz, Clémence, Madeleine, Jessie, Suzanne, Victoria and, of course, Anthony Cheetham for starting up such a vibrant, creative, supportive house in the first place. I feel very lucky indeed.

Last, but certainly not least, my indomitable, awesome editor, Rosie de Courcy. I value your opinion above all others and thank you for taking the time to make this book come alive. It was a close one, but we did it! Thank you for making me a better storyteller and a better writer.